BLUE SKIES

Summer Desserts

and

Lessons Learned

Sign of Seven Trilogy
Blood Brothers • The Hollow • The Pagan Stone

Bride Quartet
Vision in White • Bed of Roses • Savor the Moment • Happy Ever After

The Inn Boonsboro Trilogy
The Next Always • The Last Boyfriend • The Perfect Hope

The Cousins O'Dwyer Trilogy
Dark Witch • Shadow Spell • Blood Magick

The Guardians Trilogy
Stars of Fortune • Bay of Sighs • Island of Glass

Chronicles of The One
Year One • Of Blood and Bone • The Rise of Magicks

The Dragon Heart Legacy
The Awakening • The Becoming

EBOOKS BY NORA ROBERTS

Cordina's Royal Family
Affaire Royale • Command Performance • The Playboy Prince • Cordina's Crown Jewel

The Donovan Legacy
Captivated • Entranced • Charmed • Enchanted

The O'Hurleys
The Last Honest Woman • Dance to the Piper • Skin Deep • Without a Trace

Night Tales
Night Shift • Night Shadow • Nightshade • Night Smoke • Night Shield

• Witness in Death • Judgment in Death • Betrayal in Death
• Seduction in Death • Reunion in Death • Purity in Death
• Portrait in Death • Imitation in Death • Divided in Death
• Visions in Death • Survivor in Death • Origin in Death
• Memory in Death • Born in Death • Innocent in Death •
Creation in Death • Strangers in Death • Salvation in Death
• Promises in Death • Kindred in Death • Fantasy in Death •
Indulgence in Death • Treachery in Death • New York to Dallas
• Celebrity in Death • Delusion in Death • Calculated in Death
• Thankless in Death • Concealed in Death • Festive in Death •
Obsession in Death • Devoted in Death • Brotherhood in Death
• Apprentice in Death • Echoes in Death • Secrets in Death •
Dark in Death • Leverage in Death • Connections in Death •
Vendetta in Death • Golden in Death • Shadows in Death •
Faithless in Death • Forgotten in Death •
Abandoned in Death

ANTHOLOGIES

From the Heart • A Little Magic • A Little Fate

Moon Shadows
(with Jill Gregory, Ruth Ryan Langan, and Marianne Willman)

The Once Upon Series
(with Jill Gregory, Ruth Ryan Langan, and Marianne Willman)
Once Upon a Castle • Once Upon a Star • Once Upon a Dream • Once Upon a Rose • Once Upon a Kiss • Once Upon a Midnight

Silent Night
(with Susan Plunkett, Dee Holmes, and Claire Cross)

Out of This World
(with Laurell K. Hamilton, Susan Krinard, and Maggie Shayne)

Bump in the Night
(with Mary Blayney, Ruth Ryan Langan, and Mary Kay McComas)

BLUE SKIES

Summer Desserts

and

Lessons Learned

TWO NOVELS IN ONE

NORA ROBERTS

St. Martin's Paperbacks

This is a work of fiction. All of the characters, organizations, and events portrayed in this book are either products of the author's imagination or are used fictitiously.

Published in the United States by St. Martin's Paperbacks, an imprint of St. Martin's Publishing Group

BLUE SKIES: SUMMER DESSERTS copyright © 1985 by Nora Roberts and LESSONS LEARNED copyright © 1986 by Nora Roberts.

For information, address St. Martin's Publishing Group, 120 Broadway, New York, NY 10271.

www.stmartins.com

ISBN: 978-1-250-84713-3

Our books may be purchased in bulk for promotional, educational, or business use. Please contact your local bookseller or the Macmillan Corporate and Premium Sales Department at 1-800-221-7945, ext. 5442, or by email at MacmillanSpecialMarkets@macmillan.com.

Printed in the United States of America

St. Martin's Paperbacks edition / August 2022

10 9 8 7 6 5 4 3 2 1

Summer Desserts

To Marianne Shock,
for the cheerful and clever last-minute help.

CHAPTER 1

Her name was Summer. It was a name that conjured visions of hot petaled flowers, sudden storms and long, restless nights. It also brought images of sun-warmed meadows and naps in the shade. It suited her.

As she stood, hands poised, body tensed, eyes alert, there wasn't a sound in the room. No one, absolutely no one, took their eyes off her. She might move slowly, but there wasn't a person there who wanted to chance missing a gesture, a motion. All attention, all concentration, was riveted upon that one slim, solitary figure. Strains of Chopin floated romantically through the air. The light slanted and shot through her neatly bound hair—rich, warm brown with hints and tints of gold. Two emerald studs winked at her ears.

Her skin was a bit flushed so that a rose tinge accented already prominent cheekbones and the elegant bone structure that comes only from breeding. Excitement, intense concentration, deepened the amber flecks that were sprinkled in the hazel of her eyes. The same excitement and concentration had her soft, molded lips forming a pout.

She was all in white, plain, unadorned white, but she drew the eye as irresistibly as a butterfly in full, dazzling flight.

She wouldn't speak, yet everyone in the room strained forward as if to catch the slightest sound.

The room was warm, the smells intoxicating, the atmosphere taut with anticipation.

Summer might have been alone for all the attention she paid to those around her. There was only one goal, one end. Perfection. She'd never settled for less.

With infinite care she lifted the final diamond-shape and pressed the angelica onto the Savarin to complete the design she'd created. The hours she'd already spent preparing and baking the huge, elaborate dessert were forgotten, as was the heat, the tired leg muscles, the aching arms. The final touch, the *appearance* of a Summer Lyndon creation, was of the utmost importance. Yes, it would taste perfect, smell perfect, even slice perfectly. But if it didn't look perfect, none of that mattered.

With the care of an artist completing a masterpiece, she lifted her brush to give the fruits and almonds a light, delicate coating of apricot glaze.

Still, no one spoke.

Asking no assistance—indeed, she wouldn't have tolerated any—Summer began to fill the center of the Savarin with the rich cream whose recipe she guarded jealously.

Hands steady, head erect, Summer stepped back to give her creation one last critical study. This was the ultimate test, for her eye was keener than any other's when it came to her own work. She folded her arms across her body. Her face was without expression. In the huge kitchen, the ping of a pin dropped on the tile would have reverberated like a gunshot.

Slowly her lips curved, her eyes glittered. Success. Summer lifted one arm and gestured rather dramatically. "Take it away," she ordered.

As two assistants began to roll the glittering concoction from the room, applause broke out.

Summer accepted the accolade as her due. There was a place for modesty, she knew, and she knew it didn't apply to her Savarin. It was, to put it mildly, magnificent. Magnificence was what the Italian duke had wanted for his daughter's engagement party, and magnificence was what he'd paid for. Summer had simply delivered.

"Mademoiselle." Foulfount, the Frenchman whose specialty was shellfish, took Summer by both shoulders. His eyes were round and damp with appreciation. *"Incroyable."* Enthusiastically, he kissed both her cheeks while his thick, clever fingers squeezed her skin as they might a fresh-baked loaf of bread. Summer broke out in her first grin in hours.

"Merci." Someone had opened a celebratory bottle of wine. Summer took two glasses, handing one to the French chef. "To the next time we work together, *mon ami.*"

She tossed back the wine, took off her chef's hat, then breezed out of the kitchen. In the enormous marble-floored, chandeliered dining room, her Savarin was even now being served and admired. Her last thought before leaving was— thank God someone else had to clean up the mess.

Two hours later, she had her shoes off and her eyes closed. A gruesome murder mystery lay open on her lap as her plane cruised over the Atlantic. She was going home. She'd spent almost three full days in Milan for the sole purpose of creating that one dish. It wasn't an unusual experience for her. Summer had baked *Charlotte Malakoff* in Madrid, flamed *Crêpes Fourée* in Athens and molded *île Flottante* in Istanbul. For her expenses, and a stunning fee, Summer Lyndon would create a dessert that would live in the memory long after the last bite, drop or crumb was consumed.

Have wisk, will travel, she thought vaguely and smiled through a yawn.

She considered herself a specialist, not unlike a skilled surgeon. Indeed, she'd studied, apprenticed and practiced as long as many respected members of the medical profession. Five years after passing the stringent requirements to become a Cordon Bleu chef in Paris, the city where cooking is its own art, Summer had a reputation for being as temperamental as any artist, for having the mind of a computer when it came to remembering recipes and for having the hands of an angel.

Summer half dozed in her first-class seat and fought off a desperate craving for a slice of pepperoni pizza.

She knew the flight time would go faster if she could read or sleep her way through it. She decided to mix the two, taking the light nap first. Summer was a woman who prized her sleep almost as highly as she prized her recipe for chocolate mousse.

On her return to Philadelphia, her schedule would be hectic at best. There was the bombe to prepare for the governor's charity banquet, the annual meeting of the Gourmet Society, the demonstration she'd agreed to do for public television . . . and that meeting, she remembered drowsily.

What had that bird-voiced woman said over the phone? Summer wondered. Drake—no, Blake—Cocharan. Blake Cocharan III of the Cocharan hotel chain. Excellent hotels, Summer thought without any real interest. She'd patronized a number of them in various corners of the world. Mr. Cocharan the Third had a business proposition for her.

Summer assumed that he wanted her to create some special dessert exclusively for his chain of hotels, something they could attach the Cocharan name to. She wasn't averse to the notion—under the proper circumstances. And for the proper fee. Naturally she'd have to investigate the entire Cocharan enterprise carefully before she agreed to involve her skill or her name with it. If any one of their hotels was of inferior quality . . .

With a yawn, Summer decided to think about it later—

after she'd met with The Third personally. Blake Cocharan III, she thought again with a sleepily amused smile. Plump, balding, probably dyspeptic. Italian shoes, Swiss watch, French shirts, German car—and no doubt he'd consider himself unflaggingly American. The image she created hung in her mind a moment, and, bored with it, she yawned again—then sighed as the idea of pizza once again invaded her thoughts. Summer tilted her seat back farther and determinedly willed herself to sleep.

* * *

Blake Cocharan III sat in the plush rear seat of the gunmetal-gray limo and meticulously went over the report on the newest Cocharan House being constructed in Saint Croix. He was a man who could scoop up a mess of scattered details and align them in perfect, systematic order. Chaos was simply a form of order waiting to be unjumbled with logic. Blake was a very logical man. Point A invariably led to point B, and from there to C. No matter how confused the maze, with patience and logic, one could find the route.

Because of his talent for doing just that, Blake, at thirty-five, had almost complete control of the Cocharan empire. He'd inherited his wealth and, as a result, rarely thought of it. But he'd earned his position, and valued it. Quality was a Cocharan tradition. Nothing but the finest would do for any Cocharan House, from the linen on the beds to the mortar in the foundations.

His report on Summer Lyndon told him she was the best.

Setting aside the Saint Croix packet, Blake slipped another file from the slim briefcase by his feet. A single ring, oval-faced, gold and scrolled, gleamed dully on his hand. Summer Lyndon, he mused, flipping the file open . . .

Twenty-eight, graduate of Sorbonne, certified Cordon Bleu

chef. Father, Rothschild Lyndon, respected member of British Parliament. Mother, Monique Dubois Lyndon, former star of the French cinema. Parents amicably divorced for twenty-three years. Summer Lyndon had spent her formative years between London and Paris before her mother had married an American hardware tycoon, based in Philadelphia. Summer had then returned to Paris to complete her education and currently had living quarters both there and in Philadelphia. Her mother had since married a third time, a paper baron on this round, and her father was separated from his second wife, a successful barrister.

All of Blake's probing had produced the same basic answer. Summer Lyndon was the best dessert chef on either side of the Atlantic. She was also a superb all-around chef with an instinctive knowledge of quality, a flair for creativity and the ability to improvise in a crisis. On the other hand, she was reputed to be dictatorial, temperamental and brutally frank. These qualities, however, hadn't alienated her from heads of state, aristocracy or celebrities.

She might insist on having Chopin piped into the kitchen while she cooked, or summarily refuse to work at all if the lighting wasn't to her liking, but her mousse alone was enough to make a strong man beg to grant her slightest wish.

Blake wasn't a man to beg for anything . . . but he wanted Summer Lyndon for Cocharan House. He never doubted he could persuade her to agree to precisely what he had in mind.

A formidable woman, he imagined, respecting that. He had no patience with weak wills or soft brains—particularly in people who worked for him. Not many women had risen to the position, or the reputation, that Summer Lyndon held. Women might traditionally be cooks, but men were traditionally chefs.

He imagined her thick waisted from sampling her own creations. Strong hands, he thought idly. Her skin was probably a bit pasty from all those hours indoors in kitchens. A no-nonsense woman, he was sure, with an uncompromising view on what was edible and why. Organized, logical and cultured—perhaps a bit plain due to her preoccupation with food rather than fashion. Blake imagined that they would deal with each other very well. With a glance at his watch, Blake noted with satisfaction that he was right on time for the meeting.

The limo cruised to a halt beside the curb. "I'll be no more than an hour," Blake told the driver as he climbed out.

"Yes, sir." The driver checked his watch. When Mr. Cocharan said an hour, you could depend on it.

Blake glanced up at the fourth floor as he crossed to the well-kept old building. The windows were open, he noted. Warm spring air poured in, while music—a melody he couldn't quite catch over the sounds of traffic—poured out. When Blake went in, he learned that the single elevator was out of order. He walked up four flights.

After Blake knocked, the door was opened by a small woman with a stunning face who was dressed in a T-shirt and slim black jeans. The maid on her way out for a day off? Blake wondered idly. She didn't look strong enough to scrub a floor. And if she was going out, she was going out without her shoes.

After the brief, objective glance, his gaze was drawn irresistibly back to her face. Classic, naked and undeniably sensuous. The mouth alone would make a man's blood move. Blake ignored what he considered an automatic sexual pull.

"Blake Cocharan to see Ms. Lyndon."

Summer's left brow rose—a sign of surprise. Then her lips curved slightly—a sign of pleasure.

Plump, he wasn't, she observed. Hard and lean—racketball, tennis, swimming. He was obviously a man more prone to

these than lingering over executive lunches. Balding, no. His
hair was rich black and thick. It was styled well, with slight
natural waves that added to the attractiveness of a cool, sensual face. A sweep of cheekbones, a firm line of chin. She
liked the look of the former that spoke of strength, and the
latter, just barely cleft, that spoke of charm. Black brows
were almost straight over clear, water-blue eyes. His mouth
was a bit long but beautifully shaped. His nose was very
straight—the sort she'd always thought was made to be
looked down. Perhaps she'd been right about the outward
trimmings—the Italian shoes, and so forth—but, Summer
admitted, she'd been off the mark with the man.

The assessment didn't take her long—three, perhaps four,
seconds. But her mouth curved more. Blake couldn't take his
eyes off it. It was a mouth a man, if he breathed, wanted
to taste. "Please come in, Mr. Cocharan." Summer stepped
back, swinging the door wider in invitation. "It's very considerate of you to agree to meet here. Please have a seat. I'm
afraid I'm in the middle of something in the kitchen." She
smiled, gestured and disappeared.

Blake opened his mouth—he wasn't used to being brushed
off by servants—then closed it again. He had enough time
to be tolerant. As he set down his briefcase he glanced around
the room. There were fringed lamps, a curved sofa in plush
blue velvet, a fussily carved cherrywood table. Aubusson
carpets—two—softly faded in blues and grays—were spread
over the floors. A Ming vase. Potpourri in what was certainly a Dresden compote.

The room had no order; it was a mix of European periods
and styles that should never have suited, but was instantly attractive. He saw that a pedestal table at the far end of the
room was covered with jumbled typewritten pages and hand-
written notes. Street sounds drifted in through the window.
Chopin floated from the stereo.

As he stood there, drawing it in, he was abruptly certain there was no one in the apartment but himself and the woman who had opened the door. Summer Lyndon? Fascinated with the idea, and with the aroma creeping from the kitchen, Blake crossed the room.

Six pastry shells, just touched with gold and moisture, sat on a rack. One by one Summer filled them to overflowing with what appeared to be some rich white cream. When Blake glanced at her face, he saw the concentration, the seriousness and intensity he might have associated with a brain surgeon. It should have amused him. Yet somehow, with the strains of Chopin pouring through the kitchen speakers, with those delicate, slim-fingered hands arranging the cream in mounds, he was fascinated.

She dipped a fork in a pan and dribbled what he guessed was warmed caramel over the cream. It ran lavishly down the sides and gelled. He doubted that it was humanly possible not to lust after just one taste. Again, one by one, she scooped up the tarts and placed them on a plate lined with a lacy paper doily. When the last one was arranged, she looked up at Blake.

"Would you like some coffee?" She smiled and the line of concentration between her brows disappeared. The intensity that had seemed to darken her irises lightened.

Blake glanced at the dessert plate and wondered how her waist could be hand-spannable. "Yes, I would."

"It's hot," she told him as she lifted the plate. "Help yourself. I have to run these next door." She was past him and to the doorway of the kitchen before she turned around. "Oh, there're some cookies in the jar, if you like. I'll be right back."

She was gone, and the pastries with her. With a shrug, he turned back to the kitchen, which was a shambles. Summer Lyndon might be a great cook, but she was obviously not a neat one. Still if the scent and look of the pastries had been any indication . . .

He started to root in the cupboards for a cup, then gave in to temptation. Standing in his Saville Row suit, Blake ran his finger along the edge of the bowl that had held the cream. He laid it on his tongue. With a sigh, his eyes closed. Rich, thick and very French.

He'd dined in the most exclusive restaurants, in some of the wealthiest homes, in dozens of countries all over the world. Logically, practically, honestly, he couldn't say he'd ever tasted better than what he now scooped from the bowl in this woman's kitchen. In deciding to specialize in desserts and pastries, Summer Lyndon had chosen well, he concluded. He felt a momentary regret that she'd taken those rich, fat tarts to someone else. This time when Blake started his search for a cup, he spotted the ceramic cookie jar shaped like a panda.

Normally he wouldn't have been interested. He wasn't a man with a particularly active sweet tooth. But the flavor of the cream lingered on his tongue. What sort of cookie did a woman who created the finest of haute cuisine make? With a cup of English bone china in one hand, Blake lifted off the top of the panda's head. Setting it down, he pulled out a cookie and stared in simple wonder.

No American could mistake that particular munchie. A classic? he mused. A tradition? An Oreo. Blake continued to stare at the chocolate sandwich cookie with its double dose of white center. He turned it over in his hand. The brand was unmistakably stamped into both sides. This from a woman who baked and whipped and glazed for royalty?

A laugh broke from him as he dropped the Oreo back into the panda. Throughout his career he'd had to deal with more than his share of eccentrics. Running a chain of hotels wasn't just a matter of who checked in and who checked out. There were designers, artists, architects, decorators, chefs, musicians, union representatives. Blake considered himself knowledgeable of people. It wouldn't take him long to learn what made Summer tick.

She dashed back into the kitchen just as he was finally pouring the coffee. "I'm sorry to have kept you waiting, Mr. Cocharan. I know it was rude." She smiled, as if she had no doubt she'd be forgiven, as she poured her own coffee. "I had to get those pastries finished for my neighbor. She's having a small engagement tea this afternoon—with prospective in-laws." Her smile turned to a grin and, sipping her black coffee, she plucked the top from the panda. "Did you want a cookie?"

"No. Please, you go ahead."

Taking him at his word, Summer chose one and nibbled. "You know," she said thoughtfully, "these are uniformly excellent for their kind." She gestured with the half cookie she had left. "Shall we go sit down and discuss your proposition?"

She moved fast, he mused with approval. Perhaps he'd at least been on the mark about the no-nonsense attitude. With a nod of acknowledgment, Blake followed her. He was successful in his profession, not because he was a third-generation Cocharan, but because he had a quick and analytical mind. Problems were systematically solved. At the moment, he had to decide just how to approach a woman like Summer Lyndon.

She had a face that belonged in the shade of a tree on the Bois de Boulogne. Very French, very elegant. Her voice had the round, clear tones that spoke unmistakably of European education and upbringing—a wisp of France again but with the discipline of Britain. Her hair was pinned up, a concession to the heat and humidity, he imagined—though she had the windows open, ignoring the available air-conditioning. The studs in her ears were emeralds, round and flawless. There was a good-sized tear in the sleeve of her T-shirt.

Sitting on the couch, she folded her legs under her. Her bare toes were painted with a wild rose enamel, but her fingernails were short and unvarnished. He caught the allure of her scent—a touch of the caramel from the pastries, but under it something unmistakably French, unapologetically sexual.

How did one approach such a woman? Blake reflected. Did he use charm, flattery or figures? She was reputed to be a perfectionist and occasionally a firebrand. She'd refused to cook for an important political figure because he wouldn't fly her personal kitchen equipment to his country. She'd charged a Hollywood celebrity a small fortune to create a twenty-tiered wedding cake extravaganza. And she'd just hand-baked and hand-delivered a plate of pastries to a neighbor for a tea. Blake would much prefer to have the key to her before he made his offer. He knew the advantages of taking a circular route. Indeed some might call it stalking.

"I'm acquainted with your mother," Blake began easily as he continued to gauge the woman beside him.

"Really?" He caught both amusement and affection in the word. "I shouldn't be surprised," she said as she nibbled on the cookie again. "My mother always patronized a Cocharan House when we traveled. I believe I had dinner with your grandfather when I was six or seven." The amusement didn't fade as she sipped at her coffee. "Small world."

An excellent suit, Summer decided, relaxing against the back of the sofa. It was well cut and conservative enough to have gained her father's approval. The form it was molded to was well built and lean enough to have gained her mother's.

It was perhaps the combination of the two that drew her interest.

Good God, he is attractive, she thought as she took another considering survey of his face. Not quite smooth, not quite rugged, his power sat well on him. That was something she recognized—in herself and in others. She respected someone who sought and got his own way, as she judged Blake did. She respected herself for the same reason. Attractive, she thought again—but she felt that a man like Blake would be so, regardless of physical appearance.

Her mother would have called him *séduisant,* and accurately so. Summer would have called him dangerous. A difficult combination to resist. She shifted, perhaps unconsciously, to put more distance between them. Business, after all, was business.

"You're familiar then with the standards of a Cocharan House," Blake began. Quite suddenly he wished her scent wasn't so alluring or her mouth so tempting. He didn't care to have business muddled with attraction, no matter how pleasant.

"Of course." Summer set down her coffee because drinking it only seemed to accentuate the odd little flutter in her stomach. "I invariably stay at them myself."

"I've been told your standards of quality are equally high."

This time when Summer smiled there was a hint of arrogance to it. "I'm the very best at what I do because I have no intention of being otherwise."

The first key, Blake decided with satisfaction. Professional vanity. "So my information tells me, Ms. Lyndon. The very best is all that interests me."

"So." Summer propped an elbow on the back of the sofa then rested her head on the palm. "How exactly do I interest you, Mr. Cocharan?" She knew the question was loaded, but couldn't resist. When a woman was constantly taking risks and making experiments in her professional life, the habit often leaked through.

Six separate answers skimmed through his mind, none of which had any bearing on his purpose for being there. Blake set down his coffee. "The restaurants at the Cocharan Houses are renowned for their quality and service. However, recently the restaurant here in our Philadelphia complex seems to be suffering from a lack of both. Frankly, Ms. Lyndon, it's my opinion that the food has become too pedestrian—too boring. I plan to do some remodeling, both in physical structure and in staff."

"Wise. Restaurants, like people, often become too complacent."

"I want the best head chef available." He aimed a level look. "My research tells me that's you."

Summer lifted a brow, not in surprise this time but in consideration. "That's flattering, but I freelance, Mr. Cocharan. And I specialize."

"Specialize, yes, but you do have both experience and knowledge in all areas of haute cuisine. As for the freelancing, you'd be free to continue that to a large extent, at least after the first few months. You'd need to establish your own staff and create your own menu. I don't believe in hiring an expert, then interfering."

She was frowning again—concentration, not annoyance. It was tempting, very tempting. Perhaps it was just the travel weariness from her trip back from Italy, but she'd begun to grow a bit tired—bored?—with the constant demands of flying to any given country to make that one dish. It seemed he'd hit her at the right moment to stir her interest in concentrating on one place, and one kitchen, for a span of time.

It would be interesting work—if he were being truthful about the free hand she'd have—redoing a kitchen and the menu in an old, established and respected hotel. It would take her perhaps six months of intense effort, and then . . . It was the "and then" that made her hesitate again. If she gave that much time and effort to a full-time job, would she still retain her flair for the spectacular? That, too, was something to consider.

She'd always had a firm policy against committing herself to any one establishment—a wariness of commitments ribboned through all areas of her life. If you locked yourself into something, to someone, you opened yourself to all manner of complications.

Besides, Summer reasoned, if she wanted to affiliate herself with a restaurant, she could open and run her own. She hadn't done it yet because it would tie her too long to one place, attach her too closely to one project. She preferred traveling, creating one superb dish at a time, then moving on. The next country, the next dish. That was her style. Why should she consider altering it now?

"A very flattering offer, Mr. Cocharan—"

"A mutually advantageous one," he interrupted, perceptive enough to catch the beginning of a refusal. With deliberate ease, he tossed out a six-digit annual salary that rendered Summer momentarily speechless—not a simple task.

"And generous," she said when she found her voice again.

"One doesn't get the best unless one's willing to pay for it. I'd like you to think about this, Ms. Lyndon." He reached in his briefcase and pulled out a sheaf of papers. "This is a draft of an agreement. You might like to have your attorney look it over, and of course, points can be negotiated."

She didn't want to look at the damn contract because she could feel, quite tangibly, that she was being maneuvered into a corner—a very plush one. "Mr. Cocharan, I do appreciate your interest, but—"

"After you've thought it over, I'd like to discuss it with you again, perhaps over dinner. Say, Friday?"

Summer narrowed her eyes. The man was a steamroller, she decided. A very attractive, very sleek steamroller. No matter how elegant the machinery, you still got flattened if you were in the path. Haughtiness emanated from her. "I'm sorry, I'm working Friday evening—the governor's charity affair."

"Ah, yes." He smiled, though his stomach had tightened. He had a suddenly vivid, completely wild image of making love to her on the ground of some moist, shadowy forest. That alone nearly made him consider accepting her refusal. And that alone made him all the more determined not to. "I can pick you up there. We can have a late supper."

"Mr. Cocharan," Summer said in a frigid voice, "you're going to have to learn to take no for an answer."

Like hell, he thought grimly, but gave her a rather rueful, rather charming smile. "My apologies, Ms. Lyndon, if I seem to be pressuring you. You were my first choice, you see, and I tend to go with my instincts. However . . ." Seemingly reluctant, he rose. The knot of tension and anger in Summer's stomach began to loosen. "If your mind's made up . . ." He plucked the contract from the table and started to slip it into his briefcase. "Perhaps you can give me your opinion on Louis LaPointe."

"LaPointe?" The word whispered through Summer's lips like venom. Very slowly she uncurled from the sofa, then rose, her whole body stiff. "You ask me of LaPointe?" In anger, her French ancestry became more pronounced in her speech.

"I'd appreciate anything you could tell me," Blake went on amiably, knowing full well he'd scored his first real point off her. "Seeing that you and he are associates and—"

With a toss of her head, Summer said something short,

rude and to the point in her mother's tongue. The gold flecks in her eyes glimmered. Sherlock Holmes had Professor Moriarty. Superman had Lex Luthor. Summer Lyndon had Louis LaPointe.

"Slimy pig," she grated, reverting to English. "He has the mind of a peanut and the hands of a lumberjack. You want to know about LaPointe?" She snatched a cigarette from the case on the table, lighting it as she did only when extremely agitated. "He's a peasant. What else is there to know?"

"According to my information, he's one of the five top chefs in Paris." Blake pressed because a good pressure point was an invaluable weapon. "His *Canard en Croûte* is said to be unsurpassable."

"Shoe leather." She all but spat out the words, and Blake had to school every facial muscle to prevent the grin. Professional vanity, he thought again. She had her share. Then as she drew in a deep breath, he had to school the rest of his muscles to hold off a fierce surge of desire. Sensuality— perhaps she had more than her share. "Why are you asking me about LaPointe?"

"I'm flying to Paris next week to meet with him. Since you're refusing my offer—"

"You'll offer this—" she wagged a finger at the contract still in Blake's hand "—to him?"

"Admittedly he's my second choice, but there are those on the board who feel Louis LaPointe is more qualified for the position."

"Is that so?" Her eyes were slits now behind a screen of smoke. She plucked the contract from his hand, then dropped it beside her cooling coffee. "The members of your board are perhaps ignorant?"

"They are," he managed, "perhaps mistaken."

"Indeed." Summer took a drag of her cigarette, then released smoke in a quick stream. She detested the taste. "You can pick me up at nine o'clock on Friday at the governor's kitchen, Mr. Cocharan. We'll discuss this matter further."

"My pleasure, Ms. Lyndon." He inclined his head, careful to keep his face expressionless until he'd closed the front door behind him. He laughed his way down four flights of steps.

CHAPTER 2

Making a good dessert from scratch isn't a simple matter. Creating a masterpiece from flour, eggs and sugar is something else again. Whenever Summer picked up a bowl or a whisk or beater, she felt it her duty to create a masterpiece. Adequate, as an adjective in conjunction with her work, was the ultimate insult. Adequate, to Summer, was the result achieved by a newlywed with a cookbook first opened the day after the honeymoon. She didn't simply bake, mix or freeze—she conceived, developed and achieved. An architect, an engineer, a scientist did no more, no less. When she'd chosen to study the art of haute cuisine, she hadn't done so lightly, and she hadn't done so without the goal of perfection in mind. Perfection was still what she sought whenever she lifted a spoon.

She'd already spent the better part of her day in the kitchen of the governor's mansion. Other chefs fussed with soups and sauces—or each other. All of Summer's talent was focused on the creation of the finale, the exquisite mix of tastes and textures, the overall aesthetic beauty of the bombe.

The mold was already lined with the moist cake she'd

baked, then systematically sliced into a pattern. This had been done with templates as meticulously as when an engineer designs a bridge. The mousse, a paradise of chocolate and cream, was already inside the dessert's dome. This deceptively simple element had been chilling since early morning. Between the preparations, the mixing, making and building, Summer had been on her feet essentially that long.

Now, she had the beginnings of her bombe on a waist-high table, with a large stainless steel bowl of crushed berries at her elbow. At her firm instructions, Chopin drifted through the kitchen speakers. The first course was already being enjoyed in the dining room. She could ignore the confusion reigning around her. She could shrug off the pressure of having her part of the meal complete and perfect at precisely the right moment. That was all routine. But as she stood there, prepared to begin the next step, her concentration was scattered.

LaPointe, she thought with gritted teeth. Naturally it was anger that had kept her attention from being fully focused all day, the idea of having Louis LaPointe tossed in her face. It hadn't taken Summer long to realize that Blake Cocharan had used the name on purpose. Knowing it, however, didn't make the least bit of difference to her reaction . . . except perhaps that her venom was spread over two men rather than one.

Oh, he thinks he's very clever, Summer decided, thinking of Blake—as she had too often that week. She took three cleansing breaths as she studied the golden dome in front of her. Asking me, *me,* to give LaPointe a reference. Despicable French swine, she muttered silently, referring to LaPointe. As she scooped up the first berries she decided that Blake must be an equal swine even to be considering dealing with the Frenchman.

She could remember every frustrating, annoying contact

she'd had with the beady-eyed, undersized LaPointe. As she carefully coated the outside of the cake with crushed berries, Summer considered giving him a glowing recommendation. It would teach that sneaky American a lesson to find himself stuck with a pompous ass like LaPointe. While her thoughts raged, her hands were delicately smoothing the berries, rounding out and firming the shape.

Behind her one of the assistants dropped a pan with a clatter and a bang and suffered a torrent of abuse. Neither Summer's thoughts nor her hands faltered.

Smug, self-assured jerk, she thought grimly of Blake. In a steady flow, she began layering rich French cream over the berries. Her face, though set in concentration, betrayed anger in the flash in her eyes. A man like him delighted in maneuvering and outmaneuvering. It showed, she thought, in that oh-so-smooth delivery, in that gloss of sophistication. She gave a disdainful little snort as she began to smooth out the cream.

She'd rather have a man with a few rough edges than one so polished that he gleamed. She'd rather have a man who knew how to sweat and bend his back than one with manicured nails and five-hundred-dollar suits. She'd rather have a man who . . .

Summer stopped smoothing the cream while her thoughts caught up with her consciousness. Since when had she considered having any man, and why, for God's sake, was she using Blake for comparisons? Ridiculous.

The bombe was now a smooth white dome waiting for its coating of rich chocolate. Summer frowned at it as an assistant whisked empty bowls out of her way. She began to blend the frosting in a large mixer as two cooks argued over the thickness of the sauce for the entrée.

For that matter, her thoughts ran on, it was ridiculous how often she'd thought of him the past few days, remembering foolish details . . . His eyes were almost precisely the shade of the water in the lake on her grandfather's estate in Devon. How pleasant his voice was, deep, with that faint but unmistakable inflection of the American Northeast. How his mouth curved in one fashion when he was amused, and another when he smiled politely.

It was difficult to explain why she'd noticed those things, much less why she'd continued to think of them days afterward. As a rule, she didn't think of a man unless she was with him—and even then she only allowed him a carefully regulated portion of her concentration.

Now, Summer reminded herself as she began to layer on frosting, wasn't the time to think of anything but the bombe. She'd think of Blake when her job was finished, and she'd deal with him over the late supper she'd agreed to. Oh, yes—her mouth set—she'd deal with him.

Blake arrived early deliberately. He wanted to see her work. That was reasonable, even logical. After all, if he were to contract Summer to Cocharan House for a year, he should see firsthand what she was capable of, and how she went about it. It wasn't at all unusual for him to check out potential employees or associates on their own turf. If anything, it was characteristic of him. Good business sense.

He continued to tell himself so, over and over, because there was a lingering doubt as to his own motivations. Perhaps he had left her apartment in high good spirits knowing he'd outmaneuvered her in the first round. Her face, at the mention of her rival LaPointe, had been priceless. And it was her face that he hadn't been able to push out of his mind for nearly a week.

Uncomfortable, he decided as he stepped into the huge, echoing kitchen. The woman made him uncomfortable. He'd like to know the reason why. Knowing the reasons and motivations was essential to him. With them neatly listed, the answer to any problem would eventually follow.

He appreciated beauty—in art, in architecture and certainly in the female form. Summer Lyndon was beautiful. That shouldn't have made him uncomfortable. Intelligence was something he not only appreciated but invariably demanded in anyone he associated with. She was undoubtedly intelligent. No reason for discomfort there. Style was something else he looked for—he'd certainly found it in her.

What was it about her . . . the eyes? he wondered as he passed two cooks in a heated argument over pressed duck. That odd hazel that wasn't precisely a definable color—those gold flecks that deepened or lightened according to her mood. Very direct, very frank eyes, he mused. Blake respected that. Yet the contrast of moody color that wasn't really a color intrigued him. Perhaps too much.

Sexuality? It was a foolish man who was wary because of a natural feminine sexuality, and he'd never considered himself a foolish man. Nor a particularly susceptible one. Yet the first time he'd seen her he'd felt that instant curl of desire, that immediate pull of man for woman. Unusual, he thought dispassionately. Something he'd have to consider carefully— then dispose of. There wasn't room for desire between business associates.

And they would be that, he thought as his lips curved. Blake counted on his own powers of persuasion, and his casual mention of LaPointe, to turn Summer Lyndon his way. She was already turning that way, and after tonight, he reflected, then stopped dead. For a moment it felt as though someone had delivered him a very quick, very stunning blow to the base of the spine. He'd only had to look at her.

She was half-hidden by the dessert she worked on. Her face was set, intent. He saw the faint line that might've been temper or concentration run down between her brows. Her eyes were narrowed, the lashes swept down so that the expression was unreadable. Her mouth, that soft, molded mouth that she seemed never to paint, was forming a pout. It was utterly kissable.

She should have looked plain and efficient, all in white. The chef's hat over her neatly bound hair could have given an almost comic touch. Instead she looked outrageously beautiful. Standing there, Blake could hear the Chopin that was her trademark, smell the pungent scents of cooking, feel the tension in the air as temperamental cooks fussed and labored over their creations. All he could think, and think quite clearly, was how she would look naked, in his bed, with only candles to vie with the dark.

Catching himself, Blake shook his head. *Stop it,* he thought with grim amusement. *When you mix business and pleasure, one or both suffers.* That was something Blake invariably avoided without effort. He held the position he did because he could recognize, weigh and dismiss errors before they were ever made. And he could do so with a cold-blooded ruthlessness that was as clean as his looks.

The woman might be as delectable as the concoction she was creating, but that wasn't what he wanted—correction, what he could afford to want—from her. He needed her skill, her name and her brain. That was all. For now, he comforted himself with that thought as he fought back waves of a more insistent and much more basic need.

As he stood, as far outside of the melee as possible, Blake watched her patiently, methodically apply and smooth on layer after layer. There was no hesitation in her hands— something he noticed with approval even as he noted the fine-boned elegant shape of them. There was no lack of confidence in her stance. Looking on, Blake realized that she might have been alone for all the noise and confusion around her mattered.

The woman, he decided, could build her spectacular bombe on the Ben Franklin Parkway at rush hour and never miss a step. Good. He couldn't use some hysterical female who folded under pressure.

Patiently he waited as she completed her work. By the time Summer had the pastry bag filled with white icing and had begun the final decorating, most of the kitchen staff were on hand to watch. The rest of the meal was a fait accompli. There was only the finale now.

On the last swirl, she stepped back. There was a communal sigh of appreciation. Still, she didn't smile as she walked completely around the bombe, checking, rechecking. Perfection. Nothing less was acceptable.

Then Blake saw her eyes clear, her lips curve. At the scattered applause, she grinned and was more than beautiful— she was approachable. He found that disturbed him even more.

"Take it in." With a laugh, she stretched her arms high to work out a dozen stiffened muscles. She decided she could sleep for a week.

"Very impressive."

Arms still high, Summer turned slowly to find herself facing Blake. "Thank you." Her voice was very cool, her eyes wary. Sometime between the berries and the frosting, she'd decided to be very, very careful with Blake Cocharan III. "It's meant to be."

"In looks," he agreed. Glancing down, he saw the large bowl of chocolate frosting that had yet to be removed. He ran his finger around the edge, then licked it off. The taste was enough to melt the hardest hearts. "Fantastic."

She couldn't have prevented the smile—a little boy's trick

from a man in an exquisite suit and silk tie. "Naturally," she told him with a little toss of her head. "I only make the fantastic. Which is why you want me—correct, Mr. Cocharan?"

"Mmm." The sound might have been agreement, or it might have been something else. Wisely, both left it at that. "You must be tired, after being on your feet for so long."

"A perceptive man," she murmured, pulling off the chef's hat.

"If you'd like, we'll have supper at my penthouse. It's private, quiet. You'd be comfortable."

She lifted a brow, then sent a quick, distrustful look over his face. Intimate suppers were something to be considered carefully. She might be tired, Summer mused, but she could still hold her own with any man—particularly an American businessman. With a shrug, she pulled off her stained apron. "That's fine. It'll only take me a minute to change."

She left him without a backward glance, but as he watched, she was waylaid by a small man with a dark moustache who grabbed her hand and pressed it dramatically to his lips. Blake didn't have to overhear the words to gauge the intent. He felt a twist of annoyance that, with some effort, he forced into amusement.

The man was speaking rapidly while working his way up Summer's arm. She laughed, shook her head and gently nudged him away. Blake watched the man gaze after her like a forlorn puppy before he clutched his own chef's hat to his heart.

Quite an effect she has on the male of the species, Blake mused. Again dispassionately, he reflected that there was a certain type of woman who drew men without any visible effort. It was an innate . . . skill, he supposed was the correct term. A skill he didn't admire or condemn, but simply mistrusted. A woman like that could manipulate with the flick of the wrist. On a personal level, he preferred women who were more obvious in their gifts.

He positioned himself well out of the way while the cacophony and confusion of cleaning up began. It was a skill he figured wouldn't hurt in her position as head chef of his Philadelphia Cocharan House.

In nine more than the minute she'd claimed she'd be, Summer strolled back into the kitchen. She'd chosen the thin poppy-colored silk because it was perfectly simple—so simple it had a tendency to cling to every curve and draw every eye. Her arms were bare but for one ornately carved gold bracelet she wore just above the elbow. Drop spiral earrings fell almost to her shoulders. Unbound now, her hair curled a bit around her face from the heat and humidity of the kitchen.

She knew the result was part eccentric, part alluring. Just as she knew it transmitted a primal sexuality. She dressed as she did—from jeans to silks—for her own pleasure and at her own whim. But when she saw the fire, quickly banked, in Blake's eyes, she was perversely satisfied.

No iceman, she mused—of course she wasn't interested in him in any personal way. She simply wanted to establish herself as a person, an individual, rather than a name he wanted neatly signed on a contract. Her work clothes were jumbled into a canvas tote she carried in one hand, while over her other shoulder hung a tiny exquisitely beaded purse. In a rather regal gesture, she offered Blake her hand.

"Ready?"

"Of course." Her hand was cool, small and smooth. He thought of streaming sunlight and wet, fragrant grass. Because of it, his voice became cool and pragmatic. "You're lovely."

She couldn't resist. Humor leaped into her eyes. "Of

course." For the first time she saw him grin—fast, appealing. Dangerous. In that moment she wasn't quite certain who held the upper hand.

"My driver's waiting outside," Blake told her smoothly. Together they walked from the brightly lit, noisy kitchen out into the moonlit street. "I take it you were satisified with your part of the governor's meal. You didn't choose to stay for the criticism or compliments."

As she stepped into the back of the limo, Summer sent him an incredulous look. "Criticism? The bombe is my specialty, Mr. Cocharan. It's always superb. I need no one to tell me that." She got in the car, smoothed her skirt and crossed her legs.

"Of course," Blake murmured, sliding beside her, "it's a complicated dish." He went on conversationally, "If my memory serves me, it takes hours to prepare properly."

She watched him remove a bottle of champagne from ice and open it with only a muffled pop. "There's very little that can be superb in a short amount of time."

"Very true." Blake poured champagne into two tulip glasses and, handing Summer one, smiled. "To a lengthy association."

Summer gave him a frank look as the streetlights flickered into the car and over his face. A bit Scottish warrior, a bit English aristocrat, she decided. Not a simple combination. Then again, simplicity wasn't always what she looked for. With only a brief hesitation, she touched her glass to his. "Perhaps," she said. "You enjoy your work, Mr. Cocharan?" She sipped, and without looking at the label, identified the vintage of the wine she drank.

"Very much." He watched her as he drank, noting that she'd done no more than sweep some mascara over her lashes when she'd changed. For an instant he was distracted by the speculation of what her skin would feel like under his fingers. "It's obvious by what I caught of that session in there that you enjoy yours."

"Yes." She smiled, appreciating him and what she thought would be an interesting struggle for power. "I make it a policy to do only what I enjoy. Unless I'm very much mistaken, you have the same policy."

He nodded, knowing he was being baited. "You're very perceptive, Ms. Lyndon."

"Yes." She held her glass out for a refill. "You have excellent taste in wines. Does that extend to other areas?"

His eyes locked on hers as he filled her glass. "All other areas?"

Her mouth curved slowly as she brought the champagne to it. Summer enjoyed the effervescence she could feel just before she tasted it. "Of course. Would it be accurate to say that you're a discriminating man?"

What the hell was she getting at? "If you like," Blake returned smoothly.

"A businessman," she went on. "An executive. Tell me, don't executives . . . delegate?"

"Often."

"And you? Don't you delegate?"

"That depends."

"I wondered why Blake Cocharan III himself would take the time and trouble to woo a chef into his organization."

He was certain she was laughing at him. More, he was certain she wanted him to know it. With an effort, he suppressed his annoyance. "This project is a personal pet of mine. Since I want only the best for it, I take the time and trouble to acquire the best personally."

"I see." The limo glided smoothly to the curb. Summer handed Blake her empty glass as the driver opened her door. "Then how strange that you would even mention LaPointe if only the best will serve you." With the haughty grace a woman can only be born with, Summer alighted. That, she thought smugly, should poke a few holes in his arrogance.

The Cocharan House of Philadelphia stood only twelve stories and had a weathered brick facade. It had been built to blend and accent the colonial architecture that was the heart of the city. Other buildings might zoom higher, might gleam with modernity, but Blake Cocharan had known what he'd wanted. Elegance, style and discretion. That was Cocharan House. Summer was forced to approve. In a great many things, she preferred the old world to the new.

The lobby was quiet, and if the gold was a bit dull, the rugs a bit soft and faded looking, it was a deliberate and canny choice. Old, established wealth was the ambience. No amount of gloss, gleam or gilt would have been more effective.

Taking Summer's arm, Blake passed through with only a nod here and there to the many "Good evening, Mr. Cocharans" he received. After inserting a key into a private elevator, he led her inside. They were enveloped by silence and smoked glass.

"A lovely place," Summer commented. "It's been years since I've been inside. I'd forgotten." She glanced around the elevator and saw their reflections trapped deep in gray glass. "But don't you find it confining to live in a hotel—to live, that is, where you work?"

"No. Convenient."

A pity, Summer mused. When she wasn't working, she wanted to remove herself from the kitchens and timers. She'd never been one—as her mother and father had been—to bring her work home with her.

The elevator stopped so smoothly that the change was hardly noticeable. The doors slid open silently. "Do you have the entire floor to yourself?"

"There're three guest suites as well as my penthouse,"

Blake explained as they walked down the hall. "None of them are occupied at the moment." He inserted a key into a single panel of a double oak door then gestured her inside.

The lights were already dimmed. He'd chosen his colors well, she thought as she stepped onto the thick pewter-toned carpet. Grays from silvery pale to smoky dominated in the low, spreading sofa, the chairs, the walls. With the lights low it had a dreamlike effect that was both sensuous and soothing.

It might have been dull, even bland, but there were splashes of color cleverly interspersed. The deep midnight blue of the drapes, the pearl-like tones of the army of cushions lining the sofa, the rich, primal green of an ivy tangling down the rungs of a breakfront. Then there were the glowing colors of the one painting, a French Impressionist that dominated one wall.

There was none of the clutter she would have chosen for herself, but a sense of style she admired immediately. "Unusual, Mr. Cocharan," Summer complimented as she automatically stepped out of her shoes. "And effective."

"Thank you. Another drink, Ms. Lyndon? The bar's fully stocked, or there's champagne if you prefer."

Still determined to come out of the evening on top, Summer strolled to the sofa and sat. She sent him a cool, easy smile. "I always prefer champagne."

While Blake dealt with the bottle and cork, she took an extra moment to study the room again. Not an ordinary man, she decided. Too often ordinary was synonymous with boring. Summer was forced to admit that because she'd associated herself with the bohemian, the eccentric, the creative for most of her life, she'd always thought of people in business as innately boring.

No, Blake Cocharan wouldn't be dull. She almost regretted it. A dull man, no matter how attractive, could be handled with the minimum of effort. Blake was going to be difficult. Particularly since she'd yet to come to a firm decision on his proposition.

"Your champagne, Ms. Lyndon." When she lifted her eyes to his, Blake had to fight back a frown. The look was too measuring, too damn calculating. Just what was the woman up to now? And why in God's name did she look so right, so temptingly right, curled on his sofa with pillows at her back? "You must be hungry," he said, astonished that he needed the defense of words. "If you'd tell me what you'd like, the kitchen will prepare it. Or I can get you a menu, if you'd prefer."

"A menu won't be necessary." She sipped more cold, frothy French champagne. "I'd like a cheeseburger."

Blake watched the silk shift as she nestled into the corner of the sofa. "A what?"

"Cheeseburger," Summer repeated. "With a side order of fries, shoestring." She lifted her glass to examine the color of the liquid. "Do you know, this was a truly exceptional year."

"Ms. Lyndon . . ." With strained patience, Blake dipped his hands in his pockets and kept his voice even. "Exactly what game are you playing?"

She sipped slowly, savoring. "Game?"

"Do you seriously want me to believe that you, a gourmet, a Cordon Bleu chef, want to eat a cheeseburger and shoestring fries?"

"I wouldn't have said so otherwise." When her glass was empty, Summer rose to refill it herself. She moved, he noted, lazily, with none of that sharp, almost military motion she'd used when cooking. "Your kitchen does have lean prime beef, doesn't it?"

"Of course." Certain she was trying to annoy him, or make

a fool of him, Blake took her arm and turned her to face him. "Why do you want a cheeseburger?"

"Because I like them," she said simply. "I also like tacos and pizza and fried chicken—particularly when someone else is cooking them. That sort of thing is quick, tasty and convenient." She grinned, relaxed by the wine, amused by his reaction. "Do you have a moral objection to junk food, Mr. Cocharan?"

"No, but I'd think you would."

"Ah, I've shattered your image of a gastronomic snob." She laughed, a very appealing, purely feminine sound. "As a chef, I can tell you that rich sauces and heavy creams aren't easy on the digestion either. Besides that, I cook professionally. For long periods of time I'm surrounded by the finest of haute cuisine. Delicacies, foods that have to be prepared with absolute perfection, split-second timing. When I'm not working, I like to relax." She drank champagne again. "I'd prefer a cheeseburger, medium rare, to *Filet aux Champignons* at the moment, if you don't mind."

"Your choice," he muttered and moved the phone to order. Her explanation had been reasonable, even logical. There was nothing that annoyed him more than having his own style of manuevering used against him.

With her glass in hand, Summer wandered to the window. She liked the looks of a city at night. The buildings rose and spread in the distance and traffic wound its way silently on the intersecting roads. Lights, darkness, shadows.

She couldn't have counted the number of cities she'd been in or viewed from a similar spot, but her favorite remained Paris. Yet she'd chosen to live for long lengths of time in the States—she liked the contrast of people and cultures and attitudes. She liked the ambition and enthusiasm of Americans, which she saw typified in her mother's second husband.

Ambition was something she understood. She had a lot of her own. She understood this to be the reason she looked for men with more creative ability than ambition in her personal relationships. Two competitive, career-oriented people made an uneasy couple. She'd learned that early on watching her own parents with each other, and their subsequent spouses. When she chose permanence in a relationship—something Summer considered was at least a decade away—she wanted someone who understood that her career came first. Any cook, from a child making a peanut butter sandwich to a master chef, had to understand priorities. Summer had understood her own all of her life.

"You like the view?" Blake stood behind her, where he'd been studying her for a full five minutes. Why should she seem different from any other woman he'd ever brought to his home? Why should she seem more elusive, more alluring? And why should her presence alone make it so difficult for him to keep his mind on the business he'd brought her there for?

"Yes." She didn't turn because she realized abruptly just how close he was. It was something she should have sensed before, Summer thought with a slight frown. If she turned, they'd be face-to-face. There'd be a brush of bodies, a meeting of eyes. The quick scramble of nerves made her sip the champagne again. Ridiculous, she told herself. No man made her nervous.

"You've lived here long enough to recognize the points of interest," Blake said easily, while his thoughts centered on how the curve of her neck would taste, would feel under the brush of his lips.

"Of course. I consider myself a Philadelphian when I'm in Philadelphia. I'm told by some of my associates that I've become quite Americanized."

Blake listened to the flow of the European accented voice, drew in the subtle, sexy scent of Paris that was her perfume. The dim light touched on the gold scattered through her hair. Like her eyes, he thought. He had only to turn her around and look at her face to see her sculptured, stunning look. And he wanted, overwhelmingly, to see that face.

"Americanized," Blake murmured. His hands were on her shoulders before he could stop them. The silk slid cool under his palms as he turned her. "No . . ." His gaze flicked down, over her hair and eyes, and lingered on her mouth. "I think your associates are very much mistaken."

"Do you?" Her fingers had tightened on the stem of her glass, her mouth had heated. Willpower alone kept her voice steady. Her body brushed his once, then twice as he began to draw her closer. Needs, tightly controlled, began to smolder. While her mind raced with the possibilities, Summer tilted her head back and spoke calmly. "What about the business we're here to discuss, Mr. Cocharan?"

"We haven't started on business yet." His mouth hovered over hers for a moment before he shifted to whisper a kiss just under one eyebrow. "And before we do, it might be wise to settle this one point."

Her breathing was clogging, backing up in her lungs. Drawing away was still possible, but she began to wonder why she should consider it. "Point?"

"Your lips—will they taste as exciting as they look?"

Her lashes were fluttering down, her body softening. "Interesting point," she murmured, then tilted her head back in invitation.

Their lips were only a breath apart when the sharp knock sounded at the door. Something cleared in Summer's brain—reason—while her body continued to hum. She smiled, concentrating hard on that one slice of sanity.

"The service in a Cocharan House is invariably excellent."

"Tomorrow," Blake said as he drew reluctantly away, "I'm going to fire my room service manager."

Summer laughed, but took a shaky sip of wine when he left her to answer the door. Close, she thought, letting out a long, steadying breath. Much too close. It was time to steer the evening into business channels and keep it there. She gave herself a moment while the waiter set up the meal on the table.

"Smells wonderful," Summer commented, crossing the room as Blake tipped and dismissed the waiter. Before sitting, she glanced at his meal. Steak, rare, a steaming potato popping out of its skin, buttered asparagus. "Very sensible." She shot him a teasing grin over her shoulder as he held out her chair.

"We can order dessert later."

"Never touch them," she said, tongue in cheek. With a generous hand she spread mustard over her bun. "I read over your contract."

"Did you?" He watched as she cut the burger neatly in two then lifted a half. It shouldn't surprise him, Blake mused. She did, after all, keep Oreos in her cookie jar.

"So did my attorney."

Blake added some ground pepper to his steak before cutting into it. "And?"

"And it seems to be very much in order. Except . . ." She allowed the word to hang while she took the first bite. Closing her eyes, Summer simply enjoyed.

"Except?" Blake prompted.

"*If* I were to consider such an offer, I'd need considerably more room."

Blake ignored the *if*. She was considering it, and they both knew it. "In what area?"

"Certainly you're aware that I do quite a bit of traveling."

Summer dashed salt on the French fries, tasted and approved. "Often it's a matter of two or three days when I go to, say, Venice and prepare a *Gâteau St. Honoré*. Some of my clients book me months in advance. On the other hand, there are some that deal more spontaneously. A few of these—" Summer bit into the cheeseburger again "—I'll accommodate because of personal affection or professional challenge."

"In other words you'd want to fly to Venice or wherever when you felt it necessary." However incongruous he felt the combination was, Blake poured more champagne into her glass while she ate.

"Precisely. Though your offer does have some slight interest for me, it would be impossible, even, I feel, unethical, to turn my back on established clients."

"Understood." She was crafty, Blake thought, but so was he. "I should think a reasonable arrangement could be worked out. You and I could go over your current schedule."

Summer nibbled on a fry, then dusted her fingers on a white linen napkin. "You and I?"

"That would keep it simpler. Then if we agreed to discuss whatever other occasions might crop up during the year on an individual basis . . ." He smiled as she picked up the second half of her cheeseburger. "I like to think I'm a reasonable man, Ms. Lyndon. And, to be frank, I personally would prefer signing you with my hotel. At the moment, the board's leaning toward LaPointe, but—"

"Why?" The word was a demand and an accusation. Nothing could have pleased Blake more.

"Characteristically, the great chefs are men." She cursed, bluntly and brutally in French. Blake merely nodded. "Yes, exactly. And, through some discreet questioning, we've learned that Monsieur LaPointe is very interested in the position."

"The swine would scramble at a chance to roast chestnuts on a street corner if only to have his picture in the paper." Tossing down her napkin, she rose. "You think perhaps I don't understand your strategy, Mr. Cocharan." The regal lifting of her head accentuated her long, slender neck. Blake remembered quite vividly how that skin had felt under his fingers. "You throw LaPointe in my face thinking that I'll grab your offer as a matter of ego, of pride."

He grinned because she looked magnificent. "Did it work?"

Her eyes narrowed, but her lips wanted badly to curve. "LaPointe is a philistine. *I* am an artist."

"And?"

She knew better than to agree to anything in anger. Knew better, but . . . "You accommodate my schedule, Mr. Cocharan the Third, and I'll make your restaurant the finest establishment of its kind on the East Coast." And damn it, she could do it. She found she wanted to do it to prove it to both of them.

Blake rose, lifting both glasses. "To your art, mademoiselle." He handed her a glass. "And to my business. May it be a profitable union for both of us."

"To success," she amended, clinking glass to glass. "Which, in the end, is what we both look for."

CHAPTER 3

*W*ell, *I've done it,* Summer thought, scowling. She swept back her hair and secured it with two mother-of-pearl combs. Critically she studied her face in the mirror to check her makeup. She'd learned the trick of accenting her best features from her mother. When the occasion called for it, and she was in the mood, Summer exploited the art. Although she felt the face that was reflected at her would do, she frowned anyway.

Whether it had been anger or ego or just plain cussedness, she'd agreed to tie herself to the Cocharan House, and Blake, for the next year. Maybe she did want the challenge of it, but already she was uncomfortable with the long-term commitment and the obligations that went with it.

Three hundred sixty-five days. No, that was too overwhelming, she decided. Fifty-two weeks was hardly a better image. Twelve months. Well, she'd just have to live with it. No, she'd have to do better than that, Summer decided as she wandered back into the studio where she'd be taping a demonstration for public TV. She had to live up to her vow to give the Philadelphia Cocharan House the finest restaurant on the East Coast.

And so she would, she told herself with a flick of her

hair over her shoulder. So she damn well would. Then she'd thumb her nose at Blake Cocharan III. The sneak.

He'd manipulated her. Twice, he'd manipulated her. Even though she'd been perfectly aware of it the second time, she'd strolled down the garden path anyway. Why? Summer ran her tongue over her teeth and watched the television crew set up for the taping.

The challenge, she decided, twisting her braided gold chain around one slim finger. It would be a challenge to work with him and stay on top. Competing was her greatest weakness, after all. That was one reason she'd chosen to excel in a career that was characteristically male-dominated. Oh, yes, she liked to compete. Best of all, she liked to win.

Then there was that ripe masculinity of his. Polished manners couldn't hide it. Tailored clothes couldn't cloak it. If she were honest—and she decided she would be for the moment—Summer had to admit she'd enjoy exploring it.

She knew her effect on men. A genetic gift, she'd always thought, from her mother. It was rare that she paid much attention to her own sexuality. Her life was too full of the pressures of her work and the complete relaxation she demanded between clients. But it might be time, Summer mused now, to alter things a bit.

Blake Cocharan III represented a definite challenge. And how she'd love to shake up that smug male arrogance. How she'd like to pay him back for maneuvering her to precisely where he'd wanted her. As she considered varied ways and means to do just that, Summer idly watched the studio audience file in.

They had the capacity for about fifty, and apparently they'd have a full house this morning. People were talking in undertones, the mumbles and shuffles associated with theaters and churches. The director, a small, excitable man whom Summer had worked with before, hustled from grip to gaffer, light to camera, tossing his arms in gestures that signaled pleasure or dread. Only extremes. When he came over to her, Summer listened to his quick, nervous instructions with half an ear. She wasn't thinking of him, nor was she thinking of the vacherin she was to prepare on camera. She was still thinking of the best way to handle Blake Cocharan.

Perhaps she should pursue him, subtly—but not so subtly that he wouldn't notice. Then when his ego was inflated, she'd . . . she'd totally ignore him. A fascinating idea.

"The first baked shell is in the center storage cabinet."

"Yes, Simon, I know." Summer patted the director's hand while she went over the plan for flaws. It had a big one. She could remember all too clearly that giddy sensation that had swept over her when he'd nearly—just barely—kissed her a few evenings before. If she played the game that way, she just might find herself muddling the rules. So . . .

"The second is right beneath it."

"Yes, I know." Hadn't she put it there herself to cool after baking? Summer gave the frantic director an absent smile. She could ignore Blake right from the start. Treat him—not with contempt, but with disinterest. The smile became a bit menacing. Her eyes glinted. That should drive him crazy.

"All the ingredients and equipment are exactly where you put them."

"Simon," Summer began kindly, "stop worrying. I can build a vacherin in my sleep."

"We roll tape in five minutes—"

"Where is she!"

Both Summer and Simon looked around at the bellowing voice. Her grin was already forming before she saw its owner. "Carlo!"

"Aha." Dark and wiry and as supple as a snake, Carlo Franconi wound his way around people and over cable to grab Summer and pull her jarringly against his chest. "My little French pastry." Fondly he patted her bottom.

Laughing, she returned the favor. "Carlo, what're you doing in downtown Philadelphia on a Wednesday morning?"

"I was in New York promoting my new book, *Pasta by the Master*." He drew back enough to wiggle his eyebrows at her. "And I said, Carlo, you are just around the corner from the sexiest woman who ever held a pastry bag. So I come."

"Just around the corner," Summer repeated. It was typical of him. If he'd been in Los Angeles, he'd have done the same thing. They'd studied together, cooked together, and perhaps if their friendship had not become so solid and important, they might have slept together. "Let me look at you."

Obligingly, Carlo stepped back to pose. He wore straight, tight jeans that flattered narrow hips, a salmon-colored silk shirt and a cloth fedora that was tilted rakishly over his dark, almond-shaped eyes. An outrageous diamond glinted on his finger. As always, he was beautiful, male and aware of it.

"You look fantastic, Carlo. *Fantastico*."

"But of course." He ran a finger down the brim of his hat. "And you, my delectable puff pastry—" he took her hands and pressed each palm to his lips "—*esquisita*."

"But of course." Laughing again, she kissed him full on the mouth. She knew hundreds of people, professionally, socially, but if she'd been asked to name a friend, it would have been Carlo Franconi who'd have come to her mind. "It's good to see you, Carlo. What's it been? Four months? Five? You were in Belgium the last time I was in Italy?"

"Four months and twelve days," he said easily. "But who counts? It's only that I lusted for your Napoleons, your eclairs, your—" he grabbed her again and nibbled on her fingers "—chocolate cake."

"It's vacherin this morning," she said dryly, "and you're welcome to some when the show's over."

"Ah, your meringue. To die for." He grinned wickedly. "I will sit in the front row and cross my eyes at you."

Summer pinched his cheek. "Try to lighten up, Carlo. You're so stuffy."

"Ms. Lyndon, please."

Summer glanced at Simon, whose breathing was becoming shallower as the countdown began. "It's all right, Simon, I'm ready. Get your seat, Carlo, and watch carefully. You might learn something this time."

He said something short and rude and easily translated as they went their separate ways. Relaxed, Summer stood behind her work surface and watched the floor director count off the seconds. Easily ignoring the face Carlo made at her, Summer began the show, talking directly to the camera.

She took this part of her profession as seriously as she took creating the royal wedding cake for a European princess. If she were to teach the average person how to make something elaborate and exciting, she would do it well.

She did look exquisite, Carlo thought. Then she always did. And confident, competent, cool. On one hand, he was glad to find it true, for he was a man who disliked things or people who changed too quickly—particularly if he had nothing to do with it. On the other hand, he worried about her.

As long as he'd known Summer—good God, had it been ten years?—she'd never allowed herself a personal involvement. It was difficult for a volatile, emotional man like himself to fully understand her quality of reserve, her apparent disinterest in romantic encounters. She had passion. He'd seen it explode in temper, in joy, but never had he seen it directed toward a man.

A pity, he thought as he watched her build the meringue rings. A woman, he felt, was wasted without a man—just as a man was wasted without a woman. He'd shared himself with many.

Once over kirsch cake and Chablis, she'd loosened up enough to tell him that she didn't think that men and women were meant for permanent relationships. Marriage was an institution too easily dissolved and, therefore, not an institution at all but a hypocrisy perpetuated by people who wanted to pretend they could make commitments. Love was a fickle emotion and, therefore, untrustworthy. It was something exploited by people as an excuse to act foolishly or unwisely. If she wanted to act foolish, she'd do so without excuses.

At the time, because he'd been on the down end of an affair with a Greek heiress, Carlo had agreed with her. Later, he'd realized that while his agreement had been the temporary result of sour grapes, Summer had meant precisely what she'd said.

A pity, he thought again as Summer took out the previously baked rings from beneath the counter and began to build the shell. If he didn't feel about her as he would about a sister, it would be a pleasure to show her the . . . appealing side of the man/woman mystique. Ah, well—he settled back—that was for someone else.

Keeping an easy monologue with the camera and the studio audience, Summer went through the stages of the dessert. The completed shell, decorated with strips of more meringue and dotted with candied violets, was popped into an oven. The one that she'd baked and cooled earlier was brought out to complete the final stage. She filled it, arranged the fruit, covered it all with rich raspberry sauce and whipped cream to the murmured approval of her audience. The camera came in for a close-up.

"Brava!" Carlo stood, applauding as the dessert sat tempting and complete on the counter. *"Bravissima!"*

Summer grinned and, pastry bag in hand, took a deep bow as the camera clicked off.

"Brilliant, Ms. Lyndon." Simon rushed up to her, whipping off his earphones as he came. "Just brilliant. And, as always, perfect."

"Thank you, Simon. Shall we serve this to the audience and crew?"

"Yes, yes, good idea." He snapped his fingers at his assistant. "Get some plates and pass this out before we have to clear for the next show. Aerobic dancing," he muttered and dashed off again.

"Beautiful, *cara,*" Carlo told her as he dipped a finger into the whipped cream. "A masterpiece." He took a spoon from the counter and took a hefty serving directly from the vacherin. "Now, I will take you to lunch and you can fill me in on your life. Mine—" he shrugged, still eating "—is so exciting it would take days. Maybe weeks."

"We can grab a slice of pizza around the corner." Summer pulled off her apron and tossed it on the counter. "As it happens, there's something I'd like your advice about."

"Advice?" Though the idea of Summer's asking advice of him, of anyone, stunned him, Carlo only lifted a brow. "Naturally," he said with a silky smile as he drew her along. "Who else would an intelligent woman come to for advice—or for anything—but Carlo?"

"You're such a pig, darling."

"Careful." He slipped on dark glasses and adjusted his hat. "Or you pay for the pizza."

Within moments, Summer was taking her first bite and bracing herself as Carlo zoomed his rented Ferrari into Philadelphia traffic. Carlo managed to steer and eat and shift gears with maniacal skill. "So tell me," he shouted over the boom of the radio, "what's on your mind?"

"I've taken a job," Summer yelled back at him. Her hair whipped across her face and she tossed it back again.

"A job? So, you take lots of jobs?"

"This is different." She shifted, crossing her legs beneath her and turning sideways as she took the next bite. "I've agreed to revamp and manage a hotel restaurant for the next year."

"Hotel restaurant?" Carlo frowned over his slice of pizza as he cut off a station wagon. "What hotel?"

She took a deep sip of soda through a straw. "The Cochran House here in Philadelphia."

"Ah." His expression cleared. "First class, *cara*. I should never have doubted you."

"A year, Carlo."

"Goes quickly when one has one's health," he finished blithely.

She let the grin come first. "Damn it, Carlo, I painted myself into a corner because, well, I just couldn't resist the idea of trying it and this—this American steamroller tossed LaPointe in my face."

"LaPointe?" Carlo snarled as only an Italian can. "What does that Gallic slug have to do with this?"

Summer licked sauce from her thumb. "I was going to turn down the offer at first, then Blake—that's the steamroller—asked me for my opinion on LaPointe, since he was also being considered for the position."

"And did you give it to him?" Carlo asked with relish.

"I did, and I kept the contract to look it over. The next hitch was that it was a tremendous offer. With the budget I have, I could turn a two-room slum into a gourmet palace." She frowned, not noticing when Carlo zoomed around a compact with little more than wind between metal. "In addition to that, there's Blake himself."

"The steamroller."

"Yes. I can't control the need to get the best of him. He's smart, he's smug and, damn it, he's sexy as hell."

"Oh, yes?"

"I have this tremendous urge to put him in his place."

Carlo breezed through a yellow light as it was turning red. "Which is?"

"Under my thumb." With a laugh, Summer polished off her pizza. "So because of those things, I've locked myself into a year-long commitment. Are you going to eat the rest of that?"

Carlo glanced down to the remains of his pizza, then took a healthy bite. "Yes. And the advice you wanted?"

After drawing through the straw again, Summer discovered she'd hit bottom. "If I'm going to stay sane while locked into a project for a year, I need a diversion." Grinning, she stretched her arms to the sky. "What's the most foolproof way to make Blake Cocharan III crawl?"

"Heartless woman," Carlo said with a smirk. "You don't need my advice for that. You already have men crawling in twenty countries."

"No, I don't."

"You simply don't look behind you, *cara mia.*"

Summer frowned, not certain she liked the idea after all. "Turn left at the corner, Carlo, we'll drop in on my new kitchen."

The sights and smells were familiar enough, but within moments, Summer saw a dozen changes she'd make. The lighting was good, she mused as she walked arm-in-arm with Carlo. And the space. But they'd need an eye-level wall-oven there—brick lined. A replacement for the electric oven, and certainly more kitchen help. She glanced around, checking the corners of the ceiling for speakers. None. That, too, would change.

"Not bad, my love." Carlo took down a large chef's knife and checked it for weight and balance. "You have the rudiments here. It's a bit like getting a new toy for Christmas and having to assemble it, *sì?*"

"Hmmm." Absently she picked up a skillet. Stainless steel, she noted and set it down again. The pans would have to be replaced with copper washed with tin. She turned and thudded firmly into Blake's chest.

There was a fraction of a second when she softened, enjoying the sensation of body against body. His scent, sophisticated, slightly aloof, pleased her. Then came the annoyance that she hadn't sensed him behind her as she felt she should have. "Mr. Cocharan." She drew away, masking both the attraction and the annoyance with a polite smile. "Somehow I didn't think to find you here."

"My staff keeps me well informed, Ms. Lyndon. I was told you were here."

The idea of being reported on might have grated, but Summer only nodded. "This is Carlo Franconi," she began. "One of the finest chefs in Italy."

"*The* finest chef in Italy," Carlo corrected, extending his hand. "A pleasure to meet you, Mr. Cocharan. I've often enjoyed the hospitality of your hotels. Your restaurant in Milan makes a very passable linguini."

"Very passable is a great compliment from Carlo," Summer explained. "He doesn't think anyone can make an Italian dish but himself."

"Not think, know." Carlo lifted the lid on a steaming pot and sniffed. "Summer tells me she'll be associated with your restaurant here. You're a fortunate man."

Blake looked down at Summer, glancing at the lean, tanned hand Carlo had placed on her shoulder. Jealousy is a sensation that can be recognized even if it has never been experienced before. Blake didn't care for it, or the cause. "Yes, I am. Since you're here, Ms. Lyndon, you might like to sign the final contract. It would save us both a meeting later."

"All right. Carlo?"

"Go, do your business. They do a rack of lamb over

there—it interests me." Without a backward glance, he went to add his two cents.

"Well, he's happy," Summer commented as she walked through the kitchen with Blake.

"Is he in town on business?"

"No, he just wanted to see me."

It was said carelessly, and truthfully, and had the effect of knotting Blake's stomach muscles. So she liked slick Italians, he thought grimly, and slipped a proprietary hand over her arm without being aware of it. That was certainly her business. His was to get her into the kitchens as quickly as possible.

In silence he led her though the lobby and into the hotel offices. Quiet and efficient. Those were brief impressions before she was led into a large, private room that was obviously Blake's.

The colors were bones and creams and browns, the decor a bit more modern than his apartment, but she could recognize his stamp on it. Without being asked, Summer walked over and took a chair. It was hardly past noon, but it occurred to her that she'd been on her feet for almost six consecutive hours.

"Handy that I happened to drop by when you were around," she began, sliding her toes out of her shoes. "It simplifies this contract business. Since I've agreed to do it, we might as well get started." *Then there will be only three hundred and sixty-four days,* she added silently, and sighed.

He didn't like her careless attitude about the contract any more than he liked her careless affection toward the Italian. Blake walked over to his desk and lifted a packet of papers. When he looked back at her, some of his anger drained. "You look tired, Summer."

The lids she allowed to droop lifted again. His first, his only, use of her given name intrigued her. He said it as though he was thinking of the heat and the storms. She felt her chest tighten and blamed it on fatigue. "I am. I was baking meringue at seven o'clock this morning."

"Coffee?"

"No, thanks. I'm afraid I've overdone that already today." She glanced at the papers he held, then smiled with a trace of self-satisfaction. "Before I sign those, I should warn you I'm going to order some extensive changes in the kitchen."

"One of the essential reasons you're to sign them."

She nodded and held out her hand. "You might not be so amiable when you get the bill."

Taking a pen from a holder on his desk, Blake gave it to her. "I think we're both after the same thing, and would both agree cost is secondary."

"I might think so." With a flourish, she looped her name on the line. "But I'm not signing the checks. So—" she passed the contract back to him "—it's official."

"Yes." He didn't even glance at her signature before he dropped the paper on his desk. "I'd like to take you to dinner tonight."

She rose, though she found her legs a bit reluctant to hold weight again. "We'll have to put the seal on our bargain another time. I'll be entertaining Carlo." Smiling, she held out her hand. "Of course, you're welcome to join us."

"It has nothing to do with business." Blake took her hand, then surprised them both by taking her other one. "And I want to see you alone."

She wasn't ready for this, Summer realized. She was supposed to begin the maneuvers, in her own time, on her own turf. Now she was forced to realign her strategy and to deal with the blood warming just under her skin. Determined not to be outflanked this time, she tilted her head and smiled. "We are alone."

His brow lifted. Was that a challenge, or was she plainly mocking him? Either way, this time, he wasn't going to let it go. Deliberately he drew her into his arms. She fit there smoothly. It was something each of them noticed, something they both found disturbing.

Her eyes were level on his, but he saw, fascinated, that the gold flecks had deepened. Amber now, they seemed to glow against the cloudy, changeable hazel of her irises. Hardly aware of what he did, Blake brushed the hair away from her cheek in a gesture that was as sweet and as intimate as it was uncharacteristic.

Summer fought not to be affected by something so casual. A hundred men had touched her, in greeting, in friendship, in anger and in longing. There was no reason why the mere brush of a fingertip over her skin should have her head spinning. An effort of will kept her from melting into his arms or from jerking away. She remained still, watching him. Waiting.

When his mouth lowered toward hers, she knew she was prepared. The kiss would be different, naturally, because he was different. It would be new because he was new. But that was all. It was still a basic form of communication between man and woman. A touch of lips, a pressure, a testing of another's taste; it was no different from the kiss of the first couple, and so it went through culture and time.

And the moment she experienced that touch of lips, that pressure, that taste, she knew she was mistaken. Different? New? Those words were much too mild. The brush of lips, for it was no more at first, changed the fabric of everything. Her thoughts veered off into a chaos that seemed somehow right. Her body grew hot, from within and without, in the space of a heartbeat. The woman who'd thought she knew exactly what to expect, sighed with the unexpected. And reached out.

"Again," she murmured when his lips hovered a breath from hers. With her hands on either side of his face, she drew him to her, through the smoke and into the fire.

He'd thought she'd be cool and smooth and fragrant. He'd been so sure of it. Perhaps that was why the flare of heat had knocked him back on his heels. Smooth she was. Her skin was like silk when he ran his hands up her back to cup her neck. Fragrant. She had a scent that he would, from that moment on, always associate with this woman. But not cool. There was nothing cool about the mouth that clung to his, or the breath that mixed with his as two pairs of lips parted. There was something mindless here. He couldn't grip it, couldn't analyze it, could only experience it.

With a deep, almost feline sound of pleasure, she ran her hands through his hair. God, she'd thought there wasn't a taste she hadn't already known, a texture she hadn't already felt. But his, his was beyond her scope and now, just now, within her reach. Summer wallowed in it and let her lips and tongue draw in the sweetness.

More. She'd never known greed. She'd grown up in a world of affluence where enough was always available. For the first time in her life, Summer knew true hunger, true need. Those things brought pain, she discovered. A deep well of it that spread from the core. *More.* The thought ran through her mind again with the knowledge that the more she took, the more she would ache for.

Blake felt her stiffen. Not knowing the cause, he tightened his hold. He wanted her now, at once, more than he'd ever wanted or had conceived of wanting any woman. She shifted in his arms, resisting for the first time since he'd drawn her here. Throwing her head back, she looked up into the passion and impatience of Blake's eyes.

"Enough."

"No." His hand was still tangled possessively in her hair. "No, it's not."

"No," she agreed on an unsteady breath. "That's why you have to let me go."

He released her, but didn't back away. "You'll have to explain that."

She had more control now—barely, Summer realized shakily, but it was better than none. It was time to establish the rules—her rules—quickly and precisely. "Blake, you're a businessman, I'm an artist. Each of us has priorities. This—" she took a step back and stood straight "—can't be one of them."

"Want to bet?"

Her eyes narrowed more in surprise than annoyance. Odd that she'd missed the ruthlessness in him. It would be best if she considered that later, when there was some distance between them. "We'll be working together for a specific purpose," she went on smoothly. "But we're two different people with two very different outlooks. You're interested in a profit, naturally, and in the reputation of your company. I'm interested in creating the proper showcase for my art, and my own reputation. We both want to be successful. Let's not cloud the issue."

"That issue's perfectly clear," Blake countered. "So's this one. I want you."

"Ah." The sound came out slowly. Deliberately she reached for her neglected purse. "Straight and to the point."

"It would be a bit ridiculous to take a more circular route at the moment." Amusement was overtaking frustration. He was grateful for that because it would give him the edge he'd begun to lose the minute he'd tasted her. "You'd have to be unconscious not to realize it."

"And I'm not." Still, she backed away, relying on poise to

get her out before she lost whatever slim advantage she had. "But it's your kitchen—and it'll be *my* kitchen—that's my main concern right now. With the amount of money you're paying me, you should be grateful I understand the priorities. I'll have a tentative list of changes and new equipment you'll have to order on Monday."

"Fine. We'll go to dinner Saturday."

Summer paused at the door, turned and shook her head. "No."

"I'll pick you up at eight."

It was rare that anyone ignored a statement she'd made. Rather than temper, Summer tried the patient tone she remembered from her governess. It was bound to infuriate. "Blake, I said no."

If he was infuriated, he concealed it well. Blake merely smiled at her—as one might smile at a fussy child. Two, it seemed, could play the same game with equal skill. "Eight," he repeated and sat on the corner of his desk. "We can even have tacos if you like."

"You're very stubborn."

"Yes, I am."

"So am I."

"Yes, you are. I'll see you Saturday."

She had to put a lot of effort into the glare because she wanted to laugh. In the end, Summer found satisfaction by slamming the door, quite loudly.

CHAPTER 4

"Incredible nerve," Summer mumbled. She took another bite of her hot dog, scowled and swallowed. "The man has incredible nerve."

"You shouldn't let it affect your appetite, *cara*." Carlo patted her shoulder as they strolled along the sidewalk toward the proud, weathered bricks of Independence Hall.

Summer bit into the hot dog again. When she tossed her head, the sun caught at the ends of her hair and flicked them with gold. "Shut up, Carlo. He's so *arrogant*." With her free hand, she gestured wildly while continuing to munch, almost vengefully, on the dog and bun. "Carlo, I don't take orders from anyone, especially some tailored, polished American executive with dictatorial tendencies and incredible blue eyes."

Carlo lifted a brow at her description, then shot an approving look at a leggy blonde in a short pink skirt who passed them. "Of course not, *mi amore*," he said absently, craning his neck to follow the blonde's progress down the street. "This Philadelphia of yours has the most fascinating tourist attractions, *sì*?"

"I make my own decisions, run my own life," Summer grumbled, jerking his arm when she saw where his attention had wandered. "I take requests, Franconi, not orders."

"It's always been so." Carlo gave a last wistful look over his shoulder. Perhaps he could talk Summer into stopping somewhere, a park bench, an outdoor café, where he could get a more . . . complete view of Philadelphia's attractions. "You must be tired of walking, love," he began.

"I'm definitely not having dinner with him tonight."

"That should teach him to push Summer Lyndon around." The park, Carlo thought, might have the most interesting of possibilities.

She gave him a dangerous stare. "You're amused because you're a man."

"*You're* amused," Carlo corrected, grinning. "And interested."

"I am not."

"Oh, yes, *cara mia,* you are. Why don't we sit so I can take in the . . . beauty and attractions of your adopted city? After all—" he tipped the brim of his hat at a strolling brunette in brief shorts "—I'm a tourist, *si?*"

She caught the gleam in his eyes, and the reason for it. After letting out a huff of breath, Summer turned a sharp right. "I'll show you tourist attractions, *amico.*"

"But Summer . . ." Carlo caught sight of a redhead in snug jeans walking a poodle. "The view from out here is very educational and uplifting."

"I'll lift you up," she promised and ruthlessly dragged him inside. "The Second Continental Congress met here in 1775, when the building was known as the Pennsylvania State House."

There was an echoing of feet, of voices. A group of schoolchildren flocked by led by a prim, stern-faced teacher wearing practical shoes. "Fascinating," Carlo muttered. "Why don't we go to the park, Summer. It's a beautiful day." For female joggers in tiny shorts and tiny shirts.

"I'd consider myself a poor friend if I didn't give you a

brief history lesson before you leave this evening, Carlo."
She linked her arm more firmly through his. "It was actually
July 8, not July 4, 1776, that the Declaration of Independence
was read to the crowd in the yard outside this building."

"Incredible." Hadn't that brunette been heading for the
park? "I can't tell you how interesting I find this American
history, but some fresh air perhaps—"

"You can't leave Philadelphia without seeing the Liberty
Bell." Taking him by the hand, Summer dragged him along.
"A symbol of freedom is international, Carlo." She didn't
even hear his muttered assent as her thoughts began to swing
back to Blake again. "Just what was he trying to prove with
that gloss and machismo?" she demanded. "Telling me he'd
pick me up at eight after I'd refused to go." Gritting her teeth,
she put her hands on her hips and glared at Carlo. "Men—
you're all basically the same, aren't you?"

"But no, *carissima*." Amused, he gave her a charming
smile and ran his fingers down her cheek. "We are all unique,
especially Franconi. There are women in every city of the
world who can attest to that."

"Pig," she said bluntly, refusing to be swayed with humor.
She sidled closer to him, unconcerned that there was a group
of three female college students hanging on every word.
"Don't throw your women up to me, you Italian lecher."

"Ah, but, Summer . . ." He brought her palm to his lips,
watching the three young women over it. "The word is . . .
connoisseur."

Her comment was an unladylike snort. "You—men," she
corrected, jerking her hand from his, "think of women as
something to toy with, enjoy for a while, then disregard. No
one's ever going to play that game with me."

Grinning from ear to ear, Carlo took both her hands and
kissed them. "Ah, no, no, *cara mia*. A woman, she is like the
most exquisite of meals."

Summer's eyes narrowed. As the three girls edged closer she struggled with a grin of her own. "A meal? You dare to compare a woman with a meal?"

"An exquisite one," Carlo reminded her. "One you anticipate with great excitement, one you linger over, savor, even worship."

Her brows arched. "And when your plate's clean, Carlo?"

"It stays in your memory." Touching his thumb and forefinger together, he kissed them dramatically. "Returns in your dreams and keeps you forever searching for an equally sensual experience."

"Very poetic," she said dryly. "But I'm not going to be anyone's entrée."

"No, my Summer, you are the most forbidden of desserts, and therefore, the most desirable." Irrepressible, he winked at the trio of girls. "This Cocharan, do you not think his mouth waters whenever he looks at you?"

Summer gave a short laugh, took two steps away, then stopped. The image had an odd, primitive appeal. Intrigued, she looked back over her shoulder. "Does it?"

Because he knew he'd distracted her, Carlo slipped an arm around her waist and began to lead her from the building. There was still time for fresh air and leggy joggers in the park. Behind them, the three girls muttered in disappointment. "*Cara,* I am a man who has made a study of *amore.* I know what I see in another man's eyes."

Summer fought off a surge of pleasure and shrugged. "You Italians insist on giving a pretty label to basic lust."

With a huge sigh, Carlo led her outside. "Summer, for a woman with French blood, you have no romance."

"Romance belongs in books and movies."

"Romance," Carlo corrected, "belongs everywhere." Though she'd spoken lightly, Carlo understood that she was being perfectly frank. It worried him and, in the way of friend for friend, disappointed him. "You should try candle-light and wine and soft music, Summer. Let yourself experience it. It won't hurt you."

She gave him a strange sidelong smile as they walked. "Won't it?"

"You can trust Carlo like you trust no one else."

"Oh, I do." Laughing again, she swung an arm around his shoulders. "I trust no one else, Franconi."

That too, was the unvarnished truth. Carlo sighed again but spoke with equal lightness. "Then trust yourself, *cara*. Be guided by your own instincts."

"But I do trust myself."

"Do you?" This time it was Carlo who slanted a look at her. "I think you don't trust yourself to be alone with the American."

"With Blake?" He could feel her stiffen with outrage under the arm he still held around her waist. "That's absurd."

"Then why are you so upset about the idea of having a simple dinner with him?"

"Your English is suffering, Carlo. Upset's the wrong word. I'm annoyed." She made herself relax under his arm again, then tilted her chin. "I'm annoyed because he assumed I'd have dinner with him, then continued to assume I would even after I'd refused. It's a normal reaction."

"I believe your reaction to him is very normal. One might say even—ah—basic." He took out his dark glasses and adjusted them meticulously. Perhaps squint lines added character to a face, but he wanted none on his. "I saw what was in your eyes as well that day in the kitchen."

Summer scowled at him, then lifted her chin a bit higher. "You don't know what you're talking about."

"I'm a gourmet," Carlo corrected with a sweep of his free arm. "Of food, yes, but also of love."

"Just stick to your pasta, Franconi."

He only grinned and patted her flank. "*Carissima,* my pasta never sticks."

She uttered a single French word in the most dulcet tones. It was one most commonly seen scrawled in Parisian alleyways. In tune with each other, they walked on, but both were speculating about what would happen that evening at eight.

* * *

It was quite deliberate, well thought out and very satisfying. Summer put on her shabbiest jeans and a faded T-shirt that was unraveled at the hem on one sleeve. She didn't bother with even a pretense of makeup. After seeing Carlo off at the airport, she'd gone through the drive-in window at a local fast-food restaurant and had picked up a cardboard container of fried chicken, complete with French fries and a tiny plastic bowl of coleslaw.

She opened a can of diet soda and flicked the television on to a syndicated rerun of a situation comedy.

Picking up a drumstick, Summer began to nibble. She'd considered dressing to kill, then breezing by him when he came to the door with the careless comment that she had a date. Very self-satisfying. But this way, Summer decided as she propped up her feet, she could be comfortable and insult him at the same time. After a day spent walking around the city while Carlo ogled and flirted with every female between six and sixty, comfort was every bit as important as the insult.

Satisfied with her strategy, Summer settled back and waited for the knock. It wouldn't be long, she mused. If she was any judge of character, she'd peg Blake as a man who was obsessively prompt. And fastidious, she added, taking a pleased survey of her cluttered, comfortably disorganized apartment.

Let's not forget smug, she reminded herself as she polished off the drumstick. He'd arrive in a sleek tailored suit with the shirt crisp and monogrammed on the cuffs. There wouldn't be a smudge on the Italian leather of his shoes. Not a hair out of place. Pleased, she glanced down at the tattered hem on her oldest jeans. A pity they didn't have a few good holes in them.

Grinning gleefully, she reached for her soda. Holes or not, she certainly didn't look like a woman waiting anxiously to impress a man. And that, Summer concluded, was what a man like Blake expected. Surprising him would give her a great deal of pleasure. Infuriating him would give her even more.

When the knock came, Summer glanced around idly before unfolding her legs. Taking her time, she rose, stretched, then moved to the door.

For the second time, Blake wished he'd had a camera to catch the look of blank astonishment on her face. She said nothing, only stared. With a hint of a smile on his lips, Blake tucked his hands into the pockets of his snug, faded jeans. There was no one, he reflected, whom he'd ever gotten more pleasure out of outwitting. So much so, it was tempting to make a career out of it.

"Dinner ready?" He took an appreciative sniff of the air. "Smells good."

Damn his arrogance—and his perception, Summer thought. How did he always manage to stay one step ahead of her? Except for the fact that he wore tennis shoes—tattered ones—he was dressed almost identically to her. It was only more annoying that he looked every bit as natural, and every bit as attractive, in jeans and a T-shirt as he did in an elegant business suit. With an effort, Summer controlled her temper, and twin surges of humor and desire. The rules might have changed, but the game wasn't over.

"*My* dinner's ready," she told him coolly. "I don't recall inviting you."

"I did say eight."

"I did say no."

"Since you objected to going out—" he took both her hands before breezing inside "—I thought we'd just eat in."

With her hands caught in his, Summer stood in the open doorway. She could order him to leave, she considered. Demand it . . . And he might. Although she didn't mind being rude, she didn't see much satisfaction in winning a battle so directly. She'd have to find another, more devious, more gratifying method to come out on top.

"You're very persistent, Blake. One might even say pigheaded."

"One might. What's for dinner?"

"Very little." Freeing one hand, Summer gestured toward the take-out box.

Blake lifted a brow. "Your penchant for fast food's very intriguing. Ever thought of opening your own chain—Minute Croissants? Drive Through Pastries?"

She wouldn't be amused. "You're the businessman," she reminded him. "I'm an artist."

"With a teenager's appetite." Strolling over, Blake plucked a drumstick from the box. He settled on the couch, then propped his feet on the coffee table. "Not bad," he decided after the first bite. "No wine?"

No, she didn't want to be amused, was determined not to be, but watching him make himself at home with her dinner, Summer fought off a grin. Maybe her plan to insult him hadn't worked, but there was no telling what the evening might bring. She only needed one opening to give him a good, solid jab. "Diet soda." She sat down and lifted the can. "There's more in the kitchen."

"This is fine." Blake took the drink from her and sipped.

"Is this how one of the greatest dessert chefs spends her evenings?"

Lifting a brow, Summer took the can back from him. "*The* greatest dessert chef spends her evenings as she pleases."

Blake crossed one ankle over the other and studied her. The flecks in her eyes were more subtle this evening— perhaps because she was relaxed. He liked to think he could make them glow again before the night was over. "Yes, I'm sure you do. Does that extend to other areas?"

"Yes." Summer took another piece of chicken before handing Blake a paper napkin. "I've decided your company's tolerable—for the moment."

Watching her, he took another bite. "Have you?"

"That's why you're here eating half my meal." She ignored his chuckle and propped her own feet on the table beside his. There was something cozy about the setting that appealed to her—something intimate that made her wary. She was too cautious a woman to allow herself to forget the effect that one kiss had had on her. She was too stubborn a woman to back down.

"I'm curious about why you insisted on seeing me tonight." A commercial on floor wax flicked across the television screen. Summer glanced at it before turning to Blake. "Why don't you explain?"

He took a plastic fork and sampled the coleslaw. "The professional reason or the personal one?"

He answered a question with a question too often, she decided. It was time to pin him down. "Why don't you take it one at a time?"

How did she eat this stuff? he wondered as he dropped the fork back into the box. When you looked at her, you could see her in the most elegant of restaurants—flowers, French wine, starchily correct waiters. She'd be wearing silk and toying with some luscious dessert.

Summer rubbed the bottom of one bare foot over the top of the other while she took another bite of chicken. Blake smiled even as he asked himself why she attracted him.

"Business first then. We'll be working together closely for several months at least. I think it's wise if we get to know each other—find out how the other works so we can make the proper adjustments when necessary."

"Logical." Summer plucked out a couple of French fries before offering the box to Blake. "It's just as well that you find out up front that I don't make adjustments at all. I work only one way—my way. So . . . personal?"

He enjoyed her confidence and the complete lack of compromise. He planned to explore the first and undo the second. "Personally, I find you a beautiful, interesting woman." Dipping his hand into the box, he watched her. "I want to take you to bed." When she said nothing, he nibbled on a fry. "And I think we should get to know each other first." Her stare was direct and unblinking. He smiled. "Logical?"

"Yes, and egotistical. You seem to have your share of both qualities. But—" she wiped her fingers on the napkin before she picked up the soda again "—you're honest. I admire honesty in other people." Rising, she looked down at him. "Finished?"

His gaze remained as cool as hers while he handed her the box. "Yeah."

"I happen to have a couple of éclairs in the fridge, if you're interested."

"Supermarket special?"

Her lips curved, slowly, slightly. "No. I do have some standards. They're mine."

"Then I could hardly insult you by turning them down."

This time she laughed. "I'm sure diplomacy's your only motive."

"That, and basic gluttony," he added as she walked away.

She's a cool one, Blake reflected, thinking back to her reaction, or lack of one, to his statement about taking her to bed. The coolness, the control, intrigued him. Or perhaps more accurately, challenged him.

Was it a veneer? If it was, he'd like the opportunity to strip off the layers. Slowly, he decided, even lazily, until he found the passion beneath. It would be there—he imagined it would be like one of her desserts—dark and forbidden beneath a cool white icing. Before too much time had passed, Blake intended to taste it.

Her hands weren't steady. Summer cursed herself as she opened the refrigerator. He'd shaken her—just as he'd meant to. She only hoped he hadn't been able to see through her off-hand response. Yes, he'd intended to shake her, but he'd said precisely what he'd meant. That she understood. At the moment, she didn't have the time to absorb and dissect her feelings. There was only her first reaction—not shock, not outrage, but a kind of nervous excitement she hadn't experienced in years.

Silly, Summer told herself while she arranged éclairs on two Meissen plates. She wasn't a teenager who delighted in fluttery feelings. Nor would she tolerate being informed she was about to become someone's lover. Affairs, she knew, were dangerous, time-consuming and distracting. And there always seemed to be one party who was more involved, therefore, more vulnerable, than the other. She wouldn't allow herself to be in that position.

But the little twinges of nervous excitement remained.

She was going to have to do something about Blake Cocharan, Summer decided as she poured out two cups of coffee. And she was going to have to do it quickly. The problem was—what?

As Summer arranged cups and plates on a tray, she decided to do what she did best under pressure. She'd wing it.

"You're about to have a memorable, sensuous experience."

Blake glanced up at the announcement and watched her come into the room, tray in hand. Desire hit him surprisingly hard, surprisingly fast. It warned him that if he wanted to stay in control, he'd have to play the game with skill.

"My éclairs aren't to be taken lightly," Summer continued. "Nor are they to be eaten with anything less than reverence."

He waited until she sat beside him again before he took a plate. Very skillfully done, he thought again as her scent drifted to him. "I'll do my best."

"Actually—" she brought down the side of her fork and broke off the first bite "—no effort's required. Just taste buds." Unable to resist, Summer brought the fork to his lips.

He watched her, and she him, as she fed him. The light slanted through the window behind them and caught in her eyes. More green now, Blake thought, almost feline. A man, any man, could lose himself trying to define that color, read that expression. The rich cream and flaky pastry melted in his mouth. Perfect, unique, desirable—like its creator. The first taste, like the first kiss, demanded more.

"Incredible," he murmured, and as her lips curved, he wanted them under his.

"Naturally." As she broke off another portion, Blake's hand closed over her wrist. Her pulse scrambled briefly, he could feel it, but her eyes remained cool and level.

"I'll return the favor." He said it quietly, and his fingers stayed lightly on her wrist as he took the fork in his other hand. He moved slowly, deliberately, keeping his eyes on hers, bringing the pastry to her lips, then pausing. He watched them part, saw the tip of her tongue. It would have been so easy to close his mouth over hers just then—from the rapid beat of her pulse under his fingers, he knew there'd be no resistance. Instead, he fed her the éclair, his stomach muscles tightening as he imagined the taste that was even now lying delicately on her tongue.

She'd never felt anything like this. She'd sampled her own cooking countless times, but had never had her senses so heightened. The flavor seemed to fill her mouth. Summer wanted to keep it there, exploring the sensation that had become so unexpectedly, so intensely, sexual. It took a conscious effort to swallow, and another to speak.

"More?" she asked.

His gaze flicked down from her eyes to her mouth then back again. "Always."

A dangerous game. She knew it, but opted to play. And to win. Taking her time, she fed him the next bite. Was the color of his eyes deeper? She didn't think she was imagining it, nor the waves of desire that seemed to pound over her. Did they come from her, or from him?

On the television, someone broke into raucous laughter. Neither of them noticed. It would be wise to step back now, cautiously. Even as the thought passed through her mind, she opened her mouth for the next taste.

Some things exploded on the tongue, others heated it or tantalized. This was a cool, elegant experience, no less sensual than champagne, no less primitive than ripened fruit. Her nerves began to calm, but her awareness intensified. He was wearing some subtle cologne that made her think of the woods in autumn. His eyes were the deep blue of an evening sky. When his knee brushed hers, she felt a warmth that seeped through two layers of material and touched flesh. Moment after moment passed without her being aware that they weren't speaking, only slowly, luxuriously, feeding each other. The intimacy wrapped around her, no less intense, no less exciting than lovemaking. The coffee sat cooling. Shadows spread through the room as the sun went down.

"The last bite," Summer murmured, offering it. "You approve?"

He caught the ends of her hair between his thumb and finger. "Completely."

Her skin tingled, much too pleasantly. Although she didn't shift away, Summer set the fork down with great care. She was feeling soft—too soft. And too vulnerable. "One of my clients has a secret passion for éclairs. Four times a year I go to Brittany and make him two dozen. Last fall he gave me an emerald necklace."

Blake lifted a brow as he twined a strand of her hair around his finger. "Is that a hint?"

"I'm fond of presents," she said easily. "But then, that sort of thing isn't quite ethical between business associates."

As she leaned forward for her coffee, Blake tightened his fingers in her hair and held her still. In the moment her eyes met his, he saw mild surprise and mild annoyance. She didn't like to be held down by anyone. "Our business association is only one level. We're both acutely aware of that by this time."

"Business is the first level, and the first priority."

"Maybe." It was difficult to admit, even to himself, that he was beginning to have doubts about that. "In any case, I haven't any intention of staying at level one."

If she were ever going to handle him, it would have to be now. Summer draped her arm negligently across the back of the sofa and wished her stomach would unknot. "I'm attracted to you. And I think it should be difficult, and interesting, to work around that for the next few months. You said you wanted to understand me. I rarely explain myself, but I'll make an exception." Leaning forward again, she plucked a cigarette from its holder. "Have you a light?"

It was strange how easily she drew feelings from him without warning. Now it was annoyance. Blake took out his lighter and flicked it on. He watched her pull in smoke, then blow it out quickly in a gesture he realized came more from habit than pleasure. "Go on."

"You said you knew my mother," Summer began. "You'd know of her in any case. She's a beautiful, talented, intelligent woman. I love her very much, both as a mother, and as a person who's full of the joy of life. If she has one weakness, it is men."

Summer folded her legs under her and concentrated on relaxing. "She's had three husbands, and innumerable lovers. She's always certain each relationship is forever. When she's involved with a man, she's blissfully happy. His interests are her interests, his dislikes her dislikes. Naturally, when it ends, she's crushed."

Again, Summer drew on her cigarette. She'd expected him to make some passing comment. When instead, he only listened, only watched, she went further than she'd intended. "My father is a more practical man, and yet he's been through two wives and quite a few discreet affairs. Unlike my mother, who accepts flaws—even enjoys them for a short time—he looks for perfection. Since there is no perfection in people, only in what people create, he's continually disappointed. My mother looks for elation and romance, my father looks for the perfect companion. I don't look for either of those."

"Why don't you tell me what you look for then?"

"Success," she said simply. "Romance has a beginning, so it follows it has an end. A companion demands compromise and patience. I give all my patience to my work, and I have no talent for compromise."

It should have satisfied him, even relieved him. After all, he wanted nothing more than a casual affair, no strings, no commitments. He didn't understand why he wanted to shake the words back down her throat, only knew that he did. "No romance," he said with a nod, "No companionship. That doesn't rule out the fact that you want me, and I want you."

"No." The smoke was leaving a bitter taste in her mouth. As Summer crushed out her cigarette she thought how much their discussion sounded like a negotiation. Yet wasn't that how she preferred things? "I said it would be difficult to work around, but it's also necessary. You want a service from me, Blake, and I agreed to give you that, because I want the experience and the publicity I'll get out of it. But changing the tone and face of your restaurant is going to be a long, complicated process. Combining that with my other commitments, I won't have time for any personal distractions."

"Distractions?" Why should that one word have infuriated him? It did, just as her businesslike dismissal of desire infuriated him. Perhaps she hadn't meant it as a challenge, but he couldn't take it as anything less. "Does this distract you?" He ran his finger down the side of her throat before he cupped the back of her neck.

She could feel the firm pressure of each of his fingers against her skin. And in his eyes, she could see the temper, the need. Both pulled at her. "You're paying me a great deal of money to do a job, Blake." Her voice was steady. Good. Her heartbeat wasn't. "As a businessman, you should want the complications left to a minimum."

"Complications," he repeated. He drew his other hand through her hair so that her face was tilted back. Summer felt a jolt of excitement shoot down her spine. "Is this—" he brushed his lips over her cheek "—a complication?"

"Yes." Her brain sent out the signal to pull away, but her body refused the command.

"And a distraction?"

He took his mouth on a slow journey to hers, but only nibbled. There was no pressure but the slight grip he kept on the base of her neck with fingers moving slowly, rhythmically over her skin. Summer didn't move away, though she told herself she still could. She'd never permitted herself to be seduced, and tonight was no different.

Just a sample, she thought. She knew how to taste and judge, then step away from even the most tempting of flavors. Just as she knew how to absorb every drop of pleasure from that one tiny test.

"Yes," she murmured and let her eyes flutter closed. She needed no visual image now, but only the sensations. Warm, soft, moist—his mouth against hers. Firm, strong, persuasive—the fingers against her skin. Subtle, male, intriguing—the scent that clung to him. When he spoke her name, his voice flowed over her like a breeze, one that carried a trace of heat and the hint of a storm.

"How simple do you want it to be, Summer?" It was happening again, he realized. That total involvement he neither looked for nor wanted—the total involvement he couldn't resist. "There's only you and me."

"There's nothing simple about that." Even as she disagreed, her arms were going around him, her mouth was seeking his again.

It was only a kiss. She told herself that as his lips slanted lightly over hers. She could still end it, she was still in control. But first, she wanted just one more taste. Without thinking, she touched the tip of his tongue with hers, to fully explore the flavor. Her own moan sounded softly in her ears as she drew him closer. Body against body, firm and somehow right. This new thought drifted to her even as the sensation concentrated on the play of mouth to mouth.

Why had kisses seemed so basic, so simplistic before this? There were hundreds of pulse points in her body she'd remained unaware of until this moment. There were pleasures deeper, richer than she'd ever imagined that could be drawn out and exploited by the most elemental gesture between a man and a woman. She'd thought she'd known the limits of her own needs, the depth of her own passions . . . until now. Barely touching her, Blake was tearing something from her that wasn't calm, ordered and disciplined. And when it was totally free, what then?

She found herself at the verge of something she'd never come to before—where emotions commanded her mind completely. A step further and he would have all of her. Not just her body, not just her thoughts, but that most private, most well guarded possession, her heart.

She felt a greed for him and pulled away from it. If she were greedy, if she took, then he would too. He still held her, lightly enough for her to draw back, firmly enough to keep her close. She was breathless, moved. As she struggled to think clearly, Summer decided it would be foolish to try to deny either.

"I think I proved my point," she managed.

"Yours?" Blake countered as he ran a hand up her back. "Or mine?"

She took a deep breath, expelling it slowly. That one small show of emotion had desire clawing at him again. "I've mixed enough ingredients to know that business affairs and personal affairs aren't palatable. On Monday, I go to work for Cocharan. I intend to give you your money's worth. There can't be anything else."

"There's quite a bit else already." He cupped her chin in his hand so that their eyes held steady. Inside he was a mass of aching needs and confusion. With that kiss, that long, slow kiss, he'd all but forgotten his strictest rule. *Keep the emotions harnessed, both in business and in pleasure. Otherwise, you make mistakes that aren't easily rectified.* He needed time, and he realized he needed distance. "We know each other better now," he said after a moment. "When we make love, we'll understand each other."

Summer remained seated when he rose. She wasn't completely sure she could stand. "On Monday," she said in a firmer voice, "we'll be working together. That's all there is between us from this point on."

"When you deal with as many contracts as I do, Summer, you learn that paper is just that: paper. It's not going to make any difference."

He walked to the door thinking he needed some fresh air to clear his head, a drink to settle his nerves. And distance, a great deal of distance, before he forgot everything except the raging need to have her.

With his hand on the knob, Blake turned around for one last look at her. There was something in the way she frowned at him, with her eyes focused and serious, her lips soft in a half pout that made him smile.

"Monday," he told her, and was gone.

CHAPTER 5

Why in hell couldn't he stop thinking of her? Blake sat at his desk examining the details of a twenty-page contract in preparation for what promised to be a long, tense meeting in the boardroom. He wasn't taking in a single word. Uncharacteristic. He knew it, resented it and could do nothing about it.

For days Summer had been slipping into his mind and crowding out everything else. For a man who took order and self-control for granted, it was nerve-racking.

Logically, there was no reason for his obsession with her. Blake called it obsession, for lack of a better term, but it didn't please him. She was beautiful, he mused as his thoughts drifted further away from clauses and terms. He'd known hundreds of beautiful women. She was intelligent, but intelligent women had been in his life before. Desirable—even now in his neat, quiet office he could feel the first stirrings of need. But he was no stranger to desire.

He enjoyed women, as friends and as lovers. Enjoyment, Blake reflected, was perhaps the key word—he'd never looked for anything deeper in a relationship with a woman. But he wasn't certain it was the proper word to describe what was already between himself and Summer. She moved him—too strongly, too quickly—to the point where his innate control was shaken. No, he didn't enjoy that, but it didn't stop him from wanting more. Why?

Utilizing his customary method of working through a problem, Blake leaned back and, picking up a pen, began to list the possibilities.

Perhaps part of the consistent attraction was the fact that he liked outmaneuvering her. It wasn't easily done, and took quick thinking and careful planning. Up till this point, he'd countered her at every turn. Blake was realistic enough to know that that wouldn't last, but he was human enough to want to try. Just where would they clash next? he wondered. Over business . . . or over something more personal? In either case he wanted to go head to head with her just as much—well, almost as much—as he wanted to make love with her.

And perhaps another reason was that he knew the attraction was just as strong on her part—yet she continued to refuse it. He admired that strength of will in her. She mistrusted intimacy, he mused. Because of her parents' track record? Yes, partially, he decided. But he didn't think that was all of it. He'd just have to dig a bit deeper to get the whole picture.

He wanted to dig, he realized. For the first time in his life Blake wanted to know a woman completely. Her thought process, her eccentricities, what made her laugh, what annoyed, what she really wanted for and in her life. Once he knew all there was to know . . . He couldn't see past that. But he wanted to know her, understand her. And he wanted her as a lover as he'd never wanted anything else.

When the buzzer on his desk sounded, Blake answered it automatically with his thoughts still centering on Summer Lyndon.

"Your father's on his way back, Mr. Cocharan."

Blake glanced down at the contract on his desk and mentally filed it. He still needed an hour with it before the board meeting. "Thanks." Even as he released the intercom button, the door swung open. Blake Cocharan II strolled into the room and took it over.

In build and coloring, he was similar to his son. Exercise and athletics had kept him trim and hard over the years. There were threads of gray in the dark hair that was covered by a white sea captain's hat. But his eyes were young and vibrant. He walked with the easy rolling gait of a man more accustomed to decks than floors. He wore canvas on his sockless feet, and a Swiss watch on his wrist. When he grinned, the lines etched by time and squinting at the sun fanned out from his eyes and mouth. As he stood to greet him, Blake caught the salty, sea-breezy scent he always associated with his father.

"B.C." Their hands clasped, one older and rougher than the other, both firm. "Just passing through?"

"On my way to Tahiti, going to do some sailing." B.C. grinned again, appealingly, as he ran a finger along the brim of his cap. "Want to play hookey and crew for me?"

"Can't. I'm booked solid for the next two weeks."

"You work too hard, boy." In an old habit, B.C. walked over to the bar at the west side of the room and poured himself bourbon, neat.

Blake grinned at his father's back as B.C. tossed down three fingers of liquor. It was still shy of noon. "I came by it honestly."

With a chuckle, B.C. poured a second drink. When it had been his office, he'd stocked only the best bourbon. He was glad his son carried on the tradition. "Maybe—but I learned to play just as hard."

"You paid your dues, B.C."

"Yeah." Twenty-five years of ten-hour days, he reflected.

Of hotel rooms, airports and board meetings. "So did the old man—so've you." He turned back to his son. Like looking into a mirror that's twenty years past, he thought, and smiled rather than sighed. "I've told you before, you can't wrap your life up in hotels." He sipped appreciatively at the bourbon this time, then swirled it. "Gives you ulcers."

"Not so far." Sitting again, Blake steepled his fingers, watching his father over them. He knew him too well, had apprenticed under him, watched him wheel and deal. Tahiti might be his destination, but he hadn't stopped off in Philadelphia without a reason. "You came in for the board meeting."

B.C. nodded before he found some salted almonds under the bar. "Have to put in my two cents worth now and again." He popped two nuts in his mouth and bit down with relish. He was always grateful that the teeth were still his and his eyesight was keen. If a man had those, and a forty-foot sloop, he needed little else. "If we buy the Hamilton chain, it's going to mean twenty more hotels, over two thousand more employees. A big step."

Blake lifted a brow. "Too big?"

With a laugh, B.C. dropped down into a chair across from the desk. "I didn't say that, don't think that—and apparently you don't think so either."

"No, I don't." Blake waved away his father's offering of almonds. "Hamilton's an excellent chain, simply mismanaged at this point. The buildings themselves are worth the outlay." He gave his father a mild, knowledgeable look. "You might check out the Hamilton Tahiti while you're there."

Grinning, B.C. leaned back. The boy was sharp, he thought, pleased. But then he came by that honestly, too. "Thought crossed my mind. By the way, your mother sends her love."

"How is she?"

"Up to her neck in a campaign to save another crumbling ruin." The grin widened. "Keeps her off the streets. Going to meet me on the island next week. Hell of a first mate, your mother." He nibbled on another almond, pleased to think of having some time alone with his wife in the tropics. "So, Blake, how's your sex life?"

Too used to his father to be anything but amused, Blake inclined his head. "Adequate, thanks."

With a short laugh, B.C. downed the rest of his drink. "Adequate's a disgrace to the Cocharan name. We do everything in superlatives."

Blake drew out a cigarette. "I've heard stories."

"All true," his father told him, gesturing with the empty glass. "One day I'll have to tell you about this dancer in Bangkok in '39. In the meantime, I've heard you plan to do some face-lifting right here."

"The restaurant." Blake nodded and thought of Summer. "It promises to be . . . fascinating work."

B.C. caught the tone and began to gently probe. "I can't disagree that the place needs a little glitzing up. So you hired on a French chef to oversee the operation."

"Half French."

"A woman?"

"That's right." Blake blew out smoke, aware which path his father was trying to lead him down.

B.C. stretched out his legs. "Knows her business, does she?"

"I wouldn't have hired her otherwise."

"Young?"

Blake drew on his cigarette and suppressed a smile. "Moderately, I suppose."

"Attractive?"

"That depends on your definition—I wouldn't call her attractive." Too tame a word, Blake thought, much, much too tame. Mesmerizing, alluring—those suited her more. "I can tell you that she's dedicated to her profession, an ambitious perfectionist and that her éclairs . . ." His thoughts drifted back to that intoxicating interlude. "Her éclairs are an experience not to be missed."

"Her éclairs," B.C. repeated.

"Fantastic." Blake leaned back in his chair. "Absolutely fantastic." He kept the grin under control as his buzzer sounded again.

"Ms. Lyndon is here, Mr. Cocharan."

Monday morning, he thought. Business as usual. "Send her in."

"Lyndon." B.C. set down his glass. "That's the cook, isn't it?"

"Chef," Blake corrected. "I'm not sure if she answers to the term 'cook.' "

The knock was brief before Summer walked in. She carried a slim leather folder in one hand. Her hair was braided and rolled at the nape of her neck so that the hints of gold threaded through the brown. Her suit in a deep plum color was Chanel, simple and exquisite over a high-necked lace blouse that rose to frame her face. The strict professionalism of her attire made Blake instantly speculate on what she wore beneath—something brief, silky and sexy, the same color as her skin.

"Blake." Following her own self-lecture on priorities, Summer held out her hand. Impersonal, businesslike and formal. She wasn't going to think about what happened when his mouth touched hers. "I've brought you the list of changes of equipment and suggestions we spoke about."

"Fine." He saw her turn her head as B.C. rose from his chair. And he saw the gleam light his father's eyes as it always did when he was in the company of a beautiful woman. "Summer Lyndon, Blake Cocharan II. B.C., Ms. Lyndon will be managing the kitchen here at the Philadelphia Cocharan House."

"Mr. Cocharan." Summer found her hand enveloped in a large, calloused one. He looks, she realized with a jolt, exactly as Blake will in thirty years. Distinguished, weathered, with that perennial touch of polish. Then B.C. grinned, and she understood that Blake would still be dangerous in three decades.

"B.C.," he corrected, lifting her fingers to his lips. "Welcome to the family."

Summer shot Blake a quick look. "Family?"

"We consider anyone associated with Cocharan House part of the family." B.C. gestured to the chair he'd vacated. "Please, sit down. Let me get you a drink."

"Thank you. Perhaps some Perrier." She watched B.C. cross the room before she sat and laid the folder on her lap. "I believe you're acquainted with my mother, Monique Dubois."

That stopped him. B.C. turned, the bottle of Perrier still in his hand, the glass in the other still empty. "Monique? You're Monique's girl? I'll be damned."

And so he might be, B.C. thought. Years before—was it nearly twenty now?—during a period of marital upheaval on both sides, he'd had a brief, searing affair with the French actress. They'd parted on amicable terms and he'd reconciled with his wife. But the two weeks with Monique had been . . . memorable. Now he was in his son's office pouring Perrier for her daughter. Fate, he thought wryly, was a tricky sonofabitch.

If Summer had suspected before that her mother and Blake's father had once been lovers, she was now certain of it. Her thoughts on fate directly mirrored his as she crossed her legs. Like mother, like daughter? she wondered. Oh, no, not in this case. B.C. was still staring at her. For a reason she didn't completely understand, she decided to make it easy for him.

"Mother is a loyal client of Cocharan Houses; she'll stay nowhere else. I've already mentioned to Blake that we once had dinner with your father. He was very gracious."

"When it suits him," B.C. returned, relieved. *She knows,* he concluded before his gaze strayed to Blake's. There he saw a frown of concentration that was all too familiar. *And so will he if I don't watch my step,* B.C. decided. *Hot water,* he mused. *After twenty years I could still be in hot water.* His wife was the love of his life, his best friend, but twenty years wasn't long enough to be safe from a transgression.

"So—" he finished pouring the Perrier, then brought it to her "—you decided against following in your mother's footsteps and became a chef instead."

"I'm sure Blake would agree that following in a parent's footsteps is often treacherous."

Instinct told Blake that it wasn't business she spoke of now. A look passed between his father and Summer that he couldn't comprehend. "It depends where the path leads," Blake countered. "In my case I preferred to look at it as a challenge."

"Blake takes after his grandfather," B.C. put in. "He has that cagey kind of logic."

"Yes," Summer murmured. "I've seen it in action."

"Apparently you made the right choice," B.C. went on. "Blake told me about your éclairs."

Slowly, Summer turned her head until she was facing Blake again. The muscles in her stomach, in her thighs, tightened with the memory. Her voice remained calm and cool. "Did he? Actually, my specialty is the bombe."

Blake met her gaze directly. "A pity you didn't have one available the other night."

There were vibrations there, B.C. thought, that didn't need

to bounce off a third party. "Well, I'll let you two get on with
your business. I've some people to see before the board meeting. A pleasure meeting you, Summer." He took her hand
again and held it as his eyes held hers. "Please, give my best
to your mother."

She saw his eyes were like Blake's, in color, in shape, in
appeal. Her lips curved. "I will."

"Blake, I'll see you this afternoon."

He only murmured an assent, watching Summer rather
than his father. The door closed before he spoke. "Why do
I feel as though there were messages being passed in front
of me?"

"I have no idea," Summer said coolly as she lifted the
folder. "I'd like you to glance over these papers while I'm
here, if you have time." Zipping open the folder, she pulled
them out. "That way, if there are any questions or any dis-
agreements, we can get through them now before I begin
downstairs."

"All right." Blake picked up the first sheet but studied her
over it. "Is that suit supposed to keep me at a distance?"

She sent him a haughty look. "I have no idea what you're
talking about."

"Yes, you do. And another time I'd like to peel it off you,
layer by layer. But at the moment, we'll play it your way."
Without another word, he lowered his gaze to the paper and
started to read.

"Arrogant swine," Summer said distinctly. When he didn't
even bother to look up, she folded her arms over her chest.
She wanted a cigarette to give her something to do with her
hands, but refused herself the luxury. She would sit like a
stone, and when the time came, she would argue for every
one of the changes she'd listed. And win every one of them.
On that level *she* was in complete control.

She wanted to hate him for realizing she'd worn the

elegant, career-oriented suit to set a certain tone. Instead, she had to respect him for being perceptive enough to pick up on small details. She wanted to hate him for making her want so badly with only a look and a few words. It wasn't possible when she'd spent the remainder of the weekend alternately wishing she'd never met him and wishing he'd come back and bring her that excitement again. He was a problem; there was no denying it. She understood that you solved problems one step at a time. Step one, her kitchen—accent on the personal pronoun.

"Two new gas ovens," he murmured as he scanned the sheet. "One electric oven and two more ranges of each kind." Without lowering it, he glanced at her over the top of the page.

"I believe I explained to you before the need for both gas and electric ovens. First, yours are antiquated. Second, in a restaurant of this size the need for two gas ovens is imperative."

"You specify brands."

"Of course, I know what I like to work with."

He only lifted a brow, thinking that procurement was going to grumble. "All new pots and pans?"

"Definitely."

"Perhaps we should have a yard sale," Blake mumbled as he went back to the sheet. He hadn't the vaguest idea what a *sautoir* was or why she required three of them. "And this particular heavy-duty mixer?"

"Essential. The one you have is adequate. I don't accept adequate."

He smothered a laugh as he recalled his father's view on adequate in relation to love lives. "Did you list so much of this in French to confuse me?"

"I listed in French," Summer countered, "because French is correct."

He made an indefinable sound as he passed over the next

sheet. "In any case, I've no intention of quibbling over equipment in French or English."

"Good. Because I've no intention of working with any less than the best." She smiled at him and settled back. First point taken.

Blake flipped over the second sheet and went on to the third. "You intend to rip out the existing counters, have the new ranges built in, add an island and an additional six feet of counter space."

"More efficient," Summer said easily.

"And time-consuming."

"In a hurry? You hired me, Blake, not Minute Chef." His quick grin made her eyes narrow. "My function is to organize your kitchen, which means making it as efficient and creative as I know how. Once the nuts and bolts of that are done, I'll beef up your menu."

"And this—" he flipped through the five typed sheets "— is all necessary for that?"

"I don't bother with anything that isn't necessary when it comes to business. If you don't agree," she said as she rose, "we can terminate the agreement. Hire LaPointe," she suggested, firing up. "You'll have an ostentatious, overpriced, second-rate kitchen that produces equally ostentatious, overpriced and second-rate meals."

"I have to meet this LaPointe," Blake murmured as he stood. "You'll get what you want, Summer." As a satisfied smile formed on her lips, he narrowed his eyes. "And you damn well better deliver what you promised."

The fire leapt back, accenting the gold in her irises. And as he saw it, he wanted.

"I've given you my word. Your middle-class restaurant with its mediocre prime rib and soggy pastries will be serving the finest in haute cuisine within six months."

"Or?"

So he wanted collateral, Summer thought, and heaved a breath. "Or my services for the term of the contract are gratis. Does that satisfy you?"

"Completely." Blake held out a hand. "As I said, you'll have precisely what you've asked for, down to the last egg beater."

"A pleasure doing business with you." Summer tried to draw her hand away and found it caught firm. "Perhaps you don't," she began, "but I have work to do. You'll excuse me?"

"I want to see you."

She let her hand remain passively in his rather than risk a struggle she might lose. "You have seen me."

"Tonight."

"Sorry." She smiled again, though her teeth were beginning to clench. "I have a date."

She felt the quick increase in pressure of his fingers over hers and was perversely pleased. "All right, when?"

"I'll be in the kitchen every day, and some evenings, to oversee the remodeling. You need only ride the elevator down."

He drew her closer, and though the desk remained between them, Summer felt that the ground beneath was a bit less firm. "I want to see you alone," he said quietly. Lifting her hand to his lips, he kissed her fingers slowly, one by one. "Away from here, outside of business hours."

If Blake Cocharan II had been anything like Blake Cocharan III in his youth, Summer could understand how her mother had become so quickly, so heatedly involved. The yearning was there, and the temptation—but she wasn't Monique. In this case, she was determined history would not repeat itself. "I've explained to you why that's not possible. I don't enjoy covering the same ground twice."

"Your pulse is racing," Blake pointed out as he ran a finger across her wrist.

"It generally does when I become annoyed."

"Or aroused."

Tilting her head, she sent him a killing look. "Would you amuse yourself with LaPointe in this way?"

Temper stirred and he suppressed it, knowing she wanted him to be angry. "At the moment, I don't care whether you're a chef or a plumber or a brain surgeon. At the moment," he repeated, "I only care that you're a woman, and one who I desire very much."

She wanted to swallow because her throat had gone dry but fought off the need. "At the moment I *am* a chef with a specific job to do. I'll ask you again to excuse me so I can begin to do it."

This time, Blake thought as he released her hand. But, by God, this time was the last time. "Sooner or later, Summer."

"Perhaps," she agreed as she picked up her leather folder. "Perhaps not." In one quick gesture, she zipped it closed. "Enjoy your day, Blake." As if her legs weren't weak and watery, she strolled to the door and out.

Summer continued to walk calmly through the outer office, over the plush carpet, past the busy secretaries and through the reception area. Once in the elevator, she leaned back against the wall and let out the long, tense breath she'd been holding. Nerves jumping, she began the ride down.

That was over, she told herself. She'd faced him in his office and won every point.

Sooner or later, Summer.

She let out another breath. Almost every point, she corrected. The important thing now was to concentrate on her kitchen, and to keep busy. It wasn't going to help matters if she allowed herself to think of him as she had over the weekend.

As her nerves began to calm, Summer straightened away from the wall. She'd handled herself well, she'd made herself clear and *she'd* walked out on him. All in all, a successful morning. She pressed a hand against her stomach, where a few muscles were still jumping. Damn it, things would be simpler if she didn't want him so badly.

When the doors slid open, she stepped out, then wound her way around to the kitchen. In the prelunch bustle, she went unnoticed. She approved of the noise. A quiet kitchen to Summer meant there was no communication. Without that, there was no cooperation. For a moment, she stood just inside the doorway to watch.

She approved of the smells. It was a mixture of lunchtime aromas over the still-lingering odors of breakfast. Bacon, sausage and coffee. She caught the scent of baking chicken, of grilled meat, of cakes fresh from the oven. Narrowing her eyes, she envisioned the room as it would be in a short time. Made to her order. Better, Summer decided with a nod.

"Ms. Lyndon."

Distracted, she frowned up at a big man in white apron and cap. "Yes?"

"I'm Max." His chest expanded, his voice stiffened. "Head chef."

Ego in danger, she thought as she extended a hand. "How do you do, Max. I missed you when I was in last week."

"Mr. Cocharan has instructed me to give you full cooperation during this—transition period."

Marvelous, she thought with an inward moan. Resentment in a kitchen was as difficult to deal with as a deflated soufflé. Left to herself, she might have been able to keep injured feelings to a minimum, but the damage had already been done. She made a mental note to give Blake her opinion of his tact and diplomacy.

"Well, Max, I'd like to go over the proposed structural changes with you, since you know the routine here better than anyone else."

"Structural changes?" he repeated. His full, round face flushed. The moustache over his mouth quivered. She caught the gleam of a single gold tooth. "In *my* kitchen?"

My kitchen, Summer mentally corrected, but smiled. "I'm sure you'll be pleased with the improvements—and the new equipment. You must have found it frustrating trying to create something special with outdated appliances."

"This oven," he said and gestured dramatically toward it, "this range—both have been here since I began at Cocharan. We are none of us outdated."

So much for cooperation, Summer thought wryly. If it was too late for a friendly transition of authority, she'd have to go with the *coup*. "We'll be receiving three new ovens," she began briskly. "Two gas, one electric. The electric will be used exclusively for desserts and pastries. This counter," she continued, walking toward it without looking back to see if Max was following, "will be removed and the ranges I specified built into a new counter—butcher block. The grill remains. There'll be an island here to provide more working area and to make use of what is now essentially wasted space."

"There is no wasted space in my kitchen."

Summer turned and aimed her haughtiest stare. "That isn't a matter for debate. Creativity will be the first priority of this kitchen, efficiency the second. We'll be expected to produce quality meals during the remodeling—difficult but not impossible if everyone makes the necessary adjustments. In the meantime, you and I will go over the current menu with an eye toward adding excitement and flair to what is now pedestrian."

She heard him suck in his breath but continued before he could rage. "Mr. Cocharan contracted me to turn this restaurant into the finest establishment in the city. I fully intend to do just that. Now, I'd like to observe the staff in lunch preparations." Unzipping her leather folder, Summer pulled out a note pad and pen. Without another word she began walking through the busy kitchen.

The staff, she decided after a few moments, was well trained and more orderly than many. Credit Max. Cleanliness was obviously a first priority. Another point for Max. She watched a cook expertly bone a chicken. Not bad, Summer decided. The grill was sizzling, pots steaming. Lifting a lid, she ladeled out a small portion of the soup du jour. She sampled it, holding the taste on her tongue a moment.

"Basil," she said simply, then walked away. Another cook drew apple pies from an oven. The scent was strong and wholesome. Good, she mused, but any experienced grandmother could do the same. What was needed was some pizzazz. People would come to this restaurant for what they wouldn't get at home. Charlottes, Clafouti, flambées.

The structural changes came from her practical side, but the menu—the menu stemmed from her creativity, which was always paramount.

As she surveyed the kitchen, the staff, drew in the smells, absorbed the sounds, Summer felt the first real stirrings of excitement. She would do it, and she would do it for her own satisfaction just as much as in answer to Blake's challenge. When she was finished, this kitchen would bear her mark. It would be different entirely from jetting from one place to the next to create a single memorable dish. This would have continuity, stability. A year from now, five years from now, this kitchen would still retain her touch, her influence.

The thought pleased her more than she'd expected. She'd never looked for continuity, only the flash of an individual triumph. And wouldn't she be behind the scenes here? She might be in the kitchen in Milan or Athens, but the guests in the dining room knew who was preparing the Charlotte Royal. Clients wouldn't come into the restaurant anticipating a Summer Lyndon dessert, but a Cocharan Hotel meal.

Even as she mulled the thought over in her mind, she found it didn't matter. Why, she was still unsure. For now, she only knew the pleasurable excitement of planning. *Think about it later,* she advised herself as she made a final note. There were months to worry about consequences, reasons, pitfalls. She wanted to begin, get elbow deep in a project she now, for whatever reason, considered peculiarly her own.

Slipping her folder under her arm, she walked out. She couldn't wait to start working on menus.

CHAPTER 6

Russian Beluga Malasol Caviar—that should be available from lunch to late-night dining. All night through room service.

Summer made another scrawled note. During the past two weeks, she'd changed the projected menu a dozen times. After one abortive session with Max, she'd opted to go solo on the task. She knew the ambience she wanted to create, and how to do so through food.

To save herself time, she'd set up a small office in a storage room off the kitchen. There, she could oversee the staff and the beginnings of the remodeling while having enough privacy to work on what was now her pet project.

Avoiding Blake had been easy because she'd kept herself so thoroughly busy. And it appeared he was just as involved in some complicated corporate deal. Buying out another hotel chain, if rumor were fact. Summer had little interest in that, for her concentration focused on items like medallions of veal in champagne sauce.

As long as the remodeling was going on, the staff remained in a constant state of panic or near panic. She'd come to accept that. Most of the kitchens she'd worked in were full of the tension and terror only a cook would understand.

Perhaps it was that creative tension, and the terror of failure, that helped form the best meals.

For the most part, she left the staff supervision to Max. She interfered with the routine he'd established as little as possible, incorporating the changes she'd initiated unobtrusively. She'd learned the qualities of diplomacy and power from her father. If it placated Max at all, it wasn't apparent in his attitude toward Summer. That remained icily polite. Summer shrugged this off and concentrated on perfecting the entrées her kitchen would offer.

Calf's Liver Berlinoise. An excellent entrée, not as popular certainly as a broiled filet or prime rib, but excellent. As long as she didn't have to eat it, Summer thought with a smirk as she noted it down.

Once she'd organized the meat and poultry, she'd put her mind to the seafood. And naturally there had to be a cold buffet available twenty-four hours a day through room service. That was something else to work out. Soups, appetizers, salads—all of those had to be considered, decided on and confirmed before she began on the desserts. And at the moment, she'd have traded any of the elegant offerings jotted down in front of her for a cheeseburger on a sesame seed bun and a bag of chips.

"So this is where you've been hiding." Blake leaned against the doorway. He'd just completed a grueling four-hour meeting and had fully intended to go up to his suite for a long shower and a quiet, solitary meal. Instead, he'd found himself heading for the kitchen, and Summer.

She looked as she had the first time he'd seen her—her hair down, her feet bare. On the table in front of her were reams of scrawled-on paper and a half-empty glass of diluted soda. Behind her, boxes were stacked, sacks piled. The room smelled faintly of pine cleaner and cardboard. In her own way, she looked competent and completely in charge.

"Not hiding," she corrected. "Working." Tired, she thought. He looked tired. It showed around the eyes. "Been busy? We haven't seen you down here for the past couple of weeks."

"Busy enough." Stepping inside, he began to poke through her notes.

"Wheeling and dealing from what I hear." She leaned back, realizing all at once that her back ached. "Taking over the Hamilton chain."

He glanced up, then shrugged and looked back at her notes again. "It's a possibility."

"Discreet." She smiled, wishing she weren't quite so glad to see him again. "Well, while you've been playing Monopoly, I've been dealing with more intimate matters." When he glanced at her again, with his brow raised exactly as she'd expected it to be, she laughed. "Food, Blake, is the most basic and personal of desires, no matter what anyone might say to the contrary. For many, eating is a ritual experienced three times a day. It's a chef's job to make each experience memorable."

"For you, eating's a jaunt through adolescence."

"As I said," Summer continued mildly, "food is very personal."

"Agreed." After another glance around the room, he looked back at her. "Summer, it's not necessary for you to work in a storage room. It's a simple matter to set you up in a suite."

She pushed through the papers, looking for her list on poultry. "This is convenient to the kitchen."

"There's not even a window. The place is packed with boxes."

"No distractions." She shrugged. "If I'd wanted a suite, I'd have asked for one. For the moment, this suits me." And it's several hundred feet away from you, she added silently. "Since you're here, you might want to see what I've been doing."

He lifted a sheet of paper that listed appetizers. *"Coquilles St. Jacques, Escargots Bourguignonne, Pâté de Campagne.* Is it too personal a question to ask if you ever eat what you recommend?"

"From time to time, if I trust the chef. You'll see, if you go more thoroughly through my notes, that I want to offer a more sophisticated menu, because the American palate is becoming more sophisticated."

Blake smiled at the term *American,* and the way she said it, before he sat across from her. "Is it?"

"It's been a slow process," she said dryly. "Today, you can find a good food processor in almost every kitchen. With one, and a competent cookbook, even you could make an acceptable mousse."

"Amazing."

"Therefore," she continued, ignoring him, "to lure people into a restaurant where they'll pay, and pay well to be fed, you have to offer them the superb. A few blocks down the street, they can get a wholesome, filling meal for a fraction of what they'll pay in the Cocharan House." Summer folded her hands and rested her chin on them. "So you have to give them a very special ambience, incomparable service and exquisite food." She picked up her soda and sipped. "Personally, I'd rather pick up a take-out pizza and eat it at home, but . . ." She shrugged.

Blake scanned the next sheet. "Because you like pizza, or you like being alone?"

"Both. Now—"

"Do you stay out of restaurants because you spend so much time in a kitchen behind them or because you simply don't like being in a group?"

She opened her mouth to answer and found she didn't know. Uncomfortable, she toyed with her soda. "You're getting more personal, and off the point."

"I don't think so. You're telling me we have to appeal to people who're becoming sophisticated enough to make dishes that were once almost exclusively professionally prepared, as well as draw in clientele who might prefer a quick, less expensive meal around the corner. You, due to your profession and your taste, fall into both categories. What would a restaurant have to offer not only to bring you in, but to make you want to come back?"

A logical question. Summer frowned at it. She hated logical questions because they left you no choice but to answer. "Privacy," she answered at length. "It isn't an easy thing to accomplish in a restaurant, and of course, not everyone looks for it. Many go out to eat to see and be seen. Some, like myself, prefer at least the illusion of solitude. To accomplish both, you have to have a certain number of tables situated in such a way that they seem removed from the rest."

"Easily enough done with the right lighting, a clever arrangement of foliage."

"The key words are right and clever."

"And privacy is your prerequisite in choosing a restaurant."

"I don't generally eat in them," Summer said with a restless movement of her shoulders. "But if I do, privacy ranks equally with atmosphere, food and service."

"Why?"

She began to push the papers together on her desk and stack them. "That's definitely a personal question."

"Yes." He covered her hands with one of his to still them. "Why?"

She stared at him a moment, certain she wouldn't answer. Then she found herself drawn by the quiet look and the gentle touch. "I suppose it stems back to eating in so many restaurants as a child. And I suppose one of the reasons I first became interested in cooking was as a defense against the interminable ritual of eating out. My mother was—is—of the type who goes out to see and be seen. My father often considered eating out a business. So much of my parents' lives, and therefore mine, was public. I simply prefer my own way."

Now that he was touching her, he wanted more. Now that he was learning of her, he wanted all. He should have known better than to believe it would be otherwise. He'd nearly convinced himself that he had his feelings for her under control. But now, sitting in the cramped storage room with kitchen sounds just outside the door, he wanted her as much—more—than ever.

"I wouldn't consider you an introvert, or a recluse."

"No." She didn't even notice that she'd laced her fingers with his. There was something so comfortable, so right about the gesture. "I simply like to keep my private life just that. Mine and private."

"Yet, in your field, you're quite a celebrity." He shifted and under the table his leg brushed against hers. He felt the warmth glow through him and the need double.

Without thinking, she moved her leg so that it brushed his again. The muscles in her thighs loosened. "Perhaps. Or you might say my desserts are celebrities."

Blake lifted their joined hands and studied them. Hers was shades lighter than his, inches smaller and more narrow. She wore a sapphire, oval, deeply blue in an ornate antique setting that made her fingers look that much more elegant. "Is that what you want?"

She moistened her lips, because when his eyes came back to hers they were intense and as darkly blue as the stone on her hand. "I want to be successful. I want to be considered the very best at what I do."

"Nothing more?"

"No, nothing." Why was she breathless? she asked herself frantically. Young girls got breathless—or romantics. She was neither.

"When you have that?" Blake rose, drawing her to her feet without effort. "What else?"

Because they were standing, she had to angle her head to keep her eyes level with his. "It's enough." As she said it, Summer had her first doubts of the truth of that statement. "What about you?" she countered. "Aren't you looking for success—more success? The finest hotels, the finest restaurants."

"I'm a businessman." Slowly, he walked around the table until nothing separated them. Their hands were still joined. "I have a standard to maintain or improve. I'm also a man." He reached for her hair, then let it flow through his fingers. "And there're things other than account books I think about."

They were close now. Her body brushed his and caused her skin to hum. She forgot all the rules she'd set out for both of them and reached up to touch his cheek. "What else do you think about?"

"You." His hand was at her waist, then sliding gently up her back as he drew her closer. "I think very much about you, and this."

Lips touched—softly. Eyes remained open and aware. Pulses throbbed. Desire tugged.

Lips parted—slowly. A look said everything there was to say. Pulses hammered. Desire tore free.

She was in his arms, clinging, greedy, burning. Every hour of the past two weeks, all the work, the planning, the rules, melted away under a blaze of passion. If she sensed impatience in him, it only matched her own. The kiss was hard, long, desperate. Body strained against body in exquisite torment.

Tighter. Whether she said the word aloud or merely thought it, he seemed to understand. His arms curved around her, crushing her to him as she wanted to be. She felt the lines and planes of his body mold to hers even as his mouth molded to hers, and somehow she seemed softer than she'd ever imagined herself to be.

Feminine, sultry, delicate, passionate. Was it possible to be all at once? The need grew and expanded—for him—for a taste and touch she'd found nowhere else. The sound she made against his lips came as much from confusion as from pleasure.

Good God, how could a woman take him so far with only a kiss? He was already more than half-mad for her. Control was losing its meaning in a need that was much more imperative. Her skin would slide like silk under his hands—he knew it. He had to feel it.

He slipped a hand under her sweater and found her. Beneath his palm, her heartbeat pounded. Not enough. The thought raced through his mind that it would never be enough. But questions, reason, were for later. Burying his face against her throat, he tasted her skin. The scent he remembered lingered there, enticing him further, drawing him closer to the edge where there could be no turning back. The fatigue he'd felt when he'd entered the room vanished. The tension he felt whenever she was near evaporated. At that moment, he considered her completely his without realizing he'd wanted exclusive possession.

Her hair brushed over his face, cloud soft, fragrant. It made him think of Paris, right before the heat of summer took over from spring. But her skin was hot and vibrating, making him envision long, humid nights when lovemaking would be slow, endlessly slow. He wanted her there, in the cramped little room where the floor was littered with boxes.

She couldn't think. Summer could feel her bones dissolve and her mind empty. Sensation after sensation poured over her. She could have drowned in them. Yet she wanted more—she could feel her body craving more, wanting all.

Storm, thunder, heat. Just once . . . the longing seeped into her with whispering promises and dark pleasure. She could let herself be his, take him as hers. Just once. And then . . .

With a moan, she tore her mouth from his and buried her face against his shoulder. Once with Blake would haunt her for the rest of her life.

"Come upstairs," Blake murmured. Tilting her head back, he ran kisses over her face. "Come up with me where I can make love with you properly. I want you in my bed, Summer. Soft, naked, mine."

"Blake . . ." She turned her face away and tried to steady her breathing. What had happened to her—when—how? "This is a mistake—for both of us."

"No." Taking her by the shoulders, he kept her facing him. "This is right—for both of us."

"I can't get involved—"

"You already are."

She let out a deep breath. "No further than this. It's already more than I intended."

When she started to back away, he held her firmly in front of him. "I need a reason, Summer, a damn good one."

"You confuse me." Summer blurted it out before she realized it, then swore at the admission. "Damn it, I don't like to be confused."

"And I ache for you." His voice was as impatient as hers, his body as tense. "I don't like to ache."

"We've got a problem," she managed, dragging a hand through her hair.

"I want you." Something in the way he said it made her hand pause in midair and her gaze lift to his. There was nothing casual in those three words. "I want you more than I've ever wanted anyone. I'm not comfortable with that."

"A big problem," she whispered and sat unsteadily on the edge of the table.

"There's one way to solve it."

She managed a smile. "Two ways," she corrected. "And I think mine's the safest."

"Safest." Reaching down, he ran a fingertip over the curve of her cheek. "You want safety, Summer?"

"Yes." It was easily said because she'd discovered it was true. Safety was something she'd never thought about until Blake, because she'd never felt endangered until then. "I've made myself a lot of promises, Blake, set a lot of goals. Instinct tells me you could interfere. I always go with my instincts."

"I've no intention of interfering with your goals."

"Nevertheless, I have a few very strict rules. One of them is never to become intimate with a business associate or a client. In one point of view, you fall into both categories."

"How do you intend to prevent it from happening? Intimacies come in a lot of degrees, Summer. You and I have already reached some of them."

How could she deny it? She wanted to run from it. "We managed to keep out of each other's way for two weeks," she pointed out. "It's simply a matter of continuing to do so. Both of us are very busy at the moment, so it shouldn't be too difficult."

"Eventually one of us is going to break the rules."

And it could be me just as easily as it could be him, she thought. "I can't think about eventually, only about now. I'll stay downstairs and do my job. You stay upstairs and do yours."

"Like hell," Blake muttered and took a step forward. Summer was halfway to her feet when a knock sounded on her door.

"Mr. Cocharan, there's a phone call for you. Your secretary says it's urgent."

Blake controlled his fury. "I'll be there." He gave Summer a long, hard look. "We're not finished."

She waited until he'd reached the door. "I can turn this place into a palace or a greasy spoon," she said quietly. "It's your choice."

Turning around, he measured her. "Blackmail?"

"Insurance," she corrected and smiled. "Play it my way, Blake and everybody's happy."

"Your point, Summer," he acknowledged with a nod. "This time."

When the door closed behind him, she sat again. She may have outmaneuvered him this time, she mused, but the game was far from over.

* * *

Summer gave herself another hour before she left her temporary office to go back to the kitchen. Busboys wheeled in and out with trays of dirty dishes. The dishwasher hummed busily. Pots simmered. Someone sang as she basted a chicken. Two hours to the dinner rush. In another hour, the panic and confusion would set in.

It was then, when the scent of food hit her, that Summer realized she hadn't eaten. Deciding to kill two birds with one stone, she began to root through the cupboards. She'd find something for a late lunch, and see just how provisions were organized.

She couldn't complain about the latter. The cupboards were not only well stocked, they were systematically stocked. Max had a number of excellent qualities, she thought. A pity an open mind wasn't among them. She continued to scan shelf after shelf, but the item she was looking for was nowhere to be found.

"Ms. Lyndon?"

Hearing Max's voice behind her, Summer slowly closed the cabinet door. She didn't have to turn around to see the cold politeness in his eyes or the tight disapproval of his mouth. She was going to have to do something about this situation before long, she decided. But at the moment she was a bit tired, quite a bit hungry and not in the mood to deal with it.

"Yes, Max." She opened the next door and surveyed the stock.

"Perhaps I can help you find what you're looking for."

"Perhaps. Actually, I'm checking to see how well stocked we are while searching out a jar of peanut butter. Apparently—" she closed that door and went on to the next "—we're very well stocked indeed, and very well organized."

"My kitchen is completely organized," Max began stiffly. "Even in the midst of all this—this carpentry."

"The carpentry's almost finished," she said easily. "I think the new ovens are working out well."

"To some, new is always better."

"To some," she countered, "progress is always a death knell. Where do I find the peanut butter, Max? I really want a sandwich."

This time she did turn, in time to see his eyebrows rise and his mouth purse. "Below," he said with a hint of a smirk as he pointed. "We keep such things on hand for the children's menu."

"Good." Unoffended, Summer crouched down and found it. "Would you like to join me?"

"Thank you, no. I have work to do."

"Fine." Summer took two slices of bread and began to spread the peanut butter. "Tomorrow, nine o'clock, you and I will go over the proposed menus in my office."

"I'm very busy at nine."

"No," she corrected mildly. "We're very busy from seven to nine, then things tend to ease off, particularly midweek, until the lunch rush. Nine o'clock," she repeated over his huff of breath. "Excuse me, I have to get some jelly for this."

Leaving Max gritting his teeth, Summer went to one of the large refrigerators. Pompous, narrow-minded ass, she thought as she found a restaurant-sized jar of grape jelly. As long as he continued to be uncooperative and stiff, things were going to be difficult. More than once, she'd expected Max to turn in his resignation—and there were times, though she hated to be so hard line, that she wished he would.

The changes in the kitchen were already making a difference, she thought as she closed the second slice of bread over the jelly and peanut butter. Any fool could see that the extra range, the more efficient equipment, tightened the flow of preparation and improved the quality of food. Annoyed, she bit into her sandwich just as excited chatter broke out behind her.

"Max'll be furious. *Fur-i-ous*."

"Nothing he can do about it now."

"Except yell and throw things."

Perhaps it was the underlying glee in the last statement that made Summer turn. She saw two cooks huddled over the stove. "What'll Max be furious about?" she asked over another mouthful of sandwich.

The two faces turned to her. Both were flushed either from the heat of the stove or excitement. "Maybe you ought to tell him, Ms. Lyndon," one of the cooks said after a moment of indecision. The glee was still there, she noticed, barely suppressed.

"Tell him what?"

"Julio and Georgia eloped—we just got word from Julio's brother. They took off for Hawaii."

Julio and Georgia? After a quick flip through her mental file, Summer placed them as two cooks who worked the four-to-eleven shift. A glance at her watch told her they were already fifteen minutes late.

"I take it they won't be coming in today."

"They quit." One of the cooks snapped his fingers. "Just like that." He glanced across the room where Max was babying a rack of lamb. "Max'll hit the roof."

"He won't solve anything up there," she murmured. "So we're two short for the dinner shift."

"Three," the second cook corrected. "Charlie called in sick an hour ago."

"Wonderful." Summer finished off her sandwich, then rolled up her sleeves. "Then the rest of us better get to work."

With an apron covering her jeans and sweater, Summer took over one section of the new counter. Perhaps it wasn't her usual style, she mused as she began mixing the first oversized bowl of cake batter, but circumstances called for immediate action. And, she thought as she licked some batter from her knuckle, they damn well better get the stereo speakers in before the end of the week. Summer might bake without Chopin in an emergency once, but she wouldn't do it twice.

She was arranging several layers of Black Forest cake in the oven when Max spoke over her shoulder.

"You're making yourself some dessert now?" he began.

"No." Summer set the timer, then moved back to the counter to start preparations on chocolate mousse. "It seems there's been a wedding and an illness—though I don't think the first has anything to do with the second. We're shorthanded tonight. I'm taking over the desserts, Max, and I don't exchange small talk when I'm working."

"Wedding? What wedding?"

"Julio and Georgia eloped to Hawaii, and Charlie's sick. I have this mousse to deal with at the moment."

"Eloped!" he exploded. "Eloped without my permission?"

She took the time to look over her shoulder. "I suppose Charlie should have checked with you before he got sick as well. Save the hysterics, Max, and have someone peel me some apples. I want to do a *Charlotte de Pommes* after this."

"Now you're changing my menu!" he exploded.

She whirled, fire in her eyes. "I have a dozen different desserts to make in a very short time. I'd advise you to stay out of my way while I do it. I'm not known for graciousness when I'm cooking."

He sucked in his stomach and pulled back his shoulders. "We'll see what Mr. Cocharan has to say about this."

"Terrific. Keep him out of my way, too, for the next three hours or someone's going to end up with a face full of my best whipped cream." Spinning back around, she went to work.

There wasn't time, she couldn't take the time, to study and approve each dessert as it was completed. Later, Summer would think of the hours as assembly line work. At the moment, she was too pressed to think. Julio and Georgia had been the dessert chefs. It was now up to her to do the work of two people in the same amount of time.

She ignored the menu and went with what she knew she could make from memory. The diners that evening were in for a surprise, but as she finished topping the second Black Forest cake, Summer decided it would be a pleasant one. She arranged the cherries quickly, cursing the need to rush. Impossible to create when one was on such a ridiculous timetable, she thought, and muttered bad-temperedly under her breath.

By six, the bulk of the baking was done and she concentrated on the finishing touches of a line of desserts designed to satisfy an army. Chocolate icing there, a dab of cream here, a garnish, a spoon of jam or jelly. She was hot, her arms aching. Her once-white apron was streaked and splashed. No one spoke to her, because she wouldn't answer. No one approached her, because she tended to snarl.

Occasionally she would indicate with a wave of her arm a section of dishes that were to be taken away. This was done instantly, and without a sound. If there was talk, it was done in undertones and out of her hearing. None of them had ever seen anything quite like Summer Lyndon on a roll.

"Problems?"

Summer heard Blake speak quietly over her shoulder but didn't turn. "Cars are made this way," she mumbled, "not desserts."

"Early reports from the dining room are more than favorable."

She grunted and rolled out pastry dough for tarts. "The next time I'm in Hawaii, I'm going to look up Julio and Georgia and knock their heads together."

"A bit testy, aren't you?" he murmured and earned a lethal glare. "And hot." He touched her cheek with a fingertip. "How long have you been at it?"

"Since a bit after four." After shrugging his hand away she began to rapidly cut out pastry shells. Blake watched, surprised. He'd never seen her work quickly before. "Move."

He stepped back but continued to watch her. By his calculations, she'd worked on the menus in the windowless storage room for more than six hours, and had now been on her feet for nearly three. Too small, he thought as a protective urge moved through him. Too delicate.

"Summer, can't someone else take over now? You should rest."

"No one touches my desserts." This was said in such a strong, authoritative voice that the image of a delicate flower vanished. He grinned despite himself.

"Anything I can do?"

"I'll want some champagne in an hour. Dom Perignon, '73."

He nodded as an idea began to form in his mind. She smelled like the desserts lined on the counter in front of her. Tempting, delicious. Since he'd met her, Blake had discovered he possessed a very demanding sweet tooth. "Have you eaten?"

"A sandwich a few hours ago," she said testily. "Do you think I could eat at a time like this?"

He glanced at the sumptuous array of cakes and pastries. He could smell delicately roasted meats, spicy sauces. Blake shook his head. "No, of course not. I'll be back."

Summer muttered something, then fluted the edges of her pastry shells.

CHAPTER 7

By eight o'clock, Summer was finished, and not in the best of humors. For nearly four hours, she'd whipped, rolled, fluted and baked. Often, she'd spent twice that time, and twice that effort, perfecting one single dish. That was art. This, on the other hand, had been labor, plain and simple.

She felt no flash of triumph, no glow of self-satisfaction, but simply fatigue. An army cook, she thought disdainfully; it was hardly different from producing the quickest and easiest for the masses. At the moment, if she never saw the inside of another egg again, it would be too soon.

"There should be enough made up to get us through the dinner hour, and room service tonight," she told Max briskly as she pulled off her soiled apron. Critically she frowned at a line of fruit tarts. More than one of them were less than perfect in shape. If there'd been time, she'd have discarded them and made others. "I want someone in touch with personnel first thing in the morning to see about hiring two more dessert chefs."

"Mr. Cocharan has already contacted personnel." Max stood stiffly, not wanting to give an inch, though he'd been impressed with how quickly and efficiently she'd avoided what could easily have been a catastrophe. He clung tightly to his resentment, even though he had to admit—to himself—that she baked the best apricot tart he'd ever tasted.

"Fine." Summer ran a hand over the back of her neck. The skin there was damp, the muscles drawn taut. "Nine o'clock tomorrow, Max, in my office. Let's see if we can get organized. I'm going home to soak in a hot tub until morning."

Blake had been leaning against the wall, watching her work. It had been fascinating to see just how quickly the temperamental artist had put her nose to the grindstone and produced.

She'd shown him two things he hadn't expected—a speed and lack of histrionics when she'd been forced to deal with a less than ideal situation, and a calm acceptance of what was obviously a touchy area with Max. However much she played the role of prima donna, when her back was against the wall, she handled herself very well.

When she removed her apron, he stepped forward. "Give you a lift?"

Summer glanced over at him as she pulled the pins from her hair. It fell to her shoulders, tousled, and a bit damp at the ends from the heat. "I have my car."

"And I have mine." The arrogance, with that trace of aloofness, was still there, even when he smiled.

"And a bottle of Dom Perignon, '73. My driver can pick you up in the morning."

She told herself she was only interested in the wine. The cool smile had nothing to do with her decision. "Properly chilled?" she asked, arching her brow. "The champagne, that is."

"Of course."

"You're on, Mr. Cocharan. I never turn down champagne."

"The car's out in the back." He took her hand rather than her arm as she'd expected. Before she could make any counter move, he was leading her from the kitchen. "Would it embarrass you if I said I was very impressed with what you did this evening?"

She was used to accolades, even expected them. Somehow, she couldn't remember ever getting so much pleasure from one before. She moved her shoulders, hoping to lighten her own response. "I make it my business to be impressive. It doesn't embarrass me."

Perhaps if she hadn't been tired, he wouldn't have seen through the glib answer so easily. When they reached his car, Blake turned and took her by the shoulders. "You worked very hard in there."

"Just part of the service."

"No," he corrected, soothing the muscles. "That's not what you were hired for."

"When I signed the contract, that became my kitchen. What goes out of it has to satisfy my standards, my pride."

"Not an easy job."

"You wanted the best."

"Apparently I got it."

She smiled, though she wanted badly just to sit down. "You definitely got it. Now, you did say something about champagne?"

"Yes, I did." He opened the door for her. "You smell of vanilla."

"I earned it." When she sat, she let out a long, pleasurable sigh. Champagne, she thought, a hot bath with mountains of bubbles, and smooth, cool sheets. In that order. "Chances are," she murmured, "even as we speak, someone in there is taking the first bite of my Black Forest cake."

Blake shut the driver's door, then glanced at her as he started the ignition. "Does it feel odd?" he asked. "Having strangers eat something you spent so much time and care creating?"

"Odd?" Summer stretched back, enjoying the plush luxury

of the seat and the view of the dusky sky through the sun roof. "A painter creates on canvas for whoever will look, a composer creates a symphony for whoever will listen."

"True enough." Blake maneuvered his way onto the street and into the traffic. The sun was red and low. The night promised to be clear. "But wouldn't it be more gratifying to be there when your desserts are served?"

She closed her eyes, completely relaxed for the first time in hours. "When one cooks in one's own kitchen for friends, relatives, it can be a pleasure or a duty. Then there might be the satisfaction of watching something you've cooked being appreciated. But again, it's a pleasure or a duty, not a profession."

"You rarely eat what you cook."

"I rarely cook for myself," she countered. "Except the simpler things."

"Why?"

"When you cook for yourself, there's no one there to clean up the mess."

He laughed and turned into a parking lot. "In your own odd way you're a very practical woman."

"In every way I'm a practical woman." Lazily, she opened her eyes. "Why did we stop?"

"Hungry?"

"I'm always hungry after I work." Turning her head, she saw the blue neon sign of a pizza parlor.

"Knowing your tastes by now, I thought you'd find this the perfect accompaniment to the champagne."

She grinned as the fatigue was replaced with the first real stirrings of hunger. "Absolutely perfect."

"Wait here," he told her as he opened the door. "I had someone call ahead and order it when I saw you were nearly finished."

Grateful, and touched, Summer leaned back and closed

her eyes again. When was the last time she'd allowed anyone to take care of her? she wondered. If memory served her, the last time she'd been pampered she'd been eight, and cranky with a case of chicken pox. Independence had always been expected of her, by her parents, and by herself. But tonight, this one time, it was a rather sweet feeling to let someone else make the arrangements with her comfort in mind.

And she had to admit, she hadn't expected simple consideration from Blake. Style, yes, credit where credit was due, yes—but not consideration. He'd put in a hard day himself, she thought, remembering how tired he'd looked that afternoon. Still, he'd waited long past the time when he could have had his own dinner in comfort, relaxed in his own way. He'd waited until she was finished.

Surprises, she mused. Blake Cocharan III definitely had some surprises up his sleeve. She'd always been a sucker for them.

When Blake opened the car door, the scent of pizza rolled pleasurably inside. Summer took the box from him, then leaned over and kissed his cheek. "Thanks."

"I should've tried pizza before," he murmured.

She settled back again, letting her eyes close and her lips curve. "Don't forget the champagne. Those are two of my biggest weaknesses."

"I've made a note of it." Blake pulled out of the parking lot and joined the traffic again. Her simple gratitude shouldn't have surprised him. It certainly shouldn't have moved him. He had the feeling she would have had the same low-key, pleased reaction if he'd presented her with a full-length sable or a bracelet of blue-white diamonds. With Summer, it wouldn't be the gift, but the nature of the giving. He found he liked that idea very much. She wasn't a woman who was easily impressed, he mused, yet she was a woman who could be easily pleased.

Summer did something she rarely did unless she was completely alone. She relaxed, fully. Though her eyes were closed,
she was no longer sleepy, but aware. She could feel the smooth
motion of the car beneath her, hear the rumble of traffic outside the windows. She had only to draw in a breath to smell
the tangy scent of sauce and spice. The car was spacious, but
she could sense the warmth of Blake's body across the seat.

Pleasant. That was the word that drifted through her mind.
So pleasant, there seemed to be no need for caution, for defenses. It was a pity, she reflected, that they weren't driving
aimlessly . . .

Strange, she'd never chosen to do anything aimlessly. And
yet, tonight, to drive . . . along along, deserted beach—with
the moon full, shining off the water, and the sand white.
You'd be able to hear the surf ebb and flow, and see the hundreds of stars you so rarely noticed in the city. You'd smell
the salt and feel the spray. The moist, warm air would flow
over your skin.

She felt the car swing off the road, then purr to a stop. For
an extra moment, Summer held on to the fantasy.

"What're you thinking?"

"About the beach," she answered. "Stars." She caught herself, surprised that she'd indulged in what could only be
termed romanticism. "I'll take the pizza," she said, straight-
ening. "You can bring the champagne."

He put a hand on her arm, lightly but it stopped her. Slowly
he ran a finger down it. "You like the beach?"

"I never really thought about it." At the moment, she
found she'd like nothing better than to rest her head against
his shoulder and watch waves surge against the shore. Star
counting. Why should she want to indulge in something so
foolish now when she never had before? "For some reason,
it just seemed like the night for it." And she wondered if she
were answering his question or her own.

"Since there's no beach, we'll just have to come up with something else. How's your imagination?"

"Good enough." Quite good enough, Summer thought, to see where she'd end up if she didn't change the mood—hers as well as his. "And at the moment, I imagine the pizza's getting cold, and the champagne warm." Opening the door, she climbed out with the box in hand. Once inside the building, Summer started up the stairs.

"Does the elevator ever work?" Blake shifted the bag in his arm and joined her.

"Off and on—mostly it's off. Personally, I don't trust it."

"In that case, why'd you pick the fourth floor?"

She smiled as they rounded the second landing. "I like the view—and the fact that salesmen are usually discouraged when they're faced with more than two flights of steps."

"You could've chosen a more modern building, with a view, a security system and a working elevator."

"I look at modern tools as essential, a new car, well tuned, as imperative." Drawing out her keys, Summer jiggled them lightly as they approached her door. "As to living arrangements, I'm a bit more open-minded. My flat in Paris has temperamental plumbing and the most exquisite cornices I've ever seen."

When she opened the door, the scent of roses was overwhelming. There were a dozen white in a straw basket, a dozen red in a Sevres vase, a dozen yellow in a pottery jug and a dozen pink in Venetian glass.

"Run into a special at the florist's?"

Summer raised her brows as she set the pizza on the dinette. "I never buy flowers for myself. These are from Enrico."

Blake set the bag next to the box and drew out the champagne. "All?"

"He's a bit flamboyant—Enrico Gravanti—you might've heard of him. Italian shoes and bags."

Two hundred million dollars worth of shoes and bags, as Blake recalled. He flicked a finger down a rose petal. "I hadn't heard Gravanti was in town. He normally stays at the Cocharan House."

"No, he's in Rome." As she spoke, Summer went into the kitchen for plates and glasses. "He wired these when I agreed to make the cake for his birthday next month."

"Four dozen roses for a cake?"

"Five," Summer corrected as she came back in. "There's another dozen in the bedroom. They're rather lovely, a kind of peach color." In anticipation, she held out both glasses. "And, after all, it is one of my cakes."

With a nod of acknowledgment, Blake loosened the cork. Air fizzed out while the champagne bubbled toward the lip of the bottle. "So, I take it you'll be going to Italy to bake it."

"I don't intend to ship it air freight." She watched the pale gold liquid rise in the glass as Blake poured. "I should only be in Rome two days, three at most." Raising the glass to her lips, she sipped, eyes closed, senses keen. "Excellent." She sipped again before she opened her eyes and smiled. "I'm starving." After lifting the lid on the box, she breathed deep. "Pepperoni."

"Somehow I thought it suited you."

With a laugh, an easy one, she sat down. "Very perceptive. Shall I serve?"

"Please." And as she began to, Blake flicked on his lighter and set the three staggered-length tapers she had on the table burning. "Champagne and pizza," he said as he turned off the lights. "That demands candlelight, don't you think?"

"If you like." When he sat, Summer lifted her first piece. The cheese was hot enough to make her catch her breath, the sauce tangy. "Mmmm. Wonderful."

"Has it occurred to you that we spend a great deal of our time together eating?"

"Hmm—well, it's something I thoroughly enjoy. I always try to look at eating as a pleasure rather than a physical necessity. It adds something."

"Pounds, usually."

She shrugged and reached for the champagne. "Of course, if one isn't wise enough to take one's pleasure in small doses. Greed is what adds pounds, ruins the complexion and makes one miserable."

"You don't succumb to greed?"

She remembered abruptly that it had been just that, exactly that, that she'd felt for him. But she'd controlled it, Summer reminded herself. She hadn't succumbed. "No." She ate slowly, savoring. "I don't. In my profession, it would be disastrous."

"How do you keep your pleasure in small doses?"

She wasn't sure she trusted the way the question came out. Taking her time, she set a second piece on each plate. "I'd rather have one spoonful of a superb chocolate soufflé than an entire plateful of food that doesn't have flair."

Blake took another bite of pizza. "And this has flair?"

She smiled because it was so obviously not the sort of meal he was used to. "An excellent balance of spices—perhaps just a tad heavy on the oregano—a good marriage of sauce and crust, the proper handling of cheese and the bite of pepperoni. With the proper use of the senses, almost any meal can be memorable."

"With the proper use of the senses," Blake countered, "other things can be memorable."

She reached for her glass again, her eyes laughing over the rim. "We're speaking of food. Taste, of course, is paramount, but appearance . . ." He linked his hand with hers and she found herself watching him. "Your eyes tell you first of the desire to taste." His face was lean, the eyes a deep blue she found continuously compelling. . . .

"Then a scent teases you, entices you." His was dark, woodsy, tempting. . . .

"You hear the way champagne bubbles into a glass and you want to experience it." Or the way he said her name, quietly.

"After all this," she continued in a voice that was beginning to take on a faint huskiness, a faint trace of feeling, "you have the taste, the texture to explore." And his mouth held a flavor she couldn't forget.

"So—" he lifted her hand and pressed his mouth to the palm "—your advice is to savor every aspect of the experience in order to absorb all the pleasure. Then . . ." Turning her hand over, he brushed his lips, then the tip of his tongue, over her knuckles. "The most basic of desires becomes unique."

In an arrow-straight line, the heat shot up her arm. "No experience is acceptable otherwise."

"And atmosphere?" Lightly, with just a fingertip, he traced the shape of her ear. "Wouldn't you agree that the proper setting can enhance the same experience? Candlelight, for instance."

Their faces were closer now. She could see the soft shifting light casting shadows, mysteries. "Outside devices can often add more intensity to a mood."

"You could call it romance." He took his fingertip down the length of her jawline.

"You could." Champagne never went to her head, yet her head was light. Slowly, luxuriously, her body was softening. She made an effort to remember why she should allow neither to happen, but no answer came.

"And romance, for some, is another very elemental need."

"For some," he murmured when his lips followed the trail of his fingertip.

"But not for you." He nipped at her lips and found them soft, and warm.

"No, not for me." But her sigh was as soft and warm as her lips.

"A practical woman." He was raising her to her feet so that their bodies could touch.

"Yes." She tilted her head back, inviting the exploration of his lips.

"Candlelight doesn't move you?"

"It's only an attractive device." She curved her arms up his back to bring him closer. "As chefs, we're taught that such things can lend the right mood to our meals."

"And it wouldn't matter if I told you that you were beautiful? In the full sun where your skin's flawless—in candlelight, which turns it to porcelain. It wouldn't matter," he continued as he ran a line of moist heat down her throat, "if I told you you excite me as no other woman ever has? Just looking at you makes me want, touching you drives me mad."

"Words," she managed, though her head was spinning. "I don't need—"

Then his mouth covered hers. The one long, deep kiss made lies of all her practical claims. Tonight, though she'd never wanted such things before, she wanted the romance of soft words, soft lights. She wanted the slow, savoring loving that emptied the mind and made a furnace of the body. Tonight she wanted, and there was only one man. If tomorrow there were consequences, tomorrow was hours away. He was here.

She didn't resist as he lifted her. Tonight, if only for a short while, she'd be fragile, soft. She heard him blow out the candles and the light scent of melted wax followed them toward the bedroom.

Moonlight. The silvery sorcery of moonlight slipped through the windows. Roses. The fragile fragrance of roses floated on the air. Music. The muted magic of Beethoven drifted in from the apartment below.

There was a breeze. Summer felt it whisper over her face as he placed her on the bed. Atmosphere, she thought hazily. If she had planned on a night of lovemaking, she could have set the stage no better. Perhaps . . . She drew him down to join her. . . . Perhaps it was fate.

She could see his eyes. Deep blue, direct, involving. He watched her while doing no more than tracing the shape of her face, of her lips, with his finger. Had anyone ever shown her that kind of tenderness? Had she ever wanted it?

No. And if the answer was no, the answer had abruptly changed. She wanted this new experience, the sweetness she'd always disregarded, and she wanted the man who would bring her both.

Taking his face in her hands, she studied him. This was the man she would share this one completely private moment with, the one who would soon know her body as well as her vulnerabilities. She might have wavered over the trust, reminded herself of the pitfalls—if she'd been able to resist the need, and the strength, she saw in his eyes.

"Kiss me again," she murmured. "No one's ever made me feel the way you do when you kiss me."

He felt a surge of pleasure, intense, stunning. Lowering his head, he touched his lips to hers, toying with them, watching her as she watched him while their emotions heightened and their need sharpened. Should he have known she'd be even more beautiful in the moonlight, with her hair spread over a pillow? Could he have known that desire for her would be an ache unlike any desire he'd known? Was it still as simple as desire, or had he crossed some line he'd been unaware of? There were no answers now. Answers were for the daylight.

With a moan, he deepened the kiss and felt her body yield beneath his even as her mouth grew avid. Little tongues of passion flickered, still subdued beneath a gentleness they both seemed to need. Odd, because neither of them had needed it before, or often thought to show it.

Her hands were light on his face, over his neck, then slowly combing through his hair. Though his body was hard on hers, there was no demand yet.

Savor me. The thought ran silkily through her mind even as Blake's lips journeyed over her face. Slowly. She'd never known a man with such patience or an arousal so heady. Mouth against mouth, then mouth against skin—each drew her deeper and still deeper into a languor that encompassed both body and mind.

Touch me. And he seemed to understand this fresh need. His hands moved, but still without hurry, over her shoulders, down her sides, then up again to whisper over her breasts— until it was no longer enough for either of them. Then word- lessly they began to undress each other.

Fingers of moonlight fell across exposed flesh—a shoul- der, the length of an arm, a lean torso. Luxuriously, Summer ran her hands over Blake's chest and learned the muscle and form. Lazily, he explored the length of her and learned the subtle curves and silk. Even when the last barrier of clothing was drawn away, they didn't rush. So much to touch, taste— and time had no meaning.

The breeze flitted in, but they grew warmer. Wherever her fingers wandered, his flesh would burn, then cool only to burn again. As he took his lips over her, finding pleasure, learning secrets, she began to heat. And demand crept into both of them.

More urgently now, with quick moans, trembling breaths, they took each other further. He hadn't known he could be led, and she'd always refused to be, yet now, one guided the other to the same destination.

Summer felt reality slipping away from her, but had no will to stop it. The music penetrated only faintly into her consciousness, but his murmurs were easily heard. It was his scent, no longer the roses, that titillated. She would feel whatever she was meant to feel, go wherever she was meant to go, as long as he was with her. Along with the strongest physical desire she'd ever known was an emotional need that exploded inside her. She couldn't question it, couldn't refuse it. Her body, mind, heart, ached for him.

With his name trembling on her lips, she took him into her. Then, for both of them, the pleasure was so acute that sanity was forgotten. Sensation—waves, floods, storms—whipped through her. The calm had become a hurricane to revel in. Together, they were swept away.

* * *

Had hours passed or minutes? Summer lay in the filtered moonlight and tried to orient herself. She'd never felt quite like this. Sated, exhilarated, exhausted. Once she'd have said it was impossible to be all at once.

She could feel the brush of Blake's hair against her shoulder, the whisper of his breath against her cheek. His scent and hers were mixed now, so that the roses were only an accent. The music had stopped, but she thought she could still hear the echo. His body was pressed into hers, but his weight was a pleasure. She knew, without effort, she could wrap her arms around him and stay just so for the rest of her life. So through the hazy pleasure came the first stirrings of fear.

Oh, God, how far had she gone in such a short time? She'd always been so certain her emotions were perfectly safe. It wasn't the first time she'd been with a man, but she was too aware that it was the first time she'd made love in the true sense of the word.

Mistake. She forced the word into her head even as her heart tried to block it. She had to think, had to be practical.

Hadn't she seen what uncontrolled emotions and dreams had done to two intelligent people? Both her parents had spent years moving from relationship to relationship looking for . . . what?

This, her heart told her, but again she blocked it out. She knew better than to look for something she didn't believe existed. Permanency, commitment—they were illusions. And illusions had no place in her life.

Closing her eyes a moment, she waited for herself to settle. She was a grown woman, sophisticated enough to understand and accept mutual desire that held no strings. *Treat it lightly,* she warned herself. *Don't pretend it's more than it is.*

But she couldn't resist smoothing his hair as she spoke. "Odd how pizza and champagne affect me."

Raising his head, Blake grinned at her. At the moment, he felt he could've taken on the world. "I think it should be your staple diet." He kissed the curve of her shoulder. "It's going to be mine. Want some more?"

"Pizza and champagne?"

Laughing, he nuzzled her neck. "That, too." He shifted, drawing her against his side. It was one more gesture of intimacy that had something inside her trembling.

Set out the rules, Summer told herself. *Do it now, before . . . before it would be much too easy to forget.*

"I like being with you," she said quietly.

"And I you." He could see the shadows play on the ceiling, hear the muted sound of traffic outside, but he was still saturated with her.

"Now that we've been together like this, it's going to affect our relationship one of two ways."

Puzzled, he turned his head to look at her. "One of two ways?"

"It's either going to increase the tension while we're working, or alleviate it. I'm hoping it alleviates it."

In the darkness he frowned at her. "What happened just now had absolutely nothing to do with business."

"Whatever you and I do together is bound to affect our working relationship." Moistening her lips, she tried to continue in the same light way. "Making love with you was . . . personal, but tomorrow morning we're back to being associates. This can't change that—I think it'd be a mistake to let it change the tone of our business dealings." Was she rambling? Was she making sense? She wished desperately that he would say something, anything at all. "I think we both knew this was bound to happen. Now that it has, it's cleared the air."

"Cleared the air?" Infuriated, and to his surprise, hurt, he rose on his elbow. "It did a damn sight more than that, Summer. We both know that, too."

"Let's keep it in perspective." How had she begun this so badly? And how could she keep rambling on when she only wanted to curl up next to him and hold on? "We're both unattached adults who're attracted to each other. On that level, we shouldn't expect any more from each other than's reasonable. On a business level, we both have to expect total involvement."

He wanted to push the business level down her throat. Violently. The emotion didn't please him, nor did the sudden realization that he wanted total involvement on a very personal level. With an effort, he controlled the fury. He needed to ask, and answer, some questions for himself—soon. In the meantime, he needed to keep a cool head.

"Summer, I intend to make love with you often, and when I do, business can go to hell." He ran a hand down her side and felt her body respond. If she wanted rules, he thought furiously, he'd give her rules. His. "When we're here, there isn't any hotel or any restaurant. There's just you and me. Back at Cocharan House, we'll be as professional as you want."

She wasn't certain if she wanted to calmly agree with him or scream in protest. She remained silent.

"And now," he continued, drawing her still closer, "I want to make love with you again, then I want to sleep with you. At nine o'clock tomorrow, we'll get back to business."

She might have spoken then, but his mouth touched hers. Tomorrow was hours away.

CHAPTER 8

Damn, it was frustrating. Blake had heard men complain about women, calling them incomprehensible, contradictory, baffling. Because he'd always found it possible to deal with women on a sensible level, he'd never put much credence in any of it, until Summer. Now, he found himself searching for more adjectives. Rising from his desk, Blake paced to the window and frowned out at his view of the city.

When they'd made love the first time, he realized that he'd never known that a woman could be that soft, that giving. Strong—still strong, yes, but with a fragility that had a man lying in velvet. Had it been his imagination, or had she been totally his in every way one person could belong to another? He'd have sworn that for that space of time she'd thought of nothing but him, wanted nothing but him. And yet, before their bodies had cooled, she'd been so practical, so . . . unemotional.

Damn, wasn't a man supposed to be grateful for that—a man who wanted the pleasure and companionship of a woman without all the complications? He could remember other relationships where a neat set of rules had proven invaluable, but now . . .

Below, a couple walked along the sidewalk, their arms

slung around each other's shoulders. As he watched he imagined them laughing at something no one else would understand. And as he watched, Blake thought of his own statement of the degrees of intimacy. Instinct told him that he and Summer had shared an intimacy as deep as any two people could experience. Not just a merging of bodies, but a touching, a twining, of thoughts and needs and wants that was absolute. But if his instincts had told him one thing, she had told him another. Which was he to believe?

Frustrating, he thought again and turned away from the window. He couldn't deny that he'd gone to her apartment the night before with the idea of seducing her, and putting an end to the tension between them. But he couldn't deny that he'd been seduced after five minutes alone with her. He couldn't see her and not want to touch her. He couldn't hear her laugh without wanting to taste the curve of her lips. Now that he'd made love with her, he wasn't certain a night would pass without his wanting her again.

There must be a term for what he was experiencing. Blake was always more comfortable when he could label something and therefore file it properly. The most efficient heading, the most logical category. What was it called when you thought of a woman when you should be thinking about something else? What name did you give to this constant edgy feeling?

Love . . . The word crept up on him, not entirely pleasantly. Good God. Uneasy, Blake sat again and stared at the far wall. He was in love with her. It was just as simple—and just as terrifying—as that. He wanted to be with her, to make her laugh, to make her tremble with desire. He wanted to see her eyes glow with temper, and with passion. He wanted to spend quiet evenings, and wild nights, with her. And he was deadly sure he'd want the same thing twenty years down the road.

Since the first time he'd walked down those four flights

of stairs from her apartment, he hadn't thought of another woman. Love, if it could ever be considered logical, was the logical conclusion. And he was stuck with it. Taking out a cigarette, Blake ran his fingers down the length of it. He didn't light it, but continued to stare at the wall.

Now what? he asked himself. He was in love with a woman who'd made herself crystal clear on her feelings about commitments and relationships. She wanted no part of either. He, on the other hand, believed in the permanency, and even the romance, of marriage—though he'd never considered it specifically applying to himself.

Things were different now. He was a man too well ordered, both outwardly and mentally, not to see marriage as the direct result of love. With love, you wanted stability, vows, endurance. He wanted Summer. Blake leaned back in his chair. And he firmly believed there was always a way to get what you wanted.

If he even mentioned the word love, she'd be gone in a flash. Even he wasn't completely comfortable with it as yet. Strategy, he told himself. It was all a matter of strategy—or so he hoped. He simply had to convince her that he was essential to her life, that theirs was the relationship designed to break her set of rules.

Apparently the game was still on—and he still intended to win. Frowning at the wall, he began to work his way through the problem.

Summer was having problems of her own. Four cups of strong black coffee hadn't quite brought her up to maximum working level. Ten hours' sleep suited her well, eight could be tolerated. With less than that, and she'd had a good deal less than that the night before, she edged perilously close to nastiness. Add to that a state of emotional turmoil, and Max's frigid resentment, and it didn't promise to be the most pleasant or productive morning.

"By using one of the traditional French garnitures for the roast of lamb, we'll add something European and attractive to the entrée." Summer folded her hands on some of the scattered papers on her desk. She'd brought a few of Enrico's flowers in and set them in a water glass. They helped cover some of the dusty smell.

"My roast of lamb is perfect as it is."

"For some tastes," Summer said evenly. "For mine it's only adequate. I don't accept adequate." Their eyes warred, violently. As neither gave way, she continued. "I prefer to go with *clamart,* artichoke hearts filled with buttered peas, and potatoes sautéed in butter."

"We've always used watercress and mushrooms."

Meticulously, she changed the angle of a rosebud. The small distraction helped her keep her temper. "Now, we use *clamart.*" Summer noted it down, underlined it, then went on. "As to the prime rib—"

"You will not touch my prime rib."

She started to snap back but managed to grit her teeth instead. It was common knowledge in the kitchen that the prime rib was Max's specialty, one might say his baby. The wisest course was to give in graciously on this point, and hold a hard line on others. Her British heritage of fair play came through.

"The prime rib remains precisely as it is," she told him. "My function here is to improve what needs improving while incorporating the Cocharan House standard." Well said, Summer congratulated herself while Max huffed and subsided. "In addition, we'll keep the New York strip and the filet." Sensing he was mollified, Summer hit him with the poultry entrée. "We'll continue to serve the very simple roast chicken, with the choice of potatoes or rice and the vegetables of the day, but we add pressed duck."

"Pressed duck?" Max blustered. "We have no one on staff

who's capable of preparing that dish properly, nor do we have a duck press."

"No, which is why I've ordered one, and why I'm hiring someone who can use it."

"You're bringing someone into my kitchen just for this!"

"I'm bringing someone into *my* kitchen," she corrected, "to prepare the pressed duck and the lamb dish among other things. He's leaving his current job in Chicago to come here because he trusts my judgment. You might begin to do the same." With this, she began to tidy papers. "That's all for today, Max. I'd like you to take along these notes." While the headache began to drum inside her head, she handed him a stack of papers. "If you have any suggestions on what I've listed, please jot them down." She bent back over her work as he rose and strode silently out of the room.

Perhaps she shouldn't have been so abrupt. Summer understood injured feelings and fragile egos. She might have handled it better. Yes, she might have—with a weary sigh, she rubbed her temple—if she wasn't feeling a bit injured and fragile herself. Your own fault, she reminded herself; then propping her elbows on the table, she dropped her head into the cupped hands.

Now that it was tomorrow, she had to face the consequences. She'd broken one of her own primary rules. Never become intimate with a business associate. She should have been able to shrug and say rules were made to be broken, but . . . It worried her more that it wasn't that particular rule that was causing the turmoil, but another she'd broken. Never let anyone who could really matter get too close. Blake, if she didn't draw in the lines now and hold them, could really matter.

Drinking more coffee and wishing for an aspirin, she began to go over everything again. She was certain she'd been casual enough, and clear enough, the night before over the lack of ties and obligations. But when they'd made love again, nothing she'd said had made sense. She shook her head, trying to block that out. That morning they'd been perfectly at ease with each other—two adults preparing for a workday without any morning-after awkwardness. That's what she wanted.

Too many times, she'd seen her mother glowing and bubbling at the beginning of an affair. This man was *the* man— this man was the most exciting, the most considerate, the most poetic. Until the bloom faded. Summer's belief was that if you didn't glow, you didn't fade, and life was a lot simpler.

Yet she still wanted him.

After a brief knock, one of the kitchen staff stuck his head around her door. "Ms. Lyndon, Mr. Cocharan would like to see you in his office."

Summer finished off her rapidly cooling coffee. "Yes? When?"

"Immediately."

She lifted a brow. No one summoned her immediately. People requested her, at her leisure. "I see." Her smile was icy enough to make the messenger shrink back. "Thank you."

When the door closed again, she sat perfectly still. These were working hours, she reflected, and she was under contract. It was reasonable and right that he should ask her to come to his office. That was acceptable. But she was still Summer Lyndon—she went to no one immediately.

She spent the next fifteen minutes deliberately dawdling over her papers before she rose. After strolling through the kitchen, and taking the time to check on the contents of a pot or skillet on the way, she went to an elevator. On the ride up, she glanced at her watch, pleased to note that she'd arrive nearly twenty-five minutes after the call. As the doors opened she flicked a speck of lint from the sleeve of her blouse, then sauntered out.

"Mr. Cocharan would like to speak to me?" She gave the words the intonation of a question as she smiled down at the receptionist.

"Yes, Ms. Lyndon, you're to go right through. He's been waiting."

Unsure if the last statement had been censure or warning, Summer continued down the hall to Blake's door. She gave a peremptory knock before going in. "Good morning, Blake."

When she entered, he set aside the file in front of him and leaned back in his chair. "Have trouble finding an elevator?"

"No." Crossing the room, she chose a chair and settled down. He looked, she thought, as he had the first time she'd come into his office—aloof, aristocratic. This then was the perfect level for them to deal on. "This is one of the few hotels that has elevators one doesn't grow old waiting for."

"You're aware what the term immediately means."

"I'm aware of it. I was busy."

"Perhaps I should make it clear that I don't tolerate being kept waiting by an employee."

"And I'll make two things clear," she tossed back. "I'm not merely an employee, but an artist. Secondly, I don't come at the snap of anyone's fingers."

"It's eleven-twenty," Blake began with a mildness Summer instantly suspected. "On a workday. My signature is at the base of your checks. Therefore, you do answer to me."

The faint, telltale flush crept along her cheekbones. "You'd turn my work into something to be measured in dollars and cents and minute by minute—"

"Business is business," he countered, spreading his hands. "I think you were quite clear on that subject."

She'd maneuvered herself successfully toward that particular corner, and he'd given her a helpful shove into it. As a result, her attitude only became more haughty. "You'll notice I *am* here at present. You're wasting time."

As an ice queen, she was magnificent, Blake thought. He wondered if she realized how a change of expression, a tone of voice, could alter her image. She could be half a dozen women in the course of a day. Whether she knew it or not, Summer had her mother's talent. "I received another dissatisfied call from Max," he told her flatly.

She arched a brow and looked like royalty about to dispense a beheading. "Yes?"

"He objects—strongly—to some of the proposed changes in the menu. Ah—" Blake glanced down at the pad on his desk "—pressed duck seems to be the current problem, though several others were tossed in around it."

Summer sat straighter in her chair, tilting up her chin. "I believe you contracted me to improve the quality of Cocharan House dining."

"I did."

"That is precisely what I'm doing."

The French was beginning to seep into the intonation of her voice, her eyes were beginning to glow. Despite the fact it annoyed him, she was undeniably at her most attractive this way. "I also contracted you to manage the kitchen—which means you should be able to control your staff."

"Control?" She was up, and the ice queeen was now the enraged artist. Her gestures were broad, her movements dramatic. "I would need a whip and chain to control such a narrow-minded, ill-tempered old woman who worries only about his own egocentricities. *His* way is the only way. *His* menu is carved in stone, sacrosanct. Pah!" It was a peculiarly French expletive that would have been ridiculous coming from anyone else. From Summer, it was perfect.

Blake tapped his pen against the edge of his desk while he watched the performance. He was nearly tempted to applaud. "Is this what's known as artistic temperament?"

She drew in a breath. Mockery? Would he dare? "You've yet to see true temperament, *mon ami*."

He only nodded. It was tempting to push her into full gear—but business was business. "Max has worked for Cocharan for over twenty-five years." Blake set down the pen and folded his hands—calm, in direct contrast to Summer's temper. "He's loyal and efficient, and obviously sensitive."

"Sensitive." She nearly spat the word. "I give him his prime rib and his precious chicken, but still, he's not satisfied. I will have my pressed duck and my *clamart*. *My* menu won't read like something from the corner diner."

He wondered if he recorded the conversation and played it back to her, she'd see the absurdity of it. At the moment, though he had to clear his throat to disguise a chuckle, he doubted it. "Exactly," Blake said and kept his face expressionless. "I've no desire to interfere with the menu. The point is, I've no desire to interfere at all."

Far from mollified, Summer tossed her hair behind her shoulders and glared at him. "Then why do you bother me with these trivialities?"

"These trivialities," he countered, "are your problem, not mine. As manager, part of your function is to do simply that. Manage. If your supervisory chef is consistently dissatisfied, you're not doing your job. You're free to make whatever compromises you think necessary."

"Compromises?" Her whole body stiffened. Again, he thought she looked magnificent. "I don't make compromises."

"Being hardheaded won't bring peace to your kitchen."

She let out her breath in a hiss. "Hardheaded!"

"Exactly. Now, the problem of Max is back in your court. I don't want any more phone calls."

In a low, dangerous voice, she let out a stream of French, and though he was certain it was colloquial, he caught the drift. With a toss of her head, she started toward the door.

"Summer."

She turned, and the stance reminded him of one of the mythical female archers whose aim was killingly true. She wouldn't even wince as her arrow went straight through the heart. Ice queen or warrior, he wanted her. "I want to see you tonight."

Her eyes went to slits. "You dare."

"Now that we've tabled the first issue, it's time to go onto the second. We might have dinner."

"You tabled the first issue," she retorted. "I don't table things so easily. Dinner? Have dinner with your account book. That's what you understand."

He rose and approached her without hurry. "We agreed that when we're away from here, we're not business associates."

"We're not away from here." Her chin was still angled. "I'm standing in your office, where I was summoned."

"You won't be standing in my office tonight."

"I stand wherever I choose tonight."

"So tonight," he continued easily, "we won't be business associates. Weren't those your rules?"

Personal and professional, and that tangible line of demarcation. Yes, that's the way she'd wanted it, but it wasn't as easy for her to make the separation as she'd thought it would be. "Tonight," she said with a shrug, "I may be busy."

Blake glanced at his watch. "It's nearly noon. We might consider this lunch hour." He looked back at her, half smiling. Lifting a hand, he tangled it in her hair. "During lunch hour, there's no business between us, Summer. And tonight,

I want to be with you." He touched his lips to one corner of her mouth, then the other. "I want to spend long—" his lips slanted over hers softly "—private hours with you."

She wanted it too, why pretend otherwise? She'd never believed in pretenses, only in defenses. In any event, she'd already decided to handle Max and the kitchen in her own way. Linking her hands around his neck, she smiled back at him. "Then tonight, we'll be together. You'll bring the champagne?"

She was softening, but not yielding. Blake found it infinitely more exciting than submission. "For a price."

Her laugh was wicked and warm. "A price?"

"I want you to do something for me you haven't done before."

She tilted her head, then touched the tip of her tongue to her lip. "Such as?"

"Cook for me."

Surprise lit her eyes before the laughter sprang out again. "Cook for you? Well, that's a much different request from what I expected."

"After dinner I might come up with a few others."

"So you want Summer Lyndon to prepare your dinner." She considered it as she drew away. "Perhaps I will, though such a thing usually costs much more than a bottle of champagne. Once in Houston I prepared a meal for an oil man and his new bride. I was paid in stock certificates. Blue chip."

Blake took her hand and brought it to his lips. "I bought you a pizza. Pepperoni."

"That's true. Eight o'clock then. And I'd advise you to eat a very light lunch today." She reached for the door handle, then glanced over her shoulder with a grin. "You do like *Cervelles Braisées*?"

"I might, if I knew what it was."

Still smiling, she opened the door. "Braised calf's brains. *Au revoir.*"

Blake stared at the door. She'd certainly had the last word that time.

* * *

The kitchen smelled of cooking and sounded like a drawing room. Strains of Chopin were muted as Summer rolled the boneless breasts of chicken in flour. On the range, the clarified butter was just beginning to deepen in color. Perfect. Stuffed tomatoes were already prepared and waiting in the refrigerator. Buttered peas were just beginning to simmer. She would sauté the potato balls while she sautéed the *suprêmes.*

Timing, of course, was critical. *Suprêmes de Volaille à Brun* had to be done to the instant, even a minute of overcooking and she would, like any temperamental cook, throw them out in disgust. Hot butter sizzled as she slipped the floured chicken into it.

She heard the knock but remained where she was. "It's open," she called out. Meticulously, she adjusted the heat under the skillet. "I'll take the champagne in here."

"*Chérie,* if I'd only thought to bring some."

Stunned, Summer turned and saw Monique, glorious in midnight black and silver, framed by her kitchen doorway. "Mother!" With the kitchen fork still in her hand, Summer closed the distance and enveloped her mother.

With that part bubbling, part sultry laugh she was famous for, Monique kissed both of Summer's cheeks, then drew her daughter back. "You are surprised, *oui*? I adore surprises."

"I'm astonished," Summer countered. "What're you doing in town?"

Monique glanced toward the range. "At the moment,

apparently interrupting the preparations for an intimate *tête à tête*."

"Oh!" Whipping around, Summer dashed back to the skillet and turned the chicken breasts, not a second too soon. "What I meant was, what are you doing in Philadelphia?" She checked the flame again, and was satisfied. "Didn't you once say you'd never set foot in the town of the hardware king again?"

"Time mellows one," Monique claimed with a character-istic flick of the wrist. "And I wanted to see my daughter. You are not so often in Paris these days."

"No, it doesn't seem so, does it?" Summer split her at-tention between her mother and her range, something she would have done for no one else. "You look wonderful."

Monique's smooth cheeks dimpled. "I feel wonderful, *mignonne*. In six weeks, I start a new picture."

"A new picture." Carefully Summer pressed a finger to the top of the chicken. When they sprang back, she removed them to a hot platter. "Where?"

"In Hollywood. They have pestered me, and at last I give in." Monique's infectious laugh bubbled out again. "The script is superb. The director himself came to Paris to woo me. Keil Morrison."

Tall, somewhat gangly, intelligent face, fiftyish. Summer had a clear enough picture from the glossies, and from a party for a reigning box office queen where she'd prepared *île Flottante*. From her mother's tone of voice, Summer knew the answer before she asked the question. "And the director?"

"He, too, is superb. How would you feel about a new step poppa, *chérie*?"

"Resigned," Summer said, then smiled. That was too hard a word. "Pleased, of course, if you're happy, Mother." She began to prepare the brown butter sauce while Monique expounded.

"Oh, but he is brilliant and so sensitive! I've never met a

man who so understands a woman. At last, I've found my perfect match. The man who finally brings everything I need and want into my life. The man who makes me feel like a woman."

Nodding, Summer removed the skillet from the heat and stirred in the parsley and lemon juice. "When's the wedding?"

"Last week." Monique smiled brilliantly as Summer glanced up. "We were married quietly in a little churchyard outside Paris. There were doves—a good sign. I tore myself away from Keil because I wanted to tell you in person." Stepping forward, she flashed a thin diamond-crusted band. "Elegant, *oui*? Keil doesn't believe in the—how do you say?—ostentatious."

So, for the moment, neither would Monique DuBois Lyndon Smith Clarion Morrison. She supposed, when the news broke, the glossies and trades would have a field day. Monique would eat up every line of publicity. Summer kissed her mother's cheek. "Be happy, *ma mère*."

"I'm ecstatic. You must come to California and meet my Keil, and then—" She broke off as the knock interrupted her. "Ah, this must be your dinner guest. Shall I answer for you?"

"Please." With the tongue caught between her teeth, Summer poured the sauce over the *suprêmes*. She'd serve them within five minutes or dump them down the sink.

When the door opened, Blake was treated to a slightly more voluptuous, slightly more glossy, version of Summer. The candlelight disguised the years and enhanced the classic features. Her lips curved slowly, in the way her daughter's did, as she offered her hand.

"Hello, Summer is busy in the kitchen. I'm her mother, Monique." She paused a moment as their hands met. "But you are familiar to me, yes. But yes!" she continued before Blake could speak. "The Cocharan House. You are the son—B.C.'s son. We've met before."

"A pleasure to see you again, Mademoiselle Dubois."

"This is odd, *oui?* And amusing. I stay in your hotel while in Philadelphia. Already my bags are checked in and my bed turned down."

"You'll let me know personally if there's anything I can do for you while you stay with us."

"Of course." She studied him in the brief but thorough way a woman of experience has. Like mother, like daughter, she mused. Each had excellent taste. "Please, come in. Summer is putting the finishing touches on your meal. I've always admired her skill in the kitchen. Myself, I'm helpless."

"Diabolically helpless," Summer put in as she entered with the hot platter. "She always made sure she burned things beyond recognition, and therefore, no one asked her to cook."

"An intelligent move, to my thinking," Monique said easily. "And now, I'll leave you to your dinner."

"You're welcome to join us, Mother."

"Sweet." Monique framed Summer's face in her hands and kissed both cheeks again. "But I need my beauty rest after the long flight. Tomorrow, we catch up, *non*? Monsieur Cocharan, we will all have dinner at your wonderful hotel before I go?" In her sweeping way, she was at the door. *"Bon appétit."*

"A spectacular woman," Blake commented.

"Yes." Summer went back to the kitchen for the rest of the meal. "She continually amazes me." After placing the vegetables on the table, she picked up her glass. "She's just taken her fourth husband. Shall we drink to them?"

He began to remove the foil from the bottle, but her tone had him pausing. "A bit cynical?"

"Realistic. In any case, I do wish her happiness." When he removed the cork, she took it and absently waved it under her nose. "And I envy her perennial optimism." After both glasses were filled, Summer touched hers to his. "To the new Mrs. Morrison."

"To optimism," Blake countered before he drank.

"If you like," Summer said with a shrug as she sat. She transferred one of the *suprêmes* from the platter to his plate. "Unfortunately the calf's brains looked poor today, so we have to settle for chicken."

"A pity." The first bite was tender and perfect. "Would you like some time off to spend with your mother while she's in town?"

"No, it's not necessary. Mother'll divide her time between shopping and the health spa during the day. She tells me she's about to begin a new film."

"Really." It only took him a minute to put things together. "Morrison—the director?"

"You're very quick," Summer acknowledged, toasting him.

"Summer." He laid a hand over hers. "Do you object?"

She opened her mouth to answer quickly, then thought it over. "No. No, object isn't the word. Her life's her own. I simply can't understand how or why she continually plunges into relationships, tying herself up into marriages which on the average have lasted 5.2 years apiece. Is the word optimism, I wonder, or gullibility?"

"Monique doesn't strike me as a gullible woman."

"Perhaps it's a synonym for romantic."

"No, but romantic might be synonymous with hope. Her way isn't yours."

Yet we both chose lovers from the same bloodline, Summer reminded herself. Just what would Blake's reaction be to that little gem? Keep the past in the past, Summer advised herself. And concentrate on the moment. She smiled at him. "No, it's not. And how do you find my cooking?"

Perhaps it was best to let the subject die, for a time. He needed to ease her over that block gently. "As I find everything about you," Blake told her. "Magnificent."

She laughed as she began to eat again. "It wouldn't be

advisable for you to become too used to it. I rarely prepare meals for only compliments."

"That had occured to me. So I brought what I thought was the proper token."

Summer tasted the wine again. "Yes, the champagne is excellent."

"But an inadequate token for a Summer Lyndon meal."

When she shot him a puzzled look, he reached in his inside pocket and drew out a small thin box.

"Ah, presents." Amused, she accepted the box.

"You mentioned a fondness for them." Blake saw the amusement fade as she opened the box.

Inside were diamonds—elegant, even delicate, in the form of a slender bracelet. They lay white and regal against the dark velvet of the box.

She wasn't often overwhelmed. Now, she found herself struggling through waves of astonishment. "The meal's too simple for a token like this," she managed. "If I'd known, I'd've prepared something spectacular."

"I wouldn't have thought art ever simple."

"Perhaps not, but . . ." She looked up, telling herself she wasn't supposed to be moved by such things. They were only pretty stones after all. But her heart was full. "Blake, it's lovely, exquisite. I think you've taken me too seriously when I talk of payments and gifts. I didn't do this tonight for any reason more than I wanted to do it."

"This made me think of you," he said as if she hadn't spoken. "See how cool and haughty the stones are? But . . ." He slipped the bracelet out of the box. "If you look closely, if you hold it to light, there's warmth, even fire." As he spoke, he let the bracelet dangle from his fingers so that it caught and glittered with the flames from the candles. At that moment, it might have been alive.

"So many dimensions, from every angle you can see

something different. A strong stone, and more elegant than any other." Laying the bracelet over her wrist, he clasped it. His gaze lifted and locked on hers. "I didn't do this tonight for any reason other than I wanted to do it."

She was breathless, vulnerable. Would it be like this every time he looked at her? "You begin to worry me," Summer whispered.

The one quiet statement had the need whipping through him almost out of control. He rose, then, drawing her to her feet, crushed her against him before she could agree or pro- test. "Good."

His mouth wasn't patient this time. There seemed to be a desperate need to hurry, take all, take everything. Hunger that had nothing to do with the meal still unfinished on the table sped through him. She was every desire, and every an- swer. Biting off an oath, he pulled her to the floor.

This was the whirlwind. She'd never been here before, trapped, exhilarated. Elated by the speed, trembling from the power, Summer moved with him. There was no patience with clothes this time. They were tugged and pulled and tossed aside until flesh could meet flesh. Hot and eager, her body arched against his. She wanted the wind and the fury that only he could bring her.

As his hands sped over her, she delighted in their firmness, in the strength of each individual finger. Her own demands raged equally. Her mouth raced down his throat, teeth nip- ping, tongue darting. Each unsteady breath told her that she drove him just as he drove her. There was pleasure in that, she discovered. To give passion, and to have it returned to you. Even though her mind clouded, she knew the instant his control snapped.

He was rough, but she delighted in it. She had taken him beyond the civilized only by being. His mouth was everywhere, tasting, on a crazed journey from her lips to her breasts—lingering—then lower, still lower, until she caught her breath in astonished excitement.

The world peeled away, the floor, the walls, ceiling, then the sky and the ground itself. She was beyond all that, in some spiraling tunnel where only the senses ruled. Her body had no bounds, and she had no control. She moaned, struggling for a moment to pull it back, but the first peak swept her up, tossing her blindly. Even the illusion of reason shattered.

He wanted her like this. Some dark, primitive part of him needed to know he could bring her to this throbbing, mindless world of sensations. She shuddered beneath him, gasping, yet he continued to drive her up again and again with hands and mouth only. He could see her face in the candlelight—those flickers of passion, of pleasure, of need. She was moist and heated. And he was greedy.

Her skin pulsed under him everywhere he touched. When he touched his mouth to the sensitive curve where thigh meets hip, she arched and moaned his name. The sound of it tore through him, pounding in his blood long after there was silence.

"Tell me you want me," he demanded as he raced up her shuddering body again. "And only me."

"I want you." She could think of nothing. She would have given him anything. "Only you."

They joined in a violence that went on and on, then shattered into a crystal contentment.

* * *

She lay beneath him knowing she'd never gather the strength to move. There was barely the strength to breathe. It didn't seem to matter. For the first time, she noticed the floor was hard beneath her, but it didn't inspire her to shift to a more comfortable position. Sighing, she closed her eyes. Without too much effort, she could sleep exactly where she was.

Blake moved, only to draw himself up and take his weight on his own arms. She seemed so fragile suddenly, so completely without defense. He hadn't been gentle with her, yet during the loving, she'd seemed so strong, so full of fire.

He gave himself the enjoyment of looking at her while she half dozed, wearing nothing more than diamonds at her wrist. As he watched, her eyes fluttered open and she watched him, catlike from half-lowered lids. Her lips curved. He grinned at her, then kissed them.

"What's for dessert?"

CHAPTER 9

Unfortunately, Summer was going to need a phone in her office. She preferred to work undisturbed, and phones had a habit of disturbing, but the final menu was almost completed. She was approaching the practical stage of selective marketing. With so many new things—and difficult-to-come-by items—on the bill of fare, she would have to begin the process of finding the best suppliers. It was a job she would have loved to have delegated, but she trusted her own negotiating skills, and her own intuition, more than anyone else's. When choosing a supplier of the best oysters or okra, you needed both.

After tidying her morning's work, Summer gave the stack of papers a satisifed nod. Her instincts about taking this very different sort of job had been valid. She was doing it, and doing it well. The kitchen remodeling was exactly what she'd envisioned, the staff was well trained—and with her carefully screened and selected additions would be only more so. The two new pastry chefs were better than she'd expected them to be. Julio and Georgia had sent a postcard from Hawaii, and it had been taped, with some honor, to the front of a refrigerator. Summer had only had a moment's temptation to throw darts at it.

She'd interfered very little with the setup in the dining room. The lighting there was excellent, the linen impeccable. The food—her food—alone would be all the refreshing the restaurant required.

Soon, she thought, she'd be able to have the new menus printed. She had only to pin down a few prices first and haggle over terms and delivery hours. The next step was the installation of a phone. Choosing to deal with it immediately, she headed for the door. She entered the kitchen from one end as Monique entered from the other. All work ceased.

It amused Summer, and rather pleased her, that her mother had that stunning effect on people. She could see Max standing, staring, with a kitchen spoon in one hand that dripped sauce unheeded onto the floor. And, of course, Monique knew how to make an entrance. It might be said she was a woman made for entrances.

She smiled slowly—it almost appeared hesitantly—as she stepped in, bringing the scent of Paris and spring with her. Her eyes were more gray than her daughter's and, despite the difference in years and experience, held more innocence. Summer had yet to decide if it was calculated or innate.

"Perhaps someone could help me?"

Six men stepped forward. Max came perilously close to allowing the stock from the spoon to drip on Monique's shoulder. Summer decided it was time to restore order. "Mother." She brushed her way through the circle of bodies surrounding Monique.

"Ah, Summer, just who I was looking for." Even as she took her daughter's hands, she gave the group of male faces a sweeping smile. "How fascinating. I don't believe I've ever been in a hotel kitchen before. It's so—ah—large, *oui*?"

"Please, Ms. Dubois—madame." Unable to contain himself, Max took Monique's hand. "I'd be honored to show you whatever you'd like to see. Perhaps you'd care to sample some of the soup?"

"How kind." Her smile would have melted chocolate at fifty yards. "Of course, I must see everything where my daughter works."

"Daughter?"

Obviously, Summer mused, Max had heard nothing but violins since Monique walked into the room. "My mother," Summer said clearly, "Monique Dubois. This is Max, who's in charge of the kitchen staff."

Mother? Max thought dumbly. But of course the resemblance was so strong he felt like a fool for not seeing it before. There wasn't a Dubois film he hadn't seen at least three times. "A pleasure." Rather gallantly, he kissed the offered hand. "An honor."

"How comforting to know my daughter works with such a gentleman." Though Summer's lip curled, she said nothing. "And I would love to see everything, just everything— perhaps later today?" she added before Max could begin again. "Now, I must steal Summer away for just a short time. Tell me, would it be possible to have some champagne and caviar delivered to my suite?"

"Caviar isn't on the menu," Summer put in with an arch look at Max. "As yet."

"Oh." Prettily, Monique pouted. "I suppose some pâté, or some cheese would do."

"I'll see to it personally. Right away, madame."

"So kind." With a flutter of lashes, Monique slipped her arm through Summer's and swept from the room.

"Laying it on a bit thick," Summer muttered.

Monique threw back her head and gave a bubbling laugh. "Don't be so British, *chérie*. I just did you an enormous service. I learned from the delightful young Cocharan this morning that not only is my daughter an employee at this very hotel—which you didn't bother to tell me—but that you had a few internal problems in the kitchen."

"I didn't tell you because it's only a temporary arrangement, and because it's been keeping me quite busy. As to the internal problems . . ."

"In the form of one very large Max." Monique glided into the elevator.

"I can handle them just fine by myself," Summer finished.

"But it doesn't hurt to have him impressed by your parentage." After pressing the button for her floor, Monique turned to study her daughter. "So, I look at you in the light and see that you've grown more lovely. That pleases me. If one must have a grown daughter, one should have a beautiful grown daughter."

Laughing, Summer shook her head. "You're as vain as ever."

"I'll always be vain," Monique said simply. "God willing I'll always have a reason to be. Now—" she motioned Summer out of the elevator "—I've had my morning coffee and croissants, and my massage. I'm ready to hear about this new job of yours and your new lover. From the look of you, both agree with you."

"I believe it's customary for mothers and daughters to discuss new jobs, but not new lovers."

"Pooh." Monique tossed open the door to her suite. "We were never just mother and daughter, but friends, *n'est-ce pas*? And *chère amies* always discuss new lovers."

"The job," Summer said distinctly as she dropped into a butter-soft daybed and brought up her legs, "is working out quite well. I took it originally because it intrigued me and—well because Blake threw LaPointe up in my face."

"LaPointe? The beady-eyed little man you detest so much? The one who told the Paris papers you were his . . ."

"Mistress," Summer said violently.

"Ah, yes, such a foolish word, mistress, so antiquated, don't you agree? Unless one considers that mistress is the feminine term for master." Monique smiled serenely as she draped herself on the sofa. "And were you?"

"Certainly not. I wouldn't have let him put his pudgy little hands on me if he'd been half the chef he claims to be."

"You might have sued."

"Then more people would've snickered and said where there's smoke, there's fire. The little French swine would've loved that." She was gritting her teeth, so she deliberately relaxed her jaw. "Don't get me started on LaPointe. It was enough that Blake maneuvered me into this job with him as an edge."

"A very clever man—your Blake, that is."

"He's not my Blake," Summer said pointedly. "He's his own man, just as I'm my own woman. You know I don't believe in that sort of thing." The discreet knock had Monique waving negligently and Summer rising to answer. She thought, as the tray of cheeses and fresh fruit and the bucket of iced champagne was wheeled in, that Max must have dashed around like a madman to have it served so promptly. Summer signed the check with a flourish and dismissed the waiter.

Idly Monique inspected the tray before choosing a single cube of cheese. "But you're in love with him."

Busy with the champagne cork, Summer glanced over. "What?"

"You're in love with the young Cocharan."

The cork exploded out, champagne fizzed and geysered from the bottle. Monique merely lifted her glass to be filled. "I'm not in love with him," Summer said with an underlying desperation her mother recognized.

"One is always in love with one's lover."

"No, one is not." With a bit more control, Summer poured

the wine. "Affairs don't have to be romantic and flowery. I'm fond of Blake, I respect him. I consider him an attractive, intelligent man and enjoy his company."

"It's possible to say the same of a brother, or an uncle. Even perhaps an ex-husband," Monique commented. "This is not what I think you feel for Blake."

"I feel passion for him," Summer said impatiently. "Passion is not to be equated with love."

"Ah, Summer." Amused, Monique chose a grape. "You can think with your British mind, but you feel with your French heart. This young Cocharan isn't a man any woman would lightly dismiss."

"Like father like son?" The moment it was said, Summer regretted it.

But Monique only smiled, softly, reminiscently. "It occurred to me. I haven't forgotten B.C."

"Nor he you."

Interested, Monique flipped back from the past. "You've met Blake's father?"

"Briefly. When your name was mentioned, he looked as though he'd been struck by lightning."

The soft smile became brilliant. "How flattering. A woman likes to believe she remains in a man's memory long after they part."

"You may be flattered. I can tell you I was damned uncomfortable."

"But why?"

"Mother." Restless, Summer rose again and began to pace. "I was attracted to Blake—very much attracted—and he to me. How do you think I felt when I was talking to his father, and both B.C. and I were thinking about the fact that you'd been lovers? I don't think Blake has any idea. If he did, do you realize how awkward the situation would be?"

"Why?"

On a long breath, Summer turned to her mother again. "B.C. was and is married to Blake's mother. I get the impression Blake's rather fond of his mother, and of his father."

"What does that have to do with it?" Monique's gesture was typically French—a slight shrug, a slight lifting of the hand, palm out. "I was fond of his father too. Listen to me," she continued before Summer could retort. "B.C. was always in love with his wife. I knew that then. We consoled each other, made each other laugh in what was a miserable time for both of us. I'm grateful for it, not ashamed of it. Neither should you be."

"I'm not ashamed." Frustrated, Summer dragged a hand through her hair. "I don't ask you to be, but—damn it, Mother, it's awkward."

"Life often is. You'll remind me there are rules, and so there are." She threw back her head and took on the regal haughtiness her daughter had inherited. "I don't play by the rules, and I don't apologize."

"Mother." Cursing herself, Summer went and knelt beside the couch. "I wasn't criticizing you. It's only that what's right for you, what's good for you, isn't right and good for me."

"You think I don't know that? You think I'd have you live my life?" Monique laid a hand on her daughter's head. "Perhaps I've seen more deep happiness than you've seen. But I've also seen more deep despair. I can't wish you the first without knowing you'd face the second. I want for you only what you wish for yourself."

"Some things you're afraid to wish for."

"No, but some things are more carefully wished for. I will give you some advice." She patted Summer's head, then drew her up to sit on the sofa. "When you were a little girl, I gave you none because small children have always been a mystery to me. When you grew up, you wouldn't have listened to any. Perhaps now we've come to the point between mother and daughter when each understands the other is intelligent."

With a laugh, Summer picked a strawberry from the tray. "All right, I'll listen."

"It does not make you less of a woman to need a man." When Summer frowned, she continued. "To need one to exist, yes, this is nonsense. To need one to give one scope and importance, this is dishonest. But to need a man, one man, to bring joy and passion? This is life."

"There can be joy and passion in a woman's life without a man."

"Some joy, some passion," Monique agreed. "Why settle for some? What is it that you prove by cutting off what is a natural need? Perhaps it's a foolish woman who takes a different man as a husband, four times. Again, I don't apologize, but only remind you that Summer Lyndon is not Monique Dubois. We look for different things in different ways. But we are both women. I don't regret my choices."

With a sigh, Summer laid her head on her mother's shoulder. "I want to be able to say that for myself. I've always thought I could."

"You're an intelligent woman. What choice you make will be right for you."

"My greatest fear has always been to make a mistake."

"Perhaps your greatest fear is your greatest mistake." She touched Summer's cheek again. "Come, pour me some more champagne. I'll tell you of my Keil."

*   *   *

When Summer returned to the kitchen, her mind was still playing back her conversation with Monique. It was rare that Monique pressed her for details about her personal life, and rarer still for her to offer advice. It was true that most of the hour they'd spent together had been devoted to a listing of Keil Morrison's virtues, but in those first few moments, Monique had said things designed to make Summer think—designed to make her begin to doubt her own list of priorities.

But when she approached the swinging doors leading into the kitchen, and the sounds of the argument met her, she knew her thinking would have to wait.

"My casserole's perfect."

"Too much milk, too little cheese."

"You've never been able to admit that my casseroles are better than yours."

Perhaps the scene was laughable—huge Max and little Charlie, the undersized Korean cook who came no higher than his superior's breastbone. They stood, glaring at each other, while both of them held a solid grip on a spinach casserole. It might have been laughable, Summer thought wearily, if the rest of the kitchen staff hadn't already been choosing up sides while the luncheon orders were ignored.

"Inferior work," Max retorted. He'd yet to forgive Charlie for being out sick three days running.

"Your casseroles are always inferior work. Mine are perfect."

"Too much milk," Max said solidly. "Not enough cheese."

"Problem?" Summer stepped up, lining herself between them.

"This scrawny little man who masquerades as a cook is trying to pass this mass of soggy leaves off as a spinach casserole." Max tried to tug the glass dish away and found that the scrawny little man was surprisingly strong.

"This big lump of dough who calls himself a chef is jealous because I know more about vegetables than he does."

Summer bit down hard on her bottom lip. Damn it, it was funny, but the timing was all wrong. "Perhaps the rest of you

might get back to work," she began coolly, "before what clientele we have left in the dining room evacuates to the near-
est golden arches for decent service. Now . . ." She turned
back to the two opponents. Any moment, she decided, there'd
be bared teeth and snarls. "This, I take it, is the casserole in
question."

"The dish is a casserole," Max tossed back. "What's in it
is garbage." He tugged again.

"Garbage!" The little cook squealed in outrage, then curled
his lip. "Garbage is what you pass off as prime rib. The only
thing edible on the plate is the tiny spring of parsley you part
with." He tugged back.

"Gentlemen, might I ask a question?" Without waiting
for an answer, she touched a finger to the dish. It was still
warm, but cooling fast. "Has anyone tasted the casserole?"

"I don't taste poison." Max gave the dish another yank. "I
pour poison down the sink."

"I wouldn't have this—this ox taste one spoonful of my
spinach." Charlie yanked right back. "He'd contaminate it."

"All right, children," Summer said in sweet tones that had
both men's annoyance turning on her. "Why don't I do the
testing?"

Both men eyed each other warily. "Tell him to let go of
my spinach," Charlie insisted.

"Max—"

"He lets go first. I'm his superior."

"Charlie—"

"The only thing superior is his weight." And the tug-of-
war began again.

Out of patience, Summer tossed up her hands. "All right,
enough!"

It might have been the shock of having her raise her voice,
something she'd never done in the kitchen—or it might have

been that the dish itself was becoming slippery from so much handling. Either way, at her word, the dish fell out of both men's hands with force. It struck the edge of the counter, shattering, so that glass flew even before the casserole and its contents hit the floor. In unison, Max and Charlie erupted with abuse and accusations.

Summer, distracted by the pain in her right arm, glanced down and saw the blood begin to seep from a four-inch gash. Amazed, she stared at it for a full three seconds while her mind completely rejected the idea that blood, her blood, could pour out so quickly.

"Excuse me," she managed at length. "Do you think the two of you could finish this round after I stop bleeding to death?"

Charlie looked over, a torrent of abuse trembling on his tongue. Instead, he stared wide-eyed at the wound, then broke into an excited ramble of Korean.

"If you'd stop interfering," Max began, even as he caught sight of the blood running down Summer's arm. He blanched, then to everyone's surprise, moved like lightning. Grabbing a clean cloth, he pressed it against the gash in Summer's arm. "Sit," he ordered and nudged her onto a kitchen stool. "You," he bellowed at no one in particular, "clean up this mess." Already he was fashioning a tourniquet. "Relax," he said to Summer with unaccustomed gentleness. "I want to see how deep it is."

Giddy, she nodded and kept her eyes trained on the steam from a pot across the room. It didn't really hurt so very much, she thought as her vision blurred then refocused. She'd probably imagined all that blood.

"What the hell's going on in here?" She heard Blake's voice vaguely behind her. "You can hear the commotion in here clear out to the dining room." He strode over, intending to give both Summer and Max the choice of unemployment or peaceful coexistence. The red-stained cloth stopped him cold. "Summer?"

"An accident," Max said hurriedly while Summer shook her head to clear it. "The cut's deep—she'll need stitches."

Blake was already grabbing the cloth from Max and pushing him aside. "Summer. How the hell did this happen?"

She focused on his face and registered concern and perhaps temper in his eyes before everything started to swim again. Then she made the mistake of looking down at her arm. "Spinach casserole," she said foolishly before she slid from the stool in a dead faint.

The next thing she heard was an argument. *Isn't this where I came in?* she thought vaguely. It only took her a moment to recognize Blake's voice, but the other, female and dry, was a stranger.

"I'm staying."

"Mr. Cocharan, you aren't a relative. It's against hospital policy for you to remain while we treat Ms. Lyndon. Believe me, it's only a matter of a few stitches."

A few stitches? Summer's stomach rolled. She didn't like to admit it, but when it came to needles—the kind the medical profession liked to poke into flesh—she was a complete coward. And if her sense of smell wasn't playing tricks on her, she knew where she was. The odor of antiseptics was much too recognizable. Perhaps if she just sat up and quietly walked away, no one would notice.

When she did sit up, she found herself in a small, curtained examining room. Her gaze lit on a tray that held all the shiny, terrifying tools of the trade.

Blake caught the movement out of the corner of his eye, and was beside her. "Summer, just relax."

Moistening her lips, she studied the room again. "Hospital?"

"Emergency Room. They're going to fix your arm."

She managed a smile, but kept her gaze locked on the tray. "I'd just as soon not." When she started to swing her legs over the side of the examining table, the doctor was there to stop her.

"Lie still, Ms. Lyndon."

Summer stared back at the tough, lined female face. She had frizzy hair the color of a peach, and wire-rim glasses. Summer gauged her own strength against the doctor's and decided she could win. "I'm going home now," she said simply.

"You're going to lie right there and get that arm sewed up. Now be quiet."

Well, perhaps if she recruited an ally. "Blake?"

"You need stitches, love."

"I don't want them."

"Need," the doctor corrected, briskly. "Nurse!" While she scrubbed her hands in a tiny sink, she looked back over her shoulder. "Mr. Cocharan, you'll have to wait outside."

"No." Summer managed to struggle back into a sitting position. "I don't know you," she told the white-coated woman at the sink. "And I don't know her," she added when the nurse pushed passed the curtains. "If I'm going to have to sit here while you sew up my arm with cat gut or whatever it is you use, I'm going to have someone here that I know." She tightened her grip on Blake's hand. "I know him." She lay back down but kept the death hold on Blake's hand.

"Very well." Recognizing both a strong will and basic fear, the doctor gave in. "Just turn your head away," she advised. "This won't take long. I've already used yards of cat gut today."

"Blake." Summer took a deep breath and looked straight into his eyes. She wouldn't think about what the two women on the other side of the table were doing to her arm. "I have a confession to make. I don't deal very well with this sort of thing." She swallowed again when she felt the pressure on her skin. "I have to be tranquilized to get through a dental appointment."

Out of the corner of his eye, he saw the doctor take the first stitch. "We almost had to do the same thing for Max." He ran his thumb soothingly over his knuckles. "After this, you could tell him you're going to put in a wood-burning stove and a hearth and he wouldn't give you any trouble."

"A hell of a way to get cooperation." She winced, felt her stomach roll and swallowed desperately. "Talk to me—about anything."

"We should take a weekend, soon, and go to the beach. Some place quiet, right on the ocean."

It was a good image, she struggled to focus on it. "Which ocean?"

"Any one you want. We'll do nothing for three days but lie in the sun, make love."

The young nurse glanced over, and a sigh escaped before the doctor caught her eye.

"As soon as I'm back from Rome. All you have to do is find some little island in the Pacific while I'm gone. I'd like a few palm trees and friendly natives."

"I'll look into it."

"In the meantime," the doctor put in as she snipped off a length of bandage, "keep this dressing dry, have it changed every third day and come back in two weeks to have the stitches removed. A nasty slice," she added, giving the bandage a last professional adjustment. "But you'll live."

Cautiously Summer turned her head. The wound was now covered in the sterile white gauze. It looked neat, trim and somehow competent. The nausea faded instantly. "I thought they made the stitches so they dissolved."

"It's a nice arm." The doctor rinsed off her hands in the

sink. "We wouldn't want a scar on it. I'll give you a prescription for some pain pills."

Summer set her jaw. "I won't take them."

With a shrug, the doctor dried her hands. "Suit yourself. Oh, and you might try the Solomon Islands off New Guinea." Whipping back the curtain, she strode out.

"Quite a lady," Summer muttered as Blake helped her off the table. "Terrific bedside manner. I can't think why I don't hire her as my personal physician."

The spunk was back, Blake thought with a grin, but kept a supportive arm around her waist. "She was exactly what you needed. You didn't need any more sympathy, or worry, than you were getting from me."

She frowned up at him as he led her into the parking lot. "When I bleed," she corrected, "I need a great deal of sympathy and worry."

"What you need—" he kissed her forehead before opening the car door "—is a bed, a dark room and a few hours' rest."

"I'm going back to work," she corrected. "The kitchen's probably chaos, and I have a long list of phone calls to make—as soon as you arrange to have a phone hooked up for me."

"You're going home, to bed."

"I've stopped bleeding," Summer reminded him. "And though I admit I'm a complete baby when it comes to blood and needles and doctors in white coats, that's done now. I'm fine."

"You're pale." He stopped at a light and turned to her. It wasn't entirely clear to him how he'd gotten through the last hour himself. "You arm's certainly throbbing now, or soon will be. I make it a policy—whenever one of my staff faints on the job, they have the rest of the day off."

"Very liberal and humanitarian of you. I wouldn't have fainted if I hadn't looked."

"Home, Summer."

She sat up, folded her hands and took a deep breath. Her arm *was* throbbing, but she wouldn't have admitted it now for anything. With the new ache, and annoyance, it was easy to forget that she'd clung to his hand a short time before. "Blake, I realize I've mentioned this before, but sometimes it doesn't hurt to reiterate. I don't take orders."

Silence reigned in the car for almost a full minute. Blake turned west, away from Cocharan House and toward Summer's apartment building.

"I'll just take a cab," she said lightly.

"What you'll take is a couple of aspirin, right before I draw the shades and tuck you into bed."

God, that sounded like heaven. Ignoring the image, she set her chin. "Just because I depended on you—a little—while that woman was plying her needle, doesn't mean I need a keeper."

There was a way to convince her to do as he wanted. Blake considered it. Perhaps the direct way was the best way. "I don't suppose you noticed how many stitches she put in your arm."

"No." Summer looked out the window.

"I did. I counted them as she sewed. Fifteen. You didn't notice the size of the needle, either?"

"No." Pressing a hand to her stomach she glared at him. "Dirty pool, Blake."

"If it works . . ." Then he slipped a hand over hers. "A nap, Summer. I'll stay with you if you like."

How was she supposed to deal with him when he went from being kind, to filthy, to gentle? How was she supposed to deal with herself when all she really wanted was to curl up beside him where she knew it would be safe and warm? "I'll rest." All at once, she felt she needed to, badly, but it no longer had anything to do with her arm. If he continually stirred her emotions like this, the next few months were going to be impossible. "Alone," she finished firmly. "You have enough to do back at the hotel."

When he pulled up in front of her building, she put out a hand to stop him from turning off the engine. "No, you needn't bother to come up. I'll go to bed, I promise." Because she could feel him tense with an objection, she smiled and squeezed his hand. I have to go up alone, she realized. If he came with her now, everything could change. "I'm going to take those aspirin, turn on the stereo and lie down. I'd feel better if you'd go by the kitchen and make certain everything's all right there."

He studied her face. Her skin was pale, her eyes weary. He wanted to stay with her, have her hold onto him for support again. Even as he sat beside her, he could feel the distance she was putting between them. No, he wouldn't allow that—but for now, she needed rest more than she needed him.

"If that's what you want. I'll call you tonight."

Leaning over, she kissed his cheek, then climbed from the car quickly. "Thanks for holding my hand."

CHAPTER 10

It was beginning to grate on her nerves. It wasn't as though Summer didn't enjoy attention. More than enjoying it, she'd come to expect it as a matter of course in her career. It wasn't as if she didn't enjoy being catered to. That was something she'd developed a taste for early on, growing up in households with servants. But as any good cook knows, sugar has to be dispensed with a careful hand.

Monique had extended her stay a full week, claiming that she couldn't possibly leave Philadelphia while Summer was still recovering from an injury. The more Summer tried to play down the entire incident of her arm and the stitches, the more Monique looked at her with admiration and concern. The more admiration and concern she received, the more Summer worried about that next visit to the doctor.

Though it wasn't in character, Monique had gotten into the habit of coming by Summer's office every day with healing cups of tea and bowls of healthy soup—then standing over her daughter until everything was consumed.

For the first few days, Summer had found it rather sweet—though tea and soup weren't regulars on her diet. As far as she could remember, Monique had always been loving and certainly kind, but never maternal. For this reason alone, Summer drank the tea, ate the soup and swallowed complaints along with them. But as it continued, and as Monique consistently interrupted the final stages of her planning, Summer began to lose patience. She might have been able to tolerate Monique's overreaction and mothering, if it hadn't been for the same treatment by the kitchen staff, headed by Max.

She was permitted to do nothing for herself. If she started to brew a pot of coffee, someone was there, taking over, insisting that she sit and rest. Every day at precisely noon, Max himself brought her in a tray with the luncheon speciality of the day. Poached salmon, lobster soufflé, stuffed eggplant. Summer ate—because like her mother, he hovered over her—while she had visions of a bacon double cheeseburger with a generous side order of onion rings.

Doors were opened for her, concerned looks thrown her way, conciliatory phrases heaped on her until she wanted to scream. Once when she'd been unnerved enough to snap that she had some stitches in her arm, not a terminal illness, she'd been brought yet another soothing cup of tea—with a saucer of plain vanilla cookies.

They were killing her with kindness.

Every time she thought she'd reached her limit, Blake managed to level things for her again. He wasn't callous of her injury or even unkind, but he certainly wasn't treating her as though she were the star attraction at a deathbed.

He had an uncanny instinct for choosing the right time to phone or drop in on the kitchen. He was there, calm when she needed calm, ordered when she yearned for order. He demanded things of her when everyone else insisted she couldn't lift a finger for herself. When he annoyed her, it was in an entirely different way, a way that tested and stretched her abilities rather than smothered them.

And with Blake, Summer didn't have that hampering

guilt about letting loose with her temper. She could shout at him knowing she wouldn't see the bottomless patience in his eyes that she saw in Max's. She could be unreasonable and not be worried that his feelings would be hurt like her mother's.

Without realizing it, she began to see him as a pillar of solidity and sense in a world of nonsense. And, for perhaps the first time in her life, she felt an intrinsic need for that pillar.

Along with Blake, Summer had her work to keep her temper and her nerve ends under some kind of control. She poured herself into it. There were long sessions with the printer to design the perfect menu—an elegant slate gray with the words COCHARAN HOUSE embossed on the front—thick creamy parchment paper inside listing her final choices in delicate script. Then there were the room service menus that would go into each unit—not quite so luxurious, perhaps, but Summer saw to it that they were distinguished in their own right. She talked for hours with suppliers, haggling, demanding and enjoying herself more than she would ever have guessed, until she got precisely the terms she wanted.

It gave her a glow of success—perhaps not the flash she felt on completing some spectacular dish—but a definite glow. She found that in a different way, it was equally satisfying.

And it was unpardonably annoying to be told, after the completion of a particularly long and successful negotiation, that she should take a little nap.

"Chérie." Monique glided into the storage room, just as Summer hung up the phone with the butcher, bearing the inevitable cup of herbal tea. "It's time you had a break. You mustn't push yourself so."

"I'm fine, Mother." Glancing at the tea, Summer sincerely hoped she wouldn't gag. She wanted something carbonated and cold, preferably loaded with caffeine. "I'm just going over the contracts with the suppliers. It's a bit complicated and I've still got one or two calls to make."

If she'd hoped that would be a gentle hint that she needed privacy to work, she was disappointed. "Too complicated when you've already worked so many hours today," Monique insisted and took a seat on the other side of the desk. "You forget, you've had a shock."

"I cut my arm," Summer said with strained patience.

"Fifteen stitches," Monique reminded her, then frowned with disapproval as Summer reached for a cigarette. "Those are so bad for your health, Summer."

"So's nervous tension," she muttered, then doggedly cleared her throat. "Mother, I'm sure Keil's missing you desperately just as you must be missing him. You shouldn't be away from your new husband for so long."

"Ah, yes." Monique sighed and looked dreamily at the ceiling. "For a new bride, a day away from her husband is like a week, a week can be a year." Abruptly, she pressed her hands together, shaking her head. "But my Keil, he is the most understanding of men. He knows I must stay when my daughter needs me."

Summer opened her mouth, then shut it again. Diplomacy, she reminded herself. Tact. "You've been wonderful," she began, a bit guiltily, because it was true. "I can't tell you how much I appreciate all the time, all the trouble, you've taken over this past week or so. But my arm's nearly healed now. I'm really fine. I feel terribly guilty holding you here when you should be enjoying your honeymoon."

With her light, sexy laugh, Monique waved a hand. "My sweet, you'll learn that a honeymoon isn't a time or a trip, but a state of mind. Don't concern yourself with that. Besides, do you think I could leave before they take those nasty stitches out of your arm?"

"Mother—" Summer felt the hitch in her stomach and reached for the tea in defense.

"No, no. I wasn't there for you when the doctor treated you, but—" here, her eyes filled and her lips trembled "—I will be by your side when she removes them—one at a time."

Summer had an all-too-vivid picture of herself lying once again on the examining table, the tough-faced doctor over her. Monique, frail in black, would be standing by, dabbing at her eyes with a lacy handkerchief. She wasn't sure if she wanted to scream, or just drop her head between her knees.

"Mother, you'll have to excuse me. I've just remembered, I have an appointment with Blake in his office." Without waiting for an answer, Summer dashed from the storage room.

Almost immediately Monique's eyes were dry and her lips curved. Leaning back in her chair, she laughed in delight. Perhaps she hadn't always known just what to do with a daughter when Summer had been a child, but now . . . Woman to woman, she knew precisely how to nudge her daughter along. And she was nudging her along to Blake, where Monique had no doubt her strong-willed, practical and much-loved daughter belonged.

"*À l'amour,*" she said and lifted the tea in a toast.

It didn't matter to Summer that she didn't have an appointment, only that she see Blake, talk to him and restore her sanity. "I have to see Mr. Cocharan," she said desperately as she pushed right past the receptionist.

"But, Ms. Lyndon—"

Heedless, Summer dashed through the outer office and tossed open his door without knocking. "Blake!"

He lifted a brow, motioned her inside, then continued with his telephone conversation. She looked, he thought, as if she were on the last stages of a manhunt, and on the wrong side of the bloodhounds. His first instinct might have been to comfort, to soothe, but common sense prevailed. It was all too obvious that she was getting enough of that, and detesting it.

Frustrated, she whirled around the room. Nervous energy flowed from her. She stalked to the window, then, restless, turned away from the view. Ultimately she walked to the bar and poured herself a defiant portion of vermouth. The moment she heard the phone click back on the cradle, she turned to him.

"Something has to be done!"

"If you're going to wave that around," he said mildly, indicating her glass, "you'd better drink some first. It'll be all over you."

Scowling, Summer took a long sip. "Blake, my mother has to go back to California."

"Oh?" He finished scrawling a memo. "Well, we'll be sorry to see her go."

"*No!* No, she has to go back, but she won't. She insists on staying here and nursing me into catatonia. And Max," she continued before he could comment. "Something has to be done about Max. Today—today it was shrimp salad and avocado. I can't take much more." She sucked in a breath, then continued in a dazed rambling of complaints. "Charlie looks at me as if I were Joan of Arc, and the rest of the kitchen staff is just as bad—if not worse. They're driving me crazy."

"I can see that."

The tone of voice had her pacing coming to a quick halt and her eyes narrowing. "Don't aim that coolly amused smile at me."

"Was I smiling?"

"Or that innocent look, either," she snapped back. "You were smiling inside, and nervous breakdowns are definitely not funny."

"You're absolutely right." He folded his hands on the desk. "Why don't you sit down and start from the beginning."

"Listen—" She dropped into a chair, sipped the vermouth, then was up and pacing again. "It's not that I don't appreciate kindness, but there's a saying about too much of a good thing."

"I think I've heard that."

Ignoring him, she plunged on. "You can ruin a dessert with too much pampering, too much attention, you know."

He nodded. "The same's sometimes said of a child."

"Just stop trying to be cute, damn it."

"It doesn't seem to take any effort." He smiled. She scowled.

"Are you listening to me?" she demanded.

"Every word."

"I wasn't cut out to be pampered, that's all. My mother— every day it's cup after cup of herbal tea until I have visions of sloshing when I walk. 'You should rest, Summer. You're not strong yet, Summer.' Damn it, I'm strong as an ox!"

He took out a cigarette, enjoying the show. "I'd've said so myself."

"And Max! The man's positively smothering me with good will. Lunch every day, twelve on the dot." With a groan, she pressed a hand against her stomach. "I haven't had a real meal in a week. I keep getting these insane cravings for tacos, but I'm so full of tea and lobster bisque I can't do anything about it. If one more person tells me to put up my feet and rest, I swear, I'm going to punch them right in the mouth."

Blake scrutinized the end of his cigarette. "I'll make sure I don't mention it."

"That's just it, you don't." She spun around the desk, then sat on it directly in front of him. "You're the only one around here who's treated me like a normal person since this ridiculous thing happened. You even shouted at me yesterday. I appreciate that."

"Think nothing of it."

With a half laugh, she took his hand. "I'm serious. I feel foolish enough for being so careless as to let an accident like that happen in my kitchen. You don't constantly remind me of it with pats on the head and concerned looks."

"I understand you." Blake linked his fingers with hers. "I've been making a study of you almost from the first instant we met."

The way he said it had her pulse fluctuating. "I'm not an easy person to understand."

"No?"

"I don't always understand."

"Let me tell you about Summer Lyndon, then." He measured her hand against his before he linked their fingers. "She's a beautiful woman, a bit spoiled from her upbringing and her own success." He smiled when her brows drew together. "She's strong and opinionated and intensely feminine without being calculating. She's ambitious and dedicated with a skill for concentration that reminded me once of a surgeon. And she's romantic, though she'll claim otherwise."

"That's not true," Summer began.

"She listens to Chopin when she works. Even while she chooses to have an office in a storage room, she keeps roses on her desk."

"There're reasons why—"

"Stop interrupting," he told her simply, and with a huff, she subsided. "What fears she has are kept way below the surface because she doesn't like to admit to having any. She's tough enough to hold her own against anyone, and compassionate enough to tolerate an uncomfortable situation rather than hurt someone's feelings. She's controlled, and she's passionate. She has a taste for the best champagne and junk food. There's no one I've known who's annoyed me quite so much, or who I'd trust quite so implicitly."

She let out a long breath. It wasn't the first time he'd put her in a position where words were hard to come by. "Not an entirely admirable woman."

"Not entirely," Blake agreed. "But a fascinating one."

She smiled, then sat on his lap. "I've always wanted to do this," she murmured, snuggling. "Sit on some big corporate executive's lap in an elegant office. I'm suddenly quite sure I'd rather be fascinating than admirable."

"I prefer you that way." He kissed her, but lightly.

"You've chased off my nervous breakdown again."

He brushed at her hair, thinking he was close—very close—to winning her completely. "We aim to please."

"Now if I just didn't have to go back down and face all that sugar." She sighed. "And all those earnestly concerned faces."

"What would you rather do?"

Linking her hands around his neck, she laughed and drew back. "If I could do anything I wanted?"

"Anything."

Thoughtfully she ran her tongue over her teeth then grinned. "I'd like to go to the movies, a perfectly dreadful movie, and eat pounds of buttered popcorn with too much salt."

"Okay." He gave her a friendly slap on the bottom. "Let's go find a dreadful movie."

"You mean now?"

"Right now."

"But it's only four o'clock."

He kissed her, then hauled her to her feet. "It's known as playing hookey. I'll fill you in on the way."

* * *

She made him feel young, foolishly young and irresponsible, sitting in a darkened corner of the theater with a huge barrel of popcorn on his lap and her hand in his. When he looked back over his life, Blake could remember no time when he hadn't felt secure—but irresponsible? Never that. Having a multimillion dollar business behind him had ingrained in him a very demanding sense of obligation. However much he'd benefited growing up, having enough and always the best, there'd always been the unspoken pressure to maintain that standard—for himself, and for the family business.

Because he'd always taken that position seriously, he was a cautious man. Impulsiveness had never been part of his style. But perhaps that was changing a bit—with Summer. He'd had the impulse to give her whatever she'd wanted that afternoon. If it had been a trip to Paris to eat supper at Maxim's, he'd have arranged it then and there. Then again, he should have known that a box of popcorn and a movie were more her style.

It was that style—the contrast of elegance and simplicity—that had drawn him in from the first. He knew, without question, that there would never be another woman who would move him in the same way.

Summer knew it had been days since she had fully relaxed. In fact, she hadn't been able to relax at all since the accident with anyone but Blake. He'd given her support, but more important, he'd given her space. They hadn't been together often over the past week, and she knew Blake was closing the deal with the Hamilton chain. They'd both been busy, preoccupied, pressured, yet when they were alone and away from Cocharan House, they didn't talk business. She knew how hard he'd worked on this purchase—the negotiations, the paperwork, the endless meetings. Yet he'd put all that aside—for her.

Summer leaned toward him. "Sweet."

"Hmm?"

"You," she whispered under the dialogue on the screen. "You're sweet."

"Because I found a dreadful movie?"

With a chuckle, she reached for more popcorn. "It is dreadful, isn't it?"

"Terrible, which is why the theater's nearly empty. I like it this way."

"Antisocial?"

"No, it just makes it easier—" leaning closer, he caught the lobe of her ear between his teeth "—to indulge in this sort of thing."

"Oh." Summer felt the thrill of pleasure start at her toes and climb upward.

"And this sort of thing." He nipped at the cord of her neck, enjoying her quick little intake of breath. "You taste better than the popcorn."

"And it's excellent popcorn." Summer turned her head so that her mouth could find his.

So warm, so right. Summer felt it was almost possible to say that her lips were made to fit his. If she'd believed in such things . . . If she'd believed in such things, she might have said that they'd been meant to find each other at this stage of their lives. To meet, to clash, to attract, to merge. One man to one woman, enduringly. When they were close, when his lips were heated on hers, she could almost believe it. She wanted to believe it.

He ran a hand down her hair. Soft, fresh. Just the touch of

that and no more could make him want her unreasonably. He never felt stronger than when he was with her. And he never felt more vulnerable. He didn't hear the explosion of sound and music from the speakers. She didn't see the sudden kaleidoscope of color and movement on the screen. Hampered by the small seats, they shifted in an effort to get that much closer.

"Excuse me." The young usher, who had the job until September when school started up again, shifted his feet in the aisle. Then he cleared his throat. "Excuse me."

Glancing up, Blake noticed that the house lights were on and the screen was blank. After a surprised moment, Summer pressed her mouth against his shoulder to muffle a laugh.

"Movie's over," the boy said uncomfortably. "We have to—ah—clear the theater after every show." Glancing at Summer, he decided any man might lose interest in a movie with someone like her around. Then Blake stood, tall, broad shouldered, with that one aloofly raised eyebrow. The boy swallowed. And a lot of guys didn't like to be interrupted.

"Ah—that's the rule, you know. The manager—"

"And reasonable enough," Blake interrupted when he noticed the boy's Adam's apple working.

"We'll just take the popcorn along," Summer said as she rose. She tucked the barrel under one arm and slid her other through Blake's. "Have a nice evening," she told the usher over her shoulder as they walked out.

When they were outside, she burst out laughing. "Poor child, he thought you were going to manhandle him."

"The thought crossed my mind, but only very briefly."

"Long enough for him to get nervous about it." After climbing into the car, she placed the popcorn in her lap. "You know what he thought, don't you?"

"What?"

"That we were having an illicit affair." Leaning over, she

nipped at Blake's ear. "The kind where your wife thinks you're at the office, and my husband thinks I'm shopping."

"Why didn't we go to a motel?"

"That's where we're going now." Nibbling on popcorn again, she sent him a wicked glance. "Though I think in our case we might substitute my apartment."

"I'm willing to be flexible. Summer . . ." He drew her against his side as they breezed through a light. "Just what was that movie about?"

Laughing, she let her head lay against his shoulder. "I haven't the vaguest idea."

Later, they lay naked in her bed, the curtains open to let in the light, the windows up to let in the breeze. From the apartment below came the repetitive sound of scales being played, a bit unsteadily, on the piano. Perhaps she'd dozed for a short time, because the sunlight seemed softer now, almost rosy. But she wasn't in any hurry for night to fall.

The sheets were warm and wrinkled from their bodies. The air was ripe with supper smells—grilling pork from the piano teacher's apartment, spaghetti sauce from the newlyweds next door. The breeze carried the mix of both, appealingly.

"It's nice," Summer murmured, with her head nestled in the curve of her lover's shoulder. "Just being here like this, knowing that anything there is to do can be done just as well tomorrow. You probably haven't played hookey enough." She was quite sure she hadn't.

"If I did, the business would suffer and the board would begin to grumble. Complaining's one of their favorite things."

Absently, she rubbed the bottom of her foot over the top of one of his. "I haven't asked you about the Hamilton chain because I thought you probably got enough of that at the office, and from the press, but I'd like to know if you got what you wanted."

He thought about reaching for a cigarette then decided it wasn't worth the effort. "I wanted those hotels. As it turned out, the deal satisfied all parties in the end. You can't ask for more than that."

"No." Thoughtfully, she rolled over so that she could look at him directly. Her hair brushed over his chest. "Why did you want them? Is it the acquisition itself, the property or just a matter of enjoying the wheeling and dealing? The strategy of negotiations?"

"It's all of that. Part of the enjoyment in business is setting up deals, working out the flaws, following through until you've gotten what you were aiming for. In some ways it's not that different from art."

"Business isn't art," Summer corrected archly.

"There are parallels. You set up an idea, work out the flaws, then follow through until you've created what you wanted."

"You're being logical again. In art you use the emotion in equal parts with the mind. You can't do that in business." Her shrug was typically French. Somehow she became more French whenever her craft was under discussion. "This is all facts and figures."

"You left out instinct. Facts and figures aren't enough without that."

She frowned, considering. "Perhaps, but you wouldn't follow instinct over a solid set of facts."

"Even a solid set of facts varies according to the circumstances and the players." He was thinking of her now, and himself. Reaching up, he tucked her hair behind her ear. "Instincts are very often more reliable."

And she was thinking of him now, and herself. "Often more," Summer murmured, "but not always more. That leaves room for failure."

"No amount of planning, no amount of facts, precludes failure."

"No." She laid her head on his shoulder again, trying to ward off the little trickle of panic that was trying to creep in.

He ran a hand down her back. She was still so cautious, he thought. A little more time, a little more room—a change of subject. "I have twenty new hotels to oversee, to reorganize," he began. "That means twenty more kitchens that have to be studied and graded. I'll need an expert."

She smiled a little as she lifted her head again. "Twenty is a very demanding and time-consuming number."

"Not for the best."

Tilting her head, she looked down her straight, elegant nose. "Naturally not, but the best is very difficult to come by."

"The best is currently very soft and very naked in my arms."

Her lips curved slowly, the way he most enjoyed them. "Very true. But this, I think, is not a negotiating table."

"You've a better idea how to spend the evening?"

She ran a fingertip along his jawline. "Much better."

He caught her hand in his and, drawing her finger into his mouth, nipped lightly. "Show me."

The idea appealed, and excited. It seemed that whenever they made love, she was quickly dominated by her own emotions and his skill. This time, she would set the pace, and in her own time, in her own way, she would destroy the innate control that brought her both admiration and frustration. Just the thought of it sent a thrill racing up her spine.

She brought her mouth close to his, but used her tongue to taste. Slowly, very slowly, she traced his lips. Already she could feel the heat rising. With a lazy sigh, she shifted so that her body moved over his as she trailed kisses down his jaw.

A strong face, she thought, aristocratic but not soft, intelligent, but not cold. It was a face some women would find haughty—until they looked into the eyes. She did so now and saw the intensity, the heat, even the ruthlessness.

"I want you more than I should," she heard herself say. "I have you less than I want."

Before he could speak, she crushed her mouth to his and started the journey for both of them.

He was still throbbing from her words alone. He'd wanted to hear that kind of admission from her; he'd waited to hear it. Just as he'd waited to feel this strong, pure emotion from her. It was that emotion that stripped away all his defenses even as her seeking hands and mouth exploited the weaknesses.

She touched. His skin heated.

She tasted. His blood sang.

She encompassed. His mind swam.

Vulnerable. Blake discovered the new sensation in himself. She made him so. In the soft, lowering light—near dusk—he was trapped in that midnight world of quietly raging powers. Her fingers were cool and very sure as they stroked, enticed. He could feel them slide leisurely over him, pausing to linger while she sighed. And while she sighed, she exploited. His body was weighed down with layer after layer of pleasures—to be seduced so carefully, to be desired so fully.

With long, lengthy, openmouthed kisses, she explored all of him, reveling in the firm masculinity of his body—knowing she would soon rip apart that impenetrable control. She was obsessed with it, and with him. Could it be that now, after she'd made love with him, after she'd begun to understand the powers and weaknesses in his body, she would find even more delight in learning of them again?

There seemed to be no end to the variations of her feelings, to the changes of sensations she could experience when she was with him like this. Each time, every time, was as vital and unique as the first had been. If this was a contradiction to everything she'd ever believed was true about a man and woman, she didn't question it now. She exalted in it.

He was hers. Body and mind—she felt it. Almost tangibly she could sense the polish, the civilized sheen, that was so much a part of him melt away. It was what she wanted.

There was little sanity left. As she roamed over him the need became more primitive, more primal. He wanted more, endlessly more, but the blood was drumming in his head. She was so agile, so relentless. He experienced a wave of pure helplessness for the first time in his life. Her hands were clever—so clever he couldn't hear the quick unsteadiness of her breathing. He could feel her tormenting him exquisitely, but he couldn't see the flickers of passion or depth of desire in her eyes. He was blind and deaf to everything.

Then her mouth was devouring his and everything savage that civilized men restrain tore from him. He was mad for her. In his mind were dark swirling colors, in his ears was a wild rushing like a sea crazed by a storm. Her name ripped from him like an oath as he gripped her, rolling her to her back, enclosing her, possessing her.

And there was nothing but her, to take, to drown in, to ravage and to worship until passion spun from its peak and emptied him.

CHAPTER 11

I'm starving."

It was full dark, with no moon to shed any trickle of light into the room. The darkness itself was comfortable and easy. They were still naked and tangled on Summer's bed, but the piano had been silent for an hour. There were no more supper smells in the air. Blake drew her a bit closer and kept his eyes shut, though it wasn't sleep he sought. Somehow in the silence, in the darkness, he felt closer to her.

"I'm starving," Summer repeated, a bit sulkily this time.

"You're the chef."

"Oh, no, not this time." Rising on her elbow, Summer glared at him. She could see the silhouette of his profile, the long line of chin, the straight nose, the sweep of brow. She wanted to kiss all of them again, but knew it was time to make a stand. "It's definitely your turn to cook."

"My turn?" He opened one eye, cautiously. "I could send out for pizza."

"Takes too long." She rolled on top of him to give him a smacking kiss—and a quick jab in the ribs. "I said I was starving. That's an immediate problem."

He folded his arms behind his head. He, too, could see

only a silhouette—the drape of her hair, slope of her shoulder, the curve of her breasts. It was enough. "I don't cook."

"Everyone cooks something," she insisted.

"Scrambled eggs," he said, hoping it would discourage her. "That's about it."

"That'll do." Before he could think of anything to change her mind, she was off the bed and switching on the bedside lamp.

"Summer!" He tossed his arm over his eyes to shield them and tried a halfhearted moan. She grinned at that before she turned to the closet to find a robe.

"I have eggs, and a skillet."

"I make very bad eggs."

"That's okay." She found his slacks, shook them out briefly, then tossed them on top of him. "Real hunger makes allowances."

Resigned, Blake put his feet on the floor. "Then I don't expect a critique afterward."

While she waited, he slipped into a pair of brief jockey shorts. They were dark blue, cut low at the waist, high at the thigh. Very sexy, she mused, and very discreet. Strange how such an incidental thing could reflect a personality.

"Cooks like to be cooked for," she told him as he drew on his slacks.

He shrugged into his shirt, leaving it unbuttoned. "Then don't interfere."

"Wouldn't dream of it." Hooking her arm through his, Summer led him to the kitchen. Again, she switched on lights and made him wince. "Make yourself at home," she invited.

"Aren't you going to assist?"

"No, indeed." Summer took the top off the cookie jar and plucked out the familiar sandwich cookie. "I don't work overtime and I never assist."

"Union rules?"

"My rules."

"You're going to eat cookies?" he asked as he rummaged for a bowl. "And eggs?"

"This is just the appetizer," she said with her mouth full. "Want one?"

"I'll pass." Sticking his head in the refrigerator, he found a carton of eggs and a quart of milk.

"You might want to grate a bit of cheese," Summer began, then shrugged when he sent her an arch look. "Sorry. Carry on." Blake broke four eggs into the bowl then added a dollop of milk. "One should measure, you know."

"One shouldn't talk with one's mouth full," he said mildly and began to beat the eggs.

Overbeating them, she thought but managed to restrain herself. But when it came to cooking, willpower wasn't her strong suit. "You haven't heated up the pan, either." Undaunted by being totally ignored, she took another cookie. "I can see you're going to need lessons."

"If you want something to do, make some toast."

Obligingly she took a loaf of bread from the bin and popped two pieces in the toaster. "It's characteristic of cooks to get a bit testy when they're watched, but a good chef has to overcome that—and distractions." She waited until he'd poured the egg mixture into a skillet before going to him. Wrapping her arms around his waist, she pressed her lips to the back of his neck. "All manner of distraction. And you've got the flame up too high."

"Do you like your eggs singed or burned clear through?"

With a laugh, she ran her hands up his bare chest. "Singed is fine. I have a nice little white Bordeaux you might've put in the eggs, but since you didn't, I'll just pour some into glasses." She left him to cook and, by the time Blake had finished the eggs, she had buttered toast on a plate and chilled wine in glasses. "Impressive," Summer decided as she sat at the dinette. "And aromatic."

But it's the eyes that tell you first, he remembered. "Attractive?" He watched as she spooned eggs on her plate.

"Very, and—" she took a first testing bite "—yes, and quite good, all in all. I might consider putting you on the breakfast shift, on a trial basis."

"I might consider the job, if cold cereal were the basic menu."

"You'll have to expand your horizons." She continued to eat, enjoying the hot, simple food on an empty stomach. "I believe you could be quite good at this with a few rudimentary lessons."

"From you?"

She lifted her wine, and her eyes laughed over the rim. "If you like. You certainly couldn't have a better teacher."

Her hair was still rumpled around her face—his hands had done that. Her cheeks were flushed, her eyes bright and flecked with gold. The robe threatened to slip off one shoulder, and left a teasing hint of skin exposed. As passion had stripped away his control, now emotions stripped away all logic.

"I love you, Summer."

She stared at him while the smile faded slowly. What went through her she didn't recognize. It didn't seem to be any one sensation, but a cornucopia of fears, excitement, disbelief and longings. Oddly, no one of them seemed dominant at first, but were so mixed and muddled she tried to grip any one of them and hold on to it. Not knowing what else to do, she set the glass down precisely, then stared at the wine shimmering inside.

"That wasn't a threat." He took her hand, holding it until she looked up at him again. "I don't see how it could come as that much of a surprise to you."

But it had. She expected affection. That was something she could deal with. She understood respect. But love—that was such a fragile word. Such an easily broken word. And something inside her begged for it to be taken from him, cherished, protected. Summer struggled against it.

"Blake, I don't need to hear that sort of thing the way other women do. Please—"

"Maybe you don't." He hadn't started the way he'd intended to, but now that he had, he'd finish. "But I need to say it. I've needed to for a long time now."

She drew her hand from his and nervously picked up her glass again. "I've always thought that words are the first thing that can damage a relationship."

"When they're not said," Blake countered. "It's a lack of words, a lack of meaning, that damages a relationship. This one isn't a word I use casually."

"No." She could believe that. It might have been the belief that had the fear growing stronger. Love, when it was given demanded some kind of return. She wasn't ready—she was sure she wasn't ready. "I think it's best, if we want things to go on as they are, that we—"

"I don't want things to go on as they are," he interrupted. He'd rather have felt annoyance than this panic that was sneaking in. He took a moment, trying to alleviate both. "I want you to marry me."

"No." Summer's own panic became full-blown. She stood quickly, as if that would erase the words, put back the distance. "No, that's impossible."

"It's very possible." He rose too, unwilling to have her draw away from him. "I want you to share my life, my name. I want to share children with you and all the years it takes to watch them grow."

"Stop." She threw up her hand, desperate to halt the words.

They were moving her, and she knew it would be too easy to say yes and make that ultimate mistake.

"Why?" Before she could prevent it, he'd taken her face in his hands. The touch was gentle, though there was steel beneath. "Because you're afraid to admit it's something you want, too?"

"No, it's not something I want—it's not something I believe in. Marriage—it's a license that costs a few dollars. A piece of paper. For a few thousand dollars more, you can get a divorce decree. Another piece of paper."

He could feel her trembling and cursed himself for not knowing how to get through. "You know better than that. Marriage is two people who make promises to each other, and who make the effort to keep them. A divorce is giving up."

"I'm not interested in promises." Desperate, she pushed his hands from her face and stepped back. "I don't want any made to me, and I don't want to make any. I'm happy with my life just as it is. I have my career to think of."

"That's not enough for you, and we both know it. You can't tell me you don't feel for me. I can see it. Every time I'm with you it shows in your eyes, more each time." He was handling it badly, but saw no other course open but straight ahead. The closer he came, the further away she drew. "Damn it, Summer, I've waited long enough. If my timing's not as perfect as I wanted it to be, it can't be helped."

"Timing?" She dragged a hand through her hair. "What are you talking about? You've waited?" Dropping her hands, she began to pace the room. "Has this been one of your long-term plans, all neatly thought out, all meticulously outlined? Oh, I can see it." She let out a trembling breath and whirled back to him. It no longer made any difference to her if she were unreasonable. "Did you sit in your office and go over your strategy point by point?

Was this the setting up, the looking for flaws, the following through?"

"Don't be ridiculous—"

"Ridiculous?" she tossed back. "No, I think not. You'd play the game well—disarming, confusing, charming, supportive. Patience, you'd have a lot of that. Did you wait until you thought I was at my most vulnerable?" Her breath was heaving now, and the words were tumbling out on each one. "Let me tell you something, Blake, I'm not a hotel chain you can acquire by waiting until the market's ripe."

In a slanted way she'd been killingly accurate. And the accuracy put him on the defensive. "Damn it, Summer, I want to marry you, not acquire you."

"The words are often one and the same, to my way of thinking. Your plan's a little off the mark this time, Blake. No deal. Now, I want you to leave me alone."

"We have a hell of a lot of talking to do."

"No, we have no talking to do, not about this. I work for you, for the term of the contract. That's all."

"Damn the contract!" He took her by the shoulders, shaking her once in frustration. "And damn you for being so stubborn. I love you. That's not something you can brush aside as if it doesn't exist."

To their mutual surprise, her eyes filled abruptly, poignantly. "Leave me alone," she managed as the first tears spilled out. "Leave me completely alone."

The tears undermined him as her temper never would have done. "I can't do that." But he released her when he wanted to hold her. "I'll give you some time, maybe we both need time, but we'll have to come back to this."

"Just go away." She never allowed tears in front of anyone. Though she tried to dash them away, others fell quickly. "Go away." On the repetition she turned from him, holding herself stiff until she heard the click of the door.

She looked around, and though he was gone, he was everywhere. Dropping to the couch, she let herself weep and wished she were anywhere else.

* * *

She hadn't come to Rome for the cathedrals or the fountains or the art. Nor had she come for culture or history. As Summer took a wicked cab ride from the airport into the city, she was more grateful for the crowded streets and noise than the antiquity. Perhaps she'd stayed in America too long this time. Europe was fast cars, crumbling ruins and palaces. She needed Europe again, Summer told herself. As she zipped past the Trevi Fountain she thought of Philadelphia.

A few days away, she thought. Just a few days away, doing what she was best at, and everything would fall back into perspective again. She'd made a mistake with Blake—she'd known from the beginning it had been a mistake to get involved. Now it was up to her to break it off, quickly, completely. Before long he'd be grateful to her for preventing him from making an even larger mistake. Marriage—to her. Yes, she imagined he'd be vastly relieved, within even a few weeks.

Summer sat in the back of the cab watching Rome skim by and was more miserable than she'd ever been in her life.

When the cab squealed to a halt at the curb, she climbed out. She stood for a moment, a slender woman in a white fedora and jacket with a snakeskin bag slung carelessly over one shoulder. She was dressed like a woman of confidence and experience. In her eyes was a child who was lost.

Mechanically she paid off the driver, accepted her bag and his bow, then turned away. It was only just past 10:00

a.m. in Rome, and already hot under a spectacular sky. She remembered she'd left Philadelphia in a thunderstorm. Walking up the steps to an old, distinguished building, she knocked sharply five times. After a reasonable wait, she knocked again, harder.

When the door opened, she looked at the man in the short silk robe. It was embroidered, she noticed, with peacocks. On anyone else it would've looked absurd. His hair was tousled, his eyes half-closed. A night's growth of beard shadowed his chin.

"Hello, Carlo. Wake you up?"

"Summer!" He swallowed the string of Italian abuse that had been on his tongue and grabbed her. "A surprise, *sì*?" He kissed her soundly, twice, then drew her away. "But why do you bring me a surprise at dawn?"

"It's after ten."

"Ten is dawn when you don't begin to sleep until five. But come in, come in. I don't forget you come for Gravanti's birthday."

Outside, Carlo's home was distinguished. Inside it was opulent. Dominated by marble and gold, the entrance hall only demonstrated the beginning of his penchant for the luxurious. They walked through and under arches into a living area crowded with treasures, small and large. Most of them had been given to him by pleased clients—or women. Carlo had a talent for picking lovers who remained amiable even when they were no longer lovers.

There was a brocade at the windows, Oriental carpets on the floor and a Tintoretto on the wall. Two sofas were piled with cushions deep enough to swim in. An alabaster lion, nearly two feet in height, sat beside one. A three-tiered chandelier shot out splinters of refracted light from its crystals.

She ran her finger down a porcelain ewer in delicate Chinese blue and white. "New?"

"*Sì.*"

"Medici?"

"But of course. A gift from a . . . friend."

"Your friends are always remarkably generous."

He grinned. "But then, so am I."

"Carlo?"

The husky, impatient voice came from up the curving marble stairs. Carlo glanced up, then looked back at Summer and grinned again.

Summer removed her white fedora. "A friend, I take it."

"You'll give me a moment, *cara.*" He was heading for the steps as he spoke. "Perhaps you could go into the kitchen, make coffee."

"And stay out of the way," Summer finished as Carlo disappeared upstairs. She started toward the kitchen, then went back to take her suitcase with her. There wasn't any use leaving Carlo with something like luggage to explain to his friend.

The kitchen was as spectacular as the rest of the house and as large as the average hotel room. Summer knew it as well as she knew her own. It was all in ebonies and ivories with what appeared to be acres of counter space. It boasted two ovens, a restaurant-sized refrigerator, two sinks and a dishwasher that could handle the aftermath of an embassy dinner. Carlo Franconi had never been one to do anything in a small way.

Summer opened a cabinet for the coffee beans and grinder. On impulse, she decided to make crepes. Carlo, she mused, might be just a little while.

When he did come, she was just finishing up at the stove. "Ah, *bella,* you cook for me. I'm honored."

"I had a twinge of guilt about disrupting your morning. Besides—" She slipped crepes, pregnant with warm apples and cinnamon, onto plates. "I'm hungry." Summer set them on a scrubbed worktable while Carlo pulled up chairs. "I should apologize for coming like this without warning. Was your friend annoyed?"

He flashed a grin as he sat. "You don't give me enough credit."

"Scusi." She passed the small pitcher of cream. "So, we'll be working together for Enrico's birthday."

"My veal, with spaghetti. Enrico has a weakness for my spaghetti. Every Friday, he is in my restaurant eating." Carlo started immediately on the crêpe. "And you make the dessert."

"A birthday cake." Summer drank coffee while her crepe cooled untouched. Suddenly, she had no appetite for it. "Enrico requested something special, created just for him. Knowing his vanity, and his fondness for chocolate and whipped cream, it was easy to come up with it."

"But the dinner isn't for two more days. You come early?"

She shrugged and toyed with her coffee. "I wanted to spend some time in Europe."

"I see." And he thought he did. She was looking a bit hollow around the eyes. A sign of romantic trouble. "Everything goes well in Philadelphia?"

"The remodeling's done, the new menus printed. I think the kitchen staff is going to do very well. I hired Maurice from Chicago. You remember?"

"Oh, yes, pressed duck."

"It's an exciting menu," she went on. "Just the sort I'd have if I ever decided to have a place of my own. I suppose I developed a bit of respect for you, Carlo, when I started to deal with the paperwork."

"Paperwork." He finished off his crepes and eyed hers. "Ugly but necessary. You aren't eating, Summer."

"Hmm? No, I guess it's a touch of jet lag." She waved at her plate. "Go ahead."

Taking her at her word, he switched plates. "You solved the problem of Max?"

Absently she touched her arm. The stitches, thank God, were a thing of the past. "We're managing. Mother came to visit for a while. She always makes an impression."

"Monique! So, how is she?"

"Married again," Summer said simply and lifted her coffee. "A director this time, another American."

"She's happy?"

"Naturally." The coffee was strong—stronger than she'd grown used to in America. She thought in frustration that nothing was as it once was for her. "They're starting a film together in another few weeks."

"Perhaps her wisest choice. Someone who would understand her artistic temperament, her needs." He lingered over the perfect melding of spices and fruit. "And how is your American?"

Summer set down her coffee and stared at Carlo. "He wants to marry me."

Carlo choked on a bite of crepe and grabbed for his cup. "So—congratulations."

"Don't be silly." Unable to sit, she rose, sticking her hands in the pockets of her long, loose jacket. "I'm not going to."

"No?" Going to the stove, Carlo poured them both more coffee. "Why not? You find him unattractive, maybe? Bad tempered, stupid?"

"Of course not." Impatient, she curled and uncurled her fingers inside the jacket pockets. "That has nothing to do with it."

"What has?"

"I've no intention of getting married to anyone. That's one merry-go-round I can do without."

"You don't choose to grab for the brass ring, maybe because you're afraid you'd miss."

She lifted her chin. "Be careful, Carlo."

He shrugged at the icy tone. "You know I say what I think. If you'd wanted to hear something else, you wouldn't have come here."

"I came here because I wanted a few days with a friend, not to discuss marriage."

"You're losing sleep over it."

She'd picked up her cup and now slammed it down again. Coffee spilled over the sides. "It was a long flight and I've been working hard. And, yes, maybe I'm upset over the whole thing," she continued before Carlo could speak. "I hadn't expected this from him, hadn't wanted it. He's an honest man, and I know when he says he loves me and wants to marry me, he means it. For the moment. That doesn't make it any easier to say no."

Her fury didn't unnerve him. Carlo was well used to passionate emotions from women—he preferred them. "And you—how do you feel about him?"

She hesitated, then walked to the window. She could look out on Carlo's garden from there—a quiet, isolated spot that served as a border between the house and the busy streets of Rome. "I have feelings for him," Summer murmured. "Stronger feelings than are wise. If anything, they only make it more important that I break things off now. I don't want to hurt him, Carlo, any more than I want to be hurt myself."

"You're so sure love and marriage would hurt?" He put his hands on her shoulders and kneaded them lightly. "When you look so hard at the what-ifs in life, *cara mia,* you miss much living. You have someone who loves you, and though you won't say the words, I think you love him back. Why do you deny yourself?"

"Marriage, Carlo." She turned, her eyes earnest. "It's not for people like us, is it?"

"People like us?"

"We're so wrapped up in what it is we do. We're used to coming and going as we please, when we please. We have no one to answer to, no one to consider but ourselves. Isn't that why you've never married?"

"I could say I'm a generous man, and feel it would be too selfish to limit my gifts to only one woman." She smiled, fully, the way he'd wanted to see her smile. Gently, he brushed the hair away from her face. "But to you, the truth is I've never found anyone who could make my heart tremble. I've looked. If I found her, I'd run for a license and a priest quickly."

With a sigh, she turned back to the window. The flowers were a tapestry of color in the strong sun. "Marriage is a fairy tale, Carlo, full of princes and peasants and toads. I've seen too many of those fairy tales fade."

"We write our own stories, Summer. A woman like you knows that because you've always done so."

"Maybe. But this time I just don't know if I have the courage to turn the next page."

"Take your time. There's no better place to think about life and love than *Roma*. No better man to think about them with than Franconi. Tonight, I cook for you. Linguini—" he kissed the tips of his fingers "—to die for. You can make me one of your babas—just like when we were students, *sì*?"

Turning back to him, Summer wrapped her arms around his neck. "You know, Carlo, if I were the marrying kind, I'd take you, for your pasta alone."

He grinned. "*Carissima,* even my pasta is nothing compared to my—"

"I'm sure," she interrupted dryly. "Why don't you get dressed and take me shopping? I need to buy something fantastic while I'm in Rome. I haven't given my mother a wedding present yet."

* * *

How could he have been so stupid? Blake flicked on his lighter and watched the flame cut through the darkness. It wouldn't be dawn for an hour yet, but he'd given up on sleep. He'd given up on trying to imagine what Summer was doing in Rome while he sat wakeful in an empty suite of rooms and thought of her. If he went to Rome . . .

No, he'd promised himself he'd give her some room, especially since he'd handled everything so badly. He'd given them both some room.

More strategy, he thought derisively and drew hard on the cigarette. Was that what the whole thing was about? He'd always enjoyed challenges, problems. Summer was certainly both. Was that the reason he wanted her? If she'd agreed to marry him, he could have congratulated himself on a plan well thought out and perfectly executed. Another Cocharan acquisition. Damn it.

He rose. He paced. Smoke curled from the cigarette between his fingers, then disappeared into the half-light. He knew better than that, even if she didn't. If it were true that he'd treated the whole affair like a problem to be carefully solved, it was only because that was his make-up. But he loved her, and if he were sure of anything, it was that she loved him too. How was he going to get over that wall she'd erected?

Go back to the way things were? Impossible. He looked out at the city as the darkness began to soften. In the east, the sky was just beginning to lighten with the first hints of pink. Suddenly he realized he'd watched too many sunrises alone. Too much had changed between them now, Blake mused. Too much had been said. You couldn't take love back and lock it away for convenience's sake.

He'd stayed away from her for a full week before she'd gone to Rome. It had been much harder than he'd imagined it would be, but her tears that night had pushed him to it. Now he wondered if that had been yet another mistake. Perhaps if he'd gone to her the next day . . .

Shaking his head, he moved away from the window again. All along, his mistake had been trying to treat the situation with logic. There wasn't any logic in loving someone, only feelings. Without logic, he lost all advantage.

Madly in love. Yes, he thought the term very apt. It was all madness, an incurable madness. If she'd been with him, he could have shown her. Somehow, when she came back, he thought violently, he'd take that damn wall down piece by piece until she was forced to face the madness, too.

When the phone rang, he stared at it. Summer? "Hello."

"Blake?" The voice was a little too sulky, a little too French.

"Yes. Monique?"

"I'm sorry to disturb you, but I always forget how much time is different between west and east. I was just going to bed. You were up?"

"Yes." The sun was slowly rising, the room was pale with light. Most of the city wasn't yet awake, but he was. "Did you have a good trip back to California?"

"I slept almost the whole way. Thank God, because there have been so many parties. So little changes in Hollywood— some of the names, some of the faces. Now, to be chic, one must wear sunglasses on a string. My mother did this, but only to keep from losing them."

He smiled because Monique demanded smiles. "You don't need trends to be chic."

"How flattering." Her voice was very young and very pleased.

"What can I do for you, Monique?"

"Oh, so sweet. First I must tell you how lovely it was to stay in your hotel again. Always the service is impeccable. And Summer's arm, it's better, no?"

"Apparently. She's in Rome."

"Oh, yes, my memory. Well, she was never one to sit too long in one space, my Summer. I saw her only briefly before I left. She seemed . . . preoccupied."

He felt his stomach muscles knotting, his jaw tightening. Deliberately he relaxed both. "She's been working very hard on the kitchen."

Monique's lips curved. He gives away nothing, this one, she thought with approval. "Yes, well I may see her again for a short time. I must ask you a favor, Blake. You were so kind during my visit."

"Whatever I can do."

"The suite where I stayed, I found it so restful, so *agréable*. I wonder if you could reserve it for me again, in two days' time."

"Two days?" His brow creased, but he automatically reached for a pen to jot it down. "You're coming back east?"

"I'm so foolish, so—what is it?—absent-minded, *oui?* I have business to take care of there, and with Summer's accident, it all went out of my head. I must come back and tie up the ends that are loose. And the suite?"

"Of course, I'll see to it."

"*Merci*. And perhaps, I could ask one more thing of you. I will have a small party on Saturday evening—just a few old friends and some wine. I'd be very grateful if you could stop by for a few minutes. Around eight?"

There was nothing he wanted less at the moment than a party. But manners, upbringing and business left him only one answer. Again, he automatically noted down the date and time. "I'd be happy to."

"Marvelous. Till Saturday then, *au revoir*."

After hanging up the phone, Monique gave a tinkle of laughter. True, she was an actress, not a screenwriter, but she thought her little scenario was brilliant. Yes, absolutely brilliant.

Picking up the phone, she prepared to send a cablegram. To Rome.

CHAPTER 12

C *hérie. Must return to Philadelphia for some unfinished*
business before filming begins. Will be at Cocharan
House in my suite over the weekend. Having a little soirée
Saturday evening. Do come. 8:30. A bientôt. Mother.

And just what was she up to? Summer glanced over the
cable again as she cruised above the Atlantic. Unfinished
business? Summer could think of no business Monique would
have in Philadelphia, unless it involved husband number two.
But that was ancient history, and Monique always had someone else handle her business dealings. She'd always claimed
a good actress was a child at heart and had no head for business. It was another one of her diabolically helpless ways that
made it possible for her to do only exactly as she wanted.
What Summer couldn't figure out was why Monique would
want to come back east.

With a shrug, Summer slipped the cable back into her bag.

She didn't feel like hassling with people and cocktail
talk in just over five hours. The day before, she'd outdone
herself with the creation of a birthday cake shaped like
Enrico's palatial home outside Rome, and filled with a
wickedly wonderful combination of chocolate and cream.

It had taken her twelve hours. And for once, at the host's insistence, she'd remained and joined the party for champagne and dessert.

She'd thought it would be good for her. The people, the elegance, the celebratory atmosphere. It had done no more than show her that she didn't want to be in Rome exchanging small talk and drinking wine. She wanted to be home. Home, though it surprised her, was Philadelphia.

She didn't long for Paris and her odd little flat on the Left Bank. She wanted her fourth-floor apartment in Philadelphia, where there were memories of Blake in every corner. However foolish it made her, however unwise or impractical it was, she wanted Blake.

Now, flying home, she found that hadn't changed. It was Blake she wanted to go to when she was on the ground again. It was to Blake she wanted to tell all the foolish stories she'd heard in Enrico's dining room. It was Blake she wanted to hear laugh. It was Blake she wanted to curl up next to now that the nervous energy of the past few days was draining.

Sighing, she tilted her seat back and closed her eyes. But she would do her duty and go to her mother's suite. Perhaps Monique's little party was the perfect diversion. It would give Summer just a bit more time before she faced Blake again. Blake, and the decision she had thought was already made.

* * *

B.C. ran a finger around the inside of the snug collar of his shirt and hoped he didn't look as nervous as he felt. Seeing Monique again after all these years—having to introduce Lillian to her. *Monique, my wife, Lillian. Lillian, Monique Dubois, a former lover. Small world, isn't it?*

Though he was a man who appreciated a good joke, this one eluded him.

It seemed there was no statute of limitations on marital transgressions. It was true that he'd only strayed once, and then during an unofficial separation from his wife that had left him angry, bitter and frightened. A crime committed once, was still a crime committed.

He loved Lillian, had always loved her, but he'd never be able to deny that the brief affair with Monique had happened. And he couldn't deny that it had been exciting, passionate and memorable.

They'd never contacted each other again, though once or twice he'd seen her when he was still actively working in the business. Even that had been so long ago.

So, why had she called him now, twenty years later, insisting that he come—with his wife—to her suite at the Philadelphia Cocharan House? He ran his finger around his collar once again. Something was choking him. Monique's only explanation had been that it concerned the happiness of his son and her daughter.

That had left him with the problem of fabricating a reason for coming into town and insisting that Lillian accompany him. That hadn't been a piece of cake, because he'd married a sharp-minded, independent woman, but it was nothing compared with the next ordeal.

"Are you going to fuss with that tie all day?" B.C. jumped as his wife came up behind him. "Easy." With a laugh, she brushed the back of his jacket, smoothing it over his shoulders in a habit that took him back to their honeymoon. "You'd think you'd never spent an evening with a celebrity before. Or is it just French actresses that make you nervous?"

This one French actress, B.C. thought and turned to his

wife. She'd always been lovely, not the breath-catching beauty Monique had been, but lovely with the kind of quiet looks that remain lovely through the years. Her pure, rich brunette hair was liberally streaked with gray, but styled in such a way that the contrasting colors enhanced her looks.

Lillian had always had style. She'd been his partner, always, had stood up to him, stood by him. A strong woman. He'd needed a strong woman. She was the best damn first mate a man could ask for. He put his hands on her shoulders and kissed her, quite tenderly.

"I love you, Lily." When she touched his cheek and smiled, he took her hand, feeling like the condemned man walking his last mile. "We'd better go. We'll be late."

* * *

Blake hung up the phone in disgust. He was certain Summer would be back that evening. But though he'd called her apartment off and on for over an hour, there'd been no answer. He was out of patience, and in no mood to go down and be sociable in Monique's suite. Much like his father had done, he tugged on his tie.

When all this was over, when she was back, he was going to find a way to convince her to go away with him. He'd find that damn island in the Pacific if that's what it took. He'd *buy* the damn island and set up housekeeping. Build a chain of pizza parlors or fast-food restaurants. Maybe that would satisfy the woman.

Feeling unreasonable, and just a little mean, he strode out of the apartment.

Monique surveyed the suite and nodded. The flowers were a nice touch—not too many, just a few buds here and there to give the rooms a whiff of a garden. A touch—only a touch of romance. The wine was chilling, the glasses sparkling in the subdued lighting. And Max had outdone himself with the hors d'oeuvres, she decided. A little caviar, a little pâté, some miniature quiches—very elegant. She must remember to pay a visit to the kitchen.

As for herself—Monique touched a hand to the chignon at the base of her neck. Not her usual style, but she wanted to add the air of dignity. She felt the evening might call for it. But the black silk pants and off-the-shoulder blouse were sexy and chic. She simply couldn't resist the urge to dress with a bit of flair for the part.

The scene was set, she decided. Now it was only a matter for the players . . .

The knock came. With a slow smile, Monique went toward the door. Act one was about to begin.

"B.C.!" Her smile was brilliant, her hands thrown out to him. "How wonderful to see you again after all this time."

Her beauty was as stunning as ever. There was no resisting that smile. Though he'd been determined to be very aloof and very polite, his voice warmed. "Monique, you don't look a minute older."

"Always the charmer." She laughed, then kissed his cheek before she turned to the woman beside him. "And you are Lillian. How lovely that we meet at last. B.C. has told me so much of you, I feel we're old friends."

Lillian measured the woman across the threshold and lifted a brow. "Oh?"

No fool, this one, Monique decided instantly, and liked her. "Of course, that was all so long ago, so we must get to know each other all over again. Now please come in. B.C., you'd be kind enough to open a bottle of champagne."

A bundle of nerves, B.C. crossed the room to comply. A

drink would be an excellent idea. He'd have preferred bourbon, straight up.

"Of course, I've seen you many times," Lillian began. "I'm sure you haven't made a movie I've missed, Ms. Dubois."

"Monique, please." In a simple, gracious gesture, she plucked a rosebud from a vase and handed it to Lillian. "And I'm flattered. From time to time I would retire, this last occasion has been the longest. But always, going back to the film is like going back to an old lover."

The cork blew out of the bottle like a missile and bounced off the ceiling. Calmly Monique slipped an arm through Lillian's. Inside she was giggling like a girl. "Such an exciting sound, is it not? It always makes me happy to hear champagne being opened. We must have a toast, *n'est-çe pas?*"

She lifted a glass with a flourish, and looked, to Lillian's thinking, just like the character she'd played in *Yesterday's Dream*.

"To fate, I think," Monique decided. "And the strange way it twists us all together." She clinked her glass against B.C.'s, then his wife's, before drinking. "So tell me, you are still enchanted with sailing, B.C.?"

He cleared his throat, no longer certain if he should watch his wife or Monique. Both of them were definitely watching him. "Ah, yes. As a matter of fact, Lillian and I just got back from Tahiti."

"How charming. A perfect place for lovers, *oui?*"

Lillian sipped her wine. "Perfect."

"Et voilà," Monique said when the knock sounded. "The next guest. Please help yourself." It was now Act Two. Having the time of her life, Monique went to answer. "Blake, so kind of you to come, and how charming you look."

"Monique." He took the hand she extended and brought it to his lips even as he calculated just how long it would be before he could make his escape. "Welcome back."

"I must be certain not to wear out the welcome. You'll be surprised by my other guests, I think." With this she gestured inside.

The last two people he'd expected to see in Monique's suite were his parents. He crossed the room and bent to kiss his mother. "Very surprised. I didn't know you were in town."

"We only got in a little while ago." Lillian handed her son a glass of champagne. "We did call your suite, but the phone was busy." Just what stage is this woman setting? Lillian wondered as Monique joined them.

"Families," she said grandly, helping herself to some caviar. "I have a great fondness for them. I must tell you both how I admire your son. The young Cocharan carries on the tradition, is it not so?"

For an instant, only an instant, Lillian's eyes narrowed. She wanted to know just what tradition the French actress referred to.

"We're both very proud of Blake," B.C. said with some relief. "He's not only maintained the Cocharan standard, but expanded it. The Hamilton chain was an excellent move." He toasted his son. "Excellent. How's the turnover in the kitchen going?"

"Very smoothly." And it was the last thing he wanted to discuss. "We start serving from the new menu tomorrow."

"Then we timed our visit well," Lillian put in. "We'll have a chance to test it firsthand."

"Do you know the coincidence?" Monique asked Lillian as she offered the tray of quiches.

"Coincidence?"

"But it is amusing. It is my daughter who now manages your son's kitchen."

"Your daughter." Lillian glanced at her husband. "No, it wasn't mentioned to me."

"She is a superb chef. You would agree, Blake? She often cooks for him," she added with a deliberate smile before he could make any comment.

Lillian held the rosebud under her nose. Interesting. "Really?"

"A charming girl," B.C. put in. "She has your looks, Monique, though I could hardly credit that you had a grown daughter."

"And I was just as surprised when I first met your son." She smiled at him. "Isn't it strange where the years go?"

B.C. cleared his throat and poured more wine.

Weeks before, Blake had wondered what messages had passed between Summer and his father. Now he had no trouble recognizing what wasn't being said between B.C. and Monique. He looked at his mother first and saw her calmly drinking champagne.

His father and Summer's mother? When? he wondered as he tried to digest it. For as long as he could remember, his parents had been devoted, almost inseparable. No— abruptly he remembered a short, turbulent time during his early teens. The house had been full of tension, arguments in undertones. Then B.C. had been gone for two weeks— three? A business trip, his mother had told him, but even then he'd known better. But it had been over so quickly, he'd rarely thought of it since. Now . . . now he had a definite idea where his father had spent at least some of that time away from home. And with whom.

He caught his father's eye—the uncomfortable, half-defiant look. The man, Blake mused, was certainly paying for a slip in fidelity that was two decades old. He saw Monique smile, slowly. Just what the hell was she trying to stir up?

Almost before the anger could fully form, she laid a hand

on his arm. It was a gesture that asked him to wait, to be patient. Then came another knock. "Ah, excuse me. You would pour another glass?" Monique asked B.C. "We have one more guest tonight."

When she opened the door, Monique couldn't have been more pleased with her daughter. The simple jade silk dress was soft, narrow and subtly sexy. It made her slight pallor very romantic. "*Chérie,* so good of you not to disappoint me."

"I can't stay long, Mother, I have to get some sleep." She held out a pink-ribboned box. "But I wanted to bring you a wedding gift."

"So sweet." Monique brushed her lips over Summer's cheek. "And I have something for you. Something I hope you'll always treasure." Stepping aside, she drew Summer in.

Not like this, Summer thought desperately when the first shock of seeing Blake again rippled through her. She'd wanted to be prepared, rested, confident. She didn't want to see him here, now. And his parents—one look at the woman beside Blake and she knew she had to be B.C.'s wife. Nothing else made sense—Monique's kind of sense.

"Your game isn't amusing, Mother," she murmured in French.

"On the contrary, it might be the most important thing I've ever done. B.C.," she said in gay tones, "you've met my daughter, *oui?*"

"Yes, indeed." With a smile, he handed Summer a glass of champagne. "Nice to see you again."

"And Blake's mother," Monique continued. "Lillian, may I present my only child, Summer."

"I'm very pleased to meet you." Lillian took her hand warmly. She wasn't blind and had seen the stunned look that had passed between her son and the actress's daughter. There'd been surprise, longing and uncertainty. If Monique had set the stage for this, Lilian would do her best to help. "I've just been hearing that you're a chef and responsible for the new menu we'll be boasting of tomorrow."

"Yes." She searched for something to say. "Did you enjoy your sailing? Tahiti, wasn't it?"

"We had a marvelous time, even though B.C. tends to become Captain Bligh if you don't watch him."

"Nonsense." He slipped his arm around his wife's shoulders. "This is the only woman I'd ever trust at the wheel of one of my ships."

They adore each other. Summer realized it and found it surprised her. Their marriage was nearing its fortieth year, and obviously hadn't been without storms . . . yet they adored each other.

"It's rather beautiful, is it not, when a husband and wife can share an interest and yet be—separate people?" Monique beamed at them, then looked at Blake. "You would agree that such things keep a man and woman together, even when they have to struggle through hard times and misunderstandings?"

"I would." He looked directly at Summer. "It's a matter of love, and of respect and perhaps of . . . optimism."

"Optimism!" Monique clearly found the word perfect. "Yes, this I like. I, of course, am always so—perhaps too much. I've had four husbands, clearly too optimistic." She laughed at herself. "But then, I think I looked always first, and perhaps only, for romance. Would you say, Lillian, that it's a mistake not to look beyond that?"

"We all look for romance, love, passion." She touched her husband's arm lightly, in a gesture so natural neither of them noticed it. "Then of course respect. I suppose I'd have to add two things to that." She looked up at her husband. "Tolerance and tenacity. Marriage needs them all."

She knew. As B.C. saw the look in his wife's eyes he realized she'd always known. For twenty years, she'd known.

"Excellent." Rather pleased with herself, Monique set her gift on the table. "This is the perfect time then to open a gift celebrating my marriage. This time I intend to put all those things into it."

She wanted to leave. Summer told herself it was only a matter of turning around and walking to the door. She stood rooted, with her eyes locked on Blake's.

"Oh, but it's beautiful." Reverently, Monique lifted the tiny hand-crafted merry-go-round from the bed of tissue. The horses were ivory, trimmed in gilt—each one perfect, each one unique. At the turn of the base, it played a romantic Chopin Prelude. "But, darling, how perfect. A carousel to celebrate a marriage. The horses should be named romance, love, tenacity and so forth. I shall treasure it."

"I—" Summer looked at her mother, and suddenly none of the practicalities, none of the mistakes mattered. "Be happy, *ma mére*."

Monique touched her cheek with a fingertip, then brushed it with her lips. "And you, *mignonne*."

B.C. leaned down to whisper in his wife's ear. "You know, don't you?"

Amused, she lifted her glass. "Of course," she answered in an undertone. "You've never been able to keep secrets from me."

"But—"

"I knew then and hated you for almost a day. Do you remember whose fault it was? I don't anymore."

"God, Lily, if you'd known how guilty I was. Tonight, I was nearly suffocating with—"

"Good," she said simply. "Now, you old fool, let's get out of here so these children can iron things out. Monique—" She held out her hand, and as hands met, eyes met, things passed between them that would never have to be said. "Thank you for a lovely evening, and my best wishes to you and your husband."

"And mine to you." With a smile reminiscent of the past, she held out her arms to B.C. *"Au revoir, mon ami."*

He accepted the embrace, feeling like a man who'd just been granted amnesty. He wanted nothing more than to go up to his own suite and show his wife how much he loved her. "Perhaps we'll have lunch tomorrow," he said absently to the room at large. "Good night."

Monique began to giggle as the door shut behind him. "Love, it will always make me laugh. So—" Briskly, she began to rewrap her gift and box it. "My bags are being held for me downstairs and my plane leaves in one hour."

"An hour?" Summer began. "But—"

"My business is done." Tucking the box under her arm, she rose on her toes to kiss Blake. "You have the good fortune of possessing excellent parents." Then she kissed Summer. "And so, my sweet, do you, though they weren't suited to remain husband and wife. The suite is paid for through the night, the champagne's still cold." She glided for the door leaving a trail of Paris in her wake. Pausing in the doorway, she looked back. *"Bon appétit, mes enfants."* Monique considered it one of her very finest exits.

When the door closed, Summer stood where she was, unsure if she wanted to applaud or throw something.

"Quite a performance," Blake commented. "More wine?"

She could be as urbane and casual as he. "All right."

"And how was Rome?"

"Hot."

"And your cake?"

"Magnificent." Lifting her freshly filled glass, she took

two steps away. It was always better to talk of the unimportant when so many urgent needs were pressing. "Things running smoothly here?"

"Amazingly so. Though I think everyone'll be relieved that you're here for the first run tomorrow. Tell me—" he sipped his own wine, approving it "—when did you first know that my father and your mother had had an affair?"

That was blunt enough, she thought. Well, she would be equally blunt. "When it was happening. I was only a child, but children are astute. You could say I suspected it then. I was sure of it when I first mentioned my mother's name to your father."

He nodded, remembering the meeting in his office. "Just how much have you let that bother you?"

"It was awkward." Restlessly she moved her shoulders.

"And you were determined not to let history repeat itself."

His perception was too often killingly accurate. "Perhaps."

"But then, in a matter of speaking, it did."

With another attempt at casualness, she spread some caviar on a cracker. "But then, neither of us was married."

As if it were only general cocktail talk, Blake chose a quiche. "You know why your mother did this tonight."

Summer shook her head when he offered the tray. "Monique could never resist a scene of any kind. She set the stage, brought in the players, to show me, I think, that while marriage might not be perfect, it can be durable."

"Was she successful?" When she didn't speak, Blake set down his glass. It was time they stopped hedging, time they stopped speaking in generalities. "There hasn't been an hour since the last time I saw you that I haven't thought of you."

Her eyes met his. Helplessly she shook her head. "Blake, I don't think you should—"

"Damn it, you're going to hear me out. We're good for each other. You can't tell me you don't believe that. Maybe you were right before about the way I planned out my . . . courtship," he decided, for a lack of a better word. "Maybe I was too smug about it, too sure that if I waited for just the right moment, I'd have exactly what I wanted with the least amount of trouble. I had to be sure or I'd've gone insane trying to give you enough time to see just what we could have together."

"I was too hard that night." She wrapped her arms around herself then dropped them to her sides. "I said things because you frightened me. I didn't mean them, not all of them."

"Summer." He touched her cheek. "I meant everything I said that night. I want you now as much as I wanted you the first time."

"I'm here." She stepped closer. "We're alone."

The need twisted inside him. "I want to make love with you, but not until I know what it is you want from me. Do you want only a few nights, a few memories, like our parents had together?"

She turned away then. "I don't know how to explain."

"Tell me how you feel."

She took a moment to steady herself. "All right. When I cook, I take this ingredient and that. I have my own hands, my own skill, and putting these together, I make something perfect. If I don't find it perfect, I toss it out. There's little patience in me." She paused a moment, wondering if he could possibly understand this kind of analogy. "I've thought that if I ever decided to become involved in a relationship, there would be this ingredient and that, and again I'd put them together. But I knew it would never be perfect. So . . ." She let out a long breath. "I wondered if that too would be something to toss out."

"A relationship isn't something that has to be created in a

day, or perfected in a day. Part of the game is to keep working on it. Fifty years still isn't long enough."

"A long time to work on something that'll always be just a little flawed."

"Too much of a challenge?"

She whirled, then stopped. "You know me too well," she murmured. "Too well for my own good. Maybe too well for your own."

"You're wrong," he said quietly. "You are my own good."

Her mouth trembled open, then closed. "Please," she managed, "I want to finish this. When I was in Rome, I tried to tell myself that this was what I wanted—to go back to flying here, there, without anyone to worry about but myself and the next dish I would create. When I was in Rome," she added with a sigh, "I was more miserable than I've ever been in my life."

He couldn't prevent the grin. "Sorry to hear it."

"No, I think you're not." Turning away, she ran her fingertip around and around the rim of a champagne glass. Since she would only explain once, she wanted to be certain she explained well. "On the plane, I told myself that when I came back, we would talk, reasonably, logically. We'd work the situation out in the best manner. In my head, I thought that would be a continuation of our relationship as it was. Intimacy without strings, which is perhaps not intimacy at all." She lifted the glass and sipped some of the cold, frothy wine. "When I walked in here tonight and saw you, I knew that would be impossible. We can't see each other as we have been. In the end, that would damage us both."

"You're not walking out of my life."

Turning back, she stood toe-to-toe with him. "I would, if I could. And damn it, you're not the one who's stopping me. It's me! None of your planning, none of your logic could've changed what was inside me. Only I could change it, only what I feel could change it."

She took his hands. She took a deep breath. "I want to ride that merry-go-round with you, and I want my shot at the brass ring."

His hands slid up her arms, into her hair. "Why? Just tell me why."

"Because sometime between the moment you walked in my front door and now, I fell in love with you. No matter how foolish it is, I want to take a chance on that."

"We're going to win." His mouth sought hers, and when she trembled, he knew it was as much from nerves as passion. Soon they'd face the passion, now he would soothe the nerves. "If you like, we'll take a trial period." He began to roam her face with kisses. "We can even put it in contract form—more practical."

"Trial?" She started to draw away from him, but he held her close.

"Yes, and if during the trial period either of us wants a divorce, they simply have to wait until the end of the contract term."

Her brows came together. Could he speak of business now? Would he dare? Her chin tilted challengingly. "How long is the contract term?"

"Fifty years."

Laughing, she threw her arms around his neck. "Deal. I want it drawn up tomorrow, in triplicate. But tonight—" she began to nibble on his lips as she ran her hands beneath his jacket "—tonight we're only lovers. Truly lovers now. And the suite is ours till morning."

The kiss was long—it was slow—it was lingering.

"Remind me to send Monique a case of champagne," Blake said as he lifted Summer into his arms.

"Speaking of it . . ." Leaning over—a bit precariously—
she lifted the two half-full glasses from the table. "We
shouldn't let it get flat. And later," she continued as he carried her toward the bedroom, "much later, perhaps we can
send out for pizza."

Lessons Learned

CHAPTER 1

So he was gorgeous. And rich . . . and talented. And sexy; you shouldn't forget that he was outrageously sexy.

It hardly mattered to Juliet. She was a professional, and to a professional, a job was a job. In this case, great looks and personality were bound to help, but that was business. Strictly business.

No, personally it didn't matter a bit. After all, she'd met a few gorgeous men in her life. She'd met a few rich ones too, and so forth, though she had to admit she'd never met a man with all those elusive qualities rolled up in one. She'd certainly never had the opportunity to work with one. Now she did.

The fact was, Carlo Franconi's looks, charm, reputation and skill were going to make her job a pleasure. So she was told. Still, with her office door closed, Juliet scowled down at the eight-by-ten glossy black-and-white publicity photo. It looked to her as though he'd be more trouble than pleasure.

Carlo grinned cockily up at her, dark, almond-shaped eyes amused and appreciative. She wondered if the photographer had been a woman. His full thick hair was appealingly disheveled with a bit of curl along the nape of his neck and over his ears. Not too much—just enough to disarm.

The strong facial bones, jauntily curved mouth, straight nose and expressive brows combined to create a face destined to sabotage any woman's common sense. Gift or cultivated talent, Juliet wasn't certain, but she'd have to use it to her advantage. Author tours could be murder.

A cookbook. Juliet tried, and failed, not to sigh. Carlo Franconi's *The Italian Way,* was, whether she liked it or not, her biggest assignment to date. Business was business.

She loved her job as publicist and was content for the moment with Trinity Press, the publisher she currently worked for, after a half-dozen job changes and upward jumps since the start of her career. At twenty-eight, the ambition she'd started with as a receptionist nearly ten years before had eased very little. She'd worked, studied, hustled and sweated for her own office and position. She had them, but she wasn't ready to relax.

In two years, by her calculations, she'd be ready to make the next jump: her own public relations firm. Naturally, she'd have to start out small, but it was building the business that was exciting. The contacts and experience she gained in her twenties would help her solidify her ambitions in her thirties. Juliet was content with that.

One of the first things she'd learned in public relations was that an account was an account, whether it was a big blockbuster bestseller already slated to be a big blockbuster film or a slim volume of poetry that would barely earn out its advance. Part of the challenge, and the fun, was finding the right promotional hook.

Now, she had a cookbook and a slick Italian chef. Franconi, she thought wryly, had a track record—with women and in publishing. The first was a matter of hot interest to the society and gossip sections of the international press. It wasn't necessary to cook to be aware of Franconi's name.

The second was the reason he was being pampered on the road with a publicist.

His first two cookbooks had been solid bestsellers. For good reason, Juliet admitted. It was true she couldn't fry an egg without creating a gooey, inedible glob, but she recognized quality and style. Franconi could make linguini sound like a dish to be prepared while wearing black lace. He turned a simple spaghetti dish into an erotic event.

Sex. Juliet tipped back in her chair and wiggled her stockinged toes. That's what he had. That's just what they'd use. Before the twenty-one-day author tour was finished, she'll have made Carlo Franconi the world's sexiest cook. Any red-blooded American woman would fantasize about him preparing an intimate dinner for two. Candlelight, pasta and romance.

One last study of his publicity shot and the charmingly crooked grin assured her he could handle it.

In the meantime, there was a bit more groundwork to cover. Creating a schedule was a pleasure, adhering to one a challenge. She thrived on both.

Juliet lifted the phone, noticed with resignation that she'd broken another nail, then buzzed her assistant. "Terry, get me Diane Maxwell. She's program coordinator on the *Simpson Show* in L.A."

"Going for the big guns?"

Juliet gave a quick, unprofessional grin. "Yeah." She replaced the phone and started making hurried notes. No reason not to start at the top, she told herself. That way, if you fell on your face, at least the trip would be worth it.

As she waited, she looked around her office. Not the top, but a good ways from the bottom. At least she had a window. Juliet could still shudder thinking of some of the walled-in cubicles she'd worked in. Now, twenty stories below, New

York rushed, bumped, pushed and shoved its way through another day. Juliet Trent had learned how to do the same thing
after moving from the relatively easygoing suburb of Harris-
burg, Pennsylvania.

She might've grown up in a polite little neighborhood
where only a stranger drove over twenty-five miles per hour
and everyone kept the grass clipped close to their side of the
chain-link fences, but Juliet had acclimated easily. The truth
was she liked the pace, the energy and the "I dare you" tone
of New York. She'd never go back to the bee-humming,
hedge-clipping quiet of suburbia where everyone knew who
you were, what you did and how you did it. She preferred the
anonymity and the individuality of crowds.

Perhaps her mother had molded herself into the perfect
suburban wife, but not Juliet. She was an eighties woman,
independent, self-sufficient and moving up. There was an
apartment in the west Seventies that she'd furnished, slowly,
meticulously and, most important, personally. Juliet had
enough patience to move step by step as long as the result was
perfect. She had a career she could be proud of and an office
she was gradually altering to suit her own tastes. Leaving
her mark wasn't something she took lightly. It had taken her
four months to choose the right plants for her work space,
from the four-foot split-leaf philodendron to the delicate
white-blossomed African violet.

She'd had to make do with the beige carpet, but the six-
foot Dali print on the wall opposite her window added life
and energy. The narrow-beveled mirror gave an illusion of
space and a touch of elegance. She had her eye on a big,
gaudy Oriental urn that would be perfect for a spray of
equally gaudy peacock feathers. If she waited a bit longer,
the price might come down from exorbitant to ridiculous.
Then she'd buy it.

Juliet might put on a very practical front to everyone,

including herself, but she couldn't resist a sale. As a result, her bank balance wasn't as hefty as her bedroom closet. She wasn't frivolous. No, she would have been appalled to hear the word applied to her. Her wardrobe was organized, well tended and suitable. Perhaps twenty pairs of shoes could be considered excessive, but Juliet rationalized that she was often on her feet ten hours a day and deserved the luxury. In any case, she'd earned them, from the sturdy sneakers, the practical black pumps to the strappy evening sandals. She'd earned them with innumerable long meetings, countless waits in airports and endless hours on the phone. She'd earned them on author tours, where the luck of the draw could have you dealing with the brilliant, the funny, the inept, the boring or the rude. Whatever she had to deal with, the results had to be the same. Media, media and more media.

She'd learned how to deal with the press, from the *New York Times* reporter to the stringer on the small-town weekly. She knew how to charm the staff of talk shows, from the accepted masters to the nervous imitators. Learning had been an adventure, and since she'd allowed herself very few in her personal life, professional success was all the sweeter.

When the intercom buzzed, she caught her tongue between her teeth. Now, she was going to apply everything she'd learned and land Franconi on the top-rated talk show in the States.

Once she did, she thought as she pressed the button, he'd better make the most of it. Or she'd slit his sexy throat with his own chef's knife.

A h, *mi amore. Squisito.*" Carlo's voice was a low purr designed to accelerate the blood pressure. The bedroom voice wasn't something he'd had to develop, but something he'd been born with. Carlo had always thought a man who didn't use God-given gifts was less than a fool. *"Bellisimo,"* he murmured and his eyes were dark and dreamy with anticipation.

It was hot, almost steamy, but he preferred the heat. Cold slowed down the blood. The sun coming through the window had taken on the subtle gold texture with tints of red that spoke of the end of the day and hinted at the pleasures of night. The room was rich with scent so he breathed it in. A man was missing a great deal of life if he didn't use and appreciate all of his senses. Carlo believed in missing nothing.

He watched his love of the moment with a connoisseur's eye. He'd caress, whisper to, flatter—it never mattered to him if it took moments or hours to get what he wanted. As long as he got what he wanted. To Carlo, the process, the anticipation, the moves themselves were equally as satisfying as the result. Like a dance, he'd always thought. Like a song. An aria from *The Marriage of Figaro* played in the background while he seduced.

Carlo believed in setting the scene because life was a play not simply to be enjoyed, but to be relished.

"Bellisimo," he whispered and bent nearer what he adored. The clam sauce simmered erotically as he stirred it. Slowly, savoring the moment, Carlo lifted the spoon to his lips and with his eyes half-closed, tasted. The sound of pleasure came from low in his throat. *"Squisito."*

He moved from the sauce to give the same loving attention to his *zabaglione*. He believed there wasn't a woman alive who could resist the taste of that rich, creamy custard with the zing of wine. As usual, it was a woman he was expecting.

The kitchen was as much a den of pleasure to him as the bedroom. It wasn't an accident that he was one of the most respected and admired chefs in the world, or that he was one of the most engaging lovers. Carlo considered it a matter of destiny. His kitchen was cleverly arranged, as meticulously laid out for the seduction of sauces and spices as his bedroom was for the seduction of women. Yes, Carlo Franconi believed life was to be relished. Every drop of it.

When the knock on the front door reverberated through the high-ceilinged rooms of his home, he murmured to his pasta before he removed his apron. As he went to answer, he rolled down the silk sleeves of his shirt but didn't stop for adjustments in any of the antique mirrors that lined the walls. He wasn't so much vain, as confident.

He opened the door to a tall, stately woman with honey-toned skin and dark, glossy eyes. Carlo's heart moved as it did whenever he saw her. *"Mi amore."* Taking her hand, he pressed his mouth to the palm, while his eyes smiled into hers. *"Bella. Molto bella."*

She stood in the evening light for a moment, dark, lovely, with a smile only for him. Only a fool wouldn't have known he'd welcomed dozens of women in just this way. She wasn't a fool. But she loved him.

"You're a scoundrel, Carlo." The woman reached out to touch his hair. It was dark and thick and difficult to resist. "Is this the way you greet your mother?"

"This is the way—" he kissed her hand again "—I greet a beautiful woman." Then he wrapped both arms around her and kissed her cheeks. "This is the way I greet my mother. It's a fortunate man who can do both."

Gina Franconi laughed as she returned her son's hug. "To you, all women are beautiful."

"But only one is my mother." With his arm around her waist, he led her inside.

Gina approved, as always, the fact that his home was

spotless, if a bit too eclectic for her taste. She often wondered how the poor maid managed to keep the ornately carved archways dusted and polished and the hundreds of windowpanes unstreaked. Because she was a woman who'd spent fifteen years of her life cleaning other people's homes and forty cleaning her own, she thought of such things.

She studied one of his new acquisitions, a three-foot ivory owl with a small rodent captured in one claw. A good wife, Gina mused, would guide her son's tastes toward less eccentric paths.

"An aperitif, Mama?" Carlo walked over to a tall smoked-glass cabinet and drew out a slim black bottle. "You should try this," he told her as he chose two small glasses and poured. "A friend sent it to me."

Gina set aside her red snakeskin bag and accepted the glass. The first sip was hot, potent, smooth as a lover's kiss and just as intoxicating. She lifted a brow as she took the second sip. "Excellent."

"Yes, it is. Anna has excellent taste."

Anna, she thought, with more amusement than exasperation. She'd learned years before that it didn't do any good to be exasperated with a man, especially if you loved him. "Are all your friends women, Carlo?"

"No." He held his glass up, twirling it. "But this one was. She sent me this as a wedding present."

"A—"

"Her wedding," Carlo said with a grin. "She wanted a husband, and though I couldn't accommodate her, we parted friends." He held up the bottle as proof.

"Did you have it analyzed before you drank any?" Gina asked dryly.

He touched the rim of his glass to hers. "A clever man turns all former lovers into friends, Mama."

"You've always been clever." With a small movement of her shoulders she sipped again and sat down. "I hear you're seeing the French actress."

"As always, your hearing's excellent."

As if it interested her, Gina studied the hue of the liqueur in her glass. "She is, of course, beautiful."

"Of course."

"I don't think she'll give me grandchildren."

Carlo laughed and sat beside her. "You have six grandchildren and another coming, Mama. Don't be greedy."

"But none from my son. My only son," she reminded him with a tap of her finger on his shoulder. "Still, I haven't given you up yet."

"Perhaps if I could find a woman like you."

She shot him back arrogant look for arrogant look. "Impossible, *caro*."

His feeling exactly, Carlo thought as he guided her into talk about his four sisters and their families. When he looked at this sleek, lovely woman, it was difficult to think of her as the mother who'd raised him, almost single-handedly. She'd worked, and though she'd been known to storm and rage, she'd never complained. Her clothes had been carefully mended, her floors meticulously scrubbed while his father had spent endless months at sea.

When he concentrated, and he rarely did, Carlo could recall an impression of a dark, wiry man with a black mustache and an easy grin. The impression didn't bring on resentment or even regret. His father had been a seaman before his parents had married, and a seaman he'd remained. Carlo's belief in meeting your destiny was unwavering. But while his feelings for his father were ambivalent, his feelings for his mother were set and strong.

She'd supported each of her children's ambitions, and when

Carlo had earned a scholarship to the Sorbonne in Paris and the opportunity to pursue his interest in haute cuisine, she'd let him go. Ultimately, she'd supplemented the meager income he could earn between studies with part of the insurance money she'd received when her husband had been lost in the sea he'd loved.

Six years before, Carlo had been able to pay her back in his own way. The dress shop he'd bought for her birthday had been a lifelong dream for both of them. For him, it was a way of seeing his mother happy at last. For Gina it was a way to begin again.

He'd grown up in a big, boisterous, emotional family. It gave him pleasure to look back and remember. A man who grows up in a family of women learns to understand them, appreciate them, admire them. Carlo knew about women's dreams, their vanities, their insecurities. He never took a lover he didn't have affection for as well as desire. If there was only desire, he knew there'd be no friendship at the end, only resentment. Even now, the comfortable affair he was having with the French actress was ending. She'd be starting a film in a few weeks, and he'd be going on tour in America. That, Carlo thought with some regret, would be that.

"Carlo, you go to America soon?"

"Hmm. Yes." He wondered if she'd read his mind, knowing women were capable of doing so. "Two weeks."

"You'll do me a favor?"

"Of course."

"Then notice for me what the professional American woman is wearing. I'm thinking of adding some things to the shop. The Americans are so clever and practical."

"Not too practical, I hope." He swirled his drink. "My publicist is a Ms. Trent." Tipping back his glass, he accepted the heat and the punch. "I'll promise you to study every aspect of her wardrobe."

She gave his quick grin a steady look. "You're so good to me, Carlo."

"But of course, Mama. Now I'm going to feed you like a queen."

Carlo had no idea what Juliet Trent looked like, but put himself in the hands of fate. What he did know, from the letters he'd received from her, was that Juliet Trent was the type of American his mother had described. Practical and clever. Excellent qualities in a publicist.

Physically was another matter. But again, as his mother had said, Carlo could always find beauty in a woman. Perhaps he did prefer, in his personal life, a woman with a lovely shell, but he knew how to dig beneath to find inner beauty. It was something that made life interesting as well as aesthetically pleasing.

Still, as he stepped off the plane into the terminal in L.A., he had his hand on the elbow of a stunning redhead.

Juliet did know what he looked like, and she first saw him, shoulder to shoulder with a luxuriously built woman in pencil-thin heels. Though he carried a bulky leather case in one hand, and a flight bag over his shoulder, he escorted the redhead through the gate as though they were walking into a ballroom. Or a bedroom.

Juliet took a quick assessment of the well-tailored slacks, the unstructured jacket and open-collared shirt. The well-heeled traveler. There was a chunk of gold and diamond on his finger that should've looked ostentatious and vulgar. Somehow it looked as casual and breezy as the rest of him. She felt formal and sticky.

She'd been in L.A. since the evening before, giving her-self time to see personally to all the tiny details. Carlo Fran-coni would have nothing to do but be charming, answer questions and sign his cookbook.

As she watched him kiss the redhead's knuckles, Juliet thought he'd be signing plenty of them. After all, didn't women do the majority of cookbook buying? Carefully smoothing away a sarcastic smirk, Juliet rose. The redhead was sending one last wistful look over her shoulder as she walked away.

"Mr. Franconi?"

Carlo turned away from the woman who'd proven to be a pleasant traveling companion on the long flight from New York. His first look at Juliet brought a quick flutter of inter-est and a subtle tug of desire he often felt with a woman. It was a tug he could either control or let loose, as was appro-priate. This time, he savored it.

She didn't have merely a lovely face, but an interesting one. Her skin was very pale, which should have made her seem fragile, but the wide, strong cheekbones undid the air of fra-gility and gave her face an intriguing diamond shape. Her eyes were large, heavily lashed and artfully accented with a smoky shadow that only made the cool green shade of the irises seem cooler. Her mouth was only lightly touched with a peach-colored gloss. It had a full, eye-drawing shape that needed no artifice. He gathered she was wise enough to know it.

Her hair was caught somewhere between brown and blond so that its shade was soft, natural and subtle. She wore it long enough in the back to be pinned up in a chignon when she wished, and short enough on the top and sides so that she could style it from fussy to practical as the occasion, and her whim, demanded. At the moment, it was loose and casual, but not windblown. She'd stopped in the ladies' room for a quick check just after the incoming flight had been announced.

"I'm Juliet Trent," she told him when she felt he'd stared long enough. "Welcome to California." As he took the hand she offered, she realized she should've expected him to kiss it rather than shake. Still, she stiffened, hardly more than an instant, but she saw by the lift of brow, he'd felt it.

"A beautiful woman makes a man welcome anywhere."

His voice was incredible—the cream that rose to the top and then flowed over something rich. She told herself it only pleased her because it would record well and took his statement literally. Thinking of the redhead, she gave him an easy, not entirely friendly smile. "Then you must have had a pleasant flight."

His native language might have been Italian, but Carlo understood nuances in any tongue. He grinned at her. "Very pleasant."

"And tiring," she said remembering her position. "Your luggage should be in by now." Again, she glanced at the large case he carried. "Can I take that for you?"

His brow lifted at the idea of a man dumping his burden on a woman. Equality, to Carlo, never crossed the border into manners. "No, this is something I always carry myself."

Indicating the way, she fell into step beside him. "It's a half-hour ride to the Beverly Wilshire, but after you've settled in, you can rest all afternoon. I'd like to go over tomorrow's schedule with you this evening."

He liked the way she walked. Though she wasn't tall, she moved in long, unhurried strides that made the red side-pleated skirt she wore shift over her hips. "Over dinner?"

She sent him a quick sidelong look. "If you like."

She'd be at his disposal, Juliet reminded herself, for the next three weeks. Without appearing to think about it, she skirted around a barrel-chested man hefting a bulging garment bag and a briefcase. Yes, he liked the way she walked, Carlo thought again. She was a woman who could take care of herself without a great deal of fuss.

"At seven? You have a talk show in the morning that starts at seven-thirty so we'd best make it an early evening."

Seven-thirty A.M. Carlo thought, only briefly, about jet lag and time changes. "So, you put me to work quickly."

"That's what I'm here for, Mr. Franconi." Juliet said it cheerfully as she stepped up to the slowly moving baggage belt. "You have your stubs?"

An organized woman, he thought as he reached into the inside pocket of his loose-fitting buff-colored jacket. In silence, he handed them to her, then hefted a pull-man and a garment bag from the belt himself.

Gucci, she observed. So he had taste as well as money. Juliet handed the stubs to a skycap and waited while Carlo's luggage was loaded onto the pushcart. "I think you'll be pleased with what we have for you, Mr. Franconi." She walked through the automatic doors and signaled for her limo. "I know you've always worked with Jim Collins in the past on your tours in the States; he sends his best."

"Does Jim like his executive position?"

"Apparently."

Though Carlo expected her to climb into the limo first, she stepped back. With a bow to women professionals, Carlo ducked inside and took his seat. "Do you like yours, Ms. Trent?"

She took the seat across from him then sent him a straight-shooting, level look. Juliet could have no idea how much he admired it. "Yes, I do."

Carlo stretched out his legs—legs his mother had once said that had refused to stop growing long after it was necessary. He'd have preferred driving himself, particularly after the long, long flight from Rome where someone else had

been at the controls. But if he couldn't, the plush laziness of
the limo was the next best thing. Reaching over, he switched
on the stereo so that Mozart poured out, quiet but vibrant. If
he'd been driving, it would've been rock, loud and rambunc-
tious.

"You've read my book, Ms. Trent?"

"Yes, of course. I couldn't set up publicity and promotion
for an unknown product." She sat back. It was easy to do her
job when she could speak the simple truth. "I was impressed
with the attention to detail and the clear directions. It seemed
a very friendly book, rather than simply a kitchen tool."

"Hmm." He noticed her stockings were very pale pink
and had a tiny line of dots up one side. It would interest his
mother that the practical American businesswoman could
enjoy the frivolous. It interested him that Juliet Trent could.
"Have you tried any of the recipes?"

"No, I don't cook."

"You don't . . ." His lazy interest came to attention.
"At all?"

She had to smile. He looked so sincerely shocked.

As he watched the perfect mouth curve, he had to put the
next tug of desire in check.

"When you're a failure at something, Mr. Franconi, you
leave it to someone else."

"I could teach you." The idea intrigued him. He never offered his expertise lightly.

"To cook?" She laughed, relaxing enough to let her heel
slip out of her shoe as she swung her foot. "I don't think so."

"I'm an excellent teacher," he said with a slow smile.

Again, she gave him the calm, gunslinger look. "I don't
doubt it. I, on the other hand, am a poor student."

"Your age?" When her look narrowed, he smiled charmingly. "A rude question when a woman's reached a certain
stage. You haven't."

"Twenty-eight," she said so coolly his smile became a grin.

"You look younger, but your eyes are older. I'd find it a pleasure to give you a few lessons, Ms. Trent."

She believed him. She, too, understood nuances. "A pity our schedule won't permit it."

He shrugged easily and glanced out the window. But the L.A. freeway didn't interest him. "You put Philadelphia in the schedule as I requested?"

"We'll have a full day there before we fly up to Boston. Then we'll finish up in New York."

"Good. I have a friend there. I haven't seen her in nearly a year."

Juliet was certain he had—friends—everywhere.

"You've been to Los Angeles before?" he asked her.

"Yes. Several times on business."

"I've yet to come here for pleasure myself. What do you think of it?"

As he had, she glanced out the window without interest. "I prefer New York."

"Why?"

"More grit, less gloss."

He liked her answer, and her phrasing. Because of it, he studied her more closely. "Have you ever been to Rome?"

"No." He thought he heard just a trace of wistfulness in her voice. "I haven't been to Europe at all."

"When you do, come to Rome. It was built on grit."

Her mind drifted a bit as she thought of it, and her smile remained. "I think of fountains and marble and cathedrals."

"You'll find them—and more." She had a face exquisite enough to be carved in marble, he thought. A voice quiet and smooth enough for cathedrals. "Rome rose and fell and clawed its way back up again. An intelligent woman understands such things. A romantic woman understands the fountains."

She glanced out again as the limo pulled up in front of the hotel. "I'm afraid I'm not very romantic."

"A woman named Juliet hasn't a choice."

"My mother's selection," she pointed out. "Not mine."

"You don't look for Romeo?"

Juliet gathered her briefcase. "No, Mr. Franconi. I don't."

He stepped out ahead of her and offered his hand. When Juliet stood on the curb, he didn't move back to give her room. Instead, he experimented with the sensation of bodies brushing, lightly, even politely on a public street. Her gaze came up to his, not wary but direct.

He felt it, the pull. Not the tug that was impersonal and for any woman, but the pull that went straight to the gut and was for one woman. So he'd have to taste her mouth. After all, he was a man compelled to judge a great deal by taste. But he could also bide his time. Some creations took a long time and had complicated preparations to perfect. Like Juliet, he insisted on perfection.

"Some women," he murmured, "never need to look, only to evade and avoid and select."

"Some women," she said just as quietly, "choose not to select at all." Deliberately, she turned her back on him to pay off the driver. "I've already checked you in, Mr. Franconi," she said over her shoulder as she handed his key to the waiting bellboy. "I'm just across the hall from your suite."

Without looking at him, Juliet followed the bellboy into the hotel and to the elevators. "If it suits you, I'll make reservations here in the hotel for dinner at seven. You can just tap on my door when you're ready." With a quick check of her watch she calculated the time difference and figured she could make three calls to New York and one to Dallas before office hours were over farther east. "If you need anything, you've only to order it and charge it to the room."

She stepped from the elevator, unzipping her purse and

pulling out her own room key as she walked. "I'm sure you'll find your suite suitable."

He watched her brisk, economic movements. "I'm sure I will."

"Seven o'clock then." She was already pushing her key into the lock as the bellboy opened the first door to the suite across the hall. As she did, her mind was already on the calls she'd make the moment she'd shed her jacket and shoes.

"Juliet."

She paused, her hair swinging back as she looked over her shoulder at Carlo. He held her there, a moment longer, in silence. "Don't change your scent," he murmured. "Sex without flowers, femininity without vulnerability. It suits you."

While she continued to stare over her shoulder, he disappeared inside the suite. The bellboy began his polite introductions to the accommodations of the suite. Something Carlo said caused him to break off and laugh.

Juliet turned her key with more strength than necessary, pushed open her door, then closed it again with the length of her body. For a minute, she just leaned there, waiting for her system to level.

Professional training had prevented her from stammering and fumbling and making a fool of herself. Professional training had helped her to keep her nerves just at the border where they could be controlled and concealed. Still, under the training, there was a woman. Control had cost her. Juliet was dead certain there wasn't a woman alive who would be totally unaffected by Carlo Franconi. It wasn't balm for her ego to admit she was simply part of a large, varied group.

He'd never know it, she told herself, but her pulse had been behaving badly since he'd first taken her hand. It was still behaving badly. Stupid, she told herself and threw her bag down on a chair. Then she thought it best if she followed it. Her legs weren't steady yet. Juliet let out a long, deep breath. She'd just have to wait until they were.

So he was gorgeous. And rich . . . and talented. And outrageously sexy. She'd already known that, hadn't she? The trouble was, she wasn't sure how to handle him. Not nearly as sure as she had to be.

CHAPTER 2

She was a woman who thrived on tight scheduling, minute details and small crises. These were the things that kept you alert, sharp and interested. If her job had been simple, there wouldn't have been much fun to it.

She was also a woman who liked long, lazy baths in mountains of bubbles and big, big beds. These were the things that kept you sane. Juliet felt she'd earned the second after she'd dealt with the first.

While Carlo amused himself in his own way, Juliet spent an hour and a half on the phone, then another hour revising and fine-tuning the next day's itinerary. A print interview had come through and had to be shuffled in. She shuffled. Another paper was sending a reporter and photographer to the book signing. Their names had to be noted and remembered. Juliet noted, circled and committed to memory. The way things were shaping up, they'd be lucky to manage a two-hour breather the next day. Nothing could've pleased her more.

By the time she'd closed her thick leather-bound notebook, she was more than ready for the tub. The bed, unfortunately, would have to wait. Ten o'clock, she promised herself. By ten, she'd be in bed, snuggled in, curled up and unconscious.

She soaked, designating precisely forty-five minutes for her personal time. In the bath, she didn't plot or plan or estimate. She clicked off the busy, business end of her brain and enjoyed.

Relaxing—it took the first ten minutes to accomplish that completely. Dreaming—she could pretend the white, standard-size tub was luxurious, large and lush. Black marble perhaps and big enough for two. It was a secret ambition of Juliet's to own one like it eventually. The symbol, she felt, of ultimate success. She'd have bristled if anyone had called her goal romantic. Practical, she'd insist. When you worked hard, you needed a place to unwind. This was hers.

Her robe hung on the back of the door—jade green, teasingly brief and silk. Not a luxury as far as she was concerned, but a necessity. When you often had only short snatches to relax, you needed all the help you could get. She considered the robe as much an aid in keeping pace as the bottles of vitamins that lined the counter by the sink. When she traveled, she always took them.

After she'd relaxed and dreamed a bit, she could appreciate soft, hot water against her skin, silky bubbles hissing, steam rising rich with scent.

He'd told her not to change her scent.

Juliet scowled as she felt the muscles in her shoulders tense. Oh no. Deliberately she picked up the tiny cake of hotel soap and rubbed it up and down her arms. Oh no, she wouldn't let Carlo Franconi intrude on her personal time. That was rule number one.

He'd purposely tried to unravel her. He'd succeeded. Yes, he had succeeded, Juliet admitted with a stubborn nod. But that was over now. She wouldn't let it happen again. Her job was to promote his book, not his ego. To promote, she'd go above and beyond the call of duty with her time, her energy and her skill, but not with her emotions.

Franconi wasn't flying back to Rome in three weeks with a smug smile on his face unless it was professionally generated. That instant knife-sharp attraction would be dealt with. Priorities, Juliet mused, were the order of the day. He could add all the American conquests to his list he chose—as long as she wasn't among them.

In any case, he didn't seriously interest her. It was simply that basic, primal urge. Certainly there wasn't any intellect involved. She preferred a different kind of man—steady rather than flashy, sincere rather than charming. That was the kind of man a woman of common sense looked for when the time was right. Juliet judged the time would be right in about three years. By then, she'd have established the structure for her own firm. She'd be financially independent and creatively content. Yes, in three years she'd be ready to think about a serious relationship. That would fit her schedule nicely.

Settled, she decided, and closed her eyes. It was a nice, comfortable word. But the hot water, bubbles and steam didn't relax her any longer. A bit resentful, she released the plug and stood up to let the water drain off her. The wide mirror above the counter and sink was fogged, but only lightly. Through the mist she could see Juliet Trent.

Odd, she thought, how pale and soft and vulnerable a naked woman could look. In her mind, she was strong, practical, even tough. But she could see, in the damp, misty mirror, the fragility, even the wistfulness.

Erotic? Juliet frowned a bit as she told herself she shouldn't be disappointed that her body had been built on slim, practical lines rather than round and lush ones. She should be grateful that her long legs got her where she was going and her narrow hips helped keep her silhouette in a business suit trim and efficient. Erotic would never be a career plus.

Without makeup, her face looked too young, too trusting. Without careful grooming, her hair looked too wild, too passionate.

Fragile, young, passionate. Juliet shook her head. Not qualities for a professional woman. It was fortunate that clothes and cosmetics could play down or play up certain aspects. Grabbing a towel, she wrapped it around herself, then taking another she wiped the steam from the mirror. No more mists, she thought. To succeed you had to see clearly.

With a glance at the tubes and bottles on the counter she began to create the professional Ms. Trent.

Because she hated quiet hotel rooms, Juliet switched on the television as she started to dress. The old Bogart–Bacall movie pleased her and was more relaxing than a dozen bubble baths. She listened to the well-known dialogue while she drew on her smoke-colored stockings. She watched the shimmering restrained passion as she adjusted the straps of a sheer black teddy. While the plot twisted and turned, she zipped on the narrow black dress and knotted the long strand of pearls under her breasts.

Caught up, she sat on the edge of the bed, running a brush through her hair as she watched. She was smiling, absorbed, distracted, but it would've shocked her if anyone had said she was romantic.

When the knock sounded at her door, she glanced at her watch. 7:05. She'd lost fifteen minutes dawdling. To make up for it, Juliet had her shoes on, her earrings clipped and her bag and notebook at hand in twelve seconds flat. She went to the door ready with a greeting and an apology.

A rose. Just one, the color of a young girl's blush. When Carlo handed it to her, she didn't have anything to say at all. Carlo, however, had no problem.

"Bella." He had her hand to his lips before she'd thought to counter the move. "Some women look severe or cold in black. Others . . ." His survey was long and male, but his smile made it gallant rather than calculating. "In others it simply enhances their femininity. I'm disturbing you?"

"No, no, of course not. I was just—"

"Ah, I know this movie."

Without waiting for an invitation, he breezed past her into the room. The standard single hotel room didn't seem so impersonal any longer. How could it? He brought life, energy, passion into the air as if it were his mission.

"Yes, I've seen it many times." The two strong faces dominated the screen. Bogart's, creased, heavy-eyed, weary— Bacall's, smooth, steamy and challenging. *"Passione,"* he murmured and made the word seem like honey to be tasted. Incredibly, Juliet found herself swallowing. "A man and a woman can bring many things to each other, but without passion, everything else is tame. *Sì?"*

Juliet recovered herself. Franconi wasn't a man to discuss passion with. The subject wouldn't remain academic for long. "Perhaps." She adjusted her evening bag and her notebook. But she didn't put the rose down. "We've a lot to discuss over dinner, Mr. Franconi. We'd best get started."

With his thumbs still hooked in the pockets of his taupe slacks, he turned his head. Juliet figured hundreds of women had trusted that smile. She wouldn't. With a careless flick, he turned off the television. "Yes, it's time we started."

What did he think of her? Carlo asked himself the question and let the answer come in snatches, twined through the evening.

Lovely. He didn't consider his affection for beautiful women a weakness. He was grateful that Juliet didn't find the need to play down or turn her natural beauty into severity, nor did she exploit it until it was artificial. She'd found a pleasing balance. He could admire that.

She was ambitious, but he admired that as well. Beautiful women without ambition lost his interest quickly.

She didn't trust him. That amused him. As he drank his second glass of Beaujolais, he decided her wariness was a compliment. In his estimation, a woman like Juliet would only be wary of a man if she were attracted in some way.

If he were honest, and he was, he'd admit that most women were attracted to him. It seemed only fair, as he was attracted to them. Short, tall, plump, thin, old or young, he found women a fascination, a delight, an amusement. He respected them, perhaps only as a man who had grown up surrounded by women could do. But respect didn't mean he couldn't enjoy.

He was going to enjoy Juliet.

"*Hello, L.A.* is on first tomorrow." Juliet ran down her notes while Carlo nibbled on pâté. "It's the top-rated morning talk show on the coast, not just in L.A. Liz Marks hosts. She's very personable—not too bubbly. Los Angeles doesn't want bubbly at 8:00 A.M."

"Thank God."

"In any case, she has a copy of the book. It's important that you get the title in a couple of times if she doesn't. You have the full twenty minutes, so it shouldn't be a problem. You'll be autographing at Books, Incorporated on Wilshire Boulevard between one and three." Hastily, she made herself a note to contact the store in the morning for a last check. "You'll want to plug that, but I'll remind you just before airtime. Of course, you'll want to mention that you're beginning a twenty-one-day tour of the country here in California."

"Mmm-hmm. The pâté is quite passable. Would you like some?"

"No, thanks. Just go ahead." She checked off her list and reached for her wine without looking at him. The restaurant was quiet and elegant, but it didn't matter. If they'd been in a loud, crowded bar on the Strip, she'd still have gone on with her notes. "Right after the morning show, we go to a radio spot. Then we'll have brunch with a reporter from the *Times*. You've already had an article in the *Trib*. I've got a clipping for you. You'd want to mention your other two books, but concentrate on the new one. It wouldn't hurt to bring up some of the major cities we'll hit. Denver, Dallas, Chicago, New York. Then there's the autographing, a spot on the evening news and dinner with two book reps. The next day—"

"One day at a time," he said easily. "I'll be less likely to snarl at you."

"All right." She closed her notebook and sipped at her wine again. "After all, it's my job to see to the details, yours to sign books and be charming."

He touched his glass to hers. "Then neither of us should have a problem. Being charming is my life."

Was he laughing at himself, she wondered, or at her? "From what I've seen, you excel at it."

"A gift, *cara*." Those dark, deep-set eyes were amused and exciting. "Unlike a skill that's developed and trained."

So, he was laughing at both of them, she realized. It would be both difficult and wise not to like him for it.

When her steak was served, Juliet glanced at it. Carlo, however, studied his veal as though it were a fine old painting. No, Juliet realized after a moment, he studied it as though it were a young, beautiful woman.

"Appearances," he told her, "in food, as in people, are essential." He was smiling at her when he cut into the veal. "And, as in people, they can be deceiving."

Juliet watched him sample the first bite, slowly, his eyes

half-closed. She felt an odd chill at the base of her spine. He'd sample a woman the same way, she was certain. Slowly.

"Pleasant," he said after a moment. "No more, no less."

She couldn't prevent the quick smirk as she cut into her steak. "Yours is better of course."

He moved his shoulders. A statement of arrogance. "Of course. Like comparing a pretty young girl with a beautiful woman." When she glanced up, he was holding out his fork. Over it, his eyes studied her. "Taste," he invited and the simple word made her blood shiver. "Nothing should ever go untasted, Juliet."

She shrugged, letting him feed her the tiny bite of veal. It was spicy, just bordering on rich and hot on her tongue. "It's good."

"Good, *sì*. Nothing Franconi prepares is ever merely good. Good, I'd pour into the garbage, feed to the dogs in the alley." She laughed, delighting him. "If something isn't special, then it's ordinary."

"True enough." Without realizing it, she slipped out of her shoes. "But then, I suppose I've always looked at food as a basic necessity."

"Necessity?" Carlo shook his head. Though he'd heard such sentiment before, he still considered it a sacrilege. "Oh, *madonna,* you have much to learn. When one knows how to eat, how to appreciate, it's second only to making love. Scents, textures, tastes. To eat only to fill your stomach? Barbaric."

"Sorry." Juliet took another bite of steak. It was tender and cooked well. But it was only a piece of meat. She'd never have considered it sensual or romantic, but simply filling. "Is that why you became a cook? Because you think food's sexy?"

He winced. "Chef, *cara mia.*"

She grinned, showing him for the first time a streak of humor and mischief. "What's the difference?"

"What's the difference between a plow horse and a thoroughbred? Plaster and porcelain?"

Enjoying herself, she touched her tongue to the rim of her glass. "Some might say dollar signs."

"No, no, no, my love. Money is only a result, not a cause. A cook makes hamburgers in a greasy kitchen that smells of onions behind a counter where people squeeze plastic bottles of ketchup. A chef creates . . ." He gestured, a circle of a hand. "An experience."

She lifted her glass and swept her lashes down, but she didn't hide the smile. "I see."

Though he could be offended by a look when he chose, and be ruthless with the offender, Carlo liked her style. "You're amused. But you haven't tasted Franconi." He waited until her eyes, both wry and wary, lifted to him. "Yet."

He had a talent for turning the simplest statement into something erotic, she observed. It would be a challenge to skirt around him without giving way. "But you haven't told me why you became a chef."

"I can't paint or sculpt. I haven't the patience or the talent to compose sonnets. There are other ways to create, to embrace art."

She saw, with surprise mixed with respect, that he was quite serious. "But paintings, sculpture and poetry remain centuries after they've been created. If you make a soufflé, it's here, then it's gone."

"Then the challenge is to make it again, and again. Art needn't be put behind glass or bronzed, Juliet, merely appreciated. I have a friend . . ." He thought of Summer Lyndon—no, Summer Cocharan now. "She makes pastries like an angel. When you eat one, you're a king."

"Then is cooking magic or art?"

"Both. Like love. And I think you, Juliet Trent, eat much too little."

She met his look as he'd hoped she would. "I don't believe in overindulgence, Mr. Franconi. It leads to carelessness."

"To indulgence then." He lifted his glass. The smile was back, charming and dangerous. "Carefully."

Anything and everything could go wrong. You had to expect it, anticipate it and avoid it. Juliet knew just how much could be botched in a twenty-minute, live interview at 7:30 A.M. on a Monday. You hoped for the best and made do with the not too bad. Even she didn't expect perfection on the first day of a tour.

It wasn't easy to explain why she was annoyed when she got it.

The morning spot went beautifully. There was no other way to describe it, Juliet decided as she watched Liz Marks talk and laugh with Carlo after the camera stopped taping. If a shrewd operator could be called a natural, Carlo was indeed a natural. During the interview, he'd subtly and completely dominated the show while charmingly blinding his host to it. Twice he'd made the ten-year veteran of morning talk shows giggle like a girl. Once, once, Juliet remembered with astonishment, she'd seen the woman blush.

Yeah. She shifted the strap of her heavy briefcase on her arm. Franconi was a natural. It was bound to make her job easier. She yawned and cursed him.

Juliet always slept well in hotel rooms. *Always.* Except for last night. She might've been able to convince someone else that too much coffee and first-day jitters had kept her awake. But she knew better. She could drink a pot of coffee at ten and fall asleep on command at eleven. Her system was very disciplined. Except for last night.

She'd nearly dreamed of him. If she hadn't shaken herself awake at 2:00 A.M., she would have dreamed of him. That was no way to begin a very important, very long author tour. She told herself now if she had to choose between some silly fantasies and honest fatigue, she'd take the fatigue.

Stifling another yawn, Juliet checked her watch. Liz had her arm tucked through Carlo's and looked as though she'd keep it there unless someone pried her loose. With a sigh, Juliet decided she'd have to be the crowbar.

"Ms. Marks, it was a wonderful show." As she crossed over, Juliet deliberately held out her hand. With obvious reluctance, Liz disengaged herself from Carlo and accepted it.

"Thank you, Miss . . ."

"Trent," Juliet supplied without a waver.

"Juliet is my publicist," Carlo told Liz, though the two women had been introduced less than an hour earlier. "She guards my schedule."

"Yes, and I'm afraid I'll have to rush Mr. Franconi along. He has a radio spot in a half hour."

"If you must." Juliet was easily dismissed as Liz turned back to Carlo. "You have a delightful way of starting the morning. A pity you won't be in town longer."

"A pity," Carlo agreed and kissed Liz's fingers. Like an old movie, Juliet thought impatiently. All they needed were violins.

"Thank you again, Ms. Marks." Juliet used her most diplomatic smile as she took Carlo's arm and began to lead him out of the studio. After all, she'd very likely need Liz Marks again. "We're in a bit of a hurry," she muttered as they worked their way back to the reception area. The taping was over and she had other fish to fry. "This radio show's one of the top-rated in the city. Since it leans heavily on top forties and classic rock, its audience, at this time of day, falls mainly in the eighteen to thirty-five range. Excellent buying power. That gives us a nice mix with the audience from this morning's show which is generally in the twenty-five to fifty, primarily female category."

Listening with all apparent respect, Carlo reached the waiting limo first and opened the door himself. "You consider this important?"

"Of course." Because she was distracted by what she thought was a foolish question, Juliet climbed into the limo ahead of him. "We've a solid schedule in L.A." And she didn't see the point in mentioning there were some cities on the tour where they wouldn't be quite so busy. "A morning talk show with a good reputation, a popular radio show, two print interviews, two quick spots on the evening news and the *Simpson Show*." She said the last with a hint of relish. The *Simpson Show* offset what she was doing to the budget with limos.

"So you're pleased."

"Yes, of course." Digging into her briefcase, she took out her folder to recheck the name of her contact at the radio station.

"Then why do you look so annoyed?"

"I don't know what you're talking about."

"You get a line right . . . here," he said as he ran a fingertip between her eyebrows. At the touch, Juliet jerked back before she could stop herself. Carlo only cocked his head, watching her. "You may smile and speak in a quiet, polite voice, but that line gives you away."

"I was very pleased with the taping," she said again.

"But?"

All right, she thought, he was asking for it. "Perhaps it annoys me to see a woman making a fool of herself." Juliet stuffed the folder back into her briefcase. "Liz Marks is married, you know."

"Wedding rings are things I try to be immediately aware

of," he said with a shrug. "Your instructions were to be charming, weren't they?"

"Perhaps *charm* has a different meaning in Italy."

"As I said, you must come to Rome."

"I suppose you enjoy having women drooling all over you."

He smiled at her, easy, attractive, innocent. "But of course."

A gurgle of laughter bubbled in her throat but she swallowed it. She wouldn't be charmed. "You'll have to deal with some men on this tour as well."

"I promise not to kiss Simpson's fingers."

This time the laughter escaped. For a moment, she relaxed with it, let it come. Carlo saw, too briefly, the youth and energy beneath the discipline. He'd like to have kept her like that longer—laughing, at ease with him, and with herself. It would be a challenge, he mused, to find the right sequence of buttons to push to bring laughter to her eyes more often. He liked challenges—particularly when there was a woman connected to them.

"Juliet." Her name flowed off his tongue in a way only the European male had mastered. "You mustn't worry. Your tidily married Liz only enjoyed a mild flirtation with a man she'll more than likely never see again. Harmless. Perhaps because of it, she'll find more romance with her husband tonight."

Juliet eyed him a moment in her straight-on, no-nonsense manner. "You think quite of lot of yourself, don't you?"

He grinned, not sure if he was relieved or if he regretted the fact that he'd never met anyone like her before. "No more than is warranted, *cara*. Anyone who has character leaves a mark on another. Would you like to leave the world without making a ripple?"

No. No, that was one thing she was determined not to do. She sat back determined to hold her own. "I suppose some of us insist on leaving more ripples than others."

He nodded. "I don't like to do anything in a small way."

"Be careful, Mr. Franconi, or you'll begin to believe your own image."

The limo had stopped, but before Juliet could scoot toward the door, Carlo had her hand. When she looked at him this time, she didn't see the affable, amorous Italian chef, but a man of power. A man, she realized, who was well aware of how far it could take him.

She didn't move, but wondered how many other women had seen the steel beneath the silk.

"I don't need imagery, Juliet." His voice was soft, charming, beautiful. She heard the razor-blade cut beneath it. "Franconi is Franconi. Take me for what you see, or go to the devil."

Smoothly, he climbed from the limo ahead of her, turned and took her hand, drawing her out with him. It was a move that was polite, respectful, even ordinary. It was a move, Juliet realized, that expressed their positions. Man to woman. The moment she stood on the curb, she removed her hand.

With two shows and a business brunch under their belts, Juliet left Carlo in the bookstore, already swamped with women crowded in line for a glimpse at and a few words with Carlo Franconi. They'd handled the reporter and photographer already, and a man like Franconi wouldn't need her help with a crowd of women. Armed with change and her credit card, she went to find a pay phone.

For the first forty-five minutes, she spoke with her assistant in New York, filling her pad with times, dates and names while L.A. traffic whisked by outside the phone booth. As a bead of sweat trickled down her back, she wondered if she'd chosen the hottest corner in the city.

Denver still didn't look as promising as she'd hoped,

but Dallas . . . Juliet caught her bottom lip between her teeth as she wrote. Dallas was going to be fabulous. She might need to double her daily dose of vitamins to get through that twenty-four-hour stretch, but it would be fabulous.

After breaking her connection with New York, Juliet dialed her first contact in San Francisco. Ten minutes later, she was clenching her teeth. No, her contact at the department store couldn't help coming down with a virus. She was sorry, genuinely sorry he was ill. But did he have to get sick without leaving someone behind with a couple of working brain cells?

The young girl with the squeaky voice knew about the cooking demonstration. Yes, she knew all about it and wasn't it going to be fun? Extension cords? Oh my, she really didn't know a thing about that. Maybe she could ask someone in maintenance. A table—chairs? Well golly, she supposed she could get something, if it was really necessary.

Juliet was reaching in her bag for her purse-size container of aspirin before it was over. The way it looked now, she'd have to get to the department store at least two hours before the demonstration to make sure everything was taken care of. That meant juggling the schedule.

After completing her calls, Juliet left the corner phone booth, aspirin in hand, and headed back to the bookstore, hoping they could give her a glass of water and a quiet corner.

No one noticed her. If she'd just crawled in from the desert on her belly, no one would have noticed her. The small, rather elegant bookstore was choked with laughter. No bookseller stood behind the counter. There was a magnet in the left-hand corner of the room. Its name was Franconi.

It wasn't just women this time, Juliet noticed with interest. There were men sprinkled in the crowd. Some of them might have been dragged along by their wives, but they were having a time of it now. It looked like a cocktail party, minus the cigarette smoke and empty glasses.

She couldn't even see him, Juliet realized as she worked her way toward the back of the store. He was surrounded, enveloped. Jingling the aspirin in her hand, she was glad she could find a little corner by herself. Perhaps he got all the glory, she mused. But she wouldn't trade places with him.

Glancing at her watch, she noted he had another hour and wondered whether he could dwindle the crowd down in that amount of time. She wished vaguely for a stool, dropped the aspirin in the pocket of her skirt and began to browse.

"Fabulous, isn't he?" Juliet heard someone murmur on the other side of a book rack.

"God, yes. I'm so glad you talked me into coming."

"What're friends for?"

"I thought I'd be bored to death. I feel like a kid at a rock concert. He's got such . . ."

"Style," the other voice supplied. "If a man like that ever walked into my life, he wouldn't walk out again."

Curious, Juliet walked around the stacks. She wasn't sure what she expected—young housewives, college students. What she saw were two attractive women in their thirties, both dressed in sleek professional suits.

"I've got to get back to the office." One woman checked a trim little Rolex watch. "I've got a meeting at three."

"I've got to get back to the courthouse."

Both women tucked their autographed books into leather briefcases.

"How come none of the men I date can kiss my hand without making it seem like a staged move in a one-act play?"

"Style. It all has to do with style."

With this observation, or complaint, the two women disappeared into the crowd.

At three-fifteen, he was still signing, but the crowd had

thinned enough that Juliet could see him. Style, she was forced to agree, he had. No one who came up to his table, book in hand, was given a quick signature, practiced smile and brush-off. He talked to them. Enjoyed them, Juliet corrected, whether it was a grandmother who smelled of lavender or a young woman with a toddler on her hip. How did he know the right thing to say to each one of them, she wondered, that made them leave the table with a laugh or a smile or a sigh?

First day of the tour, she reminded herself. She wondered if he could manage to keep himself up to this level for three weeks. Time would tell, she decided and calculated she could give him another fifteen minutes before she began to ease him out the door.

Even with the half-hour extension, it wasn't easy. Juliet began to see the pattern she was certain would set the pace of the tour. Carlo would charm and delight, and she would play the less attractive role of drill sergeant. That's what she was paid for, Juliet reminded herself as she began to smile, chat and urge people toward the door. By four there were only a handful of stragglers. With apologies and an iron grip, Juliet disengaged Carlo.

"That went very well," she began, nudging him onto the street. "One of the booksellers told me they'd nearly sold out. Makes you wonder how much pasta's going to be cooked in L.A. tonight. Consider this just one more triumph today."

"*Grazie.*"

"*Prego.* However, we won't always have the leeway to run an hour over," she told him as the door of the limo shut behind her. "It would help if you try to keep an eye on the time and pick up the pace say half an hour before finishing time. You've got an hour and fifteen minutes before airtime—"

"Fine." Pushing a button, Carlo instructed the driver to cruise.

"But—"

"Even I need to unwind," he told her, then opened up a small built-in cabinet to reveal the bar. "Cognac," he decided and poured two glasses without asking. "You've had two hours to window-shop and browse." Leaning back, he stretched out his legs.

Juliet thought of the hour and a half she'd spent on the phone, then the time involved in easing customers along. She'd been on her feet for two and a half hours straight, but she said nothing. The cognac went down smooth and warm.

"The spot on the news should run four, four and a half minutes. It doesn't seem like much time, but you'd be surprised how much you can cram in. Be sure to mention the book title, and the autographing and demonstration at the college tomorrow afternoon. The sensual aspect of food, cooking and eating's a great angle. If you'll—"

"Would you care to do the interview for me?" he asked so politely she glanced up.

So, he could be cranky, she mused. "You handle interviews beautifully, Mr. Franconi, but—"

"Carlo." Before she could open her notebook, he had his hand on her wrist. "It's Carlo, and put the damn notes away for ten minutes. Tell me, my very organized Juliet Trent, why are we here together?"

She started to move her hand but his grip was firmer than she'd thought. For the second time, she got the full impression of power, strength and determination. "To publicize your book."

"Today went well, *sì?*"

"Yes, so far—"

"Today went well," he said again and began to annoy her with the frequency of his interruptions.

"I'll go on this local news show, talk for a few minutes, then have this necessary business dinner when I would much rather have a bottle of wine and a steak in my room. With you. Alone. Then I could see you without your proper little business suit and your proper little business manner."

She wouldn't permit herself to shudder. She wouldn't permit herself to react in any way. "Business is what we're here for. It's all I'm interested in."

"That may be." His agreement was much too easy. In direct contrast, he moved his hand to the back of her neck, gently, but not so gently she could move aside. "But we have an hour before business begins again. Don't lecture me on timetables."

The limo smelled of leather, she realized all at once. Of leather and wealth and Carlo. As casually as possible, she sipped from her glass. "Timetables, as you pointed out yourself this morning, are part of my job."

"You have an hour off," he told her, lifting a brow before she could speak. "So relax. Your feet hurt, so take your shoes off and drink your cognac." He set down his own drink, then moved her briefcase to the floor so there was nothing between them. "Relax," he said again but wasn't displeased that she'd stiffened. "I don't intend to make love with you in the back of a car. This time." He smiled as temper flared in her eyes because he'd seen doubt and excitement as well. "One day, one day soon, I'll find the proper moment for that, the proper place, the proper mood."

He leaned closer, so that he could just feel her breath flutter on his lips. She'd swipe at him now, he knew, if he took the next step. He might enjoy the battle. The color that ran along her cheekbones hadn't come from a tube or pot, but from passion. The look in her eyes was very close to a dare. She expected him to move an inch closer, to press her back against the seat with his mouth firm on hers. She was waiting for him, poised, ready.

He smiled while his lips did no more than hover until

he knew the tension in her had built to match the tension in him. He let his gaze shift down to her mouth so that he could imagine the taste, the texture, the sweetness. Her chin stayed lifted even as he brushed a thumb over it.

He didn't care to do the expected. In a long, easy move, he leaned back, crossed his feet at the ankles and closed his eyes.

"Take off your shoes," he said again. "My schedule and yours should merge very well."

Then, to her astonishment, he was asleep. Not feigning it, she realized, but sound asleep, as if he'd just flicked a switch.

With a click, she set her half-full glass down and folded her arms. Angry, she thought. Damn right she was angry because he hadn't kissed her. Not because she wanted him to, she told herself as she stared out the tinted window. But because he'd denied her the opportunity to show her claws.

She was beginning to think she'd love drawing some Italian blood.

CHAPTER 3

Their bags were packed and in the limo. As a precaution, Juliet had given Carlo's room a quick, last-minute going-over to make sure he hadn't left anything behind. She still remembered being on the road with a mystery writer who'd forgotten his toothbrush eight times on an eight-city tour. A quick look was simpler than a late-night search for a drugstore.

Checkout at the hotel had gone quickly and without any last-minute hitches. To her relief, the charges on Carlo's room bill had been light and reasonable. Her road budget might just hold. With a minimum of confusion, they'd left the Wilshire. Juliet could only hope check-in at the airport, then at the hotel in San Francisco would go as well.

She didn't want to think about the *Simpson Show*.

A list of demographics wasn't necessary here. She knew Carlo had spent enough time in the States off and on to know how important his brief demonstration on the proper way to prepare *biscuit tortoni* and his ten minutes on the air would be. It was the top-rated nighttime show in the country and had been for fifteen years. Bob Simpson was an American institution. A few minutes on his show could boost the sale of books even in the most remote areas. Or it could kill it.

And boy, oh boy, she thought, with a fresh gurgle of excitement, did it look impressive to have the *Simpson Show* listed on her itinerary. She offered a last-minute prayer that Carlo wouldn't blow it.

She checked the little freezer backstage to be certain the dessert Carlo had prepared that afternoon was in place and ready. The concoction had to freeze for four hours, so they'd play the before-and-after game for the viewers. He'd make it up on the air, then *voilà,* they'd produce the completed frozen dessert within minutes.

Though Carlo had already gone over the procedure, the tools and ingredients with the production manager and the director, Juliet went over them all again. The whipped cream was chilling and so far none of the crew had pilfered any macaroons. The brand of dry sherry Carlo had insisted on was stored and ready. No one had broken the seal for a quick sample.

Juliet nearly believed she could whip up the fancy frozen dessert herself if necessary and only thanked God she wouldn't have to give a live culinary demonstration in front of millions of television viewers.

He didn't seem to be feeling any pressure, she thought as they settled in the green room. No, he'd already given the little half-dressed blonde on the sofa a big smile and offered her a cup of coffee from the available machine.

Coffee? Even for Hollywood, it took a wild imagination to consider the contents of the pot coffee. Juliet had taken one sip of what tasted like lukewarm mud and set the cup aside.

The little blonde was apparently a new love interest on one of the popular nighttime soaps, and she was jittery with nerves. Carlo sat down on the sofa beside her and began

chatting away as though they were old friends. By the time
the green room door opened again, she was giggling.

The green room itself was beige—pale, unattractive beige
and cramped. The air-conditioning worked, but miserably.
Still Juliet knew how many of the famous and near-famous
had sat in that dull little room chewing their nails. Or taking
quick sips from a flask.

Carlo had exchanged the dubious coffee for plain water
and was sprawled on the sofa with one arm tossed over the
back. He looked as easy as a man entertaining in his own
home. Juliet wondered why she hadn't tossed any antacids in
her bag.

She made a pretense of rechecking the schedule while
Carlo charmed the rising star and the *Simpson Show* murmured away on the twenty-five-inch color console across
the room.

Then the monkey walked in. Juliet glanced up and saw
the long-armed, tuxedoed chimpanzee waddle in with his
hand caught in that of a tall thin man with harassed eyes and
a nervous grin. Feeling a bit nervous herself, Juliet looked
over at Carlo. He nodded to both newcomers, then went back
to the blonde without missing a beat. Even as Juliet told herself to relax, the chimp grinned, threw back his head and let
out a long, loud announcement.

The blonde giggled, but looked as though she'd cut and run
if the chimp came one step closer—tux or no tux.

"Behave, Butch." The thin man cleared his throat as he
swept his gaze around the room. "Butch just finished a picture last week," he explained to the room in general. "He's
feeling a little restless."

With a jiggle of the sequins that covered her, the blonde
walked to the door when her name was announced. With
some satisfaction, Carlo noted that she wasn't nearly as edgy

as she'd been when he'd sat down. She turned and gave him
a toothy smile. "Wish me luck, darling."

"The best."

To Juliet's disgust, the blonde blew him a kiss as she
sailed out.

The thin man seemed to relax visibly. "That's a relief.
Blondes make Butch overexcited."

"I see." Juliet thought of her own hair that could be considered blond or brown depending on the whim. Hopefully
Butch would consider it brown and unstimulating.

"But where's the lemonade?" The man's nerves came back
in full force. "They know Butch wants lemonade before he
goes on the air. Calms him down."

Juliet bit the tip of her tongue to hold back a snicker. Carlo
and Butch were eyeing each other with a kind of tolerant understanding. "He seems calm enough," Carlo ventured.

"Bundle of nerves," the man disagreed. "I'll never be able
to get him on camera."

"I'm sure it's just an oversight." Because she was used to
soothing panic, Juliet smiled. "Maybe you should ask one of
the pages."

"I'll do that." The man patted Butch on the head and went
back through the door.

"But—" Juliet half rose, then sat again. The chimp stood
in the middle of the room, resting his knuckles on the floor.
"I'm not sure he should've left Cheetah."

"Butch," Carlo corrected. "I think he's harmless enough."
He sent the chimp a quick grin. "He certainly has an excellent tailor."

Juliet looked over to see the chimp grinning and wink-
ing. "Is he twitching," she asked Carlo, "or is he flirting
with me?"

"Flirting, if he's a male of any taste," he mused. "And, as

I said, his tailoring is quite good. What do you say, Butch? You find my Juliet attractive?"

Butch threw back his head and let out a series of sounds Juliet felt could be taken either way.

"See? He appreciates a beautiful woman."

Appreciating the ridiculous, Juliet laughed. Whether he was attracted to the sound or simply felt it was time he made his move, Butch bowlegged his way over to her. Still grinning, he put his hand on Juliet's bare knee. This time, she was certain he winked.

"I never make so obvious a move on first acquaintance," Carlo observed.

"Some women prefer the direct approach." Deciding he was harmless, Juliet smiled down at Butch. "He reminds me of someone." She sent Carlo a mild look. "It must be that ingratiating grin." Before she'd finished speaking, Butch climbed into her lap and wrapped one of his long arms around her. "He's kind of sweet." With another laugh, she looked down into the chimp's face. "I think he has your eyes, Carlo."

"Ah, Juliet, I think you should—"

"Though his might be more intelligent."

"Oh, I think he's smart, all right." Carlo coughed into his hand as he watched the chimp's busy fingers. "Juliet, if you'd—"

"Of course he's smart, he's in movies." Enjoying herself, Juliet watched the chimp grin up at her. "Have I seen any of your films, Butch?"

"I wouldn't be surprised if they're blue."

She tickled Butch under the chin. "Really, Carlo, how crude."

"Just a guess." He let his gaze run over her. "Tell me Juliet, do you feel a draft?"

"No. I'd say it's entirely too warm in here. This poor thing is all wrapped up in a tux." She clucked at Butch and he clacked his teeth at her.

"Juliet, do you believe people can reveal their personalities by the clothes they wear? Send signals, if you understand what I mean."

"Hmm?" Distracted, she shrugged and helped Butch straighten his tie. "I suppose so."

"I find it interesting that you wear pink silk under such a prim blouse."

"I beg your pardon?"

"An observation, *mi amore*." He let his gaze wander down again. "Just an observation."

Sitting very still, Juliet moved only her head. In a moment, her mouth was as open as her blouse. The monkey with the cute face and excellent tailor had nimbly undone every one of the buttons.

Carlo gave Butch a look of admiration. "I must ask him how he perfected that technique."

"Why you son of a—"

"Not me." Carlo put a hand to his heart. "I'm an innocent bystander."

Juliet rose abruptly, dumping the chimp onto the floor. As she ducked into the adjoining rest room, she heard the laughter of two males—one a chimp, the other a rat.

Juliet took the ride to the airport where they would leave for San Diego in excruciatingly polite silence.

"Come now, *cara*, the show went well. Not only was the title mentioned three times, but there was that nice close-up of the book. My *tortoni* was a triumph, and they liked my anecdote on cooking the long, sensual Italian meal."

"You're a real prince with anecdotes," she murmured.

"*Amore*, it was the monkey who tried to undress you, not

I." He gave a long, self-satisfied sigh. He couldn't remember when he'd enjoyed a . . . demonstration quite so much. "If I had, we'd have missed the show altogether."

"You just had to tell that story on the air, didn't you?" She sent him a cool, killing look. "Do you know how many millions of people watch that show?"

"It was a good story." In the dim light of the limo, she saw the gleam in his eyes. "Most millions of people like good stories."

"Everyone I work with will have seen that show." She found her jaw was clenched and deliberately relaxed it. "Not only did you just—just *sit* there and let that happy-fingered little creature half strip me, but then you broadcast it on national television."

"*Madonna,* you'll remember I did try to warn you."

"I remember nothing of the kind."

"But you were so enchanted with Butch," he continued. "I confess, it was difficult not to be enchanted myself." He let his gaze roam down to her tidily buttoned blouse. "You've lovely skin, Juliet; perhaps I was momentarily distracted. I throw myself, a simple, weak man, on your mercy."

"Oh, shut up." She folded her arms and stared straight ahead, not speaking again until the driver pulled to the curb at their airline.

Juliet pulled her carry-on bag out of the trunk. She knew the chance was always there that the bags could be lost—sent to San Jose while she went to San Diego—so she always carried her absolute essentials with her. She handed over both her ticket and Carlo's so the check-in could get underway while she paid off the driver. It made her think of her budget. She'd managed to justify limo service in L.A., but it would be cabs and rented cars from here on. Goodbye, glamour, she thought as she pocketed her receipt. Hello, reality.

"No, this I'll carry."

She turned to see Carlo indicate his leather-bound box of about two feet in length, eight inches in width. "You're better off checking something that bulky."

"I never check my tools." He slung a flight bag over his shoulder and picked up the box by its handle.

"Suit yourself," she said with a shrug and moved through the automatic doors with him. Fatigue was creeping in, she realized, and she hadn't had to prepare any intricate desserts. If he were human, he'd be every bit as weary as she. He might annoy her in a dozen ways, but he didn't gripe. Juliet bit back a sigh. "We've a half hour before they'll begin boarding. Would you like a drink?"

He gave her an easy smile. "A truce?"

She returned it despite herself. "No, a drink."

"Okay."

They found a dark, crowded lounge and worked their way through to a table. She watched Carlo maneuver his box, with some difficulty, around people, over chairs and ultimately under their table. "What's in there?"

"Tools," he said again. "Knives, properly weighted, stainless steel spatulas of the correct size and balance. My own cooking oil and vinegar. Other essentials."

"You're going to lug oil and vinegar through airport terminals from coast to coast?" With a shake of her head, she glanced up at a waitress. "Vodka and grapefruit juice."

"Brandy. Yes," he said, giving his attention back to Juliet after he'd dazzled the waitress with a quick smile. "Because there's no brand on the American market to compare with my own." He picked up a peanut from the bowl on the table. "There's no brand on any market to compare with my own."

"You could still check it," she pointed out. "After all, you check your shirts and ties."

"I don't trust my tools to the hands of baggage carriers." He popped the peanut into his mouth. "A tie is a simple thing to replace, even a thing to become bored with. But an excellent whisk is entirely different. Once I teach you to cook, you'll understand."

"You've got as much chance teaching me to cook as you do flying to San Diego without the plane. Now, you know you'll be giving a demonstration of preparing linguini and clam sauce on *A.M. San Diego.* The show airs at eight, so we'll have to be at the studio at six to get things started."

As far as he could see, the only civilized cooking to be done at that hour would be a champagne breakfast for two. "Why do Americans insist on rising at dawn to watch television?"

"I'll take a poll and find out," she said absently. "In the meantime, you'll make up one dish that we'll set aside, exactly as we did tonight. On the air you'll be going through each stage of preparation, but of course we don't have enough time to finish; that's why we need the first dish. Now, for the good news." She sent a quick smile to the waitress as their drinks were served. "There's been a bit of a mix-up at the studio, so we'll have to bring the ingredients along ourselves. I need you to give me a list of what you'll need. Once I see you settled into the hotel, I'll run out and pick them up. There's bound to be an all-night market."

In his head, he went over the ingredients for his *linguini con vongole biance.* True, the American market would have some of the necessities, but he considered himself fortunate that he had a few of his own in the case at his feet. The clam sauce was his specialty, not to be taken lightly.

"Is shopping for groceries at midnight part of a publicist's job?"

She smiled at him. Carlo thought it was not only lovely, but perhaps the first time she'd smiled at him and meant it. "On the road, anything that needs to be done is the publicist's job. So, if you'll run through the ingredients, I'll write them down."

"Not necessary." He swirled and sipped his brandy. "I'll go with you."

"You need your sleep." She was already rummaging for a pencil. "Even with a quick nap on the plane you're only going to get about five hours."

"So are you," he pointed out. When she started to speak again, he lifted his brow in that strange silent way he had of interrupting. "Perhaps I don't trust an amateur to pick out my clams."

Juliet watched him as she drank. Or perhaps he was a gentleman, she mused. Despite his reputation with women, and a healthy dose of vanity, he was one of that rare breed of men who knew how to be considerate of women without patronizing them. She decided to forgive him for Butch after all.

"Drink up, Franconi." And she toasted him, perhaps in friendship. "We've a plane to catch."

"Salute." He lifted his glass to her.

They didn't argue again until they were on the plane.

Grumbling only a little, Juliet helped him stow his fancy box of tools under the seat. "It's a short flight." She checked her watch and calculated the shopping would indeed go beyond midnight. She'd have to take some of the vile tasting brewer's yeast in the morning. "I'll see you when we land."

He took her wrist when she would have gone past him. "Where are you going?"

"To my seat."

"You don't sit here?" He pointed to the seat beside him.

"No, I'm in coach." Impatient, she had to shift to let another oncoming passenger by.

"Why?"

"Carlo, I'm blocking the aisle."

"Why are you in coach?"

She let out a sigh of a parent instructing a stubborn child. "Because the publisher is more than happy to spring for a first-class ticket for a bestselling author and celebrity. There's a different style for publicists. It's called coach." Someone bumped a briefcase against her hip. Damn if she wouldn't have a bruise. "Now if you'd let me go, I could stop being battered and go sit down."

"First class is almost empty," he pointed out. "It's a simple matter to upgrade your ticket."

She managed to pull her arm away. "Don't buck the system, Franconi."

"I always buck the system," he told her as she walked down the aisle to her seat. Yes, he did like the way she moved.

"Mr. Franconi." A flight attendant beamed at him. "May I get you a drink after take-off?"

"What's your white wine?"

When she told him, he settled into his seat. A bit pedestrian, he thought, but not entirely revolting. "You noticed the young woman I was speaking with. The honey-colored hair and the stubborn chin."

Her smile remained bright and helpful though she thought it was a shame that he had his mind on another woman. "Of course, Mr. Franconi."

"She'll have a glass of wine, with my compliments."

Juliet would have considered herself fortunate to have an aisle seat if the man beside her hadn't already been sprawled out and snoring. Travel was so glamorous, she thought wryly as she slipped her toes out of her shoes. Wasn't she lucky to have another flight to look forward to the very next night?

Don't complain, Juliet, she warned herself. When you have

your own agency, you can send someone else on the down-and-dirty tours.

The man beside her snored through take-off. On the other side of the aisle a woman held a cigarette in one hand and a lighter in the other in anticipation of the No Smoking sign blinking off. Juliet took out her pad and began to work.

"Miss?"

Stifling a yawn, Juliet glanced up at the flight attendant. "I'm sorry, I didn't order a drink."

"With Mr. Franconi's compliments."

Juliet accepted the wine as she looked up toward first class. He was sneaky, she told herself. Trying to get under her defenses by being nice. She let her notebook close as she sighed and sat back.

It was working.

She barely finished the wine before touchdown, but it had relaxed her. Relaxed her enough, she realized, that all she wanted to do was find a soft bed and a dark room. In an hour—or two, she promised herself and gathered up her flight bag and briefcase.

She found Carlo was waiting for her in first class with a very young, very attractive flight attendant. Neither of them seemed the least bit travel weary.

"Ah, Juliet, Deborah knows of a marvelous twenty-four-hour market where we can find everything we need."

Juliet looked at the willowy brunette and managed a smile. "How convenient."

He took the flight attendant's hand and, inevitably Juliet thought, kissed it. *"Arrivederci."*

"Don't waste time, do you?" Juliet commented the moment they deplaned.

"Every moment lived is a moment to be enjoyed."

"What a quaint little sentiment." She shifted her bag and aimed for baggage claim. "You should have it tattooed."

"Where?"

She didn't bother to look at his grin. "Where it would be most attractive, naturally."

They had to wait longer than she liked for their luggage, and by then the relaxing effects of the wine had worn off. There was business to be seen to. Because he enjoyed watching her in action, Carlo let her see to it.

She secured a cab, tipped the skycap and gave the driver the name of the hotel. Scooting in beside Carlo, she caught his grin. "Something funny?"

"You're so efficient, Juliet."

"Is that a compliment or an insult?"

"I never insult women." He said it so simply, she was absolutely certain it was true. Unlike Juliet, he was completely relaxed and not particularly sleepy. "If this was Rome, we'd go to a dark little café, drink heavy red wine and listen to American music."

She closed her window because the air was damp and chilly. "The tour interfering with your night life?"

"So far I find myself enjoying the stimulating company."

"Tomorrow you're going to find yourself worked to a frazzle."

Carlo thought of his background and smiled. At nine, he'd spent the hours between school and supper washing dishes and mopping up kitchens. At fifteen he'd waited tables and spent his free time learning of spices and sauces. In Paris he'd combined long, hard study with work as an assistant chef. Even now, his restaurant and clients had him keeping twelve-hour days. Not all of his background was in the neatly typed bio Juliet had in her briefcase.

"I don't mind work, as long as it interests me. I think you're the same."

"I have to work," she corrected. "But it's easier when you enjoy it."

"You're more successful when you enjoy it. It shows with you. Ambition, Juliet, without a certain joy, is cold, and when achieved leaves a flat taste."

"But I am ambitious."

"Oh, yes." He turned to look at her, starting off flutters she'd thought herself too wise to experience. "But you're not cold."

For a moment, she thought she'd be better off if he were wrong. "Here's the hotel." She turned from him, relieved to deal with details. "We need you to wait," she instructed the driver. "We'll be going out again as soon as we check in. The hotel has a lovely view of the bay, I'm told." She walked into the lobby with Carlo as the bellboy dealt with their luggage. "It's a shame we won't have time to enjoy it. Franconi and Trent," she told the desk clerk.

The lobby was quiet and empty. Oh, the lucky people who were sleeping in their beds, she thought and pushed at a strand of hair that had come loose.

"We'll be checking out first thing tomorrow, and we won't be able to come back, so be sure you don't leave anything behind in your room."

"But of course you'll check anyway."

She sent him a sidelong look as she signed the form. "Just part of the service." She pocketed her key. "The luggage can be taken straight up." Discreetly, she handed the bellboy a folded bill. "Mr. Franconi and I have an errand."

"Yes, ma'am."

"I like that about you." To Juliet's surprise, Carlo linked arms with her as they walked back outside.

"What?"

"Your generosity. Many people would've slipped out without tipping the bellboy."

She shrugged. "Maybe it's easier to be generous when it's not your money."

"Juliet." He opened the door to the waiting cab and gestured her in. "You're intelligent enough. Couldn't you—how is it—stiff the bellboy then write the tip down on your expense account?"

"Five dollars isn't worth being dishonest."

"Nothing's worth being dishonest." He gave the driver the name of the market and settled back. "Instinct tells me if you tried to tell a lie—a true lie—your tongue would fall out."

"Mr. Franconi." She planted the tongue in question in her cheek. "You forget, I'm in public relations. If I didn't lie, I'd be out of a job."

"A true lie," he corrected.

"Isn't that a contradiction in terms?"

"Perhaps you're too young to know the variety of truths and lies. Ah, you see? This is why I'm so fond of your country." Carlo leaned out the window as they approached the big, lighted all-night market. "In America, you want cookies at midnight, you can buy cookies at midnight. Such practicality."

"Glad to oblige. Wait here," she instructed the driver, then climbed out opposite Carlo. "I hope you know what you need. I'd hate to get into the studio at dawn and find I had to run out and buy whole peppercorns or something."

"Franconi knows linguini." He swung an arm around her shoulder and drew her close as they walked inside. "Your first lesson, my love."

He led her first to the seafood section where he clucked and muttered and rejected and chose until he had the proper number of clams for two dishes. She'd seen women give as much time and attention to choosing an engagement ring.

Juliet obliged him by pushing the cart as he walked along beside her, looking at everything. And touching. Cans, boxes, bottles—she waited as he picked up, examined and ran his long artist's fingers over the labels as he read every ingredient. Somewhat amused, she watched his diamond wink in the fluorescent light.

"Amazing what they put in this prepackaged garbage," he commented as he dropped a box back on the shelf.

"Careful, Franconi, you're talking about my staple diet."

"You should be sick."

"Prepackaged food's freed the American woman from the kitchen."

"And destroyed a generation of taste buds." He chose his spices carefully and without haste. He opened three brands of oregano and sniffed before he settled on one. "I tell you, Juliet, I admire your American convenience, its practicality, but I would rather shop in Rome where I can walk along the stalls and choose vegetables just out of the ground, fish fresh from the sea. Everything isn't in a can, like the music."

He didn't miss an aisle, but Juliet forgot her fatigue in fascination. She'd never seen anyone shop like Carlo Franconi. It was like strolling through a museum with an art student. He breezed by the flour, scowling at each sack. She was afraid for a moment, he'd rip one open and test the contents. "This is a good brand?"

Juliet figured she bought a two-pound bag of flour about once a year. "Well, my mother always used this, but—"

"Good. Always trust a mother."

"She's a dreadful cook."

Carlo set the flour firmly in the basket. "She's a mother."

"An odd sentiment from a man no mother can trust."

"For mothers, I have the greatest respect. I have one myself. Now, we need garlic, mushrooms, peppers. Fresh."

Carlo walked along the stalls of vegetables, touching, squeezing and sniffing. Cautious, Juliet looked around for clerks, grateful they'd come at midnight rather than midday.

"Carlo, you really aren't supposed to handle everything quite so much."

"If I don't handle, how do I know what's good and what's just pretty?" He sent her a quick grin over his shoulder. "I told you, food was much like a woman. They put mushrooms in this box with wrap over it." Disgusted, he tore the wrapping off before Juliet could stop him.

"Carlo! You can't open it."

"I want only what I want. You can see, some are too small, too skimpy." Patiently, he began to pick out the mushrooms that didn't suit him.

"Then we'll throw out what you don't want when we get back to the hotel." Keeping an eye out for the night manager, she began to put the discarded mushrooms back in the box. "Buy two boxes if you need them."

"It's a waste. You'd waste your money?"

"The publisher's money," she said quickly, as she put the broken box into the basket. "He's glad to waste it. Thrilled."

He paused for a moment, then shook his head. "No, no, I can't do it." But when he started to reach into the basket, Juliet moved and blocked his way.

"Carlo, if you break open another package, we're going to be arrested."

"Better to go to jail than to buy mushrooms that will do me no good in the morning."

She grinned at him and stood firm. "No, it's not."

He ran a fingertip over her lips before she could react. "For you then, but against my better judgment."

"*Grazie*. Do you have everything now?"

His gaze followed the path his finger had traced just as slowly. "No."

"Well, what next?"

He stepped closer and because she hadn't expected it, she found herself trapped between him and the grocery cart. "Tonight is for first lessons," he murmured then ran his hands along either side of her face.

She should laugh. Juliet told herself it was ludicrous that he'd make a pass at her under the bright lights of the vegetable section of an all-night market. Carlo Franconi, a man who'd made seduction as much an art as his cooking wouldn't choose such a foolish setting.

But she saw what was in his eyes, and she didn't laugh.

Some women, he thought as he felt her skin soft and warm under his hands, were made to be taught slowly. Very slowly. Some women were born knowing; others were born wondering.

With Juliet, he would take time and care because he understood. Or thought he did.

She didn't resist, but her lips had parted in surprise. He touched his to hers gently, not in question, but with patience. Her eyes had already given him the answer.

He didn't hurry. It didn't matter to him where they were, that the lights were bright and the music manufactured. It only mattered that he explore the tastes that waited for him. So he tasted again, without pressure. And again.

She found she was bracing herself against the cart with her fingers wrapped around the metal. Why didn't she walk away? Why didn't she just brush him aside and stalk out of the store? He wasn't holding her there. On her face his hands were light, clever but not insistent. She could move. She could go. She should.

She didn't.

His thumbs trailed under her chin, tracing there. He felt the pulse, rapid and jerky, and kept his hold easy. He meant to keep it so, but even he hadn't guessed her taste would be so unique.

Neither of them knew who took the next step. Perhaps they took it together. His mouth wasn't so light on hers any longer, nor was hers so passive. They met, triumphantly, and clung.

Her fingers weren't wrapped around the cart now, but gripping his shoulders, holding him closer. Their bodies fit. Perfectly. It should have warned her. Giving without thought was something she never did, until now. In giving, she took, but she never thought to balance the ledger.

His mouth was warm, full. His hands never left her face, but they were firm now. She couldn't have walked away so easily. She wouldn't have walked away at all.

He'd thought he had known everything there was to expect from a woman—fire, ice, temptation. But a lesson was being taught to both. Had he ever felt this warmth before? This kind of sweetness? No, because if he had, he'd remember. No tastes, no sensations ever experienced were forgotten.

He knew what it was to desire a woman—many women—but he hadn't known what it was to crave. For a moment, he filled himself with the sensation. He wouldn't forget.

But he knew that a cautious man takes a step back and a second breath before he steps off a cliff. With a murmur in his own language, he did.

Shaken, Juliet gripped the cart again for balance. Cursing herself for an idiot, she waited for her breath to even out.

"Very nice," Carlo said quietly and ran a finger along her cheek. "Very nice, Juliet."

An eighties woman, she reminded herself as her heart thudded. Strong, independent, sophisticated. "I'm so glad you approve."

He took her hand before she could slam the cart down the aisle. Her skin was still warm, he noted, her pulse still unsteady. If they'd been alone . . . Perhaps it was best this way. For now. "It isn't a matter of approval, *cara mia,* but of appreciation."

"From now on, just appreciate me for my work, okay?" A jerk, and she freed herself of him and shoved the cart away. Without regard for the care he'd taken in selecting them, Juliet began to drop the contents of the cart on the conveyor belt at checkout.

"You didn't object," he reminded her. He'd needed to find his balance as well, he realized. Now he leaned against the cart and gave her a cocky grin.

"I didn't want a scene."

He took the peppers from the basket himself before she could wound them. "Ah, you're learning about lies."

When her head came up, he was surprised her eyes didn't bore right through him. "You wouldn't know truth if you fell into it."

"Darling, mind the mushrooms," he warned her as she swung the package onto the belt. "We don't want them bruised. I've a special affection for them now."

She swore at him, loudly enough that the checker's eyes widened. Carlo continued to grin and thought about lesson two.

He thought they should have it soon. Very soon.

CHAPTER 4

There were times when you knew everything could go wrong, should go wrong, and probably would go wrong, but somehow it didn't. Then there were the other times.

Perhaps Juliet was grouchy because she'd spent another restless night when she couldn't afford to lose any sleep. That little annoyance she could lay smack at Carlo's door, even though it didn't bring any satisfaction. But even if she'd been rested and cheerful, the ordeal at Gallegher's Department Store would have had her steaming. With a good eight hours' sleep, she might have kept things from boiling over.

First, Carlo insisted on coming with her two hours before he was needed. Or wanted. Juliet didn't care to spend the first two hours of what was bound to be a long, hectic day with a smug, self-assured, egocentric chef who looked as though he'd just come back from two sun-washed weeks on the Riviera.

Obviously, *he* didn't need any sleep, she mused as they took the quick, damp cab ride from hotel to mall.

Whatever the tourist bureau had to say about sunny California, it was raining—big, steady drops of it that immediately made the few minutes she'd taken to fuss with her hair worthless.

Prepared to enjoy the ride, Carlo looked out the window. He liked the way the rain plopped in puddles. It didn't matter to him that he'd heard it start that morning, just past four. "It's a nice sound," he decided. "It makes things more quiet, more . . . subtle, don't you think?"

Breaking away from her own gloomy view of the rain, Juliet turned to him. "What?"

"The rain." Carlo noted she looked a bit hollow-eyed. Good. She hadn't been unaffected. "Rain changes the look of things."

Normally, she would have agreed. Juliet never minded dashing for the subway in a storm or strolling along Fifth Avenue in a drizzle. Today, she considered it her right to look on the dark side. "This one might lower the attendance in your little demonstration by ten percent."

"So?" He gave an easy shrug as the driver swung into the parking lot of the mall.

What she didn't need at that moment was careless acceptance. "Carlo, the purpose of all this is exposure."

He patted her hand. "You're only thinking of numbers. You should think instead of my *pasta con pesto*. In a few hours, everyone else will."

"I don't think about food the way you do," she muttered. It still amazed her that he'd lovingly prepared the first linguini at 6:00 A.M., then the second two hours later for the camera. Both dishes had been an exquisite example of Italian cooking at its finest. He'd looked more like a film star on holiday than a working chef, which was precisely the image Juliet had wanted to project. His spot on the morning show had been perfect. That only made Juliet more pessimistic about the rest of the day. "It's hard to think about food at all on this kind of a schedule."

"That's because you didn't eat anything this morning."

"Linguini for breakfast doesn't suit me."

"My linguini is always suitable."

Juliet gave a mild snort as she stepped from the cab into the rain. Though she made a dash for the doors, Carlo was there ahead of her, opening one. "Thanks." Inside, she ran a hand through her hair and wondered how soon she could come by another cup of coffee. "You don't need to do anything for another two hours." And he'd definitely be in the way while things were being set up on the third floor.

"So, I'll wander." With his hands in his pockets, he looked around. As luck would have it, they'd entered straight into the lingerie department. "I find your American malls fascinating."

"I'm sure." Her voice was dry as he fingered the border of lace on a slinky camisole. "You can come upstairs with me first, if you like."

"No, no." A saleswoman with a face that demanded a second look adjusted two negligees and beamed at him. "I think I'll just roam around and see what your shops have to offer." He beamed back. "So far, I'm charmed."

She watched the exchange and tried not to clench her teeth. "All right, then, if you'll just be sure to—"

"Be in Special Events on the third floor at eleven-forty-five," he finished. In his friendly, casual way, he kissed her forehead. She wondered why he could touch her like a cousin and make her think of a lover. "Believe me, Juliet, nothing you say to me is forgotten." He took her hand, running his thumb over her knuckles. That was definitely not the touch of a cousin. "I'll buy you a present."

"It isn't necessary."

"A pleasure. Things that are necessary are rarely a pleasure."

Juliet disengaged her hand while trying not to dwell on the pleasure he could offer. "Please, don't be later than eleven-forty-five, Carlo."

"Timing, *mi amore,* is something I excel in."

I'll bet, she thought as she started toward the escalator. She'd have bet a week's pay he was already flirting with the lingerie clerk.

It only took ten minutes in Special Events for Juliet to forget Carlo's penchant for romancing anything feminine.

The little assistant with the squeaky voice was still in charge as her boss continued his battle with the flu. She was young, cheerleader pretty and just as pert. She was also in completely over her head.

"Elise," Juliet began because it was still early on enough for her to have some optimism. "Mr. Franconi's going to need a working area in the kitchen department. Is everything set?"

"Oh, yes." Elise gave Juliet a toothy, amiable grin. "I'm getting a nice folding table from Sporting Goods."

Diplomacy, Juliet reminded herself, was one of the primary rules of PR. "I'm afraid we'll need something a bit sturdier. Perhaps one of the islands where Mr. Franconi could prepare the dish and still face the audience. Your supervisor and I had discussed it."

"Oh, is that what he meant?" Elise looked blank for a moment, then brightened. Juliet began to think dark thoughts about mellow California. "Well, why not?"

"Why not," Juliet agreed. "We've kept the dish Mr. Franconi is to prepare as simple as possible. You do have all the ingredients listed?"

"Oh, yes. It sounds just delicious. I'm a vegetarian, you know."

Of course she was, Juliet thought. Yogurt was probably the high point of her day. "Elise, I'm sorry if it seems I'm rushing you along, but I really need to work out the setup as soon as possible."

"Oh, sure." All cooperation, Elise flashed her straight-toothed smile. "What do you want to know?"

Juliet offered up a prayer. "How sick is Mr. Francis?" she asked, thinking of the levelheaded, businesslike man she had dealt with before.

"Just miserable." Elise swung back her straight California-blond hair. "He'll be out the rest of the week."

No help there. Accepting the inevitable, Juliet gave Elise her straight, no-nonsense look. "All right, what have you got so far?"

"Well, we've taken a new blender and some really lovely bowls from Housewares."

Juliet nearly relaxed. "That's fine. And the range?"

Elise smiled. "Range?"

"The range Mr. Franconi needs to cook the spaghetti for this dish. It's on the list."

"Oh. We'd need elecricity for that, wouldn't we?"

"Yes." Juliet folded her hands to keep them from clenching. "We would. For the blender, too."

"I guess I'd better check with maintenance."

"I guess you'd better." Diplomacy, tact, Juliet reminded herself as her fingers itched for Elise's neck. "Maybe I'll just go over to the kitchen layouts and see which one would suit Mr. Franconi best."

"Terrific. He might want to do his interview right there."

Juliet had taken two steps before she stopped and turned back. "Interview?"

"With the food editor of the *Sun*. She'll be here at eleven-thirty."

Calm, controlled, Juliet pulled out her itinerary of the San Diego stop. She skimmed it, though she knew every word by heart. "I don't seem to have anything listed here."

"It came up at the last minute. I called your hotel at nine, but you'd already checked out."

"I see." Should she have expected Elise to phone the television studio and leave a message? Juliet looked into the personality-plus smile. No, she supposed not. Resigned, she checked her watch. The setup could be dealt with in time if she started immediately. Carlo would just have to be paged. "How do I call mall management?"

"Oh, you can call from my office. Can I do anything?"

Juliet thought of and rejected several things, none of which were kind. "I'd like some coffee, two sugars."

She rolled up her sleeves and went to work.

By eleven, Juliet had the range, the island and the ingredients Carlo had specified neatly arranged. It had taken only one call, and some finesse, to acquire two vivid flower arrangements from a shop in the mall.

She was on her third coffee and considering a fourth when Carlo wandered over. "Thank God." She drained the last from the styrofoam cup. "I thought I was going to have to send out a search party."

"Search party?" Idly he began looking around the kitchen set. "I came when I heard the page."

"You've been paged five times in the last hour."

"Yes?" He smiled as he looked back at her. Her hair was beginning to stray out of her neat bun. He might have stepped off the cover of *Gentlemen's Quarterly*. "I only just heard. But then, I spent some time in the most fantastic record store. Such speakers. Quadraphonic."

"That's nice." Juliet dragged a hand through her already frazzled hair.

"There's a problem?"

"Her name's Elise. I've come very close to murdering her half a dozen times. If she smiles at me again, I just might." Juliet gestured with her hand to brush it off. This was no time for fantasies, no matter how satisfying. "It seems things were a bit disorganized here."

"But you've seen to that." He bent over to examine the range as a driver might a car before Le Mans. "Excellent."

"You can be glad you've got electricity rather than your imagination," she muttered. "You have an interview at eleven-thirty with a food editor, Marjorie Ballister, from the *Sun*."

He only moved his shoulders and examined the blender. "All right."

"If I'd known it was coming up, I'd have bought a paper so we could have seen her column and gauged her style. As it is—"

"*Non importante*. You worry too much, Juliet."

She could have kissed him. Strictly in gratitude, but she could have kissed him. Considering that unwise, she smiled instead. "I appreciate your attitude, Carlo. After the last hour of dealing with the inept, the insane and the unbearable, it's a relief to have someone take things in stride."

"Franconi always takes things in stride." Juliet started to sink into a chair for a five-minute break.

"*Dio!* What joke is this?" She was standing again and looking down at the little can he held in his hand. "Who would sabotage my pasta?"

"Sabotage?" Had he found a bomb in the can? "What are you talking about?"

"This!" He shook the can at her. "What do you call this?"

"It's basil," she began, a bit unsteady when she lifted her gaze and caught the dark, furious look in his eyes. "It's on your list."

"Basil!" He went off in a stream of Italian. "You dare call this basil?"

Soothe, Juliet reminded herself. It was part of the job. "Carlo, it says basil right on the can."

"On the can." He said something short and rude as he dropped it into her hand. "Where in your clever notes does it say Franconi uses basil from a can?"

"It just says basil," she said between clenched teeth. "B-a-s-i-l."

"Fresh. On your famous list you'll see fresh. *Accidenti!* Only a philistine uses basil from a can for *pasta con pesto.* Do I look like a philistine?"

She wouldn't tell him what he looked like. Later, she might privately admit that temper was spectacular on him. Dark and unreasonable, but spectacular. "Carlo, I realize things aren't quite as perfect here as both of us would like, but—"

"I don't need perfect," he tossed at her. "I can cook in a sewer if I have to, but not without the proper ingredients."

She swallowed—though it went down hard—pride, temper and opinion. She only had fifteen minutes left until the interview. "I'm sorry, Carlo. If we could just compromise on this—"

"Compromise?" When the word came out like an obscenity, she knew she'd lost the battle. "Would you ask Picasso to compromise on a painting?"

Juliet stuck the can into her pocket. "How much fresh basil do you need?"

"Three ounces."

"You'll have it. Anything else?"

"A mortar and pestle, marble."

Juliet checked her watch. She had forty-five minutes to handle it. "Okay. If you'll do the interview right here, I'll take care of this and we'll be ready for the demonstration at noon." She sent up a quick prayer that there was a gourmet shop within ten miles. "Remember to get in the book title and the next stop on the tour. We'll be hitting another Galle-gher's in Portland, so it's a good tie-in. Here." Digging into her bag she brought out an eight-by-ten glossy. "Take the extra publicity shot for her in case I don't get back. Elise didn't mention a photographer."

"You'd like to chop and dice that bouncy little woman," Carlo observed, noting that Juliet was swearing very unpro-fessionally under her breath.

"You bet I would." She dug in again. "Take a copy of the book. The reporter can keep it if necessary."

"I can handle the reporter," he told her calmly enough. "You handle the basil."

It seemed luck was with her when Juliet only had to make three calls before she found a shop that carried what she needed. The frenzied trip in the rain didn't improve her disposition, nor did the price of a marble pestle. Another glance at her watch reminded her she didn't have time for temperament. Carrying what she considered Carlo's eccentricities, she ran back to the waiting cab.

At exactly ten minutes to twelve, dripping wet, Juliet rode up to the third floor of Gallegher's. The first thing she saw was Carlo, leaning back in a cozy wicker dinette chair laughing with a plump, pretty middle-aged woman with a pad and pencil. He looked dashing, amiable and most of all, dry. She wondered how it would feel to grind the pestle into his ear.

"Ah, Juliet." All good humor, Carlo rose as she walked up to the table. "You must meet Marjorie. She tells me she's eaten my pasta in my restaurant in Rome."

"Loved every sinful bite. How do you do? You must be the Juliet Trent Carlo bragged about."

Bragged about? No, she wouldn't be pleased. But Juliet set her bag on the table and offered her hand. "It's nice to meet you. I hope you can stay for the demonstration."

"Wouldn't miss it." She twinkled at Carlo. "Or a sample of Franconi's pasta."

Juliet felt a little wave of relief. Something would be salvaged out of the disaster. Unless she was way off the mark, Carlo was about to be given a glowing write-up.

Carlo was already taking the little sack of basil out of the bag. "Perfect," he said after one sniff. "Yes, yes, this is excellent." He tested the pestle weight and size. "You'll see over at our little stage a crowd is gathering," he said easily to

Juliet. "So we moved here to talk, knowing you'd see us as soon as you stepped off the escalator."

"Very good." They'd both handled things well, she decided. It was best to take satisfaction from that. A quick glance showed her that Elise was busy chatting away with a small group of people. Not a worry in the world, Juliet thought nastily. Well, she'd already resigned herself to that. Five minutes in the rest room for some quick repairs, she calculated, and she could keep everything on schedule.

"You have everything you need now, Carlo?"

He caught the edge of annoyance, and her hand, smiling brilliantly. "*Grazie, cara mia.* You're wonderful."

Perhaps she'd rather have snarled, but she returned the smile. "Just doing my job. You have a few more minutes before we should begin. If you'll excuse me, I'll just take care of some things and be right back."

Juliet kept up a brisk, dignified walk until she was out of sight, then made a mad dash for the rest room, pulling out her brush as she went in.

"What did I tell you?" Carlo held the bag of basil in his palm to judge the weight. "She's fantastic."

"And quite lovely," Marjorie agreed. "Even when she's damp and annoyed."

With a laugh, Carlo leaned forward to grasp both of Marjorie's hands. He was a man who touched, always. "A woman of perception. I knew I liked you."

She gave a quick dry chuckle, and for a moment felt twenty years younger. And twenty pounds lighter. It was a talent of his that he was generous with. "One last question, Carlo, before your fantastic Ms. Trent rushes you off. Are you still likely to fly off to Cairo or Cannes to prepare one of your dishes for an appreciative client and a stunning fee?"

"There was a time this was routine." He was silent a moment, thinking of the early years of his success. There'd been mad, glamorous trips to this country and to that, preparing fettuccine for a prince or cannelloni for a tycoon. It had been a heady, spectacular time.

Then he'd opened his restaurant and had learned that the solid continuity of his own place was so much more fulfilling than the flash of the single dish.

"From time to time I would still make such trips. Two months ago there was Count Lequine's birthday. He's an old client, an old friend, and he's fond of my spaghetti. But my restaurant is more rewarding to me." He gave her a quizzical look as a thought occurred to him. "Perhaps I'm settling down?"

"A pity you didn't decide to settle in the States." She closed her pad. "I guarantee if you opened a Franconi's right here in San Diego, you'd have clientele flying in from all over the country."

He took the idea, weighed it in much the same way he had the basil, and put it in a corner of his mind. "An interesting thought."

"And a fascinating interview. Thank you." It pleased her that he rose as she did and took her hand. She was a tough, outspoken feminist who appreciated genuine manners and genuine charm. "I'm looking forward to a taste of your pasta. I'll just ease over and try to get a good seat. Here comes your Ms. Trent."

Marjorie had never considered herself particularly romantic, but she'd always believed where there was smoke, there was fire. She watched the way Carlo turned his head, saw the change in his eyes and the slight tilt of his mouth. There was fire all right, she mused. You only had to be within five feet to feel the heat.

Between the hand dryer and her brush, Juliet had managed to do something with her hair. A touch here, a dab there, and her makeup was back in shape. Carrying her raincoat over her arm, she looked competent and collected. She was ready to admit she'd had one too many cups of coffee.

"Your interview went well?"

"Yes." He noticed, and approved, that she'd taken the time to dab on her scent. "Perfectly."

"Good. You can fill me in later. We'd better get started."

"In a moment." He reached in his pocket. "I told you I'd buy you a present."

There was a flutter of surprised pleasure she tried to ignore. Just wired from the coffee, she told herself. "Carlo, I told you not to. We don't have time—"

"There's always time." He opened the little box himself and drew out a small gold heart with an arrow of diamonds running through it. She'd been expecting something along the line of a box of chocolates.

"Oh, I—" Words were her business, but she'd lost them. "Carlo, really, you can't—"

"Never say can't to Franconi," he murmured and began to fasten the pin to her lapel. He did so smoothly, with no fumbling. After all, he was a man accustomed to such feminine habits. "It's very delicate, I thought, very elegant. So it suits you." Narrowing his eyes, he stood back, then nodded. "Yes, I was sure it would."

It wasn't possible to remember her crazed search for fresh basil when he was smiling at her in just that way. It was barely possible to remember how furious she was over the lackadaisical setup for the demonstration. Instinctively, she put up her hand and ran a finger over the pin. "It's lovely." Her lips curved, easily, sweetly, as he thought they didn't do often enough. "Thank you."

He couldn't count or even remember the number of presents he'd given, or the different styles of gratitude he'd received. Somehow, he was already sure this would be one he wouldn't forget.

"Prego."

"Ah, Ms. Trent?"

Juliet glanced over to see Elise watching her. Present or no present, it tightened her jaw. "Yes, Elise. You haven't met Mr. Franconi yet."

"Elise directed me from the office to you when I answered the page," Carlo said easily, more than appreciating Juliet's aggravation.

"Yes." She flashed her touchdown smile. "I thought your cookbook looked just super, Mr. Franconi. Everyone's dying to watch you cook something." She opened a little pad of paper with daisies on the cover. "I thought you could spell what it is so I could tell them when I announce you."

"Elise, I have everything." Juliet managed charm and diplomacy to cover a firm nudge out the door. "Why don't I just announce Mr. Franconi?"

"Great." She beamed. Juliet could think of no other word for it. "That'll be a lot easier."

"We'll get started now, Carlo, if you'd just step over there behind those counters, I'll go give the announcements." Without waiting for an assent, she gathered up the basil, mortar and pestle and walked over to the area that she'd prepared. In the most natural of moves, she set everything down and turned to the audience. Three hundred, she judged. Maybe even over. Not bad for a rainy day in a department store.

"Good afternoon." Her voice was pleasant and well pitched. There'd be no need for a microphone in the relatively small space. Thank God, because Elise had botched that minor detail as well. "I want to thank you all for coming here today, and to thank Gallegher's for providing such a lovely setting for the demonstration."

From a few feet away, Carlo leaned on a counter and

watched her. She was, as he'd told the reporter, fantastic. No one would guess she'd been up and on her feet since dawn.

"We all like to eat." This drew the murmured laughter she'd expected. "But I've been told by an expert that eating is more than a basic necessity, it's an experience. Not all of us like to cook, but the same expert told me that cooking is both art and magic. This afternoon, the expert, Carlo Franconi, will share with you the art, the magic and the experience with his own *pasta con pesto*."

Juliet started the applause herself, but it was picked up instantly. As Carlo stepped out, she melted back. Center stage was his the moment he stepped on it.

"It's a fortunate man," he began, "who has the opportunity to cook for so many beautiful women. Some of you have husbands?" At the question there was a smatter of chuckles and the lifting of hands. "Ah, well." He gave a very European shrug. "Then I must be content to cook."

She knew Carlo had chosen that particular dish because it took little time in preparation. After the first five minutes, Juliet was certain not one member of the audience would have budged if he'd chosen something that took hours. She wasn't yet convinced cooking was magic, but she was certain he was.

His hands were as skilled and certain as a surgeon's, his tongue as glib as a politician's. She watched him measure, grate, chop and blend and found herself just as entertained as she might have been with a well produced one-act play.

One woman was bold enough to ask a question. It opened the door and dozens of others followed. Juliet needn't have worried that the noise and conversations would disturb him. Obviously he thrived on the interaction. He wasn't, she decided, simply doing his job or fulfilling an obligation. He was enjoying himself.

Calling one woman up with him, Carlo joked about all truly great chefs requiring both inspiration and assistance. He told her to stir the spaghetti, made a fuss out of showing her the proper way to stir by putting his hand over hers and undoubtedly sold another ten books then and there.

Juliet had to grin. He'd done it for fun, not for sales. He was fun, Juliet realized, even if he did take his basil too seriously. He was sweet. Unconsciously, she began to toy with the gold and diamonds on her lapel. Uncommonly considerate and uncommonly demanding. Simply uncommon.

As she watched him laugh with his audience, something began to melt inside of her. She sighed with it, dreaming. There were certain men that prompted a woman, even a practical woman, to dream.

One of the women seated closer to her leaned toward a companion. "Good God, he's the sexiest man I've ever seen. He could keep a dozen lovers patiently waiting."

Juliet caught herself and dropped her hand. Yes, he could keep a dozen lovers patiently waiting. She was sure he did. Deliberately she tucked her hands in the pockets of her skirt. She'd be better off remembering she was encouraging this public image, even exploiting it. She'd be better off remembering that Carlo himself had told her he needed no imagery.

If she started believing half the things he said to her, she might just find herself patiently waiting. The thought of that was enough to stop the melting. Waiting didn't fit into her schedule.

When every last bite of pasta had been consumed, and every last fan had been spoken with, Carlo allowed himself to think of the pleasures of sitting down with a cool glass of wine.

Juliet already had his jacket.

"Well done, Carlo." As she spoke, she began to help him into it. "You can leave California with the satisfaction of knowing you were a smashing success."

He took her raincoat from her when she would've shrugged into it herself. "The airport."

She smiled at his tone, understanding. "We'll pick up our bags in the holding room at the hotel on the way. Look at it this way. You can sit back and sleep all the way to Portland if you like."

Because the thought had a certain appeal, he cooperated. They rode down to the first floor and went out the west entrance where Juliet had told the cab to wait. She let out a quick sigh of relief when it was actually there.

"We get into Portland early?"

"Seven." Rain splattered against the cab's windshield. Juliet told herself to relax. Planes took off safely in the rain every day. "You have a spot on *People of Interest,* but not until nine-thirty. That means we can have breakfast at a civilized hour and go over the scheduling."

Quickly, efficiently, she checked off her San Diego list and noted everything had been accomplished. She had time for a quick, preliminary glance at her Portland schedule before the cab pulled up to the hotel.

"Just wait here," she ordered both the driver and Carlo. She was up and out of the cab and, because they were running it close, managed to have the bags installed in the trunk within seven minutes. Carlo knew because it amused him to time her.

"You, too, can sleep all the way to Portland."

She settled in beside him again. "No, I've got some work to do. The nice thing about planes is that I can pretend I'm in my office and forget I'm thousands of feet off the ground."

"I didn't realize flying bothered you."

"Only when I'm in the air." Juliet sat back and closed her eyes, thinking to relax for a moment. The next thing she knew, she was being kissed awake.

Disoriented, she sighed and wrapped her arms around Carlo's neck. It was soothing, so sweet. And then the heat began to rise.

"Cara." She'd surprised him, but that had brought its own kind of pleasure. "Such a pity to wake you."

"Hmm?" When she opened her eyes, his face was close, her mouth still warm, her heart still thudding. She jerked back and fumbled with the door handle. "That was uncalled for."

"True enough." Leisurely, Carlo stepped out into the rain. "But it was illuminating. I've already paid the driver, Juliet," he continued when she started to dig into her purse. "The baggage is checked. We board from gate five." Taking her arm, and his big leather case, he led her into the terminal.

"You didn't have to take care of all that." She'd have pulled her arm away if she'd had the energy. Or so she told herself. "The reason I'm here is to—"

"Promote my book," he finished easily. "If it makes you feel better, I've been known to do the same when I traveled with your predecessor."

The very fact that it did, made her feel foolish as well. "I appreciate it, Carlo. It's not that I mind you lending a hand, it's that I'm not used to it. You'd be surprised how many authors are either helpless or careless on the road."

"You'd be surprised how many chefs are temperamental and rude."

She thought of the basil and grinned. "No!"

"Oh, yes." And though he'd read her thoughts perfectly, his tone remained grave. "Always flying off the handle, swearing, throwing things. It leads to a bad reputation for all of us. Here, they're boarding. If only they have a decent Bordeaux."

Juliet stifled a yawn as she followed him through. "I'll need my boarding pass, Carlo."

"I have it." He flashed them both for the flight attendant and nudged Juliet ahead. "Do you want the window or the aisle?"

"I need my pass to see which I've got."

"We have 2A and B. Take your pick."

Someone pushed past her and bumped her solidly. It brought a sinking sensation of déjà vu. "Carlo, I'm in coach, so—"

"No, your tickets are changed. Take the window."

Before she could object, he'd maneuvered her over and slipped in beside her. "What do you mean my ticket's been changed? Carlo, I have to get in the back before I cause a scene."

"Your seat's here." After handing Juliet her boarding pass he stretched out his legs. "*Dio,* what a relief."

Frowning, Juliet studied her stub—2A. "I don't know how they could've made a mistake like this. I'd better see to it right away."

"There's no mistake. You should fasten your belt," he advised, then did so himself. "I changed your tickets for the remaining flights on the tour."

Juliet reached to undo the clasp he'd just secured. "You— but you can't."

"I told you, don't say can't to Franconi." Satisfied with her belt, he dealt with his own. "You work as hard as I do—why should you travel in tourist?"

"Because I'm paid to work. Carlo, let me out so I can fix this before we take off."

"No." For the first time, his voice was blunt and final. "I prefer your company to that of a stranger or an empty seat." When he turned his head, his eyes were like his voice. "I want you here. Leave it."

Juliet opened her mouth and closed it again. Professionally, she was on shaky ground either direction she went. She was supposed to see to his needs and wants within reason. Personally, she'd counted on the distance, at least during flight time, to keep her balanced. With Carlo, even a little distance could help.

He was being kind, she knew. Considerate. But he was also being stubborn. There was always a diplomatic way to handle such things.

She gave him a patient smile. "Carlo—"

He stopped her by simply closing his mouth over hers, quietly, completely and irresistibly. He held her there a moment, one hand on her cheek, the other over the fingers which had frozen in her lap. Juliet felt the floor tilt and her head go light.

We're taking off, she thought dimly, but knew the plane hadn't left the ground.

His tongue touched hers briefly, teasingly; then it was only his lips again. After brushing a hand through her hair, he leaned back. "Now, go back to sleep awhile," he advised. "This isn't the place I'd choose to seduce you."

Sometimes, Juliet decided, silence was the best diplomacy. Without another word, she closed her eyes and slept.

CHAPTER 5

Colorado. The Rockies, Pike's Peak, Indian ruins, aspens and fast-running streams. It sounded beautiful, exciting. But a hotel room was a hotel room after all.

They'd been busy in Washington State. For most of their three-day stay, Juliet had had to work and think on her feet. But the media had been outstanding. Their schedule had been so full her boss back in New York had probably done handstands. Her report on their run on the coast would be a publicist's dream. Then there was Denver.

What coverage she'd managed to hustle there would barely justify the plane fare. One talk show at the ungodly hour of 7:00 A.M. and one miserly article in the food section of a local paper. No network or local news coverage of the autographing, no print reporter who'd confirm an appearance. Lousy.

It was 6:00 A.M. when Juliet dragged herself out of the shower and began to search through her unpacked garment bag for a suit and a fresh blouse. The cleaners was definitely a priority the minute they moved on to Dallas.

At least Carlo wasn't cooking this morning. She didn't think she could bear to look at food in any form for at least two hours.

With any luck she could come back to the hotel after the show, catch another hour's sleep and then have breakfast in her room while she made her morning calls. The autographing wasn't until noon, and their flight out wasn't until early the next morning.

That was something to hold on to, Juliet told herself as she looked for the right shade of stockings. For the first time in a week, they had an evening free with no one to entertain, no one to be entertained by. A nice, quiet meal somewhere close by and a full night's sleep. With that at the end of the tunnel, she could get through the morning.

With a grimace, she gulped down her daily dose of brewer's yeast.

It wasn't until she was fully dressed that she woke up enough to remember she hadn't dealt with her makeup. With a shrug Juliet slipped out of her little green jacket and headed for the bathroom. She stared at the front door with a combination of suspicion and bad temper when she heard the knock. Peeking through the peephole, she focused on Carlo. He grinned at her, then crossed his eyes. She only swore a little as she pulled open the door.

"You're early," she began, then caught the stirring aroma of coffee. Looking down, she saw that he carried a tray with a small pot, cups and spoons. "Coffee," she murmured, almost like a prayer.

"Yes." He nodded as he stepped into the room. "I thought you'd be ready, though room service isn't." He walked over to a table, saw that her room could fit into one section of his suite and set down the tray. "So, we deliver."

"Bless you." It was so sincere he grinned again as she crossed the room. "How did you manage it? Room service doesn't open for half an hour."

"There's a small kitchen in my suite. A bit primitive, but adequate to brew coffee."

She took the first sip, black and hot, and she closed her eyes. "It's wonderful. Really wonderful."

"Of course. I fixed it."

She opened her eyes again. No, she decided, she wouldn't spoil gratitude with sarcasm. After all, they'd very nearly gotten along for three days running. With the help of her shower, the yeast and the coffee, she was feeling almost human again.

"Relax," she suggested. "I'll finish getting ready." Expecting him to sit, Juliet took her cup and went into the bathroom to deal with her face and hair. She was dotting on foundation when Carlo leaned on the doorjamb.

"*Mi amore,* doesn't this arrangement strike you as impractical?"

She tried not to feel self-conscious as she smoothed on the thin, translucent base. "Which arrangement is that?"

"You have this—broom closet," he decided as he gestured toward her room. Yes, it was small enough that the subtle, feminine scent from her shower reached all the corners. "While I have a big suite with two baths, a bed big enough for three friends and one of those sofas that unfold."

"You're the star," she murmured as she brushed color over the slant of her cheeks.

"It would save the publisher money if we shared the suite."

She shifted her eyes in the mirror until they met his. She'd have sworn, absolutely sworn, he meant no more than that. That is, if she hadn't known him. "He can afford it," she said lightly. "It just thrills the accounting department at tax time."

Carlo moved his shoulders then sipped from his cup again. He'd known what her answer would be. Of course, he'd enjoy sharing his rooms with her for the obvious reason, but neither did it sit well with him that her accommodations were so far inferior to his.

"You need a touch more blusher on your left cheek," he said idly, not noticing her surprised look. What he'd noticed was the green silk robe that reflected in the mirror from the back of the door. Just how would she look in that? Carlo wondered. How would she look out of it?

After a narrowed-eyed study, Juliet discovered he'd been right. She picked up her brush again and evened the color. "You're a very observant man."

"Hmm?" He was looking at her again, but mentally, he'd changed her neat, high-collared blouse and slim skirt for the provocative little robe.

"Most men wouldn't notice unbalanced blusher." She picked up a grease pencil to shadow her eyes.

"I notice everything when it comes to a woman." There was still a light fog near the top of the mirror from the steam of her shower. Seeing it gave Carlo other, rather pleasant mental images. "What you're doing now gives you a much different look."

Relaxed again, she laughed. "That's the idea."

"But, no." He stepped in closer so he could watch over her shoulder. The small, casual intimacy was as natural for him as it was uncomfortable for her. "Without the pots of paint, your face is younger, more vulnerable, but no less attractive than it is with them. Different . . ." Easily, he picked up her brush and ran it through her hair. "It's not more, not less, simply different. I like both of your looks."

It wasn't easy to keep her hand steady. Juliet set down the eye-shadow and tried the coffee instead. Better to be cynical than be moved, she reminded herself and gave him a cool smile. "You seem right at home in the bathroom with a woman fixing her face."

He liked the way her hair flowed as he brushed it. "I've done it so often."

Her smile became cooler. "I'm sure."

He caught the tone, but continued to brush as he met her eyes in the glass. "Take it as you like, *cara,* but remember, I grew up in a house with five women. Your powders and bottles hold no secrets from me."

She'd forgotten that, perhaps because she'd chosen to forget anything about him that didn't connect directly with the book. Yet now it made her wonder. Just what sort of insight did a man get into women when he'd been surrounded by them since childhood? Frowning a bit, she picked up her mascara.

"Were you a close family?"

"We are a close family," he corrected. "My mother's a widow who runs a successful dress shop in Rome." It was typical of him not to mention that he'd bought it for her. "My four sisters all live within thirty kilometers. Perhaps I no longer share the bathroom with them, but little else changes."

She thought about it. It sounded cozy and easy and rather sweet. Juliet didn't believe she could relate at all. "Your mother must be proud of you."

"She'd be prouder if I added to her growing horde of grandchildren."

She smiled at that. It sounded more familiar. "I know what you mean."

"You should leave your hair just like this," he told her as he set down the brush. "You have a family?"

"My parents live in Pennsylvania."

He struggled with geography a moment. "Ah, then you'll visit them when we go to Philadelphia."

"No." The word was flat as she recapped the tube of mascara. "There won't be time for that."

"I see." And he thought he was beginning to. "You have brothers, sisters?"

"A sister." Because he was right about her hair, Juliet let it be and slipped out for her jacket. "She married a doctor and produced two children, one of each gender, before she was twenty-five."

Oh yes, he was beginning to see well enough. Though the words had been easy, the muscles in her shoulders had been tight. "She makes an excellent doctor's wife?"

"Carrie makes a perfect doctor's wife."

"Not all of us are meant for the same things."

"I wasn't." She picked up her briefcase and her purse. "We'd better get going. They said it would take about fifteen minutes to drive to the studio."

Strange, he thought, how people always believed their tender spots could go undetected. For now, he'd leave her with the illusion that hers had.

B ecause the directions were good and the traffic was light, Juliet drove the late model Chevy she'd rented with confidence. Carlo obliged by navigating because he enjoyed the poised, skilled way she handled the wheel.

"You haven't lectured me on today's schedule," he pointed out. "Turn right here at this light."

Juliet glanced in the mirror, switched lanes, then made the turn. She wasn't yet sure what his reaction would be to the fact that there barely was one. "I've decided to give you a break," she said brightly, knowing how some authors snarled and ranted when they had a dip in exposure. "You have this morning spot, then the autographing at World of Books downtown."

He waited, expecting the list to go on. When he turned to her, his brow was lifted. "And?"

"That's all." She heard the apology in her voice as she stopped at a red light. "It happens sometimes, Carlo. Things just don't come through. I knew it was going to be light here, but as it happens they've just started shooting a major film using Denver locations. Every reporter, every news team, every camera crew is covering it this afternoon. The bottom line is we got bumped."

"Bumped? Do you mean there is no radio show, no lunch with a reporter, no dinner engagement?"

"No, I'm sorry. It's just—"

"Fantastico!" Grabbing her face with both hands he kissed her hard. "I'll find out the name of this movie and go to its premiere."

The little knot of tension and guilt vanished. "Don't take it so hard, Carlo."

He felt as though he'd just been paroled. "Juliet, did you think I'd be upset? *Dio,* for a week it's been nothing but go here, rush there."

She spotted the TV tower and turned left. "You've been wonderful," she told him. The best time to admit it, she decided, was when they only had two minutes to spare. "Not everyone I've toured with has been as considerate."

She surprised him. He preferred it when a woman could do so. He twined a lock of the hair he'd brushed around his finger. "So, you've forgiven me for the basil?"

She smiled and had to stop herself from reaching up to touch the heart on her lapel. "I'd forgotten all about it."

He kissed her cheek in a move so casual and friendly she didn't object. "I believe you have. You've a kind heart, Juliet. Such things are beauty in themselves."

He could soften her so effortlessly. She felt it, fought it and, for the moment, surrendered to it. In an impulsive, uncharacteristic move, she brushed the hair on his forehead. "Let's go in. You've got to wake up Denver."

Professionally, Juliet should've been cranky at the lack of obligations and exposure in Denver. It was going to leave a few very obvious blanks on her overall report. Personally, she was thrilled.

According to schedule, she was back in her room by eight. By 8:03, she'd stripped out of her suit and had crawled, naked and happy, into her still-rumpled bed. For exactly an hour she slept deeply, and without any dreams she could remember. By ten-thirty, she'd gone through her list of phone calls and an enormous breakfast. After freshening her makeup, she dressed in her suit then went downstairs to meet Carlo in the lobby.

It shouldn't have surprised her that he was huddled in one of the cozy lounging areas with three women. It shouldn't have irked her. Pretending it did neither, Juliet strolled over. It was then she noticed that all three women were built stupendously. That shouldn't have surprised her, either.

"Ah, Juliet." He smiled, all grace, all charm. She didn't stop to wonder why she'd like to deck him. "Always prompt. Ladies." He turned to bow to all three of them. "It's been a pleasure."

"Bye-bye, Carlo." One of them sent him a look that could have melted lead. "Remember, if you're ever in Tucson . . ."

"How could I forget?" Hooking his arm with Juliet's, he strolled outside. "Juliet," he murmured, "where is Tucson?"

"Don't you ever quit?" she demanded.

"Quit what?"

"Collecting women."

He lifted a brow as he pulled open the door on the driver's side. "Juliet, one collects matchbooks, not women."

"It would seem there are some who consider them on the same level."

He blocked her way before she could slip inside. "Any who do are too stupid to matter." He walked around the side of the car and opened his own door before she spoke again.

"Who were they anyhow?"

Soberly, Carlo adjusted the brim of the buff-colored fedora he wore. "Female bodybuilders. It seems they're having a convention."

A muffled laugh escaped before she could prevent it. "Figures."

"Indeed yes, but such muscular ones." His expression was still grave as he lowered himself into the car.

Juliet remained quiet a moment, then gave up and laughed out loud. Damn, she'd never had as much fun on tour with anyone. She might as well accept it. "Tucson's in Arizona," she told him with another laugh. "And it's not on the itinerary."

They would have been on time for the autographing if they hadn't run into the detour. Traffic was clogged, rerouted and bad tempered as roads were blocked off for the film being shot. Juliet spent twenty minutes weaving, negotiating and cursing until she found she'd done no more than make a nice big circle.

"We've been here before," Carlo said idly and received a glowering look.

"Oh, really?" Her sweet tone had an undertone of arsenic.

He merely shifted his legs into a less cramped position. "It's an interesting city," he commented. "I think perhaps if you turn right at the next corner, then left two corners beyond, we'll find ourselves on the right track."

Juliet meticulously smoothed her carefully written directions when she'd have preferred to crumple them into a ball. "The book clerk specifically said—"

"I'm sure she's a lovely woman, but things seem a bit confused today." It didn't particularly bother him. The blast of a horn made her jolt. Amused, Carlo merely looked over. "As someone from New York City, you should be used to such things."

Juliet set her teeth. "I never drive in the city."

"I do. Trust me, *innamorata*."

Not on your life, Juliet thought, but turned right. It took nearly ten minutes in the crawling traffic to manage the next two blocks, but when she turned left she found herself, as Carlo had said, on the right track. She waited, resigned, for him to gloat.

"Rome moves faster" was all he said.

How could she anticipate him? she wondered. He didn't rage when you expected, didn't gloat when it was natural. With a sigh, she gave up. "Anything moves faster." She found herself in the right block, but parking space was at a premium. Weighing the ins and outs, Juliet swung over beside a car at the curb. "Look, Carlo, I'm going to have to drop you off. We're already running behind. I'll find a place to park and be back as soon as I can."

"You're the boss," he said, still cheerful after forty-five minutes of teeth-grinding traffic.

"If I'm not there in an hour, send up a flare."

"My money's on you."

Still cautious, she waited until she saw him swing into the bookstore before she fought her way into traffic again.

Twenty frustrating minutes later, Juliet walked into the dignified little bookstore herself. It was, she noted with a sinking stomach, too quiet and too empty. A clerk with a thin-striped tie and shined shoes greeted her.

"Good morning. May I help you?"

"I'm Juliet Trent, Mr. Franconi's publicist."

"Ah yes, right this way." He glided across the carpet to a set of wide steps. "Mr. Franconi's on the second level. It's unfortunate that the traffic and confusion have discouraged people from coming out. Of course, we rarely do these things." He gave her a smile and brushed a piece of lint from the sleeve of his dark blue jacket. "The last time was . . . let me see, in the fall. J. Jonathan Cooper was on tour. I'm sure you've heard of him. He wrote *Metaphysical Force and You.*"

Juliet bit back a sigh. When you hit dry ground, you just had to wait for the tide.

She spotted Carlo in a lovely little alcove on a curvy love seat. Beside him was a woman of about forty with a neat suit and pretty legs. Such things didn't warrant even a raised brow. But to Juliet's surprise, Carlo wasn't busy charming her. Instead, he was listening intently to a young boy who sat across from him.

"I've worked in the kitchens there for the last three summers. I'm not allowed to actually prepare anything, but I can watch. At home, I cook whenever I can, but with school and the job, it's mostly on weekends."

"Why?"

The boy stopped in midstream and looked blank. "Why?"

"Why do you cook?" Carlo asked. He acknowledged Juliet with a nod, then gave his attention back to the boy.

"Because . . ." The boy looked at his mother, then back at Carlo. "Well, it's important. I like to take things and put them together. You have to concentrate, you know, and be careful. But you can make something really terrific. It looks good and it smells good. It's . . . I don't know." His voice lowered in embarrassment. "Satisfying, I guess."

"Yes." Pleased, Carlo smiled at him. "That's a good answer."

"I have both your other books," the boy blurted out. "I've tried all your recipes. I even made your *pasta al tre formaggi* for this dinner party at my aunt's."

"And?"

"They liked it." The boy grinned. "I mean they really liked it."

"You want to study."

"Oh yeah." But the boy dropped his gaze to where his hands rubbed nervously over his knees. "Thing is we can't really afford college right now, so I'm hoping to get some restaurant work."

"In Denver?"

"Any place where I could start cooking instead of wiping up."

"We've taken up enough of Mr. Franconi's time." The boy's mother rose, noting there was now a handful of people milling around on the second level with Carlo's books in hand. "I want to thank you." She offered her hand to Carlo as he rose with her. "It meant a great deal to Steven to talk with you."

"My pleasure." Though he was gracious as always, he turned back to the boy. "Perhaps you'd give me your address. I know of some restaurant owners here in the States. Perhaps one of them needs an apprentice chef."

Stunned, Steven could do nothing but stare. "You're very kind." His mother took out a small pad and wrote on it. Her hand was steady, but when she handed the paper to Carlo and looked at him, he saw the emotion. He thought of his own mother. He took the paper, then her hand.

"You have a fortunate son, Mrs. Hardesty."

Thoughtful, Juliet watched them walk away, noting that Steven looked over his shoulder with the same, blank, baffled expression.

So he has a heart, Juliet decided, touched. A heart that wasn't altogether reserved for *amore*. But she saw Carlo slip the paper into his pocket and wondered if that would be the end of it.

The autographing wasn't a smashing success. Six books by Juliet's count. That had been bad enough, but then there'd been The Incident.

Looking at the all but empty store, Juliet had considered hitting the streets with a sign on her back, then the homey little woman had come along bearing all three of Carlo's books. Good for the ego, Juliet thought. That was before the woman had said something that caused Carlo's eyes to chill and his voice to freeze. All Juliet heard was the name La-Bare.

"I beg your pardon, Madame?" Carlo said in a tone Juliet had never heard from him. It could've sliced through steel.

"I said I keep all your books on a shelf in my kitchen, right next to André LaBare's. I love to cook."

"LaBare?" Carlo put his hand over his stack of books as a protective parent might over a threatened child. "You would dare put my work next to that—that peasant's?"

Thinking fast, Juliet stepped up and broke into the conversation. If ever she'd seen a man ready to murder, it was Carlo. "Oh, I see you have all of Mr. Franconi's books. You must love to cook."

"Well, yes I—"

"Wait until you try some of his new recipes. I had the *pasta con pesto* myself. It's wonderful." Juliet started to take the woman's books from under Carlo's hand and met with resistance and a stubborn look. She gave him one of her own and jerked the books away. "Your family's going to be just thrilled when you serve it," Juliet went on, keeping her voice pleasant as she led the woman out of the line of fire. "And the fettuccine . . ."

"LaBare is a swine." Carlo's voice was very clear and reached the stairs. The woman glanced back nervously.

"Men." Juliet made her voice a conspiratorial whisper. "Such egos."

"Yes." Gathering up her books, the woman hurried down the stairs and out of the store. Juliet waited until she was out of earshot before she pounced on Carlo.

"How could you?"

"How could I?" He rose, and though he skimmed just under six feet, he looked enormous. "She would *dare* speak that name to me? She would *dare* associate the work of an artist with the work of a jackass? LaBare—"

"At the moment, I don't give a damn who or what this La-Bare is." Juliet put a hand on his shoulder and shoved him back onto the love seat. "What I do care about is you scaring off the few customers we have. Now behave yourself."

He sat where he was only because he admired the way she'd ordered him to. Fascinating woman, Carlo decided, finding it wiser to think of her than LaBare. It was wiser to think of flood and famine than of LaBare.

The afternoon had dragged on and on, except for the young boy, Carlo thought and touched the paper in his pocket. He'd call Summer in Philadelphia about young Steven Hardesty.

But other than Steven and the woman who upped his blood pressure by speaking of LaBare, Carlo had found himself perilously close to boredom. Something he considered worse than illness.

He needed some activity, a challenge—even a small one. He glanced over at Juliet as she spoke with a clerk. That was no small challenge. The one thing he'd yet to be in Juliet's company was bored. She kept him interested. Sexually? Yes, that went without saying. Intellectually. That was a plus, a big one.

He understood women. It wasn't a matter of pride, but to Carlo's thinking, a matter of circumstance. He enjoyed women. As lovers, of course, but he also enjoyed them as companions, as friends, as associates. It was a rare thing when a man could find a woman to be all of those things. That's what he wanted from Juliet. He hadn't resolved it yet, only felt it. Convincing her to be his friend would be as challenging, and as rewarding, as it would be to convince her to be his lover.

No, he realized as he studied her profile. With this woman, a lover would come easier than a friend. He had two weeks left to accomplish both. With a smile, he decided to start the campaign in earnest.

Half an hour later, they were walking the three blocks to the parking garage Juliet had found.

"This time I drive," he told Juliet as they stepped inside the echoing gray building. When she started to object, he held out his hand for the keys. "Come, my love, I've just survived two hours of boredom. Why should you have all the fun?"

"Since you put it that way." She dropped the keys in his hand, relieved that whatever had set him off before was forgotten.

"So now we have a free evening."

"That's right." With a sigh she leaned back in her seat and waited for him to start the engine.

"We'll have dinner at seven. Tonight, I make the arrangements."

A hamburger in her room, an old movie and bed. Juliet let the wish come and go. Her job was to pamper and entertain as much as possible. "Whatever you like."

Carlo pulled out of the parking space with a squeal of tires that had Juliet bolting up. "I'll hold you to that, *cara*."

He zoomed out of the garage and turned right with hardly a pause. "Carlo—"

"We should have champagne to celebrate the end of our first week. You like champagne?"

"Yes, I—Carlo, the light's changing."

He breezed through the amber light, skimmed by the bumper of a battered compact and kept going. "Italian food. You have no objection?"

"No." She gripped the door handle until her knuckles turned white. "That truck!"

"Yes, I see it." He swerved around it, zipped through another light and cut a sharp right. "You have plans for the afternoon?"

Juliet pressed a hand to her throat, thinking she might be able to push out her voice. "I was thinking of making use of the hotel spa. If I live."

"Good. Me, I think I'll go shopping."

Juliet's teeth snapped together as he changed lanes in bumper-to-bumper traffic. "How do I notify next of kin?"

With a laugh, Carlo swung in front of their hotel. "Don't worry, Juliet. Have your whirlpool and your sauna. Knock on my door at seven."

She looked back toward the street. Pamper and entertain, she remembered. Did that include risking your life? Her supervisor would think so. "Maybe I should go with you."

"No, I insist." He leaned over, cupping her neck before she'd recovered enough to evade. "Enjoy," he murmured lightly against her lips. "And think of me as your skin grows warm and your muscles grow lax."

In self-defense, Juliet hurried out of the car. Before she could tell him to drive carefully, he was barreling back out into the street. She offered a prayer for Italian maniacs, then went inside.

By seven, she felt reborn. She'd sweated out fatigue in the sauna, shocked herself awake in the pool and splurged on a massage. Life, she thought as she splashed on her scent, had its good points after all. Tomorrow's flight to Dallas would be soon enough to draft her Denver report. Such as it was. Tonight, all she had to worry about was eating. After pressing a hand to her stomach, Juliet admitted she was more than ready for that.

With a quick check, she approved the simple ivory dress with the high collar and tiny pearly buttons. Unless Carlo had picked a hot dog stand it would suit. Grabbing her evening bag, she slipped across the hall to knock on Carlo's door. She only hoped he'd chosen some place close by. The last thing she wanted to do was fight Denver's downtown traffic again.

The first thing she noticed when Carlo opened his door were the rolled-up sleeves of his shirt. It was cotton, oversized and chic, but her eyes were drawn to the surprising cord of muscles in his forearms. The man did more than lift spoons and spatulas. The next thing she noticed was the erotic scents of spices and sauce.

"Lovely." Carlo took both hands and drew her inside. She pleased him, the smooth, creamy skin, the light, subtle scent, but more, the confused hesitation in her eyes as she glanced over to where the aroma of food was strongest.

"An interesting cologne," she managed after a moment. "But don't you think you've gotten a bit carried away?"

"*Innamorata,* you don't wear Franconi's spaghetti sauce, you absorb it." He kissed the back of her hand. "Anticipate it." Then the other. "Savor it." This time her palm.

A smart woman wasn't aroused by a man who used such flamboyant tactics. Juliet told herself that as the chills raced up her arms and down again. "Spaghetti sauce?" Slipping her hands from his, she linked them behind her back.

"I found a wonderful shop. The spices pleased me very much. The burgundy was excellent. Italian, of course."

"Of course." Cautious, she stepped farther into the suite. "You spent the day cooking?"

"Yes. Though you should remind me to speak to the hotel owner about the quality of this stove. All in all, it went quite well."

She told herself it wasn't wise to encourage him when she had no intention of eating alone with him in his suite. Perhaps if she'd been made out of rock she could have resisted wandering toward the little kitchenette. Her mouth watered. "Oh, God."

Delighted, Carlo slipped an arm around her waist and led her to the stove. The little kitchen itself was in shambles. She'd never seen so many pots and bowls and spoons jammed into a sink before. Counters were splattered and streaked. But the smells. It was heaven, pure and simple.

"The senses, Juliet. There's not one of us who isn't ruled by them. First, you smell, and you begin to imagine." His fingers moved lightly over her waist. "Imagine. You can almost taste it on your tongue from that alone."

"Hmm." Knowing she was making a mistake, she watched him take the lid off the pot on the stove. The tang made her close her eyes and just breathe. "Oh, Carlo."

"Then we look, and the imagination goes one step further." His fingers squeezed lightly at her waist until she opened her eyes and looked into the pot. Thick, red, simmering, the sauce was chunky with meat, peppers and spice. Her stomach growled.

"Beautiful, yes?"

"Yes." She wasn't aware that her tongue slid out over her lips in anticipation. He was.

"And we hear." Beside the sauce a pot of water began to

boil. In an expert move, he measured pasta by sight and slid it in. "Some things are destined to be mated." With a slotted spoon, he stirred gently. "Without each other, they are incomplete. But when merged . . ." he adjusted the flame, "a treasure. Pasta and the sauce. A man and a woman. Come, you'll have some burgundy. The champagne's for later."

It was time to take a stand, even though she took it by the stove. "Carlo, I had no idea this was what you intended. I think—"

"I like surprises." He handed her a glass half filled with dark red wine. "And I wanted to cook for you."

She wished he hadn't put it quite that way. She wished his voice wasn't so warm, so deep, like his eyes. Like the feelings he could urge out of her. "I appreciate that Carlo, it's just that—"

"You had your sauna?"

"Yes, I did. Now—"

"It relaxed you. It shows."

She sighed, sipping at the wine without thinking. "Yes."

"This relaxes me. We eat together tonight." He tapped his glass to hers. "Men and women have done so for centuries. It has become civilized."

Her chin tilted. "You're making fun of me."

"Yes." Ducking into the refrigerator, he pulled out a small tray. "First you'll try my antipasto. Your palate should be prepared."

Juliet chose a little chunk of zucchini. "I'd think you'd prefer being served in a restaurant."

"Now and then. There are times I prefer privacy." He set down the tray. As he did, she took a small step back. Interested, he lifted a brow. "Juliet, do I make you nervous?"

She swallowed zucchini. "Don't be absurd."

"Am I?" On impulse, he set his wine down as well and

took another step toward her. Juliet found her back pressed into the refrigerator.

"Carlo—"

"No, shh. We experiment." Gently, watching her, he brushed his lips over one cheek, then the other. He heard her breath catch then shudder out. Nerves—these he accepted. When a man and woman were attracted and close, there had to be nerves. Without them, passion was bland, like a sauce without spice.

But fear? Wasn't that what he saw in her eyes? Just a trace of it, only briefly. Nerves he'd use, play on, exploit. Fear was something different. It disturbed him, blocked him and, at the same time, moved him.

"I won't hurt you, Juliet."

Her eyes were direct again, level, though her hand was balled into a fist. "Won't you?"

He took her hand, slowly working it open. "No." In that moment, he promised both of them. "I won't. Now we'll eat."

Juliet held off the shudder until he'd turned around to stir and drain his pasta. Perhaps he wouldn't hurt her, she thought and recklessly tossed back her wine. But she might hurt herself.

He didn't fuss. He merely perfected. It occurred to Juliet, as she watched him put the last touches on the meal, that he was no different here in the little hotel kitchen than he'd been before the camera. Juliet added her help in the only way she'd have dared. She set the table.

Yes, it was a mistake, she told herself as she arranged plates. But no one but a fool would walk away from anything that smelled like that sauce. She wasn't a fool. She could handle herself. The moment of weak fear she'd felt in the kitchen was past. She'd enjoy a take-your-shoes-off meal, drink two glasses of really excellent burgundy, then go across the hall and catch eight hours' sleep. The merry-go-round would continue the next day.

She selected a marinated mushroom as Carlo brought in the platter of spaghetti. "Better," he said when she smiled at him. "You're ready to enjoy yourself."

With a shrug, Juliet sat. "If one of the top chefs in the world wants to cook me dinner, why should I complain?"

"*The* top," he corrected and gestured for her to serve herself. She did, barely conquering greed.

"Does it really relax you to stand in a kitchen?"

"It depends. Sometimes it relaxes, sometimes it excites. Always it pleases. No, don't cut." With a shake of his head, he reached over. "Americans. You roll it onto the fork."

"It falls off when I do."

"Like this." With his hands on her wrists, he guided her. Her pulse was steady, he noted, but not slow. "Now." Still holding her hand, he lifted the fork toward her mouth. "Taste."

As she did, he had the satisfaction of watching her face. Spices exploded on her tongue. Heat seeped through, mellowing to warmth. She savored it, even as she thought of the next bite. "Oh, this is no little sin."

Nothing could have delighted him more. With a laugh, he sat back and started on his own plate. "Small sins are only small pleasures. When Franconi cooks for you, food is not a basic necessity."

She was already rolling the next forkful. "You win that one. Why aren't you fat?"

"*Prego?*"

"If I could cook like this . . ." She tasted again and sighed. "I'd look like one of your meatballs."

With a chuckle, he watched her dig in. It pleased him to see someone he cared for enjoying what he'd created. After years of cooking, he'd never tired of it. "So, your mother didn't teach you to cook?"

"She tried." Juliet accepted a piece of the crusty bread he offered but set it aside as she rolled more spaghetti. First things first. "I never seemed to be very good at the things she wanted me to be good at. My sister plays the piano beautifully; I can barely remember the scales."

"So, what did you want to do instead of taking piano lessons?"

"Play third base." It came out so easily, it stunned her. Juliet had thought she'd buried that along with a dozen other childhood frustrations. "It just wasn't done," she said with a shrug. "My mother was determined to raise two well-rounded ladies who would become two well-rounded, successful wives. Win some, lose some."

"You think she's not proud of you?"

The question hit a target she hadn't known was exposed. Juliet reached for her wine. "It's not a matter of pride, but of disappointment, I suppose. I disappointed her; I confused my father. They still wonder what they did wrong."

"What they did wrong was not to accept what you are."

"Maybe," she murmured. "Or maybe I was determined to be something they couldn't accept. I've never worked it out."

"Are you unhappy with your life?"

Surprised, she glanced up. Unhappy? Sometimes frustrated, harassed and pressured. But unhappy? "No. No, I'm not."

"Then perhaps that's your answer."

Juliet took a moment to study him. He was more than gorgeous, more than sexy, more than all those qualities she'd once cynically attributed to him. "Carlo." For the first time she reached out to touch him, just his hand, but he thought it a giant step. "You're a very nice man."

"But of course I am." His fingers curled over hers because he couldn't resist. "I could give you references."

With a laugh, Juliet backed off. "I'm sure you could." With concentration, dedication and just plain greed, she cleared off her plate.

"Time for dessert."

"Carlo!" Moaning, Juliet pressed a hand to her stomach. "Please, don't be cruel."

"You'll like it." He was up and in the kitchen before she found the strength to refuse again. "It's an old, old, Italian tradition. Back to the empire. American cheesecake is sometimes excellent, but this . . ." He brought out a small, lovely cake with cherries dripping lavishly over it.

"Carlo, I'll die."

"Just a taste with the champagne." He popped the cork with an expert twist and poured two fresh glasses. "Go, sit on the sofa, be comfortable."

As she did, Juliet realized why the Romans traditionally slept after a meal. She could've curled up in a happy little ball and been unconscious in moments. But the champagne was lively, insistent.

"Here." He brought over one plate with a small slice. "We'll share."

"One bite," she told him, prepared to stand firm. Then she tasted. Creamy, smooth, not quite sweet, more nutty. Exquisite. With a sigh of surrender, Juliet took another. "Carlo, you're a magician."

"Artist," he corrected.

"Whatever you want." Using all the willpower she had left, Juliet exchanged the cake for champagne. "I really can't eat another bite."

"Yes, I remember. You don't believe in overindulgence." But he filled her glass again.

"Maybe not." She sipped, enjoying that rich, luxurious aura only champagne could give. "But now I've gotten a different perspective on indulgence." Slipping out of her shoes, she laughed over the rim of her glass. "I'm converted."

"You're lovely." The lights were low, the music soft, the scents lingering and rich. He thought of resisting. The fear that had been in her eyes demanded he think of it. But just now, she was relaxed, smiling. The desire he'd felt tug the moment he'd seen her had never completely gone away.

Senses were aroused, heightened, by a meal. That was something he understood perfectly. He also understood that a man and a woman should never ignore whatever pleasure they could give to each other.

So he didn't resist, but took her face in his hands. There he could watch her eyes, feel her skin, nearly taste her. This time he saw desire, not fear but wariness. Perhaps she was ready for lesson two.

She could have refused. The need to do so went through her mind. But his hands were so strong, so gentle on her skin. She'd never been touched like that before. She knew how he'd kiss her and the sense of anticipation mixed with nerves. She knew, and wanted.

Wasn't she a woman who knew her own mind? She took her hands to his wrists, but didn't push away. Her fingers curled around and held as she touched her mouth to his. For a moment they stayed just so, allowing themselves to savor that first taste, that first sensation. Then slowly, mutually, they asked for more.

She seemed so small when he held her that a man could forget how strong and competent she was. He found himself wanting to treasure. Desire might burn, but when she was so pliant, so vulnerable, he found himself compelled to show only gentleness.

Had any man ever shown her such care? Juliet's head

began to swim as his hands moved into her hair. Was there another man so patient? His heart was pounding against hers. She could feel it, like something wild and desperate. But his mouth was so soft, his hands so gentle. As though they'd been lovers for years, she thought dimly. And had all the time left in the world to continue to love.

No hurry, no rush, no frenzy. Just pleasure. Her heart opened reluctantly, but it opened. He began to pour through. When the phone shrilled, he swore and she sighed. They'd both been prepared to take all the chances.

"Only a moment," he murmured.

Still dreaming, she touched his cheek. "All right."

As he went to answer, she leaned back, determined not to think.

"*Cara!*" The enthusiasm in his voice, and the endearment had her opening her eyes again. With a warm laugh, Carlo went into a stream of Italian. Juliet had no choice but to think.

Affection. Yes, it was in his voice. She didn't have to understand the words. She looked around to see him smiling as he spoke to the woman on the other end. Resigned, Juliet picked up her champagne. It wasn't easy for her to admit she'd been a fool. Or for her to admit she'd been hurt.

She knew who he was. What he was. She knew how many women he'd seduced. Perhaps she was a woman who knew her own mind, and perhaps she wanted him. But she would never be eased into a long line of *others*. Setting down the champagne, she rose.

"*Si, si.* I love you."

Juliet turned away at the phrase I love you. How well it slid off his tongue, in any language. How little it meant, in any language.

"Interruptions. I'm sorry."

Juliet turned back and gave him her uncompromising look.

"Don't be. The dinner was marvelous, Carlo, thank you. You should be ready to check out by eight."

"A moment," he murmured. Crossing over, he took her by the arms. "What's this? You're angry."

"Of course not." She tried to back away and failed. It was easy to forget just how strong he was. "Why should I be?"

"Reasons aren't always necessary for a woman."

Though he'd said it in a simple tone that offered no insult, her eyes narrowed. "The expert. Well, let me tell you something about *this* woman, Franconi. She doesn't think much of a man who makes love to her one minute then pushes another lover in her face the next."

He held up his hand as he struggled to follow her drift. "I'm not following you. Maybe my English is failing."

"Your English is perfect," she spit at him. "From what I just heard, so's your Italian."

"My . . ." His grin broke out. "The phone."

"Yes. The phone. Now, if you'll excuse me."

He let her get as far as the door. "Juliet, I admit I'm hopelessly enamored of the woman I was speaking to. She's beautiful, intelligent, interesting and I've never met anyone quite like her."

Furious, Juliet whirled around. "How marvelous."

"I think so. It was my mother."

She walked back to snatch up the purse she'd nearly forgotten. "I'd think a man of your experience and imagination could do better."

"So I could." He held her again, not so gently, not so patiently. "If it was necessary. I don't make a habit to explain myself, and when I do, I don't lie."

She took a deep breath because she was abruptly certain she was hearing the truth. Either way, she'd been a fool. "I'm sorry. It's none of my business in any case."

"No, it's not." He took her chin in his hand and held it. "I saw fear in your eyes before. It concerned me. Now I think it wasn't me you were afraid of, but yourself."

"That's none of your business."

"No, it's not," he said again. "You appeal to me, Juliet, in many ways, and I intend to take you to bed. But we'll wait until you aren't afraid."

She wanted to rage at him. She wanted to weep. He saw both things clearly. "We have an early flight in the morning, Carlo."

He let her go, but stood where he was for a long time after he'd heard her door shut across the hall.

CHAPTER 6

Dallas was different. Dallas was Dallas without apology. Texas rich, Texas big and Texas arrogant. If it was the city that epitomized the state, then it did so with flair. Futuristic architecture and mind-twisting freeways abounded in a strange kind of harmony with the more sedate buildings downtown. The air was hot and carried the scents of oil, expensive perfumes and prairie dust. Dallas was Dallas, but it had never forgotten its roots.

Dallas held the excitement of a boomtown that was determined not to stop booming. It was full of down-home American energy that wasn't about to lag. As far as Juliet was concerned they could have been in downtown Timbuktu.

He acted as though nothing had happened—no intimate dinner, no arousal, no surrender, no cross words. Juliet wondered if he did it to drive her crazy.

Carlo was amiable, cooperative and charming. She knew better now. Under the amiability was a shaft of steel that wouldn't bend an inch. She'd seen it. One could say she'd felt it. It would have been a lie to say she didn't admire it.

Cooperative, sure. In his favor, Juliet had to admit that she'd never been on tour with anyone as willing to work without complaint. And touring was hard work, no matter how glamorous it looked on paper. Once you were into your second full week, it became difficult to smile unless you were cued. Carlo never broke his rhythm.

But he expected perfection—spelled his way—and wouldn't budge an inch until he got it.

Charming. No one could enchant a group of people with more style than Franconi. That alone made her job easier. No one would deny his charm unless they'd seen how cold his eyes could become. She had.

He had flaws like any other man, Juliet thought. Remembering that might help her keep an emotional distance. It always helped her to list the pros and cons of a situation, even if the situation was a man. The trouble was, though flawed, he was damn near irresistible.

And he knew it. That was something else she had to remind herself of.

His ego was no small matter. That was something she'd be wise to balance against his unrestricted generosity. Vanity about himself and his work went over the border into arrogance. It didn't hurt her sense of perspective to weigh that against his innate consideration for others.

But then, there was the way he smiled, the way he said her name. Even the practical, professional Juliet Trent had a difficult time finding a flaw to balance those little details.

The two days in Dallas were busy enough to keep her driving along on six hours' sleep, plenty of vitamins and oceans of coffee. They were making up for Denver all right. She had the leg cramps to prove it.

Four minutes on the national news, an interview with one of the top magazines in the country, three write-ups in the Dallas press and two autograph sessions that sold clean out. There was more, but those headed up her report. When she went back to New York, she'd go back in triumph.

She didn't want to think of the dinners with department

store executives that started at 10:00 P.M. and lasted until she was falling asleep in her bananas flambé. She couldn't bear to count the lunches of poached salmon or shrimp salad. She'd had to refill her pocket aspirin bottles and stock up on antacids. But it was worth it. She should have been thrilled.

She was miserable.

She was driving him mad. Polite, Carlo thought as they prepared to sit through another luncheon interview. Yes, she was polite. Her mother had taught her perfect manners even if she hadn't taught her to cook.

Competent? As far as he was concerned, he'd never known anyone, male or female, who was as scrupulously competent as Juliet Trent. He'd always admired that particular quality in a companion, insisted on it in an associate. Of course, Juliet was both. Precise, prompt, cool in a crisis and unflaggingly energetic. Admirable qualities all.

For the first time in his life he gave serious thought to strangling a woman.

Indifferent. That's what he couldn't abide. She acted as though there was nothing more between them than the next interview, the next television spot, the next plane. She acted as though there'd been no flare of need, of passion, of understanding between them. One would think she didn't want him with the same intensity that he wanted her.

He knew better. Didn't he?

He could remember her ripe, unhesitating response to him. Mouth to mouth, body to body. There'd been no indifference in the way her arms had held him. No, there'd been strength, pliancy, need, demand, but no indifference. Yet now . . .

They'd spent nearly two days exclusively in each other's company, but he'd seen nothing in her eyes, heard nothing in her voice that indicated more than a polite business association. They ate together, drove together, worked together. They did everything but sleep together.

He'd had his fill of polite. But he hadn't had his fill of Juliet.

He thought of her. It didn't bruise Carlo's pride to admit he thought of her a great deal. He often thought of women, and why not? When a man didn't think of a woman, he was better off dead.

He wanted her. It didn't worry him to admit that he wanted her more every time he thought of her. He'd wanted many women. He'd never believed in self-denial. When a man didn't want a woman, he *was* dead.

But . . . Carlo found it odd that "buts" so often followed any thoughts he had on Juliet. But he found himself dwelling on her more often than he'd have once considered healthy. Though he didn't mind wanting a woman until he ached, he found Juliet could make him ache more than he'd have once considered comfortable.

He might have been able to rationalize the threat to his health and comfort. But . . . she was so damn indifferent.

If he did nothing else in the short time they had left in Dallas, he was going to change that.

Lunch was white linen, heavy silver flatware and thin crystal. The room was done in tones of dusty rose and pastel greens. The murmur of conversation was just as quiet.

Carlo thought it a pity they couldn't have met the reporter at one of the little Tex-Mex restaurants over Mexican beer with chili and nachos. Briefly, he promised himself he'd rectify that in Houston.

He barely noticed the reporter was young and running on nerves as they took their seats. He'd decided, no matter what it took, he'd break through Juliet's inflexible shield of politeness before they stood up again. Even if he had to play dirty.

"I'm so happy you included Dallas on your tour, Mr. Franconi," the reporter began, already reaching for her water glass to clear her throat. "Mr. Van Ness sends his apologies. He was looking forward to meeting you."

Carlo smiled at her, but his mind was on Juliet. "Yes?"

"Mr. Van Ness is the food editor for the *Tribune*." Juliet spread her napkin over her lap as she gave Carlo information she'd related less than fifteen minutes before. She sent him the friendliest of smiles and hoped he felt the barbs in it. "Ms. Tribly is filling in for him."

"Of course." Carlo smoothed over the gap of attention. "Charmingly, I'm sure."

As a woman she wasn't immune to that top-cream voice. As a reporter, she was well aware of the importance of her assignment. "It's all pretty confused." Ms. Tribly wiped damp hands on her napkin. "Mr. Van Ness is having a baby. That is, what I mean is, his wife went into labor just a couple of hours ago."

"So, we should drink to them." Carlo signaled a waiter. "Margaritas?" He phrased the question as a statement, earned a cool nod from Juliet and a grateful smile from the reporter.

Determined to pull off her first really big assignment, Ms. Tribly balanced a pad discreetly on her lap. "Have you been enjoying your tour through America, Mr. Franconi?"

"I always enjoy America." Lightly he ran a finger over the back of Juliet's hand before she could move it out of reach. "Especially in the company of a beautiful woman." She started to slide her hand away then felt it pinned under his. For a man who could whip up the most delicate of soufflés, his hands were as strong as a boxer's.

Wills sparked, clashed and fumed. Carlo's voice remained mild, soft and romantic. "I must tell you, Ms. Tribly, Juliet is an extraordinary woman. I couldn't manage without her."

"Mr. Franconi's very kind." Though Juliet's voice was as mild and quiet as his, the nudge she gave him under the table wasn't. "I handle the details; Mr. Franconi's the artist."

"We make an admirable team, wouldn't you say, Ms. Tribly?"

"Yes." Not quite sure how to handle that particular line, she veered off to safer ground. "Mr. Franconi, besides writing cookbooks, you own and run a successful restaurant in Rome and occasionally travel to prepare a special dish. A few months ago, you flew to a yacht in the Aegean to cook minestrone for Dimitri Azares, the shipping magnate."

"His birthday," Carlo recalled. "His daughter arranged a surprise." Again, his gaze skimmed over the woman whose hand he held. "Juliet will tell you, I'm fond of surprises."

"Yes, well." Ms. Tribly reached for her water glass again. "Your schedule's so full and exciting. I wonder if you still enjoy the basics as far as cooking."

"Most people think of cooking as anything from a chore to a hobby. But as I've told Juliet—" His fingers twined possessively with hers "—food is a basic need. Like making love, it should appeal to all the senses. It should excite, arouse, satisfy." He slipped his thumb around to skim over her palm. "You remember, Juliet?"

She'd tried to forget, had told herself she could. Now with that light, insistent brush of thumb, he was bringing it all back. "Mr. Franconi is a strong believer in the sensuality of food. His unusual flair for bringing this out has made him one of the top chefs in the world."

"Grazie, mi amore," he murmured and brought her stiff hand to his lips.

She pressed her shoe down on the soft leather of his loafers and hoped she ground bones. "I think you, and your readers, will find that Mr. Franconi's book, *The Italian Way,* is a really stunning example of his technique, his style and his opinions, written in such a way that the average person following one of his recipes step-by-step can create something very special."

When their drinks were served, Juliet gave another tug

on her hand thinking she might catch him off guard. She should have known better.

"To the new baby." He smiled over at Juliet. "It's always a pleasure to drink to life in all its stages."

Ms. Tribly sipped lightly at her margarita in a glass the size of a small birdbath. "Mr. Franconi, have you actually cooked and tasted every recipe that's in your book?"

"Of course." Carlo enjoyed the quick tang of his drink. There was a time for the sweet, and a time for the tart. His laugh came low and smooth as he looked at Juliet. "When something's mine, there's nothing I don't learn about it. A meal, Ms. Tribly, is like a love affair."

She broke the tip of her pencil and hurriedly dug out another. "A love affair?"

"Yes. It begins slowly, almost experimentally. Just a taste, to whet the appetite, to stir the anticipation. Then the flavor changes, perhaps something light, something cool to keep the senses stirred, but not overwhelmed. Then there's the spice, the meat, the variety. The senses are aroused; the mind is focused on the pleasure. It should be lingered over. But finally, there's dessert, the time of indulgence." When he smiled at Juliet, there was no mistaking his meaning. "It should be enjoyed slowly, savored, until the palate is satisfied and the body sated."

Ms. Tribly swallowed. "I'm going to buy a copy of your book for myself."

With a laugh, Carlo picked up his menu. "Suddenly, I have a huge appetite."

Juliet ordered a small fruit salad and picked at it for thirty minutes.

"I've really got to get back." After polishing off her meal and an apricot tart, Ms. Tribly gathered up her pad. "I can't tell you how much I've enjoyed this, Mr. Franconi. I'm never going to sit down to pot roast with the same attitude again."

Amused, Carlo rose. "It was a pleasure."

"I'll be glad to send a clipping of the article to your office, Ms. Trent."

"I'd appreciate that." Juliet offered her hand, surprised when the reporter held it an extra moment.

"You're a lucky woman. Enjoy the rest of your tour, Mr. Franconi."

"Arrivederci." He was still smiling when he sat down to finish his coffee.

"You put on a hell of a show, Franconi."

He'd been expecting the storm. Anticipating it. "Yes, I think I did my—what was it you called it? Ah yes, my spiel very well."

"It was more like a three-act play." With calm, deliberate movements, she signed the check. "But the next time, don't cast me unless you ask first."

"Cast you?"

His innocence was calculated to infuriate. He never missed his mark. "You gave that woman the very clear impression that we were lovers."

"Juliet, I merely gave her the very correct impression that I respect and admire you. What she takes from that isn't my responsibility."

Juliet rose, placed her napkin very carefully on the table and picked up her briefcase. "Swine."

Carlo watched her walk out of the restaurant. No endearment could have pleased him more. When a woman called a man a swine, she wasn't indifferent. He was whistling when he walked out to join her. It pleased him even more to see her fumbling with the keys of the rented car parked at the curb. When a woman was indifferent, she didn't swear at inanimate objects.

"Would you like me to drive to the airport?"

"No." Swearing again, she jabbed the key into the lock.

She'd control her temper. She would control it. Like hell. Slamming both hands down on the roof of the car, she stared at him. "Just what was the point of that little charade?"

Squisito, he thought briefly. Her eyes were a dangerous blade-sharp green. He'd discovered he preferred a woman with temper. "Charade?"

"All that hand-holding, those intimate looks you were giving me?"

"It's not a charade that I enjoy holding your hand, and that I find it impossible not to look at you."

She refused to argue with the car between them. In a few quick steps she was around the hood and toe-to-toe with him. "It was completely unprofessional."

"Yes. It was completely personal."

It was going to be difficult to argue at all if he turned everything she said to his own advantage.

"Don't ever do it again."

"Madonna." His voice was very mild, his move very calculated. Juliet found herself boxed in between him and the car. "Orders I'll take from you when they have to do with schedules and plane flights. When it comes to more personal things, I do as I choose."

It wasn't something she'd expected; that's why she lost her advantage. Juliet would tell herself that again and again— later. He had her by both shoulders and his eyes never left hers as he gave her a quick jerk. It wasn't the smooth, calculated seduction she'd have anticipated from him. It was rough, impulsive and enervating.

His mouth was on hers, all demand. His hands held her still, all power. She had no time to stiffen, to struggle or to think. He took her with him quickly, through a journey of heat and light. She didn't resist. Later, when she would tell herself she had, it would be a lie.

There were people on the sidewalk, cars in the street.

Juliet and Carlo were unaware of everything. The heat of a Dallas afternoon soaked into the concrete beneath them. It blasted the air until it hummed. They were concerned with a fire of their own.

Her hands were at his waist, holding on, letting go. A car streaked by, country rock blasting through open windows. She never heard it. Though she'd refused wine at lunch, she tasted it on his tongue and was intoxicated.

Later, much later, he'd take time to think about what was happening. It wasn't the same. Part of him already knew and feared because it wasn't the same. Touching her was different than touching other women. Tasting her—lightly, deeply, teasingly—just tasting her was different than tasting other women. The feelings were new, though he'd have sworn he'd experienced all the feelings that any man was capable of.

He knew about sensations. He incorporated them in his work and in his life. But they'd never had this depth before. A man who found more and didn't reach for it was a fool.

He knew about intimacy. He expected, demanded it in everything he did. But it had never had this strength before.

New experiences were not to be refused, but explored and exploited. If he felt a small, nagging fear, he could ignore it. For now.

Later. They clung to each other and told themselves they'd think later. Time was unimportant after all. Now held all the meaning necessary.

He took his mouth from hers, but his hands held her still. It shocked him to realize they weren't quite steady. Women had made him ache. Women had made him burn. But no woman had ever made him tremble. "We need a place," he murmured. "Quiet, private. It's time to stop pretending this isn't real."

She wanted to nod, to simply put herself completely in his

hands. Wasn't that the first step in losing control over your own life? "No, Carlo." Her voice wasn't as strong as she would have liked but she didn't back away. "We've got to stop mixing personal feelings with business. We've got just under two weeks to go on the road."

"I don't give a damn if it's two days or two years. I want to spend it making love with you."

She brought herself back enough to remember they were standing on a public street in the middle of afternoon traffic. "Carlo, this isn't the time to discuss it."

"Now is always the time. Juliet—" He cupped her face in his hand. "It's not me you're fighting."

He didn't have to finish the thought. She was all too aware that the war was within herself. What she wanted, what was wise. What she needed, what was safe. The tug-of-war threatened to split her apart, and the two halves, put back together, would never equal the whole she understood.

"Carlo, we have a plane to catch."

He said something soft and pungent in Italian. "You'll talk to me."

"No." She lifted her hands to grip his forearms. "Not about this."

"Then we'll stay right here until you change your mind."

They could both be stubborn, and with stubbornness, they could both get nowhere. "We have a schedule."

"We have a great deal more than that."

"No, we don't." His brow lifted. "All right then, we can't. We have a plane to catch."

"We'll catch your plane, Juliet. But we'll talk in Houston."

"Carlo, don't push me into a corner."

"Who pushes?" he murmured. "Me or you?"

She didn't have an easy answer. "What I'll do is arrange for someone else to come out and finish the tour with you."

He only shook his head. "No, you won't. You're too ambitious. Leaving a tour in the middle wouldn't look good for you."

She set her teeth. He knew her too well already. "I'll get sick."

This time he smiled. "You're too proud. Running away isn't possible for you."

"It's not a matter of running." But of survival, she thought and quickly changed the phrase. "It's a matter of priorities."

He kissed her again, lightly. "Whose?"

"Carlo, we have business."

"Yes, of different sorts. One has nothing to do with the other."

"To me they do. Unlike you, I don't go to bed with everyone I'm attracted to."

Unoffended, he grinned. "You flatter me, *cara*."

She could have sighed. How like him to make her want to laugh while she was still furious. "Purely unintentional."

"I like you when you bare your teeth."

"Then you're going to enjoy the next couple of weeks." She pushed his hands away. "It's a long ride to the airport, Carlo. Let's get going."

Amiable as ever, he pulled his door open. "You're the boss."

A foolish woman might've thought she'd won a victory.

CHAPTER 7

Juliet was an expert on budgeting time. It was her business every bit as much as promotion. So, if she could budget time, she could just as easily overbudget it when the circumstances warranted. If she did her job well enough, hustled fast enough, she could create a schedule so tight that there could be no time for talk that didn't directly deal with business. She counted on Houston to cooperate.

Juliet had worked with Big Bill Bowers before. He was a brash, warmhearted braggart who handled special events for Books, Etc., one of the biggest chains in the country. Big Bill had Texas sewed up and wasn't ashamed to say so. He was partial to long, exaggerated stories, ornate boots and cold beer.

Juliet liked him because he was sharp and tough and invariably made her job easier. On this trip, she blessed him because he was also long-winded and gregarious. He wouldn't give her or Carlo many private moments.

From the minute they arrived at Houston International, the six-foot-five, two-hundred-and-sixty-pound Texan made it his business to entertain. There was a crowd of people waiting at the end of the breezeway, some already packed together and chatting, but there was no overlooking Big Bill. You only had to look for a Brahma bull in a Stetson.

"Well now, there's little Juliet. Pretty as ever."

Juliet found herself caught in a good-natured, rib-cracking bear hug. "Bill." She tested her lungs gingerly as she drew away. "It's always good to be back in Houston. You look great."

"Just clean living, honey." He let out a boom of a laugh that turned heads. Juliet found her mood lifting automatically.

"Carlo Franconi, Bill Bowers. Be nice to him," she added with a grin. "He's not only big, he's the man who'll promote your books for the largest chain in the state."

"Then I'll be very nice." Carlo offered his hand and met an enormous, meaty paw.

"Glad you could make it." The same meaty hand gave Carlo a friendly pat on the back that could have felled a good-sized sapling. Juliet gave Carlo points for not taking a nose-dive.

"It's good to be here" was all he said.

"Never been to Italy myself, but I'm partial to Eyetalian cooking. The wife makes a hell of a pot of spaghetti. Let me take that for you." Before Carlo could object, Bill had hefted his big leather case. Juliet couldn't prevent the smirk when Carlo glanced down at the case as though it were a small child boarding a school bus for the first time.

"Car's outside. We'll just pick up your bags and get going. Airports and hospitals, can't stand 'em." Bill started toward the terminal in his big, yard-long strides. "Hotel's all ready for you; I checked this morning."

Juliet managed to keep up though she still wore three-inch heels. "I knew I could depend on you, Bill. How's Betty?"

"Mean as ever," he said proudly of his wife. "With the kids up and gone, she's only got me to order around."

"But you're still crazy about her."

"A man gets used to mean after a while." He grinned, showing one prominent gold tooth. "No need to go by the hotel straight off. We'll show Carlo here what Houston's all about." As he walked he swung Carlo's case at his side.

"I'd like that." Diplomatically, Carlo moved closer to his side. "I could take that case . . ."

"No need for that. What you got in here, boy? Weighs like a steer."

"Tools," Juliet put in with an innocent smile. "Carlo's very temperamental."

"Man can't be too temperamental about his tools," Bill said with a nod. He tipped his hat at a young woman with a short skirt and lots of leg. "I've still got the same hammer my old man gave me when I was eight."

"I'm just as sentimental about my spatulas," Carlo murmured. But he hadn't, Juliet noted, missed the legs, either.

"You got a right." A look passed between the two men that was essential male and pleased. Juliet decided it had more to do with long smooth thighs than tools. "Now, I figured you two must've had your fill of fancy restaurants and creamed chicken by now. Having a little barbecue over at my place. You can take off your shoes, let down your hair and eat real food."

Juliet had been to one of Bill's *little* barbecues before. It meant grilling a whole steer along with several chickens and the better part of a pig, then washing it all down with a couple hundred gallons of beer. It also meant she wouldn't see her hotel room for a good five hours. "Sounds great. Carlo, you haven't lived until you've tasted one of Bill's steaks grilled over mesquite."

Carlo slipped a hand over her elbow. "Then we should live first." The tone made her turn her head and meet the look. "Before we attend to business."

"That's the ticket." Bill stopped in front of the conveyor belt. "Just point 'em out and we'll haul 'em in."

They lived, mingling at Bill's little barbecue with another hundred guests. Music came from a seven-piece band that never seemed to tire. Laughter and splashing rose up from a pool separated from the patio by a spread of red flowering bushes that smelled of spice and heat. Above all was the scent of grilled meat, sauce and smoke. Juliet ate twice as much as she would normally have considered because her host filled her plate then kept an eagle eye on her.

It should have pleased her that Carlo was surrounded by a dozen or so Texas ladies in bathing suits and sundresses who had suddenly developed an avid interest in cooking. But, she thought nastily, most of them wouldn't know a stove from a can opener.

It should have pleased her that she had several men dancing attendance on her. She was barely able to keep the names and faces separate as she watched Carlo laugh with a six-foot brunette in two minuscule ribbons of cloth.

The music was loud, the air heavy and warm. Giving into necessity, Juliet had dug a pair of pleated shorts and a crop top out of her bag and changed. It occurred to her that it was the first time since the start of the tour that she'd been able to sit out in the sun, soak up rays and not have a pad and pencil in her hand.

Though the blond beside her with the gleaming biceps was in danger of becoming both a bore and a nuisance, she willed herself to enjoy the moment.

It was the first time Carlo had seen her in anything other than her very proper suits. He'd already concluded, by the way she walked, that her legs were longer than one might think from her height. He hadn't been wrong. They seemed to start at her waist and continued down, smooth, slim and New York pale. The statuesque brunette beside him might not have existed for all the attention he paid her.

It wasn't like him to focus on a woman yards away when there was one right beside him. Carlo knew it, but not what to do about it. The woman beside him smelled of heat and musk—heavy and seductive. It made him think that Juliet's scent was lighter, but held just as much punch.

She had no trouble relaxing with other men. Carlo tipped back a beer as he watched her fold those long legs under her and laugh with the two men sitting on either side of her. She didn't stiffen when the young, muscle-bound hunk on her left put his hand on her shoulder and leaned closer.

It wasn't like him to be jealous. As emotional as he was, Carlo had never experienced that particular sensation. He'd also felt that a woman had just as much right to flirt and experiment as he did. He found that particular rule didn't apply to Juliet. If she let that slick-skinned, weight-lifting *buffone* put his hand on her again . . .

He didn't have time to finish the thought. Juliet laughed again, set aside her plate and rose. Carlo couldn't hear whatever she'd said to the man beside her, but she strolled into the sprawling ranch house. Moments later, the burnished, bare-chested man rose and followed her.

"Maledetto!"

"What?" The brunette stopped in the middle of what she'd thought was an intimate conversation.

Carlo barely spared her a glance. *"Scusi."* Muttering, he strode off in the direction Juliet had taken. There was murder in his eye.

Fed up with fending off the attentions of Big Bill's hot-shot young neighbor, Juliet slipped into the house through the kitchen. Her mood might have been foul, but she congratulated herself on keeping her head. She hadn't taken a chunk out of the free-handed, self-appointed Adonis. She hadn't snarled out loud even once in Carlo's direction.

Attending to business always helped steady her temper. With a check of her watch, Juliet decided she could get one collect call through to her assistant at home. She'd no more than picked up the receiver from the kitchen wall phone than she was lifted off her feet.

"Ain't much to you. But it sure is a pleasure to look at what there is."

She barely suppressed the urge to come back with her elbow. "Tim." She managed to keep her voice pleasant while she thought how unfortunate it was that most of his muscle was from the neck up. "You're going to have to put me down so I can make my call."

"It's a party, sweetheart." Shifting her around with a flex of muscle, he set her on the counter. "No need to go calling anybody when you've got me around."

"You know what I think?" Juliet gauged that she could give him a quick kick below the belt, but tapped his shoulder instead. After all, he was Bill's neighbor. "I think you should get back out to the party before all the ladies miss you."

"Got a better idea." He leaned forward, boxing her in with a hand on each side. His teeth gleamed in the style of the best toothpaste ads. "Why don't you and I go have a little party of our own? I imagine you New York ladies know how to have fun."

If she hadn't considered him such a jerk, she'd have been insulted for women in general and New York in particular. Patiently, Juliet considered the source. "We New York ladies," she said calmly, "know how to say no. Now back off, Tim."

"Come on, Juliet." He hooked a finger in the neck of her top. "I've got a nice big water bed down the street."

She put a hand on his wrist. Neighbor or not, she was going to belt him. "Why don't you go take a dive."

He only grinned as his hand slid up her leg. "Just what I had in mind."

"Excuse me." Carlo's voice was soft as a snake from the doorway. "If you don't find something else to do with your hands quickly, you might lose the use of them."

"Carlo." Her voice was sharp, but not with relief. She wasn't in the mood for a knight-in-armor rescue.

"The lady and I're having a private conversation." Tim flexed his pectorals. "Take off."

With his thumbs hooked in his pockets, Carlo strolled over. Juliet noted he looked as furious as he had over the canned basil. In that mood, there was no telling what he'd do. She swore, let out a breath and tried to avoid a scene. "Why don't we all go outside?"

"Excellent." Carlo held out a hand to help her down. Before she could reach for it, Tim blocked her way.

"You go outside, buddy. Juliet and I haven't finished talking."

Carlo inclined his head then shifted his gaze to Juliet. "Have you finished talking?"

"Yes." She'd have slid off the counter, but that would have put her on top of Tim's shoulders. Frustrated, she sat where she was.

"Apparently Juliet is finished." Carlo's smile was all amiability, but his eyes were flat and cold. "You seem to be blocking her way."

"I told you to take off." Big and annoyed, he grabbed Carlo by the lapels.

"Cut it out, both of you." With a vivid picture of Carlo bleeding from the nose and mouth, Juliet grabbed a cookie jar shaped like a ten-gallon hat. Before she could use it, Tim grunted and bent over from the waist. As he gasped, clutching his stomach, Juliet only stared.

"You can put that down now," Carlo said mildly. "It's time

we left." When she didn't move, he took the jar himself, set it aside, then lifted her from the counter. "You'll excuse us," he said pleasantly to the groaning Tim, then led Juliet outside.

"What did you do?"

"What was necessary."

Juliet looked back toward the kitchen door. If she hadn't seen it for herself . . . "You hit him."

"Not very hard." Carlo nodded to a group of sunbathers. "All his muscle is in his chest and his brain."

"But—" She looked down at Carlo's hands. They were lean-fingered and elegant with the flash of a diamond on the pinky. Not hands one associated with self-defense. "He was awfully big."

Carlo lifted a brow as he took his sunglasses back out of his pocket. "Big isn't always an advantage. The neighborhood where I grew up was an education. Are you ready to leave?"

No, his voice wasn't pleasant, she realized. It was cold. Ice cold. Instinctively hers mirrored it. "I suppose I should thank you."

"Unless of course you enjoyed being pawed. Perhaps Tim was just acting on the signals you were sending out."

Juliet stopped in her tracks. "What signals?"

"The ones women send out when they want to be pursued."

Thinking she could bring her temper to order, she gave herself a moment. It didn't work. "He might have been bigger than you," she said between her teeth. "But I think you're just as much of an ass. You're very much alike."

The lenses of his glasses were smoky, but she saw his eyes narrow. "You compare what's between us with what happened in there?"

"I'm saying some men don't take no for an answer graciously. You might have a smoother style, Carlo, but you're after the same thing, whether it's a roll in the hay or a cruise on a water bed."

He dropped his hand from her arm, then very deliberately tucked both in his pockets. "If I've mistaken your feelings, Juliet, I apologize. I'm not a man who finds it necessary or pleasurable to pressure a woman. Do you wish to leave or stay?"

She felt a great deal of pressure—in her throat, behind her eyes. She couldn't afford the luxury of giving into it. "I'd like to get to the hotel. I still have some work to do tonight."

"Fine." He left her there to find their host.

Three hours later, Juliet admitted working was impossible. She'd tried all the tricks she knew to relax. A half hour in a hot tub, quiet music on the radio while she watched the sun set from her hotel window. When relaxing failed, she went over the Houston schedule twice. They'd be running from 7:00 A.M. to 5:00 P.M., almost nonstop. Their flight to Chicago took off at 6:00.

There'd be no time to discuss, think or worry about anything that had happened within the last twenty-four hours. That's what she wanted. Yet when she tried to work on the two-day Chicago stand, she couldn't. All she could do was think about the man a few steps across the hall.

She hadn't realized he could be so cold. He was always so full of warmth, of life. True, he was often infuriating, but he infuriated with verve. Now, he'd left her in a vacuum.

No. Tossing her notebook aside, Juliet dropped her chin in her hand. No, she'd put herself there. Maybe she could have stood it if she'd been right. She'd been dead wrong. She hadn't sent any signals to the idiot Tim, and Carlo's opinion on that still made her steam, but . . . But she hadn't even thanked him for helping her when, whether she liked to admit it or not, she'd needed help. It didn't sit well with her to be in debt.

With a shrug, she rose from the table and began to pace the room. It might be better all around if they finished off the tour with him cold and distant. There'd certainly be fewer personal problems that way because there'd be nothing personal between them. There'd be no edge to their relationship because they wouldn't have a relationship. Logically, this little incident was probably the best thing that could have happened. It hardly mattered if she'd been right or wrong as long as the result was workable.

She took a glimpse around the small, tidy, impersonal room where she'd spend little more than eight hours, most of it asleep.

No, she couldn't stand it.

Giving in, Juliet stuck her room key in the pocket of her robe.

Women had made him furious before. Carlo counted on it to keep life from becoming too tame. Women had frustrated him before. Without frustrations, how could you fully appreciate success?

But hurt. That was something no woman had ever done to him before. He'd never considered the possibility. Frustration, fury, passion, laughter, shouting. No man who'd known so many women—mother, sisters, lovers—expected a relationship without them. Pain was a different matter.

Pain was an intimate emotion. More personal than passion, more elemental than anger. When it went deep, it found places inside you that should have been left alone.

It had never mattered to him to be considered a rogue, a rake, a playboy—whatever term was being used for a man who appreciated women. Affairs came and went, as affairs were supposed to. They lasted no longer than the passion that conceived them. He was a careful man, a caring man. A lover became a friend as desire waned. There might be spats and hard words during the storm of an affair, but he'd never ended one that way.

It occurred to him that he'd had more spats, more hard words with Juliet than with any other woman. Yet they'd never been lovers. Nor would they be. After pouring a glass of wine, he sat back in a deep chair and closed his eyes. He wanted no woman who compared him with a muscle-bound idiot, who confused passion for lust. He wanted no woman who compared the beauty of lovemaking to—what was it?—a cruise on a water bed. *Dio!*

He wanted no woman who could make him ache so—in the middle of the night, in the middle of the day. He wanted no woman who could bring him pain with a few harsh words.

God, he wanted Juliet.

He heard the knock on the door and frowned. By the time he'd set his glass aside and stood, it came again.

If Juliet hadn't been so nervous, she might have thought of something witty to say about the short black robe Carlo wore with two pink flamingos twining up one side. As it was, she stood in her own robe and bare feet with her fingers linked together.

"I'm sorry," she said when he opened the door.

He stepped back. "Come in, Juliet."

"I had to apologize." She let out a deep breath as she walked into the room. "I was awful to you this afternoon, and you'd helped me out of a very tricky situation with a minimum of fuss. I was angry when you insinuated that I'd led that—that idiot on in some way. I had a right to be." She folded her arms under her chest and paced the room. "It was an uncalled for remark, and insulting. Even if by the remotest possibility it had been true, you had no right to talk. After all, you were basking in your own harem."

"Harem?" Carlo poured another glass of wine and offered it.

"With that amazon of a brunette leading the pack." She sipped, gestured with the glass and sipped again. "Everywhere we go, you've got half a dozen women nipping at your ankles, but do I say a word?"

"Well, you—"

"And once, just once, I have a problem with some creep with an overactive libido, and you assume I asked for it. I thought that kind of double standard was outdated even in Italy."

Had he ever known a woman who could change his moods so quickly? Thinking it over, and finding it to his taste, Carlo studied his wine. "Juliet, did you come here to apologize, or demand that I do so?"

She scowled at him. "I don't know why I came, but obviously it was a mistake."

"Wait." He held up a hand before she could storm out again. "Perhaps it would be wise if I simply accepted the apology you came in with."

Juliet sent him a killing look. "You can take the apology I came in with and—"

"And offer you one of my own," he finished. "Then we'll be even."

"I didn't encourage him," she murmured. And pouted. He'd never seen that sulky, utterly feminine look on her face before. It did several interesting things to his system.

"And I'm not looking for the same thing he was." He came to her then, close enough to touch. "But very much more."

"Maybe I know that," she whispered, but took a step away. "Maybe I'd like to believe it. I don't understand affairs,

Carlo." With a little laugh, she dragged her hand through her hair and turned away. "I should; my father had plenty of them. Discreet," she added with a lingering taste of bitterness. "My mother could always turn a blind eye as long as they were discreet."

He understood such things, had seen them among both friends and relatives, so he understood the scars and disillusionments that could be left. "Juliet, you're not your mother."

"No." She turned back, head up. "No, I've worked long and hard to be certain I'm not. She's a lovely, intelligent woman who gave up her career, her self-esteem, her independence to be no more than a glorified housekeeper because my father wanted it. He didn't want a wife of his to work. A wife of his," she repeated. "What a phrase. Her job was to take care of him. That meant having dinner on the table at six o'clock every night, and his shirts folded in his drawer. He—damn, he's a good father, attentive, considerate. He simply doesn't believe a man should shout at a woman or a girl. As a husband, he'd never forget a birthday, an anniversary. He's always seen to it that she was provided for in the best material fashion, but he dictated my mother's lifestyle. While he was about it, he enjoyed a very discreet string of women."

"Why does your mother stay his wife?"

"I asked her that a few years ago, before I moved away to New York. She loves him." Juliet stared into her wine. "That's reason enough for her."

"Would you rather she'd have left him?"

"I'd rather she'd have been what she could be. What she might've been."

"The choice was hers, Juliet. Just as your life is yours."

"I don't want to ever be bound to anyone, *anyone* who could humiliate me that way." She lifted her head again. "I won't put myself in my mother's position. Not for anyone."

"Do you see all relationships as being so imbalanced?"

With a shrug, she drank again. "I suppose I haven't seen so many of them."

For a moment he was silent. Carlo understood fidelity, the need for it, and the lack of it. "Perhaps we have something in common. I don't remember my father well, I saw him little. He, too, was unfaithful to my mother."

She looked over at him, but he didn't see any surprise in her face. It was as though she expected such things. "But he committed his adultery with the sea. For months he'd be gone, while she raised us, worked, waited. When he'd come home, she'd welcome him. Then he'd go again, unable to resist. When he died, she mourned. She loved him, and made her choice."

"It's not fair, is it?"

"No. Did you think love was?"

"It's not something I want."

He remembered once another woman, a friend, telling him the same thing when she was in turmoil. "We all want love, Juliet."

"No." She shook her head with the confidence born of desperation. "No, affection, respect, admiration, but not love. It steals something from you."

He looked at her as she stood in the path of the lamplight. "Perhaps it does," he murmured. "But until we love, we can't be sure we needed what was lost."

"Maybe it's easier for you to say that, to think that. You've had many lovers."

It should have amused him. Instead, it seemed to accent a void he hadn't been aware of. "Yes. But I've never been in love. I have a friend—" again he thought of Summer "—once she told me love was a merry-go-round. Maybe she knew best."

Juliet pressed her lips together. "And an affair?"

Something in her voice had him looking over. For the

second time he went to her, but slowly. "Perhaps it's just one ride on the carousel."

Because her fingers weren't steady, Juliet set down the glass. "We understand each other."

"In some ways."

"Carlo—" She hesitated, then admitted the decision had already been made before she crossed the hall. "Carlo, I've never taken much time for carousels, but I do want you."

How should he handle her? Odd, he'd never had to think things through so carefully before. With some women, he'd have been flamboyant, sweeping her up, carrying her off. With another he might have been impulsive, tumbling with her to the carpet. But nothing he'd ever done seemed as important as the first time with Juliet.

Words for a woman had always come easily to him. The right phrase, the right tone had always come as naturally as breathing. He could think of nothing. Even a murmur might spoil the simplicity of what she'd said to him and how she'd said it. So he didn't speak.

He kissed her where they stood, not with the raging passion he knew she could draw from him, not with the hesitation she sometimes made him feel. He kissed her with the truth and the knowledge that longtime lovers often experience. They came to each other with separate needs, separate attitudes, but with this, they locked out the past. Tonight was for the new, and for renewing.

She'd expected the words, the flash and style that seemed so much a part of him. Perhaps she'd even expected something of triumph. Again, he gave her the different and the fresh with no more than the touch of mouth to mouth.

The thought came to her, then was discounted, that he was no more certain of his ground than she. Then he held out his hand. Juliet put hers in it. Together they walked to the bedroom.

If he'd set the scene for a night of romance, Carlo would've added flowers with a touch of spice, music with the throb of passion. He'd have given her the warmth of candlelight and the fun of champagne. Tonight, with Juliet, there was only silence and moonlight. The maid had turned down the bed and left the drapes wide. White light filtered through shadows and onto white sheets.

Standing by the bed, he kissed her palms, one by one. They were cool and carried a hint of her scent. At her wrist her pulse throbbed. Slowly, watching her, he loosened the tie of her robe. With his eyes still on hers, he brought his hands to her shoulders and slipped the material aside. It fell silently to pool at her feet.

He didn't touch her, nor did he yet look at anything but her face. Through nerves, through needs, something like comfort began to move through her. Her lips curved, just slightly, as she reached for the tie of his robe and drew the knot. With her hands light and sure on his shoulders, she pushed the silk aside.

They were both vulnerable, to their needs, to each other. The light was thin and white and washed with shadows. No other illumination was needed this first time that they looked at each other.

He was lean but not thin. She was slender but soft. Her skin seemed only more pale when he touched her. Her hand seemed only more delicate when she touched him.

They came together slowly. There was no need to rush.

The mattress gave, the sheets rustled. Quietly. Side by side they lay, giving themselves time—all the time needed to discover what pleasures could come from the taste of mouth to mouth, the touch of flesh to flesh.

Should she have known it would be like this? So easy. Inevitable. Her skin was warm, so warm wherever he brushed it. His lips demanded, they took, but with such patience. He loved her gently, slowly, as though it were her first time. As she drifted deeper, Juliet thought dimly that perhaps it was.

Innocence. He felt it from her, not physical, but emotional. Somehow, incredibly, he discovered it was the same for himself. No matter how many had come before, for either of them, they came to each other now in innocence.

Her hands didn't hesitate as they moved over him, but stroked as though she were blind and could only gain her own picture through other senses. He smelled of a shower, water and soap, but he tasted richer, of wine. Then he spoke for the first time, only her name. It was to her more moving, more poetic than any endearment.

Her body moved with his, in rhythm, keeping pace. She seemed to know, somehow, where he would touch her just before she felt his fingers trace, his palms press. Then his lips began a long, luxurious journey she hoped would never end.

She was so small. Why had he never noticed before how small she was? It was easy to forget her strength, her control, her stamina. He could give her tenderness and wait for the passion.

The line of her neck was slender and so white in the moonlight. Her scent was trapped there, at her throat. Intensified. Arousing. He could linger there while blood heated. His and hers.

He slid his tongue over the subtle curve of her breast to find the peak. When he drew it into his mouth, she moaned his name, giving them both a long, slow nudge to the edge.

But there was more to taste, more to touch. Passion, when heated, makes a mockery of control. Sounds slipped into the room—a catch of breath, a sigh, a moan—all pleasure. Their scents began to mix together—a lover's fragrance. In the moonlight, they were one form. The sheets were hot, twisted. When with tongue and fingertips he drove her over the first peak, Juliet gripped the tousled sheets as her body arched and shuddered with a torrent of sensations.

While she was still weak, still gasping, he slipped into her.

His head was spinning—a deliciously foreign sensation to him. He wanted to bury himself in her, but he wanted to see her. Her eyes were shut; her lips just parted as the breath hurried in and out. She moved with him, slowly, then faster, still faster until her fingers dug into his shoulders.

On a cry of pleasure, her eyes flew open. Looking into them, he saw the dark, astonished excitement he'd wanted to give her.

At last, giving in to the rushing need of his own body, he closed his mouth over hers and let himself go.

CHAPTER 8

Were there others who understood true passion? Wrapped in Carlo, absorbing and absorbed by Carlo, Juliet knew she hadn't until moments ago. Should it make you weak? She felt weak, but not empty.

Should she feel regret? Yes, logically she should. She'd given more of herself than she'd intended, shared more than she'd imagined, risked more than she should have dared. But she had no regrets. Perhaps later she'd make her list of the whys and why nots. For now, she wanted only to enjoy the soft afterglow of loving.

"You're quiet." His breath whispered across her temple, followed by his lips.

She smiled a little, content to let her eyes close. "So are you."

Nuzzling his cheek against her hair, he looked over to the slant of moonlight through the window. He wasn't sure which words to use. He'd never felt quite like this before with any woman. He'd never expected to. How could he tell her that and expect to be believed? He was having a hard time believing it himself. And yet . . . perhaps truth was the hardest thing to put into words.

"You feel very small when I hold you like this," he murmured. "It makes me want to hold you like this for a long, long time."

"I like having you hold me." The admission was much easier to make than she'd thought. With a little laugh, she turned her head so that she could see his face. "I like it very much."

"Then you won't object if I go on holding you for the next few hours."

She kissed his chin. "The next few minutes," she corrected. "I have to get back to my room."

"You don't like my bed?"

She stretched and cuddled and thought how wonderful it would be never to move from that one spot. "I think I'm crazy about it, but I've got a little work to do before I call it a night, then I have to be up by six-thirty, and—"

"You work too much." He cut her off, then leaned over her to pick up the phone. "You can get up in the morning just as easily from my bed as yours."

Finding she liked the way his body pressed into hers, she prepared to be convinced. "Maybe. What're you doing?"

"Shh. Yes, this is Franconi in 922. I'd like a wake-up call for six." He replaced the phone and rolled, pulling her on top of him. "There now, everything is taken care of. The phone will ring at dawn and wake us up."

"It certainly will." Juliet folded her hands over his chest and rested her chin on them. "But you told them to call at six. We don't have to get up until six-thirty."

"Yes." He slid his hands down low over her back. "So we have a half hour to—ah—wake up."

With a laugh, she pressed her lips to his shoulder. This once, she told herself, just this once, she'd let someone else do the planning. "Very practical. Do you think we might take a half hour or so to—ah—go to sleep?"

"My thoughts exactly."

When the phone did ring, Juliet merely groaned and slid down under the sheets. For the second time, she found herself buried under Carlo as he rolled over to answer it. Without complaint, she lay still, hoping the ringing of the phone had been part of a dream.

"Come now, Juliet." Shifting most of his weight from her, Carlo began to nibble on her shoulder. "You're playing mole."

She murmured in drowsy excitement as he slid his hand down to her hip. "Mole? I don't have a mole."

"Playing mole." She was so warm and soft and pliant. He'd known she would be. Mornings were made for lazy delights and waking her was a pleasure just begun.

Juliet stretched under the stroke and caress of his hands. Mornings were for a quick shower and a hasty cup of coffee. She'd never known they could be luxurious. "Playing mole?"

"An American expression." The skin over her rib cage was soft as butter. He thought there was no better time to taste it. "You pretend to be dead."

Because her mind was clouded with sleep, her system already churning with passion, it took a moment. "Possum."

"Prego?"

"Playing possum," she repeated and, guided by his hands, shifted. "A mole's different."

"So, they're both little animals."

She opened one eye. His hair was rumpled around his face, his chin darkened with a night's growth of beard. But when he smiled, he looked as though he'd been awake for hours. He looked, she admitted, absolutely wonderful.

"You want an animal?" With a sudden burst of energy, she rolled on top of him. Her hands were quick, her mouth avid. In seconds, she'd taken his breath away.

She'd never been aggressive, but found the low, surprised moan and the fast pump of his heart to her liking. Her body reacted like lightning. She didn't mind that his hands weren't as gentle, as patient as they'd been the night before. This new desperation thrilled her.

He was Franconi, known for his wide range of expertise in the kitchen and the bedroom. But she was making him wild and helpless at the same time. With a laugh, she pressed her mouth to his, letting her tongue find all the dark, lavish tastes. When he tried to shift her, to take her because the need had grown too quickly to control, she evaded. His breathless curse whispered into her mouth.

He never lost finesse with a woman. Passion, his passion, had always been melded with style. Now, as she took her frenzied journey over him, he had no style, only needs. He'd never been a man to rush. When he cooked, he went slowly, step-by-step. Enjoy, experience, experiment. He made love the same way. Such things were meant to be savored, to be appreciated by each of the five senses.

It wasn't possible to savor when you were driven beyond the civilized. When your senses were whirling and tangled, it wasn't possible to separate them. Being driven was something new for him, something intoxicating. No, he wouldn't fight it, but pull her with him.

Rough and urgent, he grabbed her hips. Within moments, they were both beyond thought, beyond reason. . . .

His breath was still unsteady, but he held her close and tight. Whatever she'd done, or was doing to him, he didn't want to lose it. The thought flickered briefly that he didn't want to lose her. Carlo pushed it aside. It was a dangerous thought. They had now. It was much wiser to concentrate on that.

"I have to go." Though she wanted nothing more than to curl up against him, Juliet made herself shift away. "We have to be downstairs at checkout in forty minutes."

"To meet Big Bill."

"That's right." Juliet reached onto the floor for her robe, slipping it onto her arms before she stood up. Carlo's lips trembled at the way she turned her back to him to tie it. It was rather endearing to see the unconscious modesty from a woman who'd just exploited every inch of his body. "You don't know how grateful I am that Bill volunteered to play chauffeur. The last thing I want to do is fight the freeway system in this town. I've had to do it before, and it's not a pretty sight."

"I could drive," he murmured, enjoying the way the rich green silk reached the top of her thighs.

"Staying alive is another reason I'm grateful for Bill. I'll call and have a bellman come up for the bags in—thirty-five minutes. Be sure—"

"You check everything because we won't be coming back," he finished. "Juliet, haven't I proven my competency yet?"

"Just a friendly reminder." She checked her watch before she remembered she wasn't wearing it. "The TV spot should be a breeze. Jacky Torrence hosts. It's a jovial sort of show that goes after the fast, funny story rather than nuts and bolts."

"Hmm." He rose, stretching. The publicist was back, he noted with a half smile, but as he reached down for his own robe, he noticed that she'd broken off. Lifting his head, he looked up at her.

Good God, he was beautiful. It was all she could think. Schedules, planning, points of information all went out of her head. In the early morning sun, his skin was more gold than brown, smooth and tight over his rib cage, nipped in at the waist to a narrow line of hip. Letting out a shaky breath, she took a step back.

"I'd better go," she managed. "We can run through today's schedule on the way to the studio."

It pleased him enormously to understand what had broken her concentration. He held the robe loosely in one hand as he took a step closer. "Perhaps we'll get bumped."

"Bite your tongue." Aiming for a light tone, she succeeded with a whisper. "That's an interesting robe."

The tone of her voice was a springboard to an arousal already begun. "You like the flamingos? My mother has a sense of humor." But he didn't put it on as he stepped closer.

"Carlo, stay right where you are. I mean it." She held up a hand as she walked backward to the doorway.

He grinned, and kept on grinning after he heard the click of the hallway door.

Between Juliet cracking the whip and Bill piloting, their Houston business went like clockwork. TV, radio and print, the media was responsive and energetic. The midafternoon autograph party turned out to be a party in the true sense of the word and was a smashing success. Juliet found herself a spot in a storeroom and ripped open the oversized envelope from her office that had been delivered to the hotel. Settling back, she began to go through the clippings her assistant had air expressed.

L.A. was excellent, as she'd expected. Upbeat and enthusiastic. San Diego might've tried for a little more depth, but they'd given him page one of the *Food* section in one spread and a below-the-fold in the *Style* section in another. No complaints. Portland and Seattle listed a recipe apiece and raved shamelessly. Juliet could've rubbed her hands together with glee if she hadn't been drinking coffee. Then she hit Denver.

Coffee sloshed out of the cup and onto her hand.

"Damn!" Fumbling in her briefcase, she found three crumpled tissues and began to mop up. A gossip column. Who'd have thought it? She gave herself a moment to think then relaxed. Publicity was publicity, after all. And the truth of the matter was, Franconi was gossip. Looking at it logically, the more times his name was in print, the more successful the tour. Resolved, Juliet began to read.

She nodded absently as she skimmed the first paragraph. Chatty, shallow, but certainly not offensive. A lot of people who might not glance at the food or cooking sections would give the gossip columns a working over. All in all, it was probably an excellent break. Then she read the second paragraph.

Juliet was up out of her folding chair. This time the coffee that dripped onto the floor went unnoticed. Her expression changed from surprised astonishment to fury in a matter of seconds. In the same amount of time, she stuffed the clippings back into their envelope. It wasn't easy, but she gave herself five minutes for control before she walked back into the main store.

The schedule called for another fifteen minutes, but Carlo had more than twenty people in line, and that many again just milling around. Fifteen minutes would have to be stretched to thirty. Grinding her teeth, Juliet stalked over to Bill.

"There you are." Friendly as always, he threw his arm over her shoulder and squeezed. "Going great guns out here. Old Carlo knows how to twinkle to the ladies without setting the men off. Damn clever sonofabitch."

"I couldn't have said it better myself." Her knuckles were white on the strap of her briefcase. "Bill, is there a phone I can use? I have to call the office."

"No problem at all. Y'all just come on back with me." He led her through Psychology, into Westerns and around

Romances to a door marked Private. "You just help yourself," he invited and showed her into a room with a cluttered metal desk, a gooseneck lamp and stacks upon stacks of books. Juliet headed straight for the phone.

"Thanks, Bill." She didn't even wait until the door closed before she started dialing. "Deborah Mortimor, please," she said to the answering switchboard. Tapping her foot, Juliet waited.

"Ms. Mortimor."

"Deb, it's Juliet."

"Hi. I've been waiting for you to call in. Looks like we've got a strong nibble with the *Times* when you come back to New York. I just—"

"Later." Juliet reached into her briefcase for a roll of antacids. "I got the clippings today."

"Great, aren't they?"

"Oh sure. They're just dandy."

"Uh-huh." Deb waited only a beat. "It's the little number in Denver, isn't it?"

She gave the rolling chair a quick kick. "Of course it is."

"Sit down, Juliet." Deb didn't have to see to know her boss was pacing.

"Sit down? I'm tempted to fly back to Denver and ring Chatty Cathy's neck."

"Killing columnists isn't good for PR, Juliet."

"It was garbage."

"No, no, it wasn't that bad. Trash maybe, but not garbage."

She struggled for control and managed to get a very slippery rein on her temper. Popping the first antacid into her mouth, she crunched down. "Don't be cute, Deb. I didn't like the insinuations about Carlo and me. *Carlo Franconi's lovely American traveling companion,*" she quoted between her teeth. "Traveling companion. It makes me sound as though I'm just along for the ride. And then—"

"I read it," Deb interrupted. "So did Hal," she added, referring to the head of publicity.

Juliet closed her eyes a moment. "And?"

"Well, he went through about six different reactions. In the end, he decided a few comments like that were bound to come up and only added to Franconi's—well, mystique might be the best term."

"I see." Her jaw clenched, her fingers tight around the little roll of stomach pills. "That's fine then, isn't it? I'm just thrilled to add to a client's mystique."

"Now, Juliet—"

"Look, just tell dear old Hal that Houston went perfectly." She was definitely going to need two pills. Juliet popped another out of the roll with her thumb. "I don't even want you to mention to him that I called about this—this tripe in Denver."

"Whatever you say."

Taking a pen, she sat down and made space on the desk. "Now, give me what you have with the *Times*."

A half hour later, Juliet was just finishing up her last call when Carlo poked his head in the office. Seeing she was on the phone, he rolled his eyes, closed the door and leaned against it. His brow lifted when he spotted the half-eaten roll of antacids.

"Yes, thank you, Ed, Mr. Franconi will bring all the necessary ingredients and be in the studio at 8:00. Yes." She laughed, though her foot was tapping out a rhythm on the floor. "It's absolutely delicious. Guaranteed. See you in two days."

When she hung up the receiver, Carlo stepped forward. "You didn't come to save me."

She gave him a long, slow look. "You seemed to be handling the situation without me."

He knew the tone, and the expression. Now all he had to

do was find the reason for them. Strolling over, he picked up the roll of pills. "You're much too young to need these."

"I've never heard that ulcers had an age barrier."

His brows drew together as he sat on the edge of the desk. "Juliet, if I believed you had an ulcer, I'd pack you off to my home in Rome and keep you in bed on bland foods for the next month. Now . . ." He slipped the roll into his pocket. "What problem is there?"

"Several," she said briskly as she began to gather up her notes. "But they're fairly well smoothed out now. We'll need to go shopping again in Chicago for that chicken dish you'd planned to cook. So, if you've finished up here, we can just—"

"No." He put a hand on her shoulder and held her in the chair. "We're not finished. Shopping for chicken in Chicago isn't what had you reaching for pills. What?"

The best defense was always ice. Her voice chilled. "Carlo, I've been very busy."

"You think after two weeks I don't know you?" Impatient, he gave her a little shake. "You dig in that briefcase for your aspirin or your little mints only when you feel too much pressure. I don't like to see it."

"It comes with the territory." She tried to shrug off his hand and failed. "Carlo, we've got to get to the airport."

"We have more than enough time. Tell me what's wrong."

"All right then." In two sharp moves, she pulled the clipping out of her case and pushed it into his hands.

"What's this?" He skimmed it first without really reading it. "One of those little columns about who is seen with whom and what they wear while they're seen?"

"More or less."

"Ah." As he began to read from the top, he nodded. "And you were seen with me."

Closing her notebook, she slipped it neatly into her

briefcase. Twice she reminded herself that losing her temper would accomplish nothing. "As your publicist, that could hardly be avoided."

Because he'd come to expect logic from her, he only nodded again. "But you feel this intimates something else."

"It *says* something else," she tossed back. "Something that isn't true."

"It calls you my traveling companion." He glanced up, knowing that wouldn't sit well with her. "It's perhaps not the full story, but not untrue. Does it upset you to be known as my companion?"

She didn't want him to be reasonable. She had no intention of emulating him. "When companion takes on this shade of meaning, it isn't professional or innocent. I'm not here to have my name linked with you this way, Carlo."

"In what way, Juliet?"

"It gives my name and goes on to say that I'm never out of arm's length, that I guard you as though you were my own personal property. And that you—"

"That I kiss your hand in public restaurants as though I couldn't wait for privacy," Carlo read at a glance. "So? What difference does it make what it says here?"

She dragged both hands through her hair. "Carlo, I'm here, with you, to do a job. This clipping came through my office, through my supervisor. Don't you know something like this could ruin my credibility?"

"No," he said simply enough. "This is no more than gossip. Your supervisor, he's upset by this?"

She laughed, but it had little to do with humor. "No, actually, it seems he's decided it's just fine. Good for your image."

"Well, then?"

"I don't want to be good for your image," she threw back

with such passion, it shocked both of them. "I won't be one of the dozens of names and faces linked with you."

"So," he murmured. "Now, we push away to the truth. You're angry with me, for this." He set the clipping down. "You're angry because there's more truth in it now than there was when it was written."

"I don't want to be on anyone's list, Carlo." Her voice had lowered, calmed. She dug balled fists into the pockets of her skirt. "Not yours, not anyone's. I haven't come this far in my life to let that happen now."

He stood, wondering if she understood how insulting her words were. No, she'd see them as facts, not as darts. "I haven't put you on a list. If you have one in your own mind, it has nothing to do with me."

"A few weeks ago it was the French actress, a month before that a widowed countess."

He didn't shout, but it was only force of will that kept his voice even. "I never pretended you were the first woman in my bed. I never expected I was the first man in yours."

"That's entirely different."

"Ah, now you find the double standard convenient." He picked up the clipping, balled it in his fist then dropped it into the wastebasket. "I've no patience for this, Juliet."

He was to the door again before she spoke. "Carlo, wait." With a polite veneer stretched thinly over fury he turned. "Damn." Hands still in her pockets, she paced from one stack of books to the other. "I never intended to take this out on you. It's totally out of line and I'm sorry, really. You might guess I'm not thinking very clearly right now."

"So it would seem."

Juliet let out a sigh, knowing she observed the cutting edge of his voice. "I don't know how to explain, except to say that my career's very important to me."

"I understand that."

"But it's no more important to me than my privacy. I don't want my personal life discussed around the office water cooler."

"People talk, Juliet. It's natural and it's meaningless."

"I can't brush it off the way you do." She picked up her briefcase by the strap then set it down again. "I'm used to staying in the background. I set things up, handle the details, do the legwork, and someone else's picture gets in the paper. That's the way I want it."

"You don't always get what you want." With his thumbs hooked in his pockets, he leaned back against the door and watched her. "Your anger goes deeper than a few lines in a paper people will have forgotten tomorrow."

She closed her eyes a moment, then turned back to him. "All right, yes, but it's not a matter of being angry. Carlo, I've put myself in a delicate position with you."

Carefully, he weighed the phrase, tested it, judged it. "Delicate position?"

"Please, don't misunderstand. I'm here, with you, because of my job. It's very important to me that that's handled in the best, the most professional manner I can manage. What's happened between us . . ."

"What has happened between us?" he prompted when she trailed off.

"Don't make it difficult."

"All right, we'll make it easy. We're lovers."

She let out a long, unsteady breath, wondering if he really believed that was easy. For him it might be just another stroll through the moonlight. For her, it was a race through a hurricane. "I want to keep that aspect of our relationship completely separate from the professional area."

It surprised him he could find such a statement endearing.

Perhaps the fact that she was half romanticist and half businesswoman was part of her appeal to him. "Juliet, my love, you sound as though you're negotiating a contract."

"Maybe I do." Nerves were beginning to run through her too quickly again. "Maybe I am, in a way."

His own anger had disappeared. Her eyes weren't nearly as certain as her voice. Her hands, he noted, were twisting together. Slowly, he walked toward her, pleased that though she didn't back away, the wariness was back. "Juliet . . ." He lifted a hand to brush through her hair. "You can negotiate terms and times, but not emotion."

"You can—regulate it."

He took both her hands, kissing them. "No."

"Carlo, please—"

"You like me to touch you," he murmured. "Whether we stand here alone, or we stand in a group of strangers. If I touch your hand, like this, you know what's in my mind. It's not always passion. There are times, I see you, I touch you, and I think only of being with you—talking, or sitting silently. Will you negotiate now how I am to touch your hand, how many times a day it's permitted?"

"Don't make me sound like a fool."

His fingers tightened on hers. "Don't make what I feel for you sound foolish."

"I—" No, she couldn't touch that. She didn't dare. "Carlo, I just want to keep things simple."

"Impossible."

"No, it's not."

"Then tell me, is this simple?" With just his fingertips on her shoulder, he leaned down to kiss her. So softly, so lightly, it was hardly a kiss at all. She felt her legs dissolve from the knees down.

"Carlo, we're not staying on the point."

He slipped his arms around her. "I like this point much better. When we get to Chicago . . ." His fingers slipped up and down her spine as he began to brush his lips over her face. "I want to spend the evening alone with you."

"We—have an appointment for drinks at ten with—"

"Cancel it."

"Carlo, you know I can't."

"Very well." He caught the lobe of her ear between his teeth. "I'll plead fatigue and make certain we have a very quick, very early evening. Then, I'll spend the rest of the night doing little things, like this."

His tongue darted inside her ear, then retreated to the vulnerable spot just below. The shudder that went through her was enough to arouse both of them. "Carlo, you don't understand."

"I understand that I want you." In a swift mood swing, he had her by the shoulders. "If I told you now that I want you more than I've wanted any other woman, you wouldn't believe me."

She backed away from that, but was caught close again. "No, I wouldn't. It isn't necessary to say so."

"You're afraid to hear it, afraid to believe it. You won't get simple with me, Juliet. But you'll get a lover you'll never forget."

She steadied a bit, meeting his look levelly. "I've already resigned myself to that, Carlo. I don't apologize to myself, and I don't pretend to have any regrets about coming to you last night."

"Then resign yourself to this." The temper was back in his eyes, hot and volatile. "I don't care what's written in the paper, what's whispered about in offices in New York. You, this moment, are all I care about."

Something shattered quietly inside her. A defense built instinctively through years. She knew she shouldn't take him literally. He was Franconi after all. If he cared about her, it was only in his way, and in his time. But something had shattered, and she couldn't rebuild it so quickly. Instead, she chose to be blunt.

"Carlo, I don't know how to handle you. I haven't the experience."

"Then don't handle me." Again, he took her by the shoulders. "Trust me."

She put her hands on his, held them a moment, then drew them away. "It's too soon, and too much."

There were times, in his work, where he had to be very, very patient. As a man, it happened much more rarely. Yet he knew if he pushed now, as for some inexplicable reason he wanted to, he'd only create more distance between them. "Then, for now, we just enjoy each other."

That's what she wanted. Juliet told herself that was exactly what she wanted—no more, no less. But she felt like weeping.

"We'll enjoy each other," she agreed. Letting out a sigh, she framed his face with her hands as he so often did with her. "Very much."

He wondered, when he lowered his brow to hers, why it didn't quite satisfy.

CHAPTER 9

Burned out from traveling, ready for a drink and elevated feet, Juliet walked up to the front desk of their Chicago hotel. Taking a quick glimpse around the lobby, she was pleased with the marble floors, sculpture and elegant potted palms. Such places usually lent themselves to big, stylish bathrooms. She intended to spend her first hour in Chicago with everything from the neck down submerged.

"May I help you?"

"You have a reservation for Franconi and Trent."

With a few punches on the keyboard, the clerk brought up their reservations on the screen. "You'll both be staying for two nights, Miss Trent?"

"Yes, that's right."

"It's direct bill. Everything's set. If you and Mr. Franconi will just fill out these forms, I'll ring for a bellman."

As he scrawled the information on the form, Carlo glanced over. From the profile, she looked lovely, though perhaps a bit tired. Her hair was pinned up in the back, fluffed out on the sides and barely mussed from traveling. She looked as though she could head a three-hour business meeting without a whimper. But then she arched her back, closing her eyes briefly as she stretched her shoulders. He wanted to take care of her.

"Juliet, there's no need for two rooms."

She shifted her shoulder bag and signed her name. "Carlo, don't start. Arrangements have already been made."

"But it's absurd. You'll be staying in my suite, so the extra room is simply extra."

The desk clerk stood at a discreet distance and listened to every word.

Juliet pulled her credit card out of her wallet and set it down on the counter with a snap. Carlo noted, with some amusement, that she no longer looked the least bit tired. He wanted to make love with her for hours.

"You'll need the imprint on this for my incidentals," she told the clerk calmly enough. "All Mr. Franconi's charges will be picked up."

Carlo pushed his form toward the clerk then leaned on the counter. "Juliet, won't you feel foolish running back and forth across the hall? It's ridiculous, even for a publisher, to pay for a bed that won't be slept in."

With her jaw clenched, she picked up her credit card again. "I'll tell you what's ridiculous," she said under her breath. "It's ridiculous for you to be standing here deliberately embarrassing me."

"You have rooms 1102 and 1108." The clerk pushed the keys toward them. "I'm afraid they're just down the hall from each other rather than across."

"That's fine." Juliet turned to find the bellman had their luggage packed on the cart and his ears open. Without a word, she strode toward the bank of elevators.

Strolling along beside her, Carlo noted that the cashier had a stunning smile. "Juliet, I find it odd that you'd be embarrassed over something so simple."

"I don't think it's simple." She jabbed the up button on the elevator.

"Forgive me." Carlo put his tongue in his cheek. "It's only that I recall you specifically saying you wanted our relationship to be simple."

"Don't tell me what I said. What I said has nothing to do with what I meant."

"Of course not," he murmured and waited for her to step inside the car.

Seeing the look on Juliet's face, the bellman began to worry about his tip. He put on a hospitality-plus smile. "So, you in Chicago long?"

"Two days," Carlo said genially enough.

"You can see a lot in a couple of days. You'll want to get down to the lake—"

"We're here on business," Juliet interrupted. "Only business."

"Yes, ma'am." With a smile, the bellman pushed his cart into the hall. "1108's the first stop."

"That's mine." Juliet dug out her wallet again and pulled out bills as the bellman unlocked her door. "Those two bags," she pointed out then turned to Carlo. "We'll meet Dave Lockwell in the bar for drinks at 10:00. You can do as you like until then."

"I have some ideas on that," he began but Juliet moved past him. After stuffing the bills in the bellman's hand, she shut the door with a quick click.

Thirty minutes, to Carlo's thinking, was long enough for anyone to cool down. Juliet's stiff-backed attitude toward their room situation had caused him more exasperation than annoyance. But then, he expected to be exasperated by women. On one hand, he found her reaction rather sweet and naive. Did she really think the fact that they were lovers would make the desk clerk or a bellman blink twice?

The fact that she did, and probably always would, was just another aspect of her nature that appealed to him. In whatever she did, Juliet Trent would always remain proper. Simmering passion beneath a tidy, clean-lined business suit. Carlo found her irresistible.

He'd known so many kinds of women—the bright young ingenue greedy to her fingertips, the wealthy aristocrat bored both by wealth and tradition, the successful career woman who both looked for and was wary of marriage. He'd known so many—the happy, the secure, the desperate and seeking, the fulfilled and the grasping. Juliet Trent with the cool green eyes and quiet voice left him uncertain as to what pigeonhole she'd fit into. It seemed she had all and none of the feminine qualities he understood. The only thing he was certain of was that he wanted her to fit, somehow, into his life.

The best way, the only way, he knew to accomplish that was to distract her with charm until she was already caught. After that, they'd negotiate the next step.

Carlo lifted the rose he'd had sent up from the hotel florist out of its bud vase, sniffed its petals once, then walked down the hall to Juliet's room.

She was just drying off from a hot, steamy bath. If she'd heard the knock five minutes before, she'd have growled. As it was, she pulled on her robe and went to answer.

She'd been expecting him. Juliet wasn't foolish enough to believe a man like Carlo would take a door in the face as final. It had given her satisfaction to close it, just as it gave her satisfaction to open it again. When she was ready.

She hadn't been expecting the rose. Though she knew it wasn't wise to be moved by a single long-stemmed flower with a bud the color of sunshine, she was moved nonetheless.

Her plans to have a calm, serious discussion with him faltered.

"You look rested." Rather than giving her the rose, he took her hand. Before she could decide whether or not to let him in, he was there.

A stand, Juliet reminded herself even as she closed the door behind him. If she didn't take a stand now, she'd never find her footing. "Since you're here, we'll talk. We have an hour."

"Of course." As was his habit, he took a survey of her room. Her suitcase sat on a stand, still packed, but with its top thrown open. It wasn't practical to unpack and repack when you were bouncing around from city to city. Though they were starting their third week on the road, the contents of the case were still neat and organized. He'd have expected no less from her. Her notebook and two pens were already beside the phone. The only things remotely out of place in the tidy, impersonal room were the Italian heels that sat in the middle of the rug where she'd stepped out of them. The inconsistency suited her perfectly.

"I can discuss things better," she began, "if you weren't wandering around."

"Yes?" All cooperation, Carlo sat and waved the rose under his nose. "You want to talk about our schedule here in Chicago?"

"No—yes." She had at least a dozen things to go over with him. For once she let business take a back seat. "Later." Deciding to take any advantage, Juliet remained standing. "First, I want to talk about that business down at the desk."

"Ah." The sound was distinctly European and as friendly as a smile. She could have murdered him.

"It was totally uncalled for."

"Was it?" He'd learned that strategy was best plotted with

friendly questions or simple agreement. That way, you could swing the final result to your own ends without too much blood being shed.

"Of course it was." Forgetting her own strategy, Juliet dropped down on the edge of the bed. "Carlo, you had no right discussing our personal business in public."

"You're quite right."

"I—" His calm agreement threw her off. The firm, moderately angry speech she'd prepared in the tub went out the window.

"I must apologize," he continued before she could balance herself. "It was thoughtless of me."

"Well, no." As he'd planned, she came to his defense. "It wasn't thoughtless, just inappropriate."

With the rose, he waved her defense away. "You're too kind, Juliet. You see, I was thinking only of how practical you are. It's one of the things I most admire about you." In getting his way, Carlo had always felt it best to use as much truth as possible. "You see, besides my own family, I've known very few truly practical women. This trait in you appeals to me, as much as the color of your eyes, the texture of your skin."

Because she sensed she was losing ground, Juliet sat up straighter. "You don't have to flatter me, Carlo. It's simply a matter of establishing ground rules."

"You see." As if she'd made his point, he sat forward to touch her fingertips. "You're too practical to expect flattery or to be swayed by it. Is it any wonder I'm enchanted by you?"

"Carlo—"

"I haven't made my point." He retreated just enough to keep his attack in full gear. "You see, knowing you, I thought you would agree that it was foolish and impractical to book separate rooms when we want to be together. You do want to be with me, don't you, Juliet?"

Frustrated, she stared at him. He was turning the entire situation around. Certain of it, Juliet groped for a handhold. "Carlo, it has nothing to do with my wanting to be with you."

His brow lifted. "No?"

"No. It has to do with the line that separates our business and our personal lives."

"A line that's difficult to draw. Perhaps impossible for me." The truth came out again, though this time unplanned. "I want to be with you, Juliet, every moment we have. I find myself resenting even the hour that you're here and I'm there. A few hours at night isn't enough for me. I want more, much more for us."

Saying it left him stunned. It hadn't been one of his clever moves, one of his easy catch-phrases. That little jewel had come from somewhere inside where it had quietly hidden until it could take him by surprise.

He rose, and to give himself a moment, stood by the window to watch a stream of Chicago traffic. It rushed, then came to fitful stops, wound and swung then sped on again. Life was like this, he realized. You could speed right along but you never knew when something was going to stop you dead in your tracks.

Juliet was silent behind him, torn between what he'd said, what he'd meant and what she felt about it. From the very beginning, she'd kept Carlo's definition of an affair in the front of her mind. Just one ride on the carousel. When the music stopped, you got off and knew you'd gotten your money's worth. Now, with a few words he was changing the scope. She wondered if either of them was ready.

"Carlo, since you say I am, I'll be practical." Drawing together her resources, she rose. "We have a week left on tour.

During that time, we've got Chicago and four other cities to deal with. To be honest, I'd rather if our only business right now was with each other."

He turned, and though she thought the smile was a bit odd, at least he smiled. "That's the nicest thing you've said to me in all these days and all these cities, Juliet."

She took a step toward him. It seemed foolish to think about risks when they had such little time. "Being with you isn't something I'll ever forget, no matter how much I might want to in years to come."

"Juliet—"

"No, wait. I want to be with you, and part of me hates the time we lose with other people, in separate rooms, in all the demands that brought us to each other in the first place. But another part of me knows that all of those things are completely necessary. Those things will still be around after we're each back in our separate places."

No, don't think about that now, she warned herself. If she did, her voice wouldn't be steady.

"No matter how much time I spend with you in your suite, I need a room of my own if for no other reason than to know it's there. Maybe that's the practical side of me, Carlo."

Or the vulnerable one, he mused. But hadn't he just discovered he had a vulnerability of his own? Her name was Juliet. "So, it will be as you want in this." And for the best perhaps. He might just need a bit of time to himself to think things through.

"No arguing?"

"Do we argue ever, *cara*?"

Her lips curved. "Never." Giving in to herself as much as him, she stepped forward and linked her arms around his neck. "Did I ever tell you that when I first started setting up this tour I looked at your publicity shot and thought you were gorgeous?"

"No." He brushed his lips over hers. "Why don't you tell me now?"

"And sexy," she murmured as she drew him closer to the bed. "Very, very sexy."

"Is that so?" He allowed himself to be persuaded onto the bed. "So you decided in your office in New York that we'd be lovers?"

"I decided in my office in New York that we'd never be lovers." Slowly, she began to unbutton his shirt. "I decided that the last thing I wanted was to be romanced and seduced by some gorgeous, sexy Italian chef who had a string of women longer than a trail of his own pasta, but—"

"Yes." He nuzzled at her neck. "I think I'll prefer the 'but.' "

"But it seems to me that you can't make definitive decisions without all the facts being in."

"Have I ever told you that your practicality arouses me to the point of madness?"

She sighed as he slipped undone the knot in her robe. "Have I ever told you that I'm a sucker for a man who brings me flowers?"

"Flowers." He lifted his head then picked up the rosebud he'd dropped on the pillow beside them. "Darling, did you want one, too?"

With a laugh, she pulled him back to her.

Juliet decided she'd seen more of Chicago in the flight into O'Hare than during the day and a half she'd been there. Cab drives from hotel to television station, from television station to department store, from department store to bookstore and back to the hotel again weren't exactly leisurely sight-seeing tours. Then and there she decided that when she took her vacation at the end of the month, she'd go somewhere steamy with sun and do nothing more energetic than laze by a pool from dawn to dusk.

The only hour remotely resembling fun was another shopping expedition where she watched Carlo select a plump three-pound chicken for his cacciatore.

He was to prepare his *pollastro alla cacciatora* from simmer to serve during a live broadcast of one of the country's top-rated morning shows. Next to the *Simpson Show* in L.A., Juliet considered this her biggest coup for the tour. *Let's Discuss It* was the hottest hour on daytime TV, and remained both popular and controversial after five consecutive seasons.

Despite the fact that she knew Carlo's showmanship abilities, Juliet was nervous as a cat. The show would air live in New York. She had no doubt that everyone in her department would be watching. If Carlo was a smash, it would be his triumph. If he bombed, the bomb was all hers. Such was the rationale in public relations.

It never occurred to Carlo to be nervous. He could make cacciatore in the dark, from memory with the use of only one hand. After watching Juliet pace the little green room for the fifth time, he shook his head. "Relax, my love, it's only chicken."

"Don't forget to bring up the dates we'll be in the rest of the cities. This show reaches all of them."

"You've already told me."

"And the title of the book."

"I won't forget."

"You should remember to mention you prepared this dish for the President when he visited Rome last year."

"I'll try to keep it in mind. Juliet, wouldn't you like some coffee?"

She shook her head and kept pacing. What else?

"I could use some," he decided on the spot.

She glanced toward the pot on a hot plate. "Help yourself."

He knew if she had something to do, she'd stop worrying, even for a few moments. And she'd stop pacing up and down in front of him. "Juliet, no one with a heart would ask a man to drink that poison that's been simmering since dawn."

"Oh." Without hesitation, she assumed the role of pamperer. "I'll see about it."

"*Grazie.*"

At the door, she hesitated. "The reporter for the *Sun* might drop back before the show."

"Yes, you told me. I'll be charming."

Muttering to herself, she went to find a page.

Carlo leaned back and stretched his legs. He'd have to drink the coffee when she brought it back, though he didn't want any. He didn't want to board the plane for Detroit that afternoon, but such things were inevitable. In any case, he and Juliet would have the evening free in Detroit—what American state was that in?

They wouldn't be there long enough to worry about it.

In any case, he would soon be in Philadelphia and there, see Summer. He needed to. Though he'd always had friends and was close to many of them, he'd never needed one as he felt he needed one now. He could talk to Summer and know what he said would be listened to carefully and not be repeated. Gossip had never bothered him in the past, but when it came to Juliet . . . When it came to Juliet, nothing was as it had been in the past.

None of his previous relationships with women had ever become a habit. Waking up in the morning beside a woman had always been pleasant, but never necessary. Every day, Juliet was changing that. He couldn't imagine his bedroom back in Rome without her, yet she'd never been there. He'd long since stopped imagining other women in his bed.

Rising, he began to pace as Juliet had.

When the door opened, he turned, expecting her. The tall, willowy blonde who entered wasn't Juliet, but she was familiar.

"Carlo! How wonderful to see you again."

"Lydia." He smiled, cursing himself for not putting the name of the *Sun*'s reporter with the face of the woman he'd spent two interesting days in Chicago with only eighteen months before. "You look lovely."

Of course she did. Lydia Dickerson refused to look anything less. She was sharp, sexy and uninhibited. She was also, in his memory, an excellent cook and critic of gourmet foods.

"Carlo, I was just thrilled when I heard you were coming into town. We'll do the interview after the show, but I just had to drop back and see you." She swirled toward him with the scent of spring lilacs and the swish of a wide-flared skirt. "You don't mind?"

"Of course not." Smiling, he took her outstretched hand. "It's always good to see an old friend."

With a laugh, she put her hands on his shoulders. "I should be angry with you, *caro*. You do have my number, and my phone didn't ring last night."

"Ah." He put his hands to her wrists, wondering just how to untangle himself. "You'll have to forgive us, Lydia. The schedule is brutal. And there's a . . . complication." He winced, thinking how Juliet would take being labeled a complication.

"Carlo." She edged closer. "You can't tell me you haven't got a few free hours for . . . an old friend. I've a tremendous recipe for *vitèllo tonnato*." She murmured the words and made the dish sound like something to be eaten in the moonlight. "Who else should I cook it for but the best chef in Italy?"

"I'm honored." He put his hands on her hips hoping to draw her away with the least amount of insult. It wouldn't occur to him until later that he'd felt none, absolutely none, of the casual desire he should have. "I haven't forgotten what a superb cook you are, Lydia."

Her laugh was low and full of memories. "I hope you haven't forgotten more than that."

"No." He let out a breath and opted to be blunt. "But you see I'm—"

Before he could finish being honest, the door opened again. With a cup of coffee in her hand, Juliet walked in, then came to a dead stop. She looked at the blonde wound around Carlo like an exotic vine. Her brow lifted as she took her gaze to Carlo's face. If only she had a camera.

Her voice was as cool and dry as her eyes. "I see you've met."

"Juliet, I—"

"I'll give you a few moments for the . . . pre-interview," she said blandly. "Try to wrap it up by eight-fifty, Carlo. You'll want to check the kitchen set." Without another word, she shut the door behind her.

Though her arms were still around Carlo's neck, Lydia looked toward the closed door. "Oops," she said lightly.

Carlo let out a long breath as they separated. "You couldn't have put it better."

At nine o'clock, Juliet had a comfortable seat midway back in the audience. When Lydia slipped into the seat beside her, she gave the reporter an easy nod, then looked back to the set. As far as she could tell, and she'd gone over every inch of it, it was perfect.

When Carlo was introduced to cheerful applause, she began to relax, just a little. But when he began preparations on the chicken, moving like a surgeon and talking to his host, his studio and television audience like a seasoned performer, her relaxation was complete. He was going to be fantastic.

"He's really something, isn't he?" Lydia murmured during the first break.

"Something," Juliet agreed.

"Carlo and I met the last time he was in Chicago."

"Yes, I gathered. I'm glad you could make it by this morning. You did get the press kit I sent in?"

She's a cool one, Lydia thought and shifted in her seat. "Yes. The feature should be out by the end of the week. I'll send you a clipping."

"I'd appreciate it."

"Miss Trent—"

"Juliet, please." For the first time, Juliet turned and smiled at her fully. "No need for formality."

"All right, Juliet, I feel like a fool."

"I'm sorry. You shouldn't."

"I'm very fond of Carlo, but I don't poach."

"Lydia, I'm sure there isn't a woman alive who wouldn't be fond of Carlo." She crossed her legs as the countdown for taping began again. "If I thought you'd even consider poaching, you wouldn't be able to pick up your pencil."

Lydia sat still for a moment, then leaned back with a laugh. Carlo had picked himself quite a handful. Served him right. "Is it all right to wish you luck?"

Juliet shot her another smile. "I'd appreciate it."

The two women might've come to amicable terms, but it wasn't easy for Carlo to concentrate on his job while they sat cozily together in the audience. His experience with Lydia had been a quick and energetic two days. He knew little more of her than her preference for peanut oil for cooking and blue bed linen. He understood how easy it was for a man to be executed without trial. He thought he could almost feel the prickle of the noose around his throat.

But he was innocent. Carlo poured the mixture of tomatoes, sauce and spices over the browned chicken and set the cover. If he had to bind and gag her, Juliet would listen to him.

He cooked his dish with the finesse of an artist completing a royal portrait. He performed for the audience like a veteran thespian. He thought the dark thoughts of a man already at the dock.

When the show was over, he spent a few obligatory moments with his host, then left the crew to devour one of his best cacciatores.

But when he went back to the green room, Juliet was nowhere in sight. Lydia was waiting. He had no choice but to deal with her, and the interview, first.

She didn't make it easy for him. But then, to his knowledge, women seldom did. Lydia chatted away as though nothing had happened. She asked her questions, noted down his answers, all the while with mischief gleaming in her eyes. At length, he'd had enough.

"All right, Lydia, what did you say to her?"

"To whom?" All innocence, Lydia blinked at him. "Oh, your publicist. A lovely woman. But then I'd hardly be one to fault your taste, darling."

He rose, swore and wondered what a desperate man should do with his hands. "Lydia, we had a few enjoyable hours together. No more."

"I know." Something in her tone made him pause and glance back. "I don't imagine either of us could count the number of few enjoyable hours we've had." With a shrug, she rose. Perhaps she understood him, even envied what she thought she'd read in his eyes, but it wasn't any reason to let him off the hook. "Your Juliet and I just chatted, darling." She dropped her pad and pencil in her bag. "Girl talk, you know. Just girl talk. Thanks for the interview, Carlo." At the door, she paused and turned back. "If you're ever back in town without a . . . complication, give me a ring. *Ciao.*"

When she left, he considered breaking something. Before he could decide what would be the most satisfying and destructive, Juliet bustled in. "Let's get moving, Carlo. The cab's waiting. It looks like we'll have enough time to get back to the hotel, check out and catch the earlier plane."

"I want to speak with you."

"Yes, fine. We'll talk in the cab." Because she was already heading down the winding corridor he had no choice but to follow.

"When you told me the name of the reporter, I simply didn't put it together."

"Put what together?" Juliet pulled open the heavy metal door and stepped out on the back lot. If it had been much hotter, she noted, Carlo could've browned his chicken on the asphalt. "Oh, that you'd known her. Well, it's so hard to remember everyone we've met, isn't it?" She slipped into the cab and gave the driver the name of the hotel.

"We've come halfway across the country." Annoyed, he climbed in beside her. "Things begin to blur."

"They certainly do." Sympathetic, she patted his hand. "Detroit and Boston'll be down and dirty. You'll be lucky to remember your own name." She pulled out her compact to give her make-up a quick check. "But then I can help out in Philadelphia. You've already told me you have a . . . friend there."

"Summer's different." He took the compact from her. "I've known her for years. We were students together. We never— Friends, we're only friends," he ended on a mutter. "I don't enjoy explaining myself."

"I can see that." She pulled out bills and calculated the tip as the cab drew up to the hotel. As she started to slide out, she gave Carlo a long look. "No one asked you to."

"Ridiculous." He had her by the arm before she'd reached the revolving doors. "You ask. It isn't necessary to ask with words to ask."

"Guilt makes you imagine all sorts of things." She swung through the doors and into the lobby.

"Guilt?" Incensed, he caught up with her at the elevators. "I've nothing to be guilty for. A man has to commit some crime, some sin, for guilt."

She listened calmly as she stepped into the elevator car and pushed the button for their floor. "That's true, Carlo. You seem to me to be a man bent on making a confession."

He went off on a fiery stream of Italian that had the other two occupants of the car edging into the corners. Juliet folded her hands serenely and decided she'd never enjoyed herself more. The other passengers gave Carlo a wide berth as the elevator stopped on their floor.

"Did you want to grab something quick to eat at the airport or wait until we land?"

"I'm not interested in food."

"An odd statement from a chef." She breezed into the hall. "Take ten minutes to pack and I'll call for a bellman." The key was in her hand and into the lock before his fingers circled her wrist. When she looked up at him, she thought she'd never seen him truly frustrated before. Good. It was about time.

"I pack nothing until this is settled."

"Until what's settled?" she countered.

"When I commit a crime or a sin, I do so with complete honesty." It was the closest he'd come to an explosion. Juliet lifted a brow and listened attentively. "It was Lydia who had her arms around me."

Juliet smiled. "Yes, I saw quite clearly how you were struggling. A woman should be locked up for taking advantage of a man that way."

His eyes, already dark, went nearly black. "You're sarcastic. But you don't understand the circumstances."

"On the contrary." She leaned against the door. "Carlo, I believe I understood the circumstances perfectly. I don't believe I've asked you to explain anything. Now, you'd better pack if we're going to catch that early plane." For the second time, she shut the door in his face.

He stood where he was for a moment, torn. A man expected a certain amount of jealousy from a woman he was involved with. He even, well, enjoyed it to a point. What he didn't expect was a smile, a pat on the head and breezy understanding when he'd been caught in another woman's arms. However innocently.

No, he didn't expect it, Carlo decided. He wouldn't tolerate it.

When the sharp knock came on the door, Juliet was still standing with a hand on the knob. Wisely, she counted to ten before she opened it.

"Did you need something?"

Carefully, he studied her face for a trap. "You're not angry."

She lifted her brows. "No, why?"

"Lydia's very beautiful."

"She certainly is."

He stepped inside. "You're not jealous?"

"Don't be absurd." She brushed a speck of lint from her sleeve. "If you found me with another man, under similar circumstances, you'd understand, I'm sure."

"No." He closed the door behind him. "I'd break his face."

"Oh?" Rather pleased, she turned away to gather a few things from her dresser. "That's the Italian temperament, I suppose. Most of my ancestors were rather staid. Hand me that brush, will you?"

Carlo picked it up and dropped it into her hand. "Staid—this means?"

"Calm and sturdy, I suppose. Though there was one—my great-great-grandmother, I think. She found her husband tickling the scullery maid. In her staid sort of way, she knocked him flat with a cast-iron skillet. I don't think he ever tickled any of the other servants." Securing the brush in a plastic case, she arranged it in the bag. "I'm said to take after her."

Taking her by the shoulders, he turned her to face him. "There were no skillets available."

"True enough, but I'm inventive. Carlo . . ." Still smiling, she slipped her arms around his neck. "If I hadn't understood exactly what was going on, the coffee I'd fetched for you would've been dumped over your head. *Capice?*"

"*Sì.*" He grinned as he rubbed his nose against hers. But he didn't really understand her. Perhaps that was why he was enchanted by her. Lowering his mouth to hers, he let the enchantment grow. "Juliet," he murmured. "There's a later plane for Detroit, yes?"

She had wondered if he would ever think of it. "Yes, this afternoon."

"Did you know it's unhealthy for the system to rush." As he spoke, he slipped the jacket from her arms so that it slid to the floor.

"I've heard something about that."

"Very true. It's much better, medically speaking, to take one's time. To keep a steady pace, but not a fast one. And, of course, to give the system time to relax at regular intervals. It could be very unhealthy for us to pack now and race to the airport." He unhooked her skirt so that it followed her jacket.

"You're probably right."

"Of course I'm right," he murmured in her ear. "It would never do for either of us to be ill on the tour."

"Disastrous," she agreed. "In fact, it might be best if we both just lay down for a little while."

"The very best. One must guard one's health."

"I couldn't agree more," she told him as his shirt joined her skirt and jacket.

She was laughing as they tumbled onto the bed.

He liked her this way. Free, easy, enthusiastic. Just as he liked her cooler, more enigmatic moods. He could enjoy her in a hundred different ways because she wasn't always the same woman. Yet she was always the same.

Soft, as she was now. Warm wherever he touched, luxurious wherever he tasted. She might be submissive one moment, aggressive the next, and he never tired of the swings.

They made love in laughter now, something he knew more than most was precious and rare. Even when the passion began to dominate, there was an underlying sense of enjoyment that didn't cloud the fire. She gave him more in a moment than he'd thought he'd ever find with a woman in a lifetime.

She'd never known she could be this way—laughing, churning, happy, desperate. There were so many things she hadn't known. Every time he touched her it was something new, though it was somehow as if his touch was all she'd ever known. He made her feel fresh and desirable, wild and weepy all at once. In the space of minutes, he could bring her a sense of contentment and a frantic range of excitements.

The more he brought, the more he gave, and the easier it became for her to give. She wasn't aware yet, nor was he, that every time they made love, the intimacy grew and spread. It was gaining a strength and weight that wouldn't break with simply walking away. Perhaps if they'd known, they would have fought it.

Instead, they loved each other through the morning with the verve of youth and the depth of familiarity.

CHAPTER 10

Juliet hung up the phone, dragged a hand through her hair and swore. Rising, she swore again then moved toward the wide spread of window in Carlo's suite. For a few moments she muttered at nothing and no one in particular. Across the room, Carlo lay sprawled on the sofa. Wisely, he waited until she'd lapsed into silence.

"Problems?"

"We're fogged in." Swearing again, she stared out the window. She could see the mist, thick and still hanging outside the glass. Detroit was obliterated. "All flights are cancelled. The only way we're going to get to Boston is to stick out our thumbs."

"Thumbs?"

"Never mind." She turned and paced around the suite.

Detroit had been a solid round of media and events, and the Renaissance Center a beautiful place to stay, but now it was time to move on. Boston was just a hop away by air, so that the evening could be devoted to drafting out reports and a good night's sleep. Except for the fact that fog had driven in from the lake and put the whole city under wraps.

Stuck, Juliet thought as she glared out the window again.

Stuck when they had an 8:00 A.M. live demonstration on a well-established morning show in Boston.

He shifted a bit, but didn't sit up. If it hadn't been too much trouble, he could've counted off the number of times he'd been grounded for one reason or another. One, he recalled, had been a flamenco dancer in Madrid who'd distracted him into missing the last flight out. Better not to mention it. Still, when such things happened, Carlo reflected, it was best to relax and enjoy the moment. He knew Juliet better.

"You're worried about the TV in the morning."

"Of course I am." As she paced, she went over every possibility. Rent a car and drive—no, even in clear weather it was simply too far. They could charter a plane and hope the fog cleared by dawn. She took another glance outside. They were sixty-five floors up, but they might as well have been sixty-five feet under. No, she decided, no television spot was worth the risk. They'd have to cancel. That was that.

She dropped down on a chair and stuck her stockinged feet up by Carlo's. "I'm sorry, Carlo, there's no way around it. We'll have to scrub Boston."

"Scrub Boston?" Lazily he folded his arms behind his head. "Juliet, Franconi scrubs nothing. Cook, yes, scrub, no."

It took her a moment to realize he was serious. "I mean cancel."

"You didn't say cancel."

She heaved out a long breath. "I'm saying it now." She wiggled her toes, finding them a bit stiff after a ten-hour day. "There's no way we can make the television spot, and that's the biggest thing we have going in Boston. There're a couple of print interviews and an autographing. We didn't expect much to move there, and we were depending on the TV spot for that. Without it . . ." She shrugged and resigned herself. "It's a wash."

Letting his eyes half close, Carlo decided the sofa was an excellent place to spend an hour or so. "I don't wash."

She shot him a level look. "You're not going to have to do anything but lie on your—back," she decided after a moment, "for the next twenty-four hours."

"Nothing?"

"Nothing."

He grinned. Moving faster than he looked capable of, he sat up, grabbed her by the arms and pulled her down with him. "Good, you lie with me. Two backs, *madonna,* are better than one."

"Carlo." She couldn't avoid the first kiss. Or perhaps she didn't put her best effort into it, but she knew it was essential to avoid the second. "Wait a minute."

"Only twenty-four hours," he reminded her as he moved to her ear. "No time to waste."

"I've got to— Stop that," she ordered when her thoughts started to cloud. "There're arrangements to be made."

"What arrangements?"

She made a quick mental sketch. True, she'd already checked out of her room. They'd only kept the suite for convenience, and until six. She could book another separate room for the night, but—she might as well admit in this case it was foolish. Moving her shoulders, she gave in to innate practicality. "Like keeping the suite overnight."

"That's important." He lifted his head a moment. Her face was already flushed, her eyes already soft. Almost as if she'd spoken aloud, he followed the train of thought. He couldn't help but admire the way her mind worked from one point to the next in such straight lines.

"I have to call New York and let them know our status. I have to call Boston and cancel, then the airport and change our flight. Then I—"

"I think you have a love affair with the phone. It's difficult for a man to be jealous of an inanimate object."

"Phones are my life." She tried to slip out from under him, but got nowhere. "Carlo."

"I like it when you say my name with just a touch of exasperation."

"It's going to be more than a touch in a minute."

He'd thought he'd enjoy that as well. "But you haven't told me yet how fantastic I was today."

"You were fantastic." It was so easy to relax when he held her like this. The phone calls could wait, just a bit. After all, they weren't going anywhere. "You mesmerized them with your linguini."

"My linguini is hypnotic," he agreed. "I charmed the reporter from the *Free Press*."

"You left him stupefied. Detroit'll never be the same."

"That's true." He kissed her nose. "Boston won't know what it's missing."

"Don't remind me," she began, then broke off. Carlo could almost hear the wheels turning.

"An idea." Resigned, he rolled her on top of him and watched her think.

"It might work," she murmured. "If everyone cooperates, it might work very well. In fact, it might just be terrific."

"What?"

"You claim to be a magician as well as an artist."

"Modesty prevents me from—"

"Save it." She scrambled up until she stradled him. "You told me once you could cook in a sewer."

Frowning, he toyed with the little gold hoop she wore in her ear. "Yes, perhaps I did. But this is only an expression—"

"How about cooking by remote control?"

His brows drew together, but he ran his hand idly to the hem of her skirt that had ridden high on her thigh. "You have extraordinary legs," he said in passing, then gave her his attention. "What do you mean by remote control?"

"Just that." Wound up with the idea, Juliet rose and grabbed her pad and pencil. "You give me all the ingredients—it's linguini again tomorrow, right?"

"Yes, my specialty."

"Good, I have all that in the file anyway. We can set up a phone session between Detroit and the studio in Boston. You can be on the air there while we're here."

"Juliet, you ask for a lot of magic."

"No, it's just basic electronics. The host of the show—Paul O'Hara—can put the dish together on the air while you talk him through it. It's like talking a plane in, you know. Forty degrees to the left—a cup of flour."

"No."

"Carlo."

Taking his time, he pried off his shoes. "You want him, this O'Hara who smiles for the camera, to cook my linguini?"

"Don't get temperamental on me," she warned, while her mind leaped ahead to possibilities. "Look, you write cookbooks so the average person can cook one of your dishes."

"Cook them, yes." He examined his nails. "Not like Franconi."

She opened her mouth, then closed it again. Tread softly on the ego, Juliet reminded herself. At least until you get your way. "Of course not, Carlo. No one expects that. But we could turn this inconvenience into a real event. Using your cookbook on the air, and some personal coaching from you via phone, O'Hara can prepare the linguini. He's not a chef or a gourmet, but an average person. Therefore, he'll be giving the audience the average person's reactions. He'll make the average person's mistakes that you can correct. If we pull it off, the sales of your cookbook are going to soar. You know you can do it." She smiled winningly. "Why you even said you could teach me to cook, and I'm helpless in the kitchen. Certainly you can talk O'Hara through one dish."

"Of course I can." Folding his arms again, he stared up at the ceiling. Her logic was infallible, her idea creative. To be truthful, he liked it—almost as much as he liked the idea of not having to fly to Boston. Still, it hardly seemed fair to give without getting. "I'll do it—on one condition."

"Which is?"

"Tomorrow morning, I talk this O'Hara through linguini. Tonight . . ." And he smiled at her. "We have a dress rehearsal. I talk you through it."

Juliet stopped tapping the end of her pencil on the pad. "You want me to cook linguini?"

"With my guidance, *cara mia,* you could cook anything."

Juliet thought it over and decided it didn't matter. The suite didn't have a kitchen this time, so he'd be counting on using the hotel's. That may or may not work. If it did, once she'd botched it, they could order room service. The bottom line was saving what she could of Boston. "I'd love to. Now, I've got to make those calls."

Carlo closed his eyes and opted for a nap. If he was going to teach two amateurs the secrets of linguini within twelve hours, he'd need his strength. "Wake me when you've finished," he told her. "We have to inspect the kitchen of the hotel."

It took her the best part of two hours, and when she hung up for the last time, Juliet's neck was stiff and her fingers numb. But she had what she wanted. Hal told her she was a genius and O'Hara said it sounded like fun. Arrangements were already in the works.

This time Juliet grinned at the stubborn fog swirling outside the window. Neither rain nor storm nor dark of night, she thought, pleased with herself. Nothing was going to stop Juliet Trent.

Then she looked over at Carlo. Something tilted inside her that had both her confidence and self-satisfaction wavering. Emotion, she reflected. It was something she hadn't written into the itinerary.

Well, maybe there was one catastrophe that wasn't in the books. Maybe it was one she couldn't work her way through with a creative idea and hustle. She simply had to take her feelings for Carlo one step at a time.

Four more days, she mused, and the ride would be over. The music would stop and it would be time to get off the carousel.

It wasn't any use trying to see beyond that yet; it was all blank pages. She had to hold on to the belief that life was built one day at a time. Carlo would go, then she would pick up the pieces and begin her life again from that point.

She wasn't fool enough to tell herself she wouldn't cry. Tears would be shed over him, but they'd be shed quietly and privately. Schedule in a day for mourning, she thought then tossed her pad away.

It wasn't healthy to think of it now. There were only four days left. For a moment, she looked down at her empty hands and wondered if she'd have taken the steps she'd taken if she'd known where they would lead her. Then she looked over at him and simply watched him sleep.

Even with his eyes closed and that irrepressible inner life he had on hold, he could draw her. It wasn't simply a matter of his looks, she realized. She wasn't a woman who'd turn her life sideways for simple physical attraction. It was a matter of style. Smiling, she rose and walked closer to him as he slept. No matter how practical she was, how much common sense she possessed, she couldn't have resisted his style.

There'd be no regrets, she reaffirmed. Not now, nor in five days' time when an ocean and priorities separated them. As years passed, and their lives flowed and altered, she'd remember a handful of days when she'd had something special.

No time to waste, he'd said. Catching her tongue in her teeth Juliet decided she couldn't agree more. Reaching up, she began to unbutton her blouse. As a matter of habit, she draped it carefully over the back of a chair before she unhooked her skirt. When that fell, she lifted it, smoothed it out and folded it. The pins were drawn out of her hair, one by one, then set aside.

Dressed in a very impractical lace camisole and string bikini she moved closer.

Carlo awoke with his blood pumping and his head whirling. He could smell her scent lightly in her hair, more heady on her skin as her mouth took command of his. Her body was already heated as she lay full length on him. Before he could draw his first thoughts together, his own body followed suit.

She was all lace and flesh and passion. There wasn't time to steady his control or polish his style. Urgent and desperate, he reached for her and found silk and delicacy, strength and demand wherever he touched.

She unbuttoned his shirt and drew it aside so that their skin could meet and arouse. Beneath hers, she felt his heartbeat race and pound until power made her dizzy. Capturing his lips once again, she thought only of driving him to madness. She could feel it spread through him, growing, building, so that it would dominate both of them.

When he rolled so that she was trapped between the back of the sofa and his body, she was ready to relinquish control. With a moan, dark and liquid, she let herself enjoy what she'd begun.

No woman had ever done this to him. He understood that as his only thoughts were to devour everything she had. His fingers, so clever, so skilled, so gentle, pulled at the lace until the thin strap tore with hardly a sound.

He found her—small soft breasts that fit so perfectly in his hands, the strong narrow rib cage and slender waist. His. The word nearly drove him mad. She was his now, as she'd been in the dream she'd woken him from. Perhaps he was still dreaming.

She smelled of secrets, small, feminine secrets no man ever fully understood. She tasted of passion, ripe, shivering passion every man craved. With his tongue he tasted that sweet subtle valley between her breasts and felt her tremble. She was strong; he'd never doubted it. In her strength, she was surrendering completely to him, for the pleasure of each.

The lace smelled of her. He could have wallowed in it, but her skin was irresistible. He drew the camisole down to her waist and feasted on her.

With her hands tangled in his hair, her body on fire, she thought only of him. No tomorrows, no yesterdays. However much she might deny it in an hour, they'd become a single unit. One depended on the other for pleasure, for comfort, for excitement. For so much more she didn't dare think of it. She yearned for him; nothing would ever stop it. But now, he was taking her, fast and furious, through doors they'd opened together. Neither of them had gone there before with another, nor would again.

Juliet gave herself over to the dark, the heat, and to Carlo.

He drew the thin strings riding on her hips, craving the essence of her. When he'd driven her over the first peak, he knew and reveled in it. With endless waves of desire, he whipped her up again, and yet again, until they were both trembling. She called out his name as he ran his lips down her leg. All of her was the thought paramount in his mind. He'd have all of her until she was willing, ready to have all of him.

"Juliet, I want you." His face was above hers again, his breath straining. "Look at me."

She was staggering on that razor's edge between reason and madness. When she opened her eyes, his face filled her vision. It was all she wanted.

"I want you," he repeated while the blood raged in his head. "Only you."

She was wrapped around him, her head arched back. For an instant, their eyes met and held. What coursed through them wasn't something they could try to explain. It was both danger and security.

"Only," she murmured and took him into her.

They were both stunned, both shaken, both content. Naked, damp and warm, they lay tangled together in silence. Words had been spoken, Juliet thought. Words that were part of the madness of the moment. She would have to take care not to repeat them when passion was spent. They didn't need words; they had four days. Yet she ached to hear them again, to say them again.

She could set the tone between them, she thought. She had only to begin now and continue. No pressure. She kept her eyes closed a moment longer. No regrets. The extra moment she took to draw back her strength went unnoticed.

"I could stay just like this for a week," she murmured. Though she meant it, the words were said lazily. Turning her head, she looked at him, smiled. "Are you ready for another nap?"

There was so much he wanted to say. So much, he thought, she didn't want to hear. They'd set the rules; he had only to follow them. Nothing was as easy as it should've been.

"No." He kissed her forehead. "Though I've never found waking from a nap more delightful. Now, I think it's time for your next lesson."

"Really?" She caught her bottom lip between her teeth. "I thought I'd graduated."

"Cooking," he told her, giving her a quick pinch where Italian males were prone to.

Juliet tossed back her hair and pinched him back. "I thought you'd forget about that."

"Franconi never forgets. A quick shower, a change of clothes and down to the kitchen."

Agreeable, Juliet shrugged. She didn't think for one minute the management would allow him to give a cooking lesson in their kitchen.

Thirty minutes later, she was proven wrong.

Carlo merely bypassed management. He saw no reason to go through a chain of command. With very little fuss, he steered her through the hotel's elegant dining room and into the big, lofty kitchen. It smelled intoxicating and sounded like a subway station.

They'd stop him here, Juliet decided, still certain they'd be dining outside or through room service within the hour. Though she'd changed into comfortable jeans, she had no plans to cook. After one look at the big room with its oversized appliances and acres of counter, she was positive she wouldn't.

It shouldn't have surprised her to be proven wrong again.

"Franconi!" The name boomed out and echoed off the walls. Juliet jumped back three inches.

"Carlo, I think we should—" But as she spoke, she looked up at his face. He was grinning from ear to ear.

"Pierre!"

As she looked on, Carlo was enveloped by a wide, white-aproned man with a drooping moustache and a face as big and round as a frying pan. His skin glistened with sweat, but he smelt inoffensively of tomatoes.

"You Italian lecher, what do you do in my kitchen?"

"Honor it," Carlo said as they drew apart. "I thought you were in Montreal, poisoning the tourists."

"They beg me to take the kitchen here." The big man with the heavy French accent shrugged tanklike shoulders. "I feel sorry for them. Americans have so little finesse in the kitchen."

"They offered to pay you by the pound," Carlo said dryly. "Your pounds."

Pierre held both hands to his abundant middle and laughed. "We understand each other, old friend. Still, I find America to my liking. You, why aren't you in Rome pinching ladies?"

"I'm finishing up a tour for my book."

"But yes, you and your cookbooks." A noise behind him had him glancing around and bellowing in French. Juliet was certain the walls trembled. With a smile, he adjusted his hat and turned back to them. "That goes well?"

"Well enough." Carlo drew Juliet up. "This is Juliet Trent, my publicist."

"So it goes very well," Pierre murmured as he took Juliet's hand and brushed his lips over it. "Perhaps I will write a cookbook. Welcome to my kitchen, *mademoiselle*. I'm at your service."

Charmed, Juliet smiled. "Thank you, Pierre."

"Don't let this one fool you," Carlo warned. "He has a daughter your age."

"Bah!" Pierre gave him a lowered brow look. "She's but sixteen. If she were a day older, I'd call my wife and tell her to lock the doors while Franconi is in town."

Carlo grinned. "Such flattery, Pierre." With his hands hooked in his back pockets, he looked around the room. "Very nice," he mused. Lifting his head, he scented the air. "Duck. Is that duck I smell?"

Pierre preened. "The specialty. *Canard au Pierre.*"

"*Fantastico.*" Carlo swung an arm around Juliet as he led her closer to the scent. "No one, absolutely no one, does to duck what Pierre can do."

The black eyes in the frying-pan face gleamed. "No, you flatter me, *mon ami.*"

"There's no flattery in truth." Carlo looked on while an assistant carved Pierre's duck. With the ease of experience, he took a small sliver and popped it into Juliet's mouth. It dissolved there, leaving behind an elusive flavor that begged for more. Carlo merely laid his tongue on his thumb to test. "Exquisite, as always. Do you remember, Pierre, when we prepared the Shah's engagement feast? Five, six years ago."

"Seven," Pierre corrected and sighed.

"Your duck and my cannelloni."

"Magnificent. Not so much paprika on that fish," he boomed out. "We are not in Budapest. Those were the days," he continued easily. "But . . ." The shrug was essentially Gallic. "When a man has his third child, he has to settle down, *oui?*"

Carlo gave another look at the kitchen, and with an expert's eye approved. "You've picked an excellent spot. Perhaps you'd let me have a corner of it for a short time."

"A corner?"

"A favor," Carlo said with a smile that would have charmed the pearls from oysters. "I've promised my Juliet to teach her how to prepare linguini."

"*Linguini con vongole biance?*" Pierre's eyes glittered.

"Naturally. It is my specialty."

"You can have a corner of my kitchen, *mon ami,* in exchange for a plate."

Carlo laughed and patted Pierre's stomach. "For you, *amico,* two plates."

Pierre clasped him by the shoulders and kissed both cheeks. "I feel my youth coming back to me. Tell me what you need."

In no time at all, Juliet found herself covered in a white apron with her hair tucked into a chef's hat. She might have felt ridiculous if she'd been given the chance.

"First you mince the clams."

Juliet looked at Carlo, then down at the mess of clams on the cutting board. "Mince them?"

"Like so." Carlo took the knife and with a few quick moves had half of the clams in small, perfect pieces. "Try."

Feeling a bit like an executioner, Juliet brought the knife down. "They're not . . . well, alive, are they?"

"*Madonna,* any clam considers himself honored to be part of Franconi's linguini. A bit smaller there. Yes." Satisfied, he passed her an onion. "Chopped, not too fine." Again, he demonstrated, but this time Juliet felt more at home. Accepting the knife, she hacked again until the onion was in pieces and her eyes were streaming.

"I hate to cook," she muttered but Carlo only pushed a clove of garlic at her.

"This is chopped very fine. Its essence is what we need, not so much texture." He stood over her shoulder, watching until he approved. "You've good hands, Juliet. Now here, melt the butter."

Following instructions, she cooked the onion and garlic in the simmering butter, stirring until Carlo pronounced it ready.

"Now, it's tender, you see. We add just a bit of flour." He held her hand to direct it as she stirred it in. "So it thickens. We add the clams. Gently," he warned before she could dump them in. "We don't want them bruised. Ah . . ." He nodded with approval. "Spice," he told her. "It's the secret and the strength."

Bending over her, he showed her how to take a pinch of this, a touch of that and create. As the scent became more pleasing, her confidence grew. She'd never remember the amounts or the ingredients, but found it didn't matter.

"How about that?" she asked, pointing to a few sprigs of parsley.

"No, that comes just at the end. We don't want to drown it. Turn the heat down, just a little more. There." Satisfied, he nodded. "The cover goes on snug, then you let it simmer while the spices wake up."

Juliet wiped the back of her hand over her damp brow. "Carlo, you talk about the sauce as though it lived and breathed."

"My sauces do," he said simply. "While this simmers, you grate the cheese." He picked up a hunk and with his eyes closed, sniffed. *"Squisito."*

He had her grate and stir while the rest of the kitchen staff worked around them. Juliet thought of her mother's kitchen with its tidy counters and homey smells. She'd never seen anything like this. It certainly wasn't quiet. Pans were dropped, people and dishes were cursed, and fast was the order of the day. Busboys hustled in and out, weighed down with trays, waiters and waitresses breezed through demanding their orders. While she watched wide-eyed, Carlo ignored. It was time to create his pasta.

Unless it was already cooked and in a meal, Juliet thought of pasta as something you got off the shelf in a cardboard box. She learned differently, after her hands were white to the wrists with flour. He had her measure and knead and roll and spread until her elbows creaked. It was nothing like the five-minute throw-it-together kind she was used to.

As she worked, she began to realize why he had such stamina. He had to. In cooking for a living the way Franconi cooked for a living, he used as much energy as any athlete did. By the time the pasta had passed his inspection, her shoulder muscles ached the way they did after a brisk set of tennis.

Blowing the hair out of her eyes and mopping away sweat, Juliet turned to him. "What now?"

"Now you cook the pasta."

She tried not to grumble as she poured water into a Dutch oven and set it on to boil.

"One tablespoon salt," Carlo instructed.

"One tablespoon salt," she muttered and poured it in. When she turned around, he handed her a glass of wine.

"Until it boils, you relax."

"Can I turn down the heat?"

He laughed and kissed her, then decided it was only right to kiss her again. She smelled like heaven. "I like you in white." He dusted flour from her nose. "You're a messy cook, my love, but a stunning one."

It was easy to forget the noisy, bustling kitchen. "Cook?" A bit primly, she adjusted her hat. "Isn't it chef?"

He kissed her again. "Don't get cocky. One linguini doesn't make a chef."

She barely finished her wine when he put her back to work. "Put one end of the linguini in the water. Yes, just so. Now, as it softens coil them in. Careful. Yes, yes, you have a nice touch. A bit more patience and I might take you on in my restaurant."

"No, thanks," Juliet said definitely as the steam rose in her face. She was almost certain she felt each separate pore opening.

"Stir easily. Seven minutes only, not a moment more." He refilled her glass and kissed her cheek.

She stirred, and drained, measured parsley, poured and sprinkled cheese. By the time she was finished, Juliet didn't think she could eat a thing. Nerves, she discovered with astonishment. She was as nervous as a new bride on her first day in the kitchen.

With her hands clasped together, she watched Carlo take a fork and dip in. Eyes closed, he breathed in the aroma. She swallowed. His eyes remained closed as he took the first sample. Juliet bit her lip. Until then, she hadn't noticed that the kitchen had become as quiet as a cathedral. A quick glimpse around showed her all activity had stopped and all eyes were on Carlo. She felt as though she were waiting to be sentenced or acquitted.

"Well?" she demanded when she couldn't stand it any longer.

"Patience," Carlo reminded her without opening his eyes. A busboy rushed in and was immediately shushed. Carlo opened his eyes and carefully set down the fork. *"Fantastico!"* He took Juliet by the shoulders and gave her the ceremonial kiss on each cheek as applause broke out.

Laughing, she pulled off her hat with a flourish. "I feel like I won a Gold Medal in the decathlon."

"You've created." As Pierre boomed orders for plates, Carlo took both her hands. "We make a good team, Juliet Trent."

She felt something creeping too close to the heart. It just didn't seem possible to stop it. "Yes, we make a good team, Franconi."

CHAPTER 11

By twelve the next day, there was absolutely nothing left to be done. Carlo's remote control demonstration on the proper way to prepare linguini had gone far beyond Juliet's hopes for success. She'd stayed glued to the television, listening to Carlo's voice beside her and through the speakers. When her supervisor called personally to congratulate her, Juliet knew she had a winner. Relaxed and satisfied, she lay back on the bed.

"Wonderful." She folded her arms, crossed her ankles and grinned. "Absolutely wonderful."

"Did you ever doubt it?"

Still grinning, she shot a look at Carlo as he finished off the last of both shares of the late breakfast they'd ordered. "Let's just say I'm glad it's over."

"You worry too much, *mi amore*." But he hadn't seen her dig for her little roll of pills in three days. It pleased him enormously to know that he relaxed her so that she didn't need them. "When it comes to Franconi's linguini, you have always a success."

"After this I'll never doubt it. Now we have five hours before flight time. Five full, completely unscheduled hours."

Rising he sat on the end of the bed and ran his fingers

along the arch of her foot. She looked so lovely when she smiled, so lovely when she let her mind rest. "Such a bonus," he murmured.

"It's like a vacation." With a sigh, she let herself enjoy the little tingles of pleasure.

"What would you like to do with our vacation of five full, unscheduled hours?"

She lifted a brow at him. "You really want to know?"

Slowly, he kissed each one of her toes. "Of course. The day is yours." He brushed his lips over her ankle. "I'm at your service."

Springing up, she threw her arms around his neck and kissed him, hard. "Let's go shopping."

Fifteen minutes later, Juliet strolled with Carlo through the first tower of the enormous circular shopping center attached to the hotel. People huddled around the maps of the complex, but she breezed around the curve and bypassed one. No maps, no schedules, no routes. Today, it didn't matter where they went.

"Do you know," she began, "with all the department stores, malls and cities we've been through, I haven't had a chance to shop?"

"You don't give yourself time."

"Same thing. Oh, look." She stopped at a window display and studied a long evening dress covered with tiny silver bangles.

"Very dashing," Carlo decided.

"Dashing," Juliet agreed. "If I were six inches taller it might not make me look like a scaled-down pillar. Shoes." She pulled him along to the next shop.

In short order, Carlo discovered Juliet's biggest weakness. The way to her heart wasn't through food, nor was it paved with furs and diamonds. Jewelry displays barely earned her glance. Evening clothes brought a brief survey while day wear and sports clothes won mild interest. But shoes were something different. Within an hour, she'd studied, fondled and critiqued at least fifty pairs. She found a pair of sneakers at 30 percent off and bought them to add to an already substantial collection. Then with a careful maneuver to pick and choose, she weeded her selection down to three pair of heels, all Italian.

"You show excellent taste." With the patience of a man accustomed to shopping expeditions, Carlo lounged in a chair and watched her vacillate between one pair then the other. Idly, he picked up one shoe and glanced at the signature inside. "He makes an elegant shoe and prefers my lasagna."

Wide-eyed, Juliet pivoted on the thin heels. "You know him?"

"Of course. Once a week he eats in Franconi's."

"He's my hero." When Carlo gave her his lifted brow look, she laughed. "I know I can put on a pair of his shoes and go eight hours without needing emergency surgery. I'll take all three," she said on impulse, then sat down to exchange the heels for her newly bought sneakers.

"You make me surprised," he commented. "So many shoes when you have only two feet. This is not my practical Juliet."

"I'm entitled to a vice." Juliet pushed the Velcro closed. "Besides, I've always known Italians make the best shoes." She leaned closer to kiss his cheek. "Now I know they make the best . . . pasta." Without a blink at the total, she charged the shoes and pocketed the receipt.

Swinging the bag between them, they wandered from tower to tower. A group of women strolled by, earning Carlo's appreciation. Shopping during lunch hour, he gauged as he tossed an extra look over his shoulder. One had to admire the American workforce.

"You'll strain your neck that way," Juliet commented easily. She couldn't help but be amused by his blatant pleasure in anything female. He merely grinned.

"It's simply a matter of knowing just how far to go."

Comfortable, Juliet enjoyed the feel of his fingers laced with hers. "I'd never argue with the expert."

Carlo stopped once, intrigued by a choker in amethysts and diamonds. "This is lovely," he decided. "My sister, Teresa, always preferred purple."

Juliet leaned closer to the glass. The small, delicate jewels glimmered, hot and cold. "Who wouldn't? It's fabulous."

"She has a baby in a few weeks," he murmured, then nodded to the discreetly anxious clerk. "I'll see this."

"Of course, a lovely piece, isn't it?" After taking it out of the locked case, he placed it reverently in Carlo's hand. "The diamonds are all superior grade, naturally, and consist of one point three carat. The amethyst—"

"I'll have it."

Thrown off in the middle of his pitch, the clerk blinked. "Yes, sir, an excellent choice." Trying not to show surprise, he took the credit card Carlo handed him along with the choker and moved farther down the counter.

"Carlo." Juliet edged closer and lowered her voice. "You didn't even ask the price."

He merely patted her hand as he skimmed the other contents in the case. "My sister's about to make me an uncle again," he said simply. "The choker suits her. Now emeralds," he began, "would be your stone."

She glanced down at a pair of earrings with stones the color of dark, wet summer grass. The momentary longing was purely feminine and easily controlled. Shoes she could justify; emeralds, no. She shook her head and laughed at him. "I'll just stick with pampering my feet."

When Carlo had his present nicely boxed and his receipt in hand, they wandered back out. "I love to shop," Juliet confessed. "Sometimes I'll spend an entire Saturday just roaming. It's one of the things I like best about New York."

"Then you'd love Rome." He'd like to see her there, he discovered. By the fountains, laughing, strolling through the markets and cathedrals, dancing in the clubs that smelled of wine and humanity. He wanted to have her there, with him. Going back alone was going back to nothing. He brought her hand to his lips as he thought of it, holding it there until she paused, uncertain.

"Carlo?" People brushed by them, and as his look became more intense, she swallowed and repeated his name. This wasn't the mild masculine appreciation she'd seen him send passing women, but something deep and dangerous. When a man looked at a woman this way, the woman was wise to run. But Juliet didn't know if it were toward him or away.

He shook off the mood, warning himself to tread carefully with her, and himself. "If you came," he said lightly, "I could introduce you to your hero. Enough of my lasagna and you'd have your shoes at cost."

Relieved, she tucked her arm through his again. "You tempt me to start saving for the airfare immediately. Oh, Carlo, look at this!" Delighted, she stopped in front of a window and pointed. In the midst of the ornate display was a three-foot Indian elephant done in high-gloss ceramic. Its blanket was a kaleidoscope of gilt and glitter and color. Opulent and regal, its head was lifted, its trunk curled high. Juliet fell in love. "It's wonderful, so unnecessarily ornate and totally useless."

He could see it easily in his living room along with the other ornate and useless pieces he'd collected over the years. But he'd never have imagined Juliet's taste running along the same path. "You surprise me again."

A bit embarrassed, she moved her shoulders. "Oh, I know it's awful, really, but I love things that don't belong anywhere at all."

"Then you must come to Rome and see my house." At her puzzled look, he laughed. "The last piece I acquired is an owl, this high." He demonstrated by holding out a palm. "It's caught a small, unfortunate rodent in its talons."

"Dreadful." With something close to a giggle, she kissed him. "I'm sure I'd love it."

"Perhaps you would at that," he murmured. "In any case, I believe the elephant should have a good home."

"You're going to buy it?" Thrilled, she clasped his hand as they went inside. The shop smelled of sandalwood and carried the tinkle of glass from wind chimes set swaying by a fan. She left him to make arrangements for shipping while she poked around, toying with long strings of brass bells, alabaster lions and ornamental tea services.

All in all, Juliet mused, it had been the easiest, most relaxing day she'd had in weeks, maybe longer. She'd remember it, that she promised herself, when she was alone again and life wound down to schedules and the next demand.

Turning, she looked at Carlo as he said something to make the clerk laugh. She hadn't thought there were men like him—secure, utterly masculine and yet sensitive to female moods and needs. Arrogant, he was certainly that, but generous as well. Passionate but gentle, vain but intelligent.

If she could have conjured up a man to fall in love with . . . oh no, Juliet warned herself with something like desperation. It wouldn't be Carlo Franconi. Couldn't be. He wasn't a man for one woman, and she wasn't a woman for any man. They both needed their freedom. To forget that would be to forget the plans she'd made and had been working toward for ten years. It was best to remember that Carlo was a ride on a carousel, and that the music only played so long.

She took a deep breath and waited for her own advice to sink in. It took longer than it should have. Determined, she smiled and walked to him. "Finished?"

"Our friend will be home soon, very soon after we are."

"Then we'll wish him bon voyage. We'd better start thinking airport ourselves."

With his arm around her shoulders, they walked out. "You'll give me our Philadelphia schedule on the plane."

"You're going to be a smash," she told him. "Though you might want to try my brewer's yeast before it's done."

I can't believe it." At eight o'clock, Juliet dropped down into a chair outside customer service. Behind her, the conveyor belt of baggage was stopped. "The luggage went to Atlanta."

"Not so hard to believe," Carlo returned. He'd lost his luggage more times than he cared to remember. He gave his leather case a pat. His spatulas were safe. "So, when do we expect our underwear?"

"Maybe by ten tomorrow morning." Disgusted, Juliet looked down at the jeans and T-shirt she'd worn on the flight. She carried her toiletries and a few odds and ends in her shoulder bag, but nothing remotely resembling a business suit. No matter, she decided. She'd be in the background. Then she took a look at Carlo.

He wore a short-sleeved sweatshirt with the word *Sorbonne* dashed across it, jeans white at the stress points and a pair of sneakers that weren't nearly as new as hers. How the hell, she wondered, was he supposed to go on the air at 8:00 A.M. dressed like that?

"Carlo, we've got to get you some clothes."

"I have clothes," he reminded her, "in my bags."

"You're on *Hello, Philadelphia* in the morning at eight,

from there we go directly to breakfast with reporters from the *Herald* and the *Inquirer*. At ten, when our bags may or may not be back, you're on *Midmorning Report*. After that—"

"You've already given me the schedule, my love. What's wrong with this?"

When he gestured toward what he wore, Juliet stood up. "Don't be cute, Carlo. We're heading for the closest department store."

"Department store?" Carlo allowed himself to be pulled outside. "Franconi doesn't wear department store."

"This time you do. No time to be choosy. What's in Philadelphia?" she muttered as she hailed a cab. "Wannamaker's." Holding the door open for him, she checked her watch. "We might just make it."

They arrived a half hour before closing. Though he grumbled, Carlo let her drag him through the old, respected Philadelphia institution. Knowing time was against them, Juliet pushed through a rack of slacks. "What size?"

"Thirty-one, thirty-three," he told her with his brow lifted. "Do I choose my own clothes?"

"Try this." Juliet held out a pair of dun-colored pleated slacks.

"I prefer the buff," he began.

"This is better for the camera. Now shirts." Leaving him holding the hanger, she pounced on the next rack. "Size?"

"What do I know from American sizes?" he grumbled.

"This should be right." She chose an elegant shade of salmon in a thin silk that Carlo was forced to admit he'd have looked twice at himself. "Go put these on while I look at the jackets."

"It's like shopping with your mother," he said under his breath as he headed for the dressing rooms.

She found a belt, thin and supple with a fancy little buckle she knew he wouldn't object to. After rejecting a half dozen jackets she came across one in linen with a casual, unstructured fit in a shade between cream and brown.

When Carlo stepped out, she thrust them at him, then stood back to take in the entire view. "It's good," she decided as he shrugged the jacket on. "Yes, it's really good. The color of the shirt keeps the rest from being drab and the jacket keeps it just casual enough without being careless."

"The day Franconi wears clothes off the rack—"

"Only Franconi could wear clothes off the rack and make them look custom-tailored."

He stopped, meeting the laughter in her eyes. "You flatter me."

"Whatever it takes." Turning him around, she gave him a quick push toward the dressing room. "Strip it off, Franconi. I'll get you some shorts."

The look he sent her was cool, with very little patience. "There's a limit, Juliet."

"Don't worry about a thing," she said breezily. "The publisher'll pick up the tab. Make it fast; we've got just enough time to buy your shoes."

She signed the last receipt five minutes after the PA system announced closing. "You're set." Before he could do so himself, she bundled up his packages. "Now, if we can just get a cab to the hotel, we're in business."

"I wear your American shoes in protest."

"I don't blame you," she said sincerely. "Emergency measures, *caro.*"

Foolishly, he was moved by the endearment. She'd never lowered her guard enough to use one before. Because of it, Carlo decided to be generous and forgive her for cracking the whip. "My mother would admire you."

"Oh?" Distracted, Juliet stood at the curb and held out her hand for a cab. "Why?"

"She's the only one who's ever poked and prodded me through a store and picked out my clothes. She hasn't done so in twenty years."

"All publicists are mothers," she told him and switched to her other arm. "We have to be."

He leaned closer and caught her earlobe between his teeth. "I prefer you as a lover."

A cab screeched to a halt at the curb. Juliet wondered if it was that which had stolen her breath. Steadying, she bundled Carlo and the packages inside. "For the next few days, I'll be both."

It was nearly ten before they checked into the Cocharan House. Carlo managed to say nothing about the separate rooms, but he made up his mind on the spot that she'd spend no time in her own. They had three days and most of that time would be eaten up with business. Not a moment that was left would be wasted.

He said nothing as they got into the elevator ahead of the bellman. As they rode up, he hummed to himself as Juliet chatted idly. At the door of his suite, he took her arm.

"Put all the bags in here, please," he instructed the bellman. "Ms. Trent and I have some business to see to immediately. We'll sort them out." Before she could say a word, he took out several bills and tipped the bellman himself. She remained silent only until they were alone again.

"Carlo, just what do you think you're doing? I told you before—"

"That you wanted a room of your own. You still have it," he pointed out. "Two doors down. But you're staying here, with me. Now, we'll order a bottle of wine and relax." He took the packages she still carried out of her hands and tossed them on a long, low sofa. "Would you prefer something light?"

"I'd prefer not to be hustled around."

"So would I." With a grin, he glanced over at his new clothes. "Emergency measures."

Hopeless, she thought. He was hopeless. "Carlo, if you'd just try to understand—"

The knock on the door stopped her. She only muttered a little as he went to answer.

"Summer!" She heard the delight in his voice and turned to see him wrapped close with a stunning brunette.

"Carlo, I thought you'd be here an hour ago."

The voice was intriguing, hints of France, a slight touch of British discipline. As she stepped away from Carlo, Juliet saw elegance, flash and style all at once. She saw Carlo take the exquisite face in his hands, as he had so often with hers, and kiss the woman long and hard.

"Ah, my little puff pastry, you're as beautiful as ever."

"And you, Franconi, are as full of . . ." Summer broke off as she spotted the woman standing in the center of the room. She smiled, and though it was friendly enough, she didn't attempt to hide the survey. "Hello. You must be Carlo's publicist."

"Juliet Trent." Odd, Carlo felt as nervous as a boy introducing his first heartthrob to his mother. "This is Summer Cocharan, the finest pastry chef on either side of the Atlantic."

Summer held out a hand as she crossed into the room. "He's flattering me because he hopes I'll fix him an éclair."

"A dozen of them," Carlo corrected. "Beautiful, isn't she, Summer?"

While Juliet struggled for the proper thing to say, Summer smiled again. She'd heard something in Carlo's voice she'd never expected to. "Yes, she is. Horrid to work with, isn't he, Juliet?"

Juliet felt the laugh come easily. "Yes, he is."

"But never dull." Angling her head, she gave Carlo a quick, intimate look. Yes, there was something here other than business. About time, too. "By the way, Carlo, I should thank you for sending young Steven to me."

Interested, Carlo set down his leather case. "He's working out then?"

"Wonderfully."

"The young boy who wanted to be a chef," Juliet murmured and found herself incredibly moved. He hadn't forgotten.

"Yes, did you meet him? He's very dedicated," Summer went on when Juliet nodded. "I think your idea of sending him to Paris for training will pay off. He's going to be excellent."

"Good." Satisfied, Carlo patted her hand. "I'll speak with his mother and make the arrangements."

Brows knit, Juliet stared at him. "You're going to send him to Paris?"

"It's the only place to study cordon bleu properly." Carlo gave a shrug as though the matter were everyday. "Then, when he's fully trained, I'll simply steal him away from Summer for my own restaurant."

"Perhaps you will," Summer smiled. "Then again, perhaps you won't."

He was going to pay for the education and training of a boy he'd met only once, Juliet thought, baffled. What sort of a man was it who could fuss for twenty minutes over the knot of his tie and give with such total generosity to a stranger? How foolish she'd been to think, even for a minute, that she really knew him.

"It's very kind of you, Carlo," she murmured after a moment.

He gave her an odd look, then shrugged it off. "Dues are meant to be paid, Juliet. I was young once and had only a mother to provide for me. Speaking of mothers," he went on smoothly, changing the topic. "How is Monique?"

"Gloriously happy still," Summer told him, and smiled thinking of her mother. "Keil was obviously the man she'd been looking for." With a laugh, she turned back to Juliet. "I'm sorry, Carlo and I go back a long way."

"Don't be. Carlo tells me you and he were students together."

"A hundred years ago, in Paris."

"Now Summer's married her big American. Where's Blake, *cara?* Does he trust you with me?"

"Not for long." Blake came through the open doorway, still elegant after a twelve-hour day. He was taller than Carlo, broader, but Juliet thought she recognized a similarity. Power, both sexual and intellectual.

"This is Juliet Trent," Summer began. "She's keeping Carlo in line on his American tour."

"Not an easy job." A waiter rolled in a bucket of champagne and glasses. Blake dismissed him with a nod. "Summer tells me your schedule in Philadelphia's very tight."

"She holds the whip," Carlo told him with a gesture toward Juliet. But when his hand came down, it brushed her shoulder in a gesture of casual and unmistakable intimacy.

"I thought I might run over to the studio in the morning and watch your demonstration." Summer accepted the glass of champagne from her husband. "It's been a long time since I've seen you cook."

"Good." Carlo relaxed with the first sip of frosty wine. "Perhaps I'll have time to give your kitchen an inspection. Summer came here to remodel and expand Blake's kitchen, then stayed on because she'd grown attached to it."

"Quite right." Summer sent her husband an amused look. "In fact, I've grown so attached I've decided to expand again."

"Yes?" Interested, Carlo lifted his brow. "Another Cocharan House?"

"Another Cocharan," Summer corrected.

It took him a moment, but Juliet saw the moment the words had sunk in. Emotion she'd always expected from him, and it was there now, in his eyes as he set down his glass. "You're having a child."

"In the winter." Summer smiled and stretched out her hand. "I haven't figured out how I'm going to reach the stove for Christmas dinner."

He took her hand and kissed it, then kissed her cheeks, one by one. "We've come a long way, *cara mia*."

"A very long way."

"Do you remember the merry-go-round?"

She remembered well her desperate flight to Rome to flee from Blake and her feelings. "You told me I was afraid to grab the brass ring, and so you made me try. I won't forget it."

He murmured something in Italian that made Summer's eyes fill. "And I've always loved you. Now make a toast or something before I disgrace myself."

"A toast." Carlo picked up his glass and slipped his free arm around Juliet. "To the carousel that doesn't end."

Juliet lifted her glass and, sipping, let the champagne wash away the ache.

Cooking before the camera was something Summer understood well. She spent several hours a year doing just that while handling the management of the kitchen in the Philadelphia Cocharan House, satisfying her own select clients with a few trips a year if the price and the occasion were important enough, and, most important of all, learning to enjoy her marriage.

Though she'd often cooked with Carlo, in the kitchen of a palace, in the less expensive area of the flat she still kept in Paris and dozens of other places, she never tired of watching him in action. While she was said to create with the intensity of a brain surgeon, Carlo had the flair of an artist. She'd always admired his expansiveness, his ease of manner, and especially his theatrics.

When he'd put the finishing touches on the pasta dish he'd named, not immodestly, after himself, she applauded with the rest of the audience. But she'd hitched a ride to the studio with him and Juliet for more reason than to feed an old friend's ego. If Summer knew anyone in the world as well as she did herself, it was Carlo. She'd often thought, in many ways, they'd risen from the same dough.

"*Bravo,* Franconi." As the crew began to serve his dish to the audience, Summer went up to give him a formal kiss on the cheek.

"Yes." He kissed her back. "I was magnificent."

"Where's Juliet?"

"On the phone." Carlo rolled his eyes to the ceiling. "*Dio,* that woman spends more time on the phone than a new bride spends in bed."

Summer checked her watch. She'd noted Carlo's schedule herself. "I don't imagine she'll be long. I know you're having a late breakfast at the hotel with reporters."

"You promised to make crêpes," he reminded her, thinking unapologetically of his own pleasure.

"So I did. In return, do you think you could find a small, quiet room for the two of us?"

He grinned and wiggled his brows. "My love, when Franconi can't oblige a lady with a quiet room, the world stops."

"My thoughts exactly." She hooked her arm through his and let him lead her down a corridor and into what turned out to be a storage room with an overhead light. "You've never lacked class, *caro.*"

"So." He made himself comfortable on a stack of boxes.

"Since I know you don't want my body, superb as it is, what's on your mind?"

"You, of course, *chérie*."

"Of course."

"I love you, Carlo."

Her abrupt seriousness made him smile and take her hands. "And I you, always."

"You remember, not so long ago when you came through Philadelphia on tour for another book?"

"You were wondering how to take the job redoing the American's kitchen when you were attracted to him and determined not to be."

"In love with him and determined not to be," she corrected. "You gave me some good advice here, and when I visited you in Rome. I want to return the favor."

"Advice?"

"Grab the brass ring, Carlo, and hold on to it."

"Summer—"

"Who knows you better?" she interrupted.

He moved his shoulders. "No one."

"I saw you were in love with her the moment I stepped into the room, the moment you said her name. We understand each other too well to pretend."

He sat a moment, saying nothing. He'd been skirting around the word, and its consequences, very carefully for days. "Juliet is special," he said slowly. "I've thought perhaps what I feel for her is different."

"Thought?"

He let out a small sound and gave up. "Known. But the kind of love we're speaking of leads to commitment, marriage, children."

Instinctively Summer touched a hand to her stomach. Carlo would understand that she still had small fears. She didn't have to speak of them. "Yes. You told me once, when I asked you why you'd never married, that no woman had made your heart tremble. Do you remember what you told me you'd do if you met her?"

"Run for a license and a priest." Rising, he slipped his hands into the pockets of the slacks Juliet had selected for him. "Easy words *before* the heart trembles. I don't want to lose her." Once said, he sighed. "It's never mattered before, but now it matters too much to make the wrong move. She's elusive, Summer. There are times I hold her and feel part of her pull away. I understand her independence, her ambition, and even admire them."

"I have Blake, but I still have my independence and my ambition."

"Yes." He smiled at her. "Do you know, she's so like you. Stubborn." When Summer lifted a brow, he grinned. "Hard in the head and so determined to be the best. Qualities I've always found strangely appealing in a beautiful woman."

"Merci, mon cher ami," Summer said dryly. "Then where's your problem?"

"You'd trust me."

She looked surprised, then moved her shoulders as though he'd said something foolish. "Of course."

"She can't—won't," Carlo corrected. "Juliet would find it easier to give me her body, even part of her heart than her trust. I need it, Summer, as much as I need what she's already given me."

Thoughtful, Summer leaned against a crate. "Does she love you?"

"I don't know." A difficult admission for a man who'd always thought he understood women so well. He smiled a little as he realized a man never fully understood the woman most important to him. With any other woman he'd have been confident he could guide and mold the emotions to his own preference. With Juliet, he was confident of nothing.

"There are times she seems very close and times she seems very detached. Until yesterday I hadn't fully begun to know my own mind."

"Which is?"

"I want her with me," he said simply. "When I'm an old man sitting by the fountains watching the young girls, I'll still want her with me."

Summer moved over to put her hands on his shoulders. "Frightening, isn't it?"

"Terrifying." Yet somehow, he thought, easier now that he'd admitted it. "I'd always thought it would be easy. There'd be love, romance, marriage and children. How could I know the woman would be a stubborn American?"

Summer laughed and dropped her forehead to his. "No more than I could know the man would be a stubborn American. But he was right for me. Your Juliet is right for you."

"So." He kissed Summer's temple. "How do I convince her?"

Summer frowned a moment, thinking. With a quick smile, she walked over to a corner. Picking up a broom, she held it out to him. "Sweep her off her feet."

Juliet was close to panic when she spotted Carlo strolling down the corridor with Summer on his arm. They might've been taking in the afternoon sun on the Left Bank. The first wave of relief evaporated into annoyance. "Carlo, I've turned this place upside down looking for you."

He merely smiled and touched a finger to her cheek. "You were on the phone."

Telling herself not to swear, she dragged a hand through

her hair. "Next time you wander off, leave a trail of bread crumbs. In the meantime, I've got a very cranky cab driver waiting outside." As she pulled him along, she struggled to remember her manners. "Did you enjoy the show?" she asked Summer.

"I always enjoy watching Carlo cook. I only wish the two of you had more time in town. As it is, your timing's very wise."

"Yes?" Carlo pushed open the door and held it for both women.

"The French swine comes through next week."

The door shut with the punch of a bullet. "LaBare?"

Juliet turned back. She'd heard him snarl that name before. "Carlo—"

He held up a hand, silencing any interruption. "What does the Gallic slug do here?"

"Precisely what you've done," Summer returned. Tossing back her hair, she scowled at nothing. "He's written another book."

"Peasant. He's fit to cook only for hyenas."

"For rabid hyenas," Summer corrected.

Seeing that both of her charges were firing up, Juliet took an arm of each. "I think we can talk in the cab."

"He will not speak to you," Carlo announced, ignoring Juliet. "I will dice him into very small pieces."

Though she relished the image, Summer shook her head. "Don't worry. I can handle him. Besides, Blake finds it amusing."

Carlo made a sound like a snake. Juliet felt her nerves fraying. "Americans. Perhaps I'll come back to Philadelphia and murder him."

Trying her best, Juliet nudged him toward the cab. "Come now, Carlo, you know you don't want to murder Blake."

"LaBare," he corrected with something close to an explosion.

"Who is LaBare?" Juliet demanded in exasperation.

"Swine," Carlo answered.

"Pig," Summer confirmed. "But I have plans of my own for him. He's going to stay at the Cocharan House." Summer spread her hands and examined her nails. "I'm going to prepare his meals personally."

With a laugh, Carlo lifted her from the ground and kissed her. "Revenge, my love, is sweeter than even your meringue." Satisfied, he set her down again. "We were students with this slug." Carlo explained to Juliet. "His crimes are too numerous to mention." With a snap, Carlo adjusted his jacket. "I refuse to be on the same continent as he."

Running out of patience, Juliet glanced at the scowling cab driver. "You won't be," she reminded him. "You'll be back in Italy when he's here."

Carlo brightened and nodded. "You're right. Summer, you'll call me and tell me how he fell on his face?"

"Naturally."

"Then it's settled." His mood altered completely, he smiled and picked up the conversation as it ended before the mention of the Frenchman's name. "Next time we come to Philadelphia," Carlo promised, "you and I will make a meal for Blake and Juliet. My veal, your bombe. You haven't sinned, Juliet, until you've tasted Summer's bombe."

There wouldn't be a next time, Juliet knew, but she managed to smile. "I'll look forward to it."

Carlo paused as Juliet opened the door of the cab. "But tonight, we leave for New York."

Summer smiled as she stepped inside. "Don't forget to pack your broom."

Juliet started to climb into the front seat. "Broom?"

Carlo took Summer's hand in his and smiled. "An old French expression."

CHAPTER 12

New York hadn't changed. Perhaps it was hotter than when Juliet had left it, but the traffic still pushed, the people still rushed and the noise still rang. As she stood at her window at the Harley, she absorbed it.

No, New York hadn't changed, but she had.

Three weeks before, she'd looked out her office window at not so different a view. Her primary thought then had been the tour, to make a success of it. For herself, she admitted. She'd wanted the splash.

She realized she'd gotten it. At that moment, Carlo was in his suite, giving an interview to a reporter for the *Times*. She'd made a half-dozen excuses why she didn't have time to sit in on it. He'd accepted her usual list of phone calls and details, but the truth had been, she'd needed to be alone.

Later, there'd be another reporter and a photographer from one of the top magazines on the stands. They had network coverage of his demonstration at Bloomingdale's. *The Italian Way* had just climbed to number five on the bestsellers list. Her boss was ready to canonize her.

Juliet tried to remember when she'd ever been more miserable.

Time was running out. The next evening, Carlo would

board a plane and she'd take the short cab ride back to her apartment. While she unpacked, he'd be thousands of miles above the Atlantic. She'd be thinking of him while he flirted with a flight attendant or a pretty seat companion. That was his way; she'd always known it.

It wasn't possible to bask in success, to begin plans on her next assignment when she couldn't see beyond the next twenty-four hours.

Wasn't this exactly what she'd always promised herself wouldn't happen? Hadn't she always picked her way carefully through life so that she could keep everything in perfect focus? She'd made a career for herself from the ground up, and everything she had, she'd earned. She'd never considered it ungenerous not to share it, but simply practical. After all, Juliet had what she considered the perfect example before her of what happened when you let go of the reins long enough to let someone else pick them up.

Her mother had blindly handed over control and had never guided her own life again. Her promising career in nursing had dwindled down to doctoring the scraped knees of her children. She'd sacrificed hunks of herself for a man who'd cared for her but could never be faithful. How close had she come to doing precisely the same thing?

If she was still certain of anything, Juliet was certain she couldn't live that way. Exist, she thought, but not live.

So whether she wanted to or not, whether she thought she could or not, she had to think beyond the next twenty-four hours. Picking up her pad, she went to the phone. There were always calls to be made.

Before she could push the first button, Carlo strolled in. "I took your key," he said before she could ask. "So I wouldn't disturb you if you were napping. But I should've known." He nodded toward the phone, then dropped into a chair. He looked so pleased with himself she had to smile.

"How'd the interview go?"

"Perfectly." With a sigh, Carlo stretched out his legs. "The reporter had prepared my ravioli only last night. He thinks, correctly, that I'm a genius."

She checked her watch. "Very good. You've another reporter on the way. If you can convince him you're a genius—"

"He has only to be perceptive."

She grinned, then on impulse rose and went to kneel in front of him. "Don't change, Carlo."

Leaning down, he caught her face in his hands. "What I am now, I'll be tomorrow."

Tomorrow he'd be gone. But she wouldn't think of it. Juliet kissed him quickly then made herself draw away. "Is that what you're wearing?"

Carlo glanced down at his casual linen shirt and trim black jeans. "Of course it's what I'm wearing. If I wasn't wearing this, I'd be wearing something else."

"Hmm." She studied him, trying to judge him with a camera's eye. "Actually, I think it might be just right for this article. Something informal and relaxed for a magazine that's generally starched collars and ties. It should be a unique angle."

"Grazie," he said dryly as he rose. "Now when do we talk about something other than reporters?"

"After you've earned it."

"You're a hard woman, Juliet."

"Solid steel." But she couldn't resist putting her arms around him and proving otherwise. "After you've finished being a hit across the hall, we'll head down to Bloomingdale's."

He nudged her closer, until their bodies fit. "And then?"

"Then you have drinks with your editor."

He ran the tip of his tongue down her neck. "Then?"

"Then you have the evening free."

"A late supper in my suite." Their lips met, clung, then parted.

"It could be arranged."

"Champagne?"

"You're the star. Whatever you want."

"You?"

She pressed her cheek against his. Tonight, this last night, there'd be no restriction. "Me."

It was ten before they walked down the hall to his suite again. Juliet had long since lost the urge to eat, but her enthusiasm in the evening hadn't waned.

"Carlo, it never ceases to amaze me how you perform. If you'd chosen show business, you'd have a wall full of Oscars."

"Timing, *innamorata*. It all has to do with timing."

"You had them eating your pasta out of your hand."

"I found it difficult," he confessed and stopped at the door to take her into his arms. "When I could think of nothing but coming back here tonight with you."

"Then you do deserve an Oscar. Every woman in the audience was certain you were thinking only of her."

"I did receive two interesting offers."

Her brow lifted. "Oh, really?"

Hopeful, he nuzzled her chin. "Are you jealous?"

She linked her fingers behind his neck. "I'm here and they're not."

"Such arrogance. I believe I still have one of the phone numbers in my pocket."

"Reach for it, Franconi, and I'll break your wrist."

He grinned at her. He liked the flare of aggression in a woman with skin the texture of rose petals. "Perhaps I'll just get my key then."

"A better idea." Amused, Juliet stood back as he opened the door. She stepped inside and stared.

The room was filled with roses. Hundreds of them in every color she'd ever imagined flowed out of baskets, tangled out of vases, spilled out of bowls. The room smelled like an English garden on a summer afternoon.

"Carlo, where did you get all these?"

"I ordered them."

She stopped as she leaned over to sniff at a bud. "Ordered them, for yourself?"

He plucked the bud out of its vase and handed it to her. "For you."

Overwhelmed, she stared around the room. "For me?"

"You should always have flowers." He kissed her wrist. "Roses suit Juliet best."

A single rose, a hundred roses, there was no in between with Carlo. Again, he moved her unbearably. "I don't know what to say."

"You like them."

"Like them? Yes, of course, I love them, but—"

"Then you have to say nothing. You promised to share a late supper and champagne." Taking her hand, he led her across the room to the table already set by the wide uncurtained window. A magnum of champagne was chilling in a silver bucket, white tapers were waiting to be lit. Carlo lifted a cover to show delicately broiled lobster tails. It was, Juliet thought, the most beautiful spot in the world.

"How did you manage to have all this here, waiting?"

"I told room service to have it here at ten." He pulled out her chair. "I, too, can keep a schedule, my love." When he'd seated her, Carlo lit the candles, then dimmed the lights so that the silver glinted. At another touch, music flowed out toward her.

Juliet ran her fingertip down the slim white column of a candle then looked at him when he joined her. He drew the cork on the champagne. As it frothed to the lip, he filled two glasses.

He'd make their last night special, she thought. It was so like him. Sweet, generous, romantic. When they parted ways, they'd each have something memorable to take with them. No regrets, Juliet thought again and smiled at him.

"Thank you."

"To happiness, Juliet. Yours and mine."

She touched her glass to his, watching him as she sipped. "You know, some women might suspect a seduction when they're dined with champagne and candlelight."

"Yes. Do you?"

She laughed and sipped again. "I'm counting on it."

God, she excited him, just watching her laugh, hearing her speak. He wondered if such a thing would mellow and settle after years of being together. How would it feel, he wondered, to wake comfortably every morning beside the woman you loved?

Sometimes, he thought, you would come together at dawn with mutual need and sleepy passion. Other times you would simply lie together, secure in the night's warmth. He'd always considered marriage sacred, almost mysterious. Now he thought it would be an adventure—one he intended to share with no one but Juliet.

"This is wonderful." Juliet let the buttery lobster dissolve on her tongue. "I've been completely spoiled."

Carlo filled her glass again. "Spoiled. How?"

"This champagne's a far cry from the little Reisling I splurge on from time to time. And the food." She took another bite of lobster and closed her eyes. "In three weeks my entire attitude toward food has changed. I'm going to end up fat and penniless supporting my habit."

"So, you've learned to relax and enjoy. Is it so bad?"

"If I continue to relax and enjoy I'm going to have to learn how to cook."

"I said I'd teach you."

"I managed the linguini," she reminded him as she drew out the last bite.

"One lesson only. It takes many years to learn properly."

"Then I guess I'll have to make do with the little boxes that say complete meal inside."

"Sacrilege, *caro,* now that your palate is educated." He touched her fingers across the table. "Juliet, I still want to teach you."

She felt her pulse skid, and though she concentrated, she couldn't level it. She tried to smile. "You'll have to write another cookbook. Next time you tour, you can show me how to make spaghetti." Ramble, she told herself. When you rambled, you couldn't think. "If you write one book a year, I should be able to handle it. When you come around this time next year, I could manage the next lesson. By then, maybe I'll have my own firm and you can hire me. After three bestsellers, you should think about a personal publicist."

"A personal publicist?" His fingers tightened on hers then released. "Perhaps you're right." He reached in his pocket and drew out an envelope. "I have something for you."

Juliet recognized the airline folder and took it with a frown. "Is there trouble on your return flight? I thought I'd . . ." She trailed off when she saw her own name on a departing flight for Rome.

"Come with me, Juliet." He waited until her gaze lifted to his. "Come home with me."

More time, she thought as she gripped the ticket. He was offering her more time. And more pain. It was time she accepted there'd be pain. She waited until she was certain she could control her voice, and her words. "I can't, Carlo. We both knew the tour would end."

"The tour, yes. But not us." He'd thought he'd feel confident, assured, even cheerful. He hadn't counted on desperation. "I want you with me, Juliet."

Very carefully, she set the ticket aside. It hurt, she discovered, to take her hand from it. "It's impossible."

"Nothing's impossible. We belong with each other."

She had to deflect the words, somehow. She had to pretend they didn't run deep inside her and swell until her heart was ready to burst. "Carlo, we both have obligations, and they're thousands of miles apart. On Monday, we'll both be back at work."

"That isn't something that must be," he corrected. "It's you and I who must be. If you need a few days to tidy your business here in New York, we'll wait. Next week, the week after, we fly to Rome."

"Tidy my business?" She rose and found her knees were shaking. "Do you hear what you're saying?"

He did, and didn't know what had happened to the words he'd planned. Demands were coming from him where he'd wanted to show her need and emotion. He was stumbling over himself where he'd always been surefooted. Even now, cursing himself, he couldn't find solid ground.

"I'm saying I want you with me." He stood and grabbed her arms. The candlelight flickered over two confused faces. "Schedules and plans mean nothing, don't you see? I love you."

She went stiff and cold, as though he'd slapped her. A hundred aches, a multitude of needs moved through her, and with them the knowledge that he'd said those words too many times to count to women he couldn't even remember.

"You won't use that on me, Carlo." Her voice wasn't strong,

but he saw fury in her eyes. "I've stayed with you until now because you never insulted me with that."

"Insult?" Astonished, then enraged, he shook her. "Insult you by loving you?"

"By using a phrase that comes much too easily to a man like you and doesn't mean any more than the breath it takes to say it."

His fingers loosened slowly until he'd dropped her arms. "After this, after what we've had together, you'd throw yesterdays at me? You didn't come to me untouched, Juliet."

"We both know there's a difference. I hadn't made my success as a lover a career." She knew it was a filthy thing to say but thought only of defense. "I told you before how I felt about love, Carlo. I won't have it churning up my life and pulling me away from every goal I've ever set. You—you hand me a ticket and say come to Rome, then expect me to run off with you for a fling, leaving my work and my life behind until we've had our fill."

His eyes frosted. "I have knowledge of flings, Juliet, of where they begin and where they end. I was asking you to be my wife."

Stunned, she took a step back, again as if he'd struck her. His wife? She felt panic bubble hot in her throat. "No." It came out in a whisper, terrified. Juliet ran to the door and across the hall without looking back.

It took her three days before she'd gathered enough strength to go back to her office. It hadn't been difficult to convince her supervisor she was ill and needed a replacement for the last day of Carlo's tour. As it was, the first thing he told her when she returned to the office days later was that she belonged in bed.

She knew how she looked—pale, hollow-eyed. But she

was determined to do as she'd once promised herself. Pick up the pieces and go on. She'd never do it huddled in her apartment staring at the walls.

"Deb, I want to start cleaning up the schedule for Lia Barrister's tour in August."

"You look like hell."

Juliet glanced up from her desk, already cluttered with schedules to be photocopied. "Thanks."

"If you want my advice, you'll move your vacation by a few weeks and get out of town. You need some sun, Juliet."

"I need a list of approved hotels in Albuquerque for the Barrister tour."

With a shrug, Deb gave up. "You'll have them. In the meantime, look over these clippings that just came in on Franconi." Looking up, she noted that Juliet had knocked her container of paperclips on the floor. "Coordination's the first thing to go."

"Let's have the clippings."

"Well, there's one I'm not sure how to deal with." Deb slipped a clipping out of the folder and frowned at it. "It's not one of ours, actually, but some French chef who's just starting a tour."

"LaBare?"

Impressed, Deb looked up. "Yeah. How'd you know?"

"Just a sick feeling."

"Anyway, Franconi's name was brought up in the interview because the reporter had done a feature on him. This LaBare made some—well, unpleasant comments."

Taking the clipping, Juliet read what her assistant had highlighted. "Cooking for peasants by a peasant," she read in a mumble. "Oil, starch and no substance . . ." There was more, but Juliet just lifted a brow. She hoped Summer's plan of revenge went perfectly. "We're better off ignoring this," she decided, and dropped the clipping in the trash. "If we passed it on to Carlo, he might challenge LaBare to a duel."

"Skewers at ten paces?"

Juliet merely sent her a cool look. "What else have you got?"

"There might be a problem with the Dallas feature," she said as she gave Juliet a folder. "The reporter got carried away and listed ten of the recipes straight out of the book."

Juliet's head flew back. "Did you say ten?"

"Count 'em. I imagine Franconi's going to blow when he sees them."

Juliet flipped through the clippings until she came to it. The feature was enthusiastic and flattering. The timid Ms. Tribly had used the angle of preparing an entire meal from antipasto to dessert. Carlo's recipes from *The Italian Way* were quoted verbatim. "What was she thinking of?" Juliet muttered. "She could've used one or two without making a ripple. But this . . ."

"Think Franconi's going to kick up a storm?"

"I think our Ms. Tribly's lucky she's a few thousand miles away. You'd better get me legal. If he wants to sue, we'll be better off having all the facts."

After nearly two hours on the phone, Juliet felt almost normal. If there was a hollowness, she told herself it was a skipped lunch—and breakfast. If she tended to miss whole phrases that were recited to her, she told herself it was hard to keep up with legalese.

They could sue, or put Ms. Tribly's neck in a sling, both of which would create a miserable mess when she had two other authors scheduled for Dallas that summer.

Carlo would have to be told, she reflected as she hung up. It wouldn't be possible, or at least ethical, to crumple up the clipping and pretend it didn't exist as she had with the one from LaBare. The problem was whether to let legal inform him, pass it off through his editor or bite the bullet and write him herself.

It wouldn't hurt to write him, she told herself as she toyed with her pen. She'd made her decision, said her piece and stepped off the carousel. They were both adults, both professionals. Dictating his name on a letter couldn't cause her any pain.

Thinking his name caused her pain.

Swearing, Juliet rose and paced to the window. He hadn't meant it. As she had consistently for days, Juliet went over and over their last evening together.

It was all romance to him. Just flowers and candlelight. He could get carried away with the moment and not suffer any consequences. I love you—such a simple phrase. Careless and calculating. He hadn't meant it the way it had to be meant.

Marriage? It was absurd. He'd slipped and slid his way out of marriage all of his adult life. He'd known exactly how she'd felt about it. That's why he'd said it, Juliet decided. He'd known it was safe and she'd never agree. She couldn't even think about marriage for years. There was her firm to think of. Her goals, her obligations.

Why couldn't she forget the way he'd made her laugh, the way he'd made her burn? Memories, sensations didn't fade even a little with the days that had passed. Somehow they gained in intensity, haunted her. Taunted her. Sometimes— too often—she'd remember just the way he'd looked as he'd taken her face in his hand.

She touched the little heart of gold and diamonds she hadn't been able to make herself put away. More time, she told herself. She just needed more time. Perhaps she'd have legal contact him after all.

"Juliet?"

Turning from the window, Juliet saw her assistant at the door. "Yes?"

"I rang you twice."

"I'm sorry."

"There's a delivery for you. Do you want them to bring it in here?"

An odd question, Juliet thought and returned to her desk. "Of course."

Deb opened the door wider. "In here."

A uniformed man wheeled a dolly into the room. Confused, Juliet stared at the wooden crate nearly as big as her desk. "Where do you want this, Miss?"

"Ah—there. There's fine."

With an expert move, he drew the dolly free. "Just sign here." He held out a clipboard as Juliet continued to stare at the crate. "Have a nice day."

"Oh—yes, thank you." She was still staring at it when Deb came back in with a small crowbar.

"What'd you order?"

"Nothing."

"Come on, open it." Impatient, Deb handed her the crowbar. "I'm dying."

"I can't think what it might be." Slipping the crowbar under the lid, Juliet began to pry. "Unless my mother sent on my grandmother's china like she's been threatening for the last couple of years."

"This is big enough to hold a set for an army."

"Probably all packing," Juliet muttered as she put her back into it. When the lid came off, she began to push at the heaps of Styrofoam.

"Does your grandmother's china have a trunk?"

"A what?"

"A trunk." Unable to wait, Deb shoved through the styrofoam herself. "Good God, Juliet, it looks like an elephant."

Juliet saw the first foolish glitter and stopped thinking. "Help me get it out."

Between the two of them, they managed to lift the big, bulky piece of ceramic out of the crate and onto her desk. "That's the most ridiculous thing I've ever seen," Deb said when she caught her breath. "It's ugly, ostentatious and ridiculous."

"Yes," Juliet murmured, "I know."

"What kind of madman would send you an elephant?"

"Only one kind," Juliet said to herself and ran her hand lovingly down the trunk.

"My two-year-old could ride on it," Deb commented and spotted the card that had come out with the packing. "Here you are. Now you'll know who to press charges against."

She wouldn't take the card. Juliet told herself she wouldn't look at it. She'd simply pack the elephant back up and ship it away. No sensible woman became emotional about a useless piece of glass three feet high.

She took the card and ripped it open.

Don't forget.

She started to laugh. As the first tears fell, Deb stood beside her without a clue. "Juliet—are you all right?"

"No." She pressed her cheek against the elephant and kept laughing. "I've just lost my mind."

When she arrived in Rome, Juliet knew it was too late for sanity. She carried one bag which she'd packed in a frenzy. If it'd been lost en route, she wouldn't have been able to identify the contents. Practicality? She'd left it behind in New York. What happened next would determine whether she returned for it.

She gave the cab driver Carlo's address and settled back for her first whirlwind ride through Rome. Perhaps she'd see it all before she went home. Perhaps she was home. Decisions had to be made, but she hoped she wouldn't make them alone.

She saw the fountains Carlo had spoken of. They rose and fell, never ending and full of dreams. On impulse she made the driver stop and wait while she dashed over to one she couldn't even name. With a wish, she flung in a coin. She watched it hit and fall to join thousands of other wishes. Some came true, she told herself. That gave her hope.

When the driver barreled up to the curb and jerked to a halt, she began to fumble with bills. He took pity on her and counted out the fare himself. Because she was young and in love, he added only a moderate tip.

Not daring to let herself stop her forward progress, Juliet ran up to the door and knocked. The dozens of things she wanted to say, had planned to say, jumbled in her mind until she knew she'd never be able to guarantee what would come out first. But when the door opened, she was ready.

The woman was lovely, dark, curvy and young. Juliet felt the impetus slip away from her as she stared. So soon, was all she could think. He already had another woman in his home. For a moment, she thought only to turn and walk away as quickly as she could. Then her shoulders straightened and she met the other woman's eyes straight on.

"I've come to see Carlo."

The other woman hesitated only a moment, then smiled beautifully. "You're English."

Juliet inclined her head. She hadn't come so far, risked so much to turn tail and run. "American."

"Come in. I'm Angelina Tuchina."

"Juliet Trent."

The moment she offered her hand, it was gripped. "Ah, yes, Carlo spoke of you."

Juliet nearly laughed. "How like him."

"But he never said you would visit. Come this way. We're just having some tea. I missed him when he was in America, you see, so I've kept him home from the restaurant today to catch up."

It amazed her that she could find it amusing. It ran through her mind that Angelina, and many others, were going to be disappointed from now on. The only woman who was going to catch up with Carlo was herself.

When she stepped into the salon, amusement became surprise. Carlo sat in a high-backed satin chair, having an intense conversation with another female. This one sat on his lap and was no more than five.

"Carlo, you have company."

He glanced up, and the smile he'd used to charm the child on his lap vanished. So did every coherent thought in his mind. "Juliet."

"Here, let me take this." Angelina slipped Juliet's bag from her hand while she gave Carlo a speculative look. She'd never seen him dazed by a woman before. "Rosa, come say good morning to Signorina Trent. Rosa is my daughter."

Rosa slipped off Carlo's lap and, staring all the way, came to Juliet. "Good morning, Signorina Trent." Pleased with her English, she turned to her mother with a spate of Italian.

With a laugh, Angelina picked her up. "She says you have green eyes like the princess Carlo told her of. Carlo, aren't you going to ask Miss Trent to sit down?" With a sigh, Angelina indicated a chair. "Please, be comfortable. You must forgive my brother, Miss Trent. Sometimes he loses himself in the stories he tells Rosa."

Brother? Juliet looked at Angelina and saw Carlo's warm, dark eyes. Over the quick elation, she wondered how many different ways you could feel like a fool.

"We must be on our way." Angelina walked over to kiss her still silent brother's cheek. As she did, she was already planning to drop by her mother's shop and relate the story of the American who'd made Carlo lose his voice. "I hope we meet again while you're in Rome, Miss Trent."

"Thank you." Juliet took her hand and met the smile, and all its implications, with an acknowledging nod. "I'm sure we will."

"We'll let ourselves out, Carlo. *Ciao.*"

He was still silent as Juliet began to wander around the room, stopping here to admire this, there to study that. Art of every culture was represented at its most opulent. It should've been overwhelming, museumlike. Instead it was friendly and lighthearted, just a bit vain and utterly suited to him.

"You told me I'd like your home," she said at length. "I do."

He managed to rise but not to go to her. He'd left part of himself back in New York, but he still had his pride. "You said you wouldn't come."

She moved one shoulder and decided it was best not to throw herself at his feet as she'd intended. "You know women, Franconi. They change their minds. You know me." She turned then and managed to face him. "I like to keep business in order."

"Business?"

Grateful she'd had the foresight, Juliet reached in her purse and drew out the Dallas clipping. "This is something you'll want to look over."

When she came no farther, he was forced to go over and take it from her. Her scent was there, as always. It reminded him of too much, too quickly. His voice was flat and brisk as he looked at her. "You came to Rome to bring me a piece of paper?"

"Perhaps you'd better look at it before we discuss anything else."

He kept his eyes on hers for a long, silent minute before

he lowered them to the paper. "So, more clippings," he began, then stopped. "What's this?"

She felt her lips curve at the change of tone. "What I thought you'd want to see."

She thought she understood the names he called the unfortunate Ms. Tribly though they were all in fast, furious Italian. He said something about a knife in the back, balled the clipping up and heaved it in a scrubbed hearth across the room. Juliet noted, as a matter of interest, that his aim was perfect.

"What does she try to do?" he demanded.

"Her job. A bit too enthusiastically."

"Job? Is it her job to quote all my recipes? And wrong!" Incensed, he whirled around the room. "She has too much oregano in my veal."

"I'm afraid I didn't notice," Juliet murmured. "In any case, you're entitled to retribution."

"Retribution." He relished the word and made a circle of his hands. "I'll fly to Dallas and squeeze my retribution from her skinny throat."

"There's that, of course." Juliet pressed her lips together to keep the laughter in. How had she ever thought she'd convince herself she could do without him? "Or a legal suit. I've given it a lot of thought, however, and feel the best way might be a very firm letter of disapproval."

"Disapproval?" He spun back to her. "Do you simply disapprove of murder in your country? She over-spiced my veal."

After clearing her throat, Juliet managed to soothe. "I understand, Carlo, but I believe it was an honest mistake all around. If you remember the interview, she was nervous and insecure. It appears to be you just overwhelmed her."

Muttering something nasty, he stuck his hands in his pockets. "I'll write to her myself."

"That might be just the right touch—if you let legal take a look at it first."

He scowled, then looked at her carefully from head to foot. She hadn't changed. He'd known she wouldn't. Somehow that fact comforted and distressed all at once. "You came to Rome to discuss lawsuits with me?"

She took her life in her hands. "I came to Rome," she said simply.

He wasn't sure he could go any closer without having to touch, and touching, take. The hurt hadn't faded. He wasn't certain it ever would. "Why?"

"Because I didn't forget." Since he wouldn't come to her, she went to him. "Because I couldn't forget, Carlo. You asked me to come and I was afraid. You said you loved me and I didn't believe you."

He curled his fingers to keep them still. "And now?"

"Now I'm still afraid. The moment I was alone, the moment I knew you'd gone, I had to stop pretending. Even when I had to admit I was in love with you, I thought I could work around it. I thought I had to work around it."

"Juliet." He reached for her, but she stepped back quickly.

"I think you'd better wait until I finish. Please," she added when he only came closer.

"Then finish quickly. I need to hold you."

"Oh, Carlo." She closed her eyes and tried to hang on. "I want to believe I can have a life with you without giving up what I am, what I need to be. But you see, I love you so much I'm afraid I'd give up everything the moment you asked me."

"*Dio,* what a woman!" Because she wasn't certain if it was a compliment or an insult, Juliet remained silent as he took a quick turn around the room. "Don't you understand that I love you too much to ask? If you weren't who you are, I wouldn't be in love with you? If I love Juliet Trent, why would I want to change her into that Juliet Trent?"

"I don't know, Carlo. I just—"

"I was clumsy." When she lifted her hands, he caught them in his to quiet her. "The night I asked you to marry me, I was clumsy. There were things I wanted to say, ways I'd wanted to say them, but it was too important. What comes easily with every woman becomes impossible with the only woman."

"I didn't think you'd meant—"

"No." Before she could resist, he'd brought her hands to his lips. "I've thought back on what I said to you. You thought I was asking you to give up your job, your home, and come to Rome to live with me. I was asking less, and much more. I should have said—Juliet, you've become my life and without you, I'm only half of what I was. Share with me."

"Carlo, I want to." She shook her head and went into his arms. "I want to. I can start over, learn Italian. There must be a publisher in Rome who could use an American."

Drawing her back by the shoulders, he stared at her. "What are you talking about, starting over? You're starting your own firm. You told me."

"It doesn't matter. I can—"

"No." He took her more firmly. "It matters a great deal, to both of us. So you'll have your own firm one day in New York. Who knows better than I how successful you'll be? I can have a wife to brag about as much as I brag about myself."

"But you have your restaurant here."

"Yes. I think perhaps you'd consider having a branch of your public relations company in Rome. Learning Italian is an excellent decision. I'll teach you myself. Who better?"

"I don't understand you. How can we share our lives if I'm in New York and you're in Rome?"

He kissed her because it had been much too long. He drew her closer because she was willing to give something he'd never have asked. "I never told you my plans that night. I've been considering opening another restaurant. Franconi's in Rome is, of course, the best. Incomparable."

She found his mouth again, dismissing any plans but that. "Of course."

"So, a Franconi's in New York would be twice the best."

"In New York?" She tilted her head back just enough to see him. "You're thinking of opening a restaurant in New York?"

"My lawyers are already looking for the right property. You see, Juliet, you wouldn't have escaped me for long."

"You were coming back."

"Once I could be certain I wouldn't murder you. We have our roots in two countries. We have our business in two countries. We'll have our lives in two countries."

Things were so simple. She'd forgotten his unending generosity. Now she remembered everything they'd already shared, thought of everything they'd yet to share. She blinked at tears. "I should've trusted you."

"And yourself, Juliet." He framed her face until his fingers slid into her hair. "*Dio,* how I've missed you. I want my ring on your finger, and yours on mine."

"How long does it take to get a license in Rome?"

Grinning, he whirled her in his arms. "I have connections. By the end of the week you'll be—what is it?—stuck with me."

"And you with me. Take me to bed, Carlo." She pressed against him, knowing she had to get still closer. "I want you to show me again what the rest of our lives will be like."

"I've thought of you, here, with me." He pressed his lips against her temple as he remembered the words she'd hurled at him on that last night. "Juliet." Troubled, he drew away, touching only her hands. "You know what I am, how I've lived. I can't take it back, nor would I if I could. There've been other women in my bed."

"Carlo." Her fingers tightened on his. "Perhaps I said foolish things once, but I'm not a fool. I don't want to be the first woman in your bed. I want to be the last. The only."

"Juliet, *mi amore,* from this moment there is only you."

She pressed his hand to her cheek. "Can you hear it?"

"What?"

"The carousel." Smiling, she held out her arms. "It's never stopped."

GREED. DESIRE. OBSESSION. REVENGE.

It's all in a night's work.

NORA ROBERTS

#1 *NEW YORK TIMES*
BESTSELLING AUTHOR

NIGHTWORK

AVAILABLE WHEREVER BOOKS ARE SOLD

In her stunning new novel, #1 *New York Times* bestselling author
NORA ROBERTS introduces an unforgettable thief who must risk everything
for a prize that matters more to him than anything he could steal.

ST. MARTIN'S PRESS